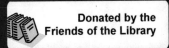

SKYLARK

SKYLARK

MEAGAN SPOONER

 carolrhoda LAB

MINNEAPOLIS

Text copyright © 2012 by Meagan Spooner

Carolrhoda Lab™ is a trademark of Lerner Publishing Group, Inc.

Carolrhoda Lab™
An imprint of Carolrhoda Books
A division of Lerner Publishing Group, Inc.
241 First Avenue North
Minneapolis, MN 55401 U.S.A.

Website address: www.lernerbooks.com

Main body text set in Janson Text 11/15.
Typeface provided by Linotype AG.

Library of Congress Cataloging-in-Publication Data

Spooner, Meagan.
    Skylark / by Meagan Spooner.
      p. cm.
      Summary: Lark Ainsley has yearned to become an adult by having her
magical energy harvested, but when she is finally chosen a special talent is
revealed and, rather than become a human battery powering the dome that
protects humanity, she escapes hoping to find the Iron Wood, a wilderness
rumored to be inhabited by others like herself.
      ISBN: 978–0–7613–8865–4 (trade hard cover : alk. paper)
      [1. Fantasy. 2. Survival—Fiction. 3. Magic—Fiction.] I. Title.
PZ7.S7642Sky 2012
[Fic]—dc23   2011044347

Manufactured in the United States of America
1 – SB – 7/15/12

For Amie

My magic, without whom I'd be
a shadow.

PART I

CHAPTER 1

The din of the clockwork dawn was loudest in the old sewers, a great whirring and clanking of gears as the artificial sun warmed up. I paused as mortar crumbled from the ceiling and hissed into the water below. Harvest Day. *This could be your last sunrise*, I told myself. *If you're lucky.*

Though I could still hear the screech of the Resource behind the sunrise, I kept moving, gritting my teeth. Not much time to waste if I wanted to see the names for the harvest and get home in time to shower off any sign I was ever down here. After a few moments the dreadful swell of energy eased, as the sun disc outside settled into its track across the dome of the Wall.

At least there'd be a little light now. I knew my way through these tunnels in pitch-black, but that didn't mean I'd turn down the occasional glimpse of sun through a grate overhead. With a jolt, I realized this could also be the last time I ever came here. My last sunrise, my last day of school, my last childish jaunt through the underground tunnels. Though I felt closer here to Basil than anywhere, it wasn't nearly enough to make me want to stay a kid. After so many years, I just wanted it to end. Let Basil's ghost lie here, quiet.

Two lefts, a right, and down. Easy. My brother's voice in my ear, I clambered on hands and knees into an access tunnel that would lead to the air cleaners under the school. The bricks were harsh and dry under my palms. The air was thick in this part of the tunnels, untreated and stale. At least these sewers hadn't served their original purpose in the better part of a century—the only smells were mildew and rotting brick. I tried to slow my pulse again. *It's just a tunnel,* Basil told me. *If you can get in, you can get out, and panicking only makes you stupid.*

Somewhere ahead I could hear the faint hum of the air machines. Another sound—above the usual metallic plinking and watery noises of the tunnels—caught my attention. My heart in my throat, I stopped moving and strained to hear through the background noise. Pixies? Panic robbed me of breath, blinding me for long seconds before logic intervened. Pixies moved silently—by the time I heard them it'd be too late. *Panicking makes you stupid.*

A footstep, sloshing, far away. Caesar, then. But that was stupid, too. Even if Caesar wanted to, he couldn't follow me through the maze of tunnels. If he stopped by our parents' place and found me missing, he'd have to report me, and by that time, I'd be long gone. And surely he wouldn't turn in his little sister?

Now the sounds became clearer. Voices echoed through the tunnels: one louder, another hissing, shushing the other. Another gentle splash, moving closer into the distance. Apparently, I wasn't the only kid on my way to the school.

I veered into a side tunnel, aiming for a less well-known route. My shoulders scraped against the bricks on either side, but I ignored it. Better a few scratches than run into any other kids down here.

Ahead, a glimmer of light outlined the end of the tunnel. I put on a little extra speed and finally lurched out of the tunnel onto my hands and knees in about six inches of mucky water.

I got to my feet and sloshed forward, drying my slimy hands against my shirt. In the distance, the sound of the air cleaner under the school drowned out any noise I made. It wasn't far now.

My path brought me to another narrow tunnel, barely large enough to fit my shoulders. I couldn't remember the last time I'd taken this side passage, but it must have been years ago. Had it always been this small? I stooped and peered into it, only able to see six feet or so through the darkness inside. *Just a tunnel.* And I had to see those names, know if this was all going to end today. I crawled inside.

I inched forward with my arms stretched out in front of me, the sound of the cleaner machinery beckoning me onward. The scrape of damp brick stung against my already raw arms, and the stale air inside reeked of rot and damp. The narrowness of the tunnel forced me to crawl, pushing myself along with the toes of my shoes and the tips of my fingers. Not surprising that no one else knew about this route.

Something snagged my pants leg, jerking me to a halt. I tugged, throat closing when whatever had caught the fabric failed to give way. The tunnel constricted my body in such a way that I couldn't even look down to see what had caught me. I jammed my leg against the wall of the tunnel and felt something hard and sharp stab at my thigh. Some iron reinforcement, perhaps, eroding its way out of the mortar. I tugged again. Nothing.

No one knew where I was. Even if Caesar guessed I'd snuck into the school, they'd be checking the popular route. I wasn't sure if anyone even knew about this way, except for Basil, and he was gone. I could be stuck down here for days—weeks. *I'm* not *going to die down here.*

I screamed out for help, my voice echoing in the tunnels. I didn't care anymore about getting caught. The idea of slowly starving to death in a brick pipe yards below the ground was worse than whatever they'd do to me for sneaking into the school. I knew there were other kids down here somewhere. Maybe they'd hear and help me.

The air was still, but for the mocking roar of the air cleaner up ahead. I was so close that the sound of my voice wouldn't carry very far over the sound of the machinery.

A jolt of panic shot down my spine, and I tried to calm myself. It felt as though I was smothering to death, forcing me to gasp for each breath. I strained my eyes until they watered, trying to stare through the darkness. Little spots began to dance in front of my eyes. My vision blurred as a roaring fog descended around my ears, accompanied by dizziness so strong I would have fallen if I could have moved.

I knew what was happening.

"When we feel the Resource taking over," the teacher always droned in a bored voice, "what do we do?"

"Start counting and picture an iron wall," half the class chorused back. The other half never bothered to pay attention.

I kept gasping for breath, trying to hold numbers in my mind. *No*, my thoughts screamed at me. *Not now.* But was it better to rot down here? The alternative was unthinkable. Illegal use of the Resource was the only offense a child could be Adjusted for.

The fog thickened, dizziness swelling and making it hard to concentrate. Panic urged it on.

Iron, I thought desperately. Images flashed through my mind, none of them what I needed. I needed cold iron, potent enough that the thought of it was enough to stop the Resource in its tracks.

Iron, like the sharp thing digging into my leg. I jammed my leg against it, trying to snuff out whatever was burning inside me. The dizziness eased, letting me blink away the blurry sparks of light obscuring my vision.

I forced myself to drag in a deep breath. *Think of Basil.* The pipe wasn't so tight I couldn't breathe. I was only imagining it. I was just stuck. I got myself in here, and I could get myself out. *Don't panic.*

I gave an experimental jerk of my leg, my pants resisting the movement. I stretched forward with my hands, seeking some kind of hole or crack in the brick of mortar that I could hold on to for leverage. There: a bit of crumbling brickwork. I raked it away with my fingertips, nails scraping against the mortar, until I had enough room to get some purchase on it.

I took another long breath in and then exhaled all the way, making myself as small as possible—and jerked.

My leg came free with a dreadful long *rip* of fabric. I scrambled forward, nails scrabbling on brick, feet scraping. Ahead of me yawned the cleaner chamber, and with a last burst of effort I spilled out onto its floor, the edge of the pipe taking several layers of skin off my arms as I did.

Air. I needed any air but the horrible, Resource-soaked air in the pipe.

Though the mechanics did their best, there were always leaks in the giant bellows moving the air. I crawled forward until I found one, and then turned over and lay there, lungs heaving and eyes shut. Gasps of fresh air brushed my face, tossing my hair around.

Safe.

After a few long moments, the trembling in my arms and legs stilled, and the burning in my lungs eased. I was lying in an inch or two of water, soaked to the bone. I opened my eyes.

The chamber housing the air cleaner was roughly spherical, with the cycling machinery taking up most of the floor space. Gears bigger than I was spun in ponderous, perpetual motion, their bottoms disappearing into grooves gouged in the stone floor. The giant bellows in the middle of it all kept the air moving, pumping recycled air into the school. The noise was deafening.

I would have lay in the muck for an hour, but I couldn't afford it. I could no longer hear the sun disc, had no way of gauging the passage of time. But I'd come this far—I wasn't going to turn back now without seeing that list, even if it meant Caesar catching me covered in sewer muck.

I sucked in a few deep breaths until my arms stopped shaking, and then reached for the maintenance ladder, just able to grab the bottom rung. I hauled myself up inch by inch, feet kicking against the wall behind it until I could get them onto the ladder.

The hatch came up inside the janitor's closet. I carefully shut it behind me and turned my attention to the door: locked, as always. But Basil had taught me about this, too. Years of practice had made it second nature. Grab the handle and pull, lower your hip, slam it into the laminate just below the lock.

Clunk. The lock's tumblers jarred into place.

The door swung open, and I slipped inside the school.

Even though I'd done this every Harvest Day for the better part of five years, praying to anything listening that I'd be harvested next, the sight of my school darkened and empty always gave me an odd chill down my spine. I slunk down the corridor, keeping to the shadows. My steps squelched lightly in the silence, leaving wet footprints against the spotless tile floor. Whoever the other group had been, they hadn't beaten me here. I felt a strange surge of pride at that thought. Basil had taught me well.

The dean's office was just down from the school's class-rooms. Its locking mechanism suffered from the same weaknesses as the closet's, and following a loud *thunk* that echoed down the hall, I ducked inside. The faint light of morning filtered in through the windows, illuminating the furniture inside.

There was a leather folder on the desk. Suddenly everything else fell away, the whole room narrowing, roaring in my ears. Nothing mattered, except that here was my ticket out of limbo.

I knew my name was on the paper inside this time. It *had* to be. It had to be. It was as though my eyes could see through the folder's cover, my name printed there dark and clear as if burned into the sheet. *Ainsley, Lark.*

My fingers shook as I picked up the folder. I didn't care that my damp skin left wet spots all over the folder and the paper inside. My eyes took forever to focus. The letters, written in neat, orderly rows, were gibberish until I forced my mind to decipher them.

Baker, Zekiel, I read, the blood roaring in my ears. Dalton, Margaret. Kennedy, Tam. Smithson, James.

My brain didn't even process that the names were in alphabetical order, that it was over before I'd read the first name. My eyes raked over each of the four names twice. I turned the paper over, but only white space greeted me. Empty.

Water dripped onto the paper, spots of translucence that blurred the names. For a strange moment, a detached part of my mind wondered if I'd started crying. Then I realized that it was dirty water from my hair, which had fallen forward over my shoulder.

As the buzzing in my head began to fade, another sound intruded upon the unnatural quiet of the empty school. It was faint first, like the sound of my own blood coursing past my eardrums. Then I picked out a humming, something almost mechanical, rising and falling. I stood listening for long, precious moments, unwilling to believe the sound.

Pixies.

CHAPTER 2

I threw the folder back onto the desk, not even bothering to make it look undisturbed. The paper inside was already water-stained and crumpled. No hiding my presence now. I took two quick steps to the door, easing it open and peering around it just enough to see a sliver of the hallway.

Dark, still, silent. Except—just there. A flash of copper, darting from one room to the next. The tiniest of hums, the sound of the Resource twined with clockwork.

I froze. A thousand half-invented stories whispered about the pixies flashed through my brain. Part of me had been hoping I was imagining it, sensing something else and jumping to the wrong conclusion. I waited, counting the seconds silently. Again it zipped out of the room and into the one across the hall. Twenty seconds it spent in each room, as steady as the ticking of a clock. Twenty seconds with the corridor free.

There were ten rooms in all, five on each side. The janitor's closet lay in between the second and third rooms on the left. I tried to gauge the distance from the dean's office to the closet.

As the pixie darted into the next room down, I took deep breaths until I was dizzy. As soon as the pixie came out and zipped into the room across the hall, I made for the closet.

My wet shoes squealed against the floor. Pixies weren't supposed to have ears, only a sensor for the Resource, but my skin burned nevertheless as though I could feel eyes on me. I skidded once for a heart-stopping second, then careened into the closet's door. Fumbling with the handle, I finally got it open and lurched inside. I slammed it behind me and stood listening, straining for sound, the side of my face and my ear pressed against the door.

A voice. "Holy shit."

I whirled to see three pairs of wide eyes glittering at me through the gloom, reflecting the faint light emanating from the crack under the door.

The other kids I'd heard in the tunnels.

"What's with all the noise?" came one voice. Without light I couldn't identify him. I didn't bother getting to know my classmates very well anymore. They inevitably got harvested and moved on without me. "Are you trying to get us all caught?"

"Sorry. I got spooked." The words were out before I could stop them. I blinked in the gloom. Why hadn't I told them about the pixie?

"Is that Lark?" demanded the same voice. He must be the leader of this little expedition.

"Who's Lark?" came another voice, younger.

"The dud, you moron." The leader grinned, a flash of slightly uneven teeth in the darkness.

Of course they all knew me. By reputation, if not by name. The unharvested freak. People on the other side of the city knew who I was. I just got older and older, watching kids three, four, five years my junior march off to their harvest ceremonies.

"Was that you screaming bloody murder down there in the tunnels?" The first boy sounded on the verge of laughter.

They'd heard me. When I believed I was trapped, possibly doomed to waste away in a tunnel below the city—they'd heard me screaming for help. And no one had come.

"Yeah," I muttered, my fingers curling into fists.

One of the other kids giggled, and I gritted my teeth. The first boy said, "Well? Did you see the list?"

I breathed in. "No," I said calmly. "I didn't. But you'd better hurry if you want to see it before anyone comes."

And without waiting for a reply, I dropped down through the hatch and let my weight pull it closed. I dangled from the hatch for a moment before swinging my legs over onto the ladder. I reached back up for the lock, shaking fingers closing over the red handle.

Just do it, I told myself, head beginning to ache from clenching my jaw so tightly. *They would've done the same to you.*

And lock them in with a pixie. My stomach roiled at the thought, a shudder of remembered terror running through me. I stared up at the hatch for a few long moments and then groaned, dropping back down to the floor, the hatch unlocked.

My heart still pounding, I set off down the larger tunnel, avoiding the one where I'd gotten stuck. My nerves were jangling, and I had to try not to think of how close I'd come to being caught. The punishments for sneaking into the school were dire—minimum rations, isolation, even giving you a lower status apprenticeship when you were harvested and made an adult. Plus there was pride. In all these years, I'd never been caught. My thoughts were lost in imagining the punishments, fear mixed with relief still ruling my mind as I hurried home.

I should have noticed something was wrong. Even though the cleaner chamber was receding further and further behind me, the sound of machinery remained. The humming grew louder as I walked, but I was so relieved at my escape that I didn't give it a second's thought.

And so when I reached an intersection of the tunnels and rounded the corner to come face to face with a pixie, I could do nothing but stare stupidly.

It had no eyes, no mouth, only a featureless, round head no bigger than my pinky fingernail. Delicate copper wings were a blur of motion as it hovered, its segmented body giving it an insectlike appearance. They were the smallest of the mechanimals invented in the extravagant decades before the wars, requiring so little of the Resource to run that they were the only ones the Institute still used. They were nothing more than curiosities then, but now they were the Institute's eyes in the city, able to detect instantly any illegal use of the Resource. Children weren't expected to report malfunctions and submit to Adjustment—children, after all, can't be expected to act responsibly. They need to be watched.

For a moment we were still, me staring at the pixie and it watching me sightlessly in return. The only sounds I could hear were the buzzing of its wings, the whirring of its gears, and the jarring, discordant twang of the Resource twisted to its mechanism.

Then it gave a malevolent whine of triumph and launched itself toward my face, so fast I almost didn't see it move. Without thinking, I threw up my hands, all of the panic, relief, despair, and fury of the past half hour exploding with no time to count to ten, no time to think of iron.

The pixie was thrown against the far wall of the tunnel with such force that it shattered, fragments tinkling against the brick and splashing in the water.

I staggered, lightheaded, a hazy mist descending over my eyes. A wave of dizziness nearly knocked me down, and I stumbled over toward where I'd seen the pixie strike. Dropping to my knees, I felt through the muck.

There was nothing left but a few hollow shards of copper shell.

Shaking, I forced myself to my feet again. The Resource. I'd used it. And not just a tiny spell to save my life in a tunnel somewhere. I'd damaged a pixie, a precious machine, the very eyes of the Institute. No, not just damaged. Obliterated.

It shouldn't have been possible. Even the strongest flow of Resource was barely enough to levitate a pencil without the help of machinery to amplify it. It was a power source—like the tightly wound spring in a watch—nothing more. The Institute had always taught us so. That the architects could be wrong was unthinkable.

At least I'd found out I wasn't a dud.

But at what cost?

• • •

I longed to linger in the shower and let the water wash away the fear as well as the tunnel muck. I'd learned long ago to save my shower ration for the days I'd be going tunnel-hopping, but even so I had only a few minutes at most. It had taken me the better part of an hour to work my way back through the tunnels, and then find a circuitous route home that would avoid having anyone see me, wet and mucky and bleeding.

I scrubbed away the mud and dirty water, my scraped arms stinging. I rinsed my hair as best as I could, in too much of a rush to coax any lather out of the cheap ration soap. After I'd finished, I stood dripping by the window. The sun disc was just clearing the buildings.

I closed my eyes, letting the light wash my face through the dingy window of my parents' apartment. If only I'd stayed stuck in that pipe, I never would've smashed that pixie. In the pipe, I had thought it better to be caught than to rot.

Now, having used the Resource, being caught would mean Adjustment.

I was supposed to be in school by now, listening to the names called for the harvest. Suffering through the same drawn-out ceremony. The fat, sugar-sweet Harvest Administrator would be there by now in her red coat, delivering her speech to the kids about sacrifice and efficiency, and the journey into adulthood. She had always terrified me, despite her pleasant demeanor. I wasn't used to seeing large people, and she got a little wider each year. In the past, fear of the Administrator was always enough to make sure I attended every Harvest Day.

But I knew I wasn't on the list, and no one would notice I was gone. All attention would be on the kids whose names were called. I was still buzzing from what I'd done, little jolts of the Resource escaping from my fingertips and my wet hair when I moved. I couldn't report to class like this. What if they could somehow sense it when I entered? What if it clung to me, like the faint stench of the tunnels still inhabiting my hair?

I drew in a shaky breath and turned away from the window. I got dressed slowly and then went into the living room. Rummaging in the box of my belongings by my sofa bed, I pulled out the paper bird Basil had made for me before he disappeared.

"Don't go," I'd begged him.

"You weren't made to live in a cage, little bird." He kept his voice low, calm. Soothing. But there was a tension behind his gaze that had frightened me. "Someone has to take the first steps beyond it."

"But who will protect me from Caesar?" Caesar, my older brother by five years, and two years older than Basil. He was almost a stranger to me and terrifying in his gruffness.

Basil crouched down to eye level with me. Even then I was short and scrawny. "What if I made you a friend to keep you company?" he asked.

It had been years since he'd last made me one of his paper animals. He'd taught himself how in school, stealing scraps of recycled paper and folding until they resembled creatures out of the history books. Elephants, tigers, dogs, squirrels, once even an eagle.

"I'm not a little kid anymore," I protested.

"I know," Basil said. "This would be a special one, different from the others. I've had this paper—" and he pulled a small, yellow-gray sheet of paper from his satchel, "—waiting for a few weeks now. The animal's already inside, waiting to be set free. You just have to see it." He looked back up at me, serious and earnest. "But she'll need someone to take care of her. Will you do that until I get back?"

I knew what he was doing, saw through his efforts to distract me, but I nodded anyway. It had been so long since I'd watched him fold. He winked at me and turned his attention to the paper. His fingers flew, forming angles by folding and folding back again, creases leaping up along edges and bisecting the center. "Slower!" I begged him, longing to see and learn the trick of it, but he just laughed and kept folding.

I couldn't see what it was until he was nearly done, at which point my breath caught in my throat.

"A lark," he said, bending the wings back up into place and then resting the paper bird on the palm of his hand. "Like you, Lark." He grinned again, and leaned toward me so he could jostle my shoulder with his.

Just before I could reach out to take the paper bird, he pulled his hand back and bent his head, gazing at it with great concentration. I felt a tingle spread outward from the base of my skull, a lightheadedness that caused my vision to spark strangely and the blood to rush past my ears. Even though I knew what I was sensing could not be true, my breath quickened. Eventually he drew in a breath and then exhaled carefully over the bird, blowing against its wings. I heard a tiny sound, like the ringing of a far-off bell. The paper bird flapped its wings once and then soared in a tiny, effortless circle over the palm of Basil's hand before gliding over to mine

I stared in horror at my brother as my spine tingled with the thrill of the forbidden. I'd never seen anyone use the Resource before. It was supposed to be impossible without the alchemists' years of training.

"How did you do that?" I breathed.

Basil grinned at me. "Magic."

My mouth hung open. I tried to remember the last time I'd even heard that word. It was strictly forbidden in school.

He winked, reaching out to tap my chin and close my mouth. "It's okay to say the word, you know. That's what it is. And they think they can control it—control us—but they're wrong."

Magic had made the bird fly from his hand. I'd always assumed he was moving the bird like the architects moved machines like the pixies, using a tiny bit of Resource to power something designed for the purpose. But I should have known better. It was, after all, only a bit of folded paper—the wings weren't designed for flight, the body too fat and the tail too long. There were no gears for the Resource to set in motion. His spell had been effortless—and considerably more impressive than floating a pencil.

But still not exactly vaporizing a pixie with a single thought.

I hadn't touched the paper bird in years, not since Basil had disappeared, but I longed for my brother to walk through the door and tell me what to do. He'd tell me not to be afraid of the pixies, that they were barely more than paper birds themselves, animated by the Institute. He'd tell me my fear was making monsters out of little tin bugs. I didn't have to let that fear control me.

I shivered, thinking of my brother's explanation for his sacrifice. *You weren't made to live in a cage, little bird.* That much, it seemed, was true.

In a city utterly dependent on its every citizen to perform their duties and fit in like clockwork, where was there room for me?

Cradling the bird in my hands, the tingle of the Resource—of magic, I corrected myself—still coursing through me, I drew a deep breath, willing my pounding heart to calm, and exhaled slowly.

My breath brushed the bird, stirring the paper wings. It so resembled the moment six years ago when the bird had come to life and taken flight that I caught my breath again, heart pounding. Had I accidentally done it again? The wings stilled, but before I could relax, the bird cocked its little head—and burst into song.

Three clear notes, and then it dissolved into a fluttering series of chirps that had me scrambling to silence it. I stopped myself before I crushed the thing, but I blew on it frantically instead, praying there was no one in a neighboring apartment to hear it. Birds had been extinct, as far as anyone knew, since the wars killed most animals and twisted the rest.

At first it shook itself with an air of indignant protest, but after a few more puffs it went still again. My head spinning, I crouched by the couch and listened.

For a moment I heard nothing. I started to stand up, my legs shaking with adrenaline.

Then came a pounding on the door. I dropped to my knees. The knock came again, loud and forceful—a city official's knock. How had they found me so quickly?

I folded the bird's wings down flat and then shoved it deep into the pocket of my pants. I scrambled to my feet and stood there, heart slamming against my ribcage. I snatched up a packet of ration crackers from the table and shoved those into my pocket too, some part of my brain reminding me that wherever I fled, I'd have to eat. The front door was the only way out of the apartment—except for the fire escape from the window in the living room. I leaped over the arm of the couch and went to the window, fingers fumbling with the latch.

As I heaved at the window, trying to get it open, a voice from outside the door called, "Lark, what the hell? Open the door!"

I knew that voice. I ran to the door, hands shaking with relief now rather than panic as I twisted the lock and threw the door open.

"Caesar!"

My brother was a tall man, his imposing stature serving him well as a Regulator. He had very carefully cultivated a mustache in an effort to fit in and be taken seriously by the more senior officials. All it earned him was years of being teased for its scraggly appearance. His eyes were so like Basil's in color and shape, but so different in character.

"What have you been up to?" he demanded. My relief vanished in an instant. Caesar lived across town now, with the other Regulators, though he still had a key to our parents' apartment—what was he doing here? He took a step into the apartment, and I fell a step back.

"Wh-what?" I gasped. "No—C, I didn't mean to, I swear. Please."

Caesar frowned, the mustache drooping dramatically. "What? No, I meant—what were you doing with the deadbolt on? I couldn't get in."

I gaped at him. "Oh," I managed.

"Why aren't you in school?" He moved past me into the living room, thrusting his hands up over his head and stretching, spine popping.

I shook my head, still trying to process. He hadn't come to bring me in for illegal use of the Resource. He didn't know about the pixie, or the paper bird.

"Keep this up and you're not going to fit when you get your assignment. Hate to send my own little sister's name to the Regulatory Board. Look, they sent me to find you, since you weren't in class. I figured you'd be at Mom and Dad's. Your name was called."

That brought me up short, panic on hold while I stared up at my brother. "My name was what?"

"Called," repeated Caesar, his voice casual. He knew what it meant to me, though. His eyes gleamed. "You're going to be harvested, though hell knows why. Just a scrawny bit of a thing, should just feed you to the shadows over the Wall and be done with it."

"Harvested," I echoed, my thoughts moving so slowly it was like swimming through syrup. Despite my flush of excitement, I knew my name hadn't been on that list. Something was wrong.

"Carriage is waiting for you downstairs. Kind of a crappy driver if you ask me, but hey—he promises he can get you to the Institute. At least you get it all to yourself."

I swallowed. "But—but the other kids?"

Caesar shook his head. "You're the only one called this time."

All happiness fled, leaving me cold, my thoughts suddenly crystal clear. I saw the paper in my mind's eye as clear as if it were in front of me again. I closed my eyes.

They knew. Somehow, they knew I'd been doing magic. I

wasn't being taken to the Institute to be harvested—I was being taken to be punished. And there was only one punishment for illegal use of the Resource: Adjustment.

"Congrats, little sis," said my brother, reaching out to ruffle my hair.

CHAPTER 3

The carriage driver was a skinny boy a few years younger than I with too large ears and hair a shocking orange. He swung a leg over his cycle, lines of muscle standing out on his skinny calves. The hitch between carriage and cycle creaked as he let his weight down onto the seat.

I wanted to run—but where would I go? There was no place in the city where the pixies wouldn't find me.

I looked over my shoulder at Caesar, hoping for some last-minute reprieve. I wanted to tell him I was in trouble, but my tongue was thick and heavy. Caesar had turned his attention to the hand-held talkie device that kept him in touch with the other cops, and didn't so much as glance at me.

The driver kicked at the starter, magic coursing through the gears of the bicycle. We pulled away slowly, the kid straining at the pedals. The pedals, like much of the rest of the carriage, were rusty and worn. The only thing in good repair was the gleaming mechanism nestled in the chains that turned magic into motion. The warm glow of copper seemed out of place within its case of rusted, ancient machinery.

I tried to imagine what it must be like to live in the Institute as the architects did, using machines like this every day. Ages ago people used horse-drawn carriages to get around. After the Wall went up, horses took up too much space and ate too much food. And so the Institute had developed these crude carriages, powered by bicycle, mechanical advantage—and a conservative dose of the Resource.

It took more power to move something directly by raw magic than it took to use magic to operate something mechanical. Clockwork was the best, with delicate gears, pendulums, and jewels that moved smoothly and efficiently, so long as something—magic—provided the impetus.

There was a time, before the wars, when the whole world was rife with technology. Most was gone now, but for the art of binding the Resource to clockwork. Without it, no one would have survived the cataclysmic events that ended the wars, destroying the countryside. We were the last city on earth. Only our architects, and the Wall they constructed, kept us safe. And they continued to do so, forming the Institute of Magic and Natural Philosophy, to preserve the remaining technologies that keep us alive. And to harvest the power they needed to do so.

Another time, I would have enjoyed a carriage ride. Carriages were free on Harvest Day for kids called to the Institute, but at all other times they cost too much for most people.

"Aren't you kinda old?"

The driver's voice yanked me back to the present. I was used to this question by now, and I ignored him. My experience in school had taught me that silence usually bred silence, and that by ignoring people I could usually make them stop talking to me.

Not so with the driver. "Your name's Lark, right? My sis just got harvested last year and she's only like nine," he said, puffing between sentences as he pedaled. "But she's cool. She's real old for her age, and smart, too. Gonna be an architect's assistant someday."

Basil had been told on more than one occasion that he could've been an architect if he'd had different parents. As it was, he had set his sights on the glass forge, and dreamed of the day he'd get picked as a vitrarius, one of the specialized glassworkers in the Institute. It would've meant that his future children, if they'd tested well enough, could've been architects, if they were lucky. So, the idea that the sister of a carriage driver had aspirations of working in the Institute was ludicrous, but I didn't say this aloud. Instead, I found myself asking, "What was your harvest like?"

The boy slowed in order to turn down a different street, and waited to answer until he'd picked up speed again. "It was spec. You're so lucky. You wouldn't believe the kind of stuff they got there. All the fruit you can eat, and syrup and these fried potato slices and—" He had to stop for breath.

"No, I meant the harvest itself, not the feast. What was it like when they stripped you?"

"Oh." No answer for a while, which I chalked up to the slight hill we were climbing. "I don't really remember much about it, I guess. The food was much more interesting. What, do you believe those kids who say it's like cutting off a hand or something?"

I laughed to hide my uneasiness. "Just curious."

I expected him to take this dismissal as a hint for silence, but he kept up his chatter the entire way. We turned down another street, and then another, until I lost track of where we were. When we turned a corner to find the Institute stretching out before us, I gasped.

I'd seen it before, but always from a distance, as if it were a two-dimensional painting instead of a complex large enough to take up a whole quarter of the city, surrounded by an ancient granite wall that must have been fifteen feet high.

My driver seemed unimpressed, but as he approached the curb outside the gate, he turned to flash a grin at me. "I know, right? Eat some of those fried potato things for me." The wistfulness in his voice caught me by surprise.

His chatter the whole way had dispelled a lot of my nervous energy. I didn't care about his sister or her school project or his dad's job at the sewage recycling plant or how he was hoping to get a better bicycle in a couple years, but I was trying so hard not to listen that I hadn't had any time to spare to worry about having broken the law.

I got out of the carriage when he pulled up to the curb. He smiled at me, all ears and orange hair, and I suddenly found myself wishing I had paid more attention to him. I knew this was where the richer people, the ones who routinely rode on the carriages, would tip a ration chit that could be exchanged for a handful of vegetables or a quarter pound of sugar. I stood there awkwardly shifting my weight from one foot to the other.

"Well, see you around," he said, cocking his head and turning back to his carriage. He knew better than to expect a tip from me.

"Right," I replied. The squashy packet of ration crackers was an uncomfortable lump in my pocket as I watched the driver—I had never even asked his name—start to pedal away.

"Wait!" I called, and he stopped, automatically checking the carriage to see if I'd left something.

"Here," I said, unwrapping the crackers so he could see them and shoving the packet at him.

He looked down at it and then back up at me, mouth hanging open. "Whoa, I can't take this from you."

"I won't need it, I'm going to be feasting in a couple hours."

"But—" His eyes were wide, almost as round as his ears, which were turning pink as he gazed at me.

"Just take it!" I turned away, embarrassed that he thought I was so poor that I couldn't tip him something.

As I hurried away, he called, "Thanks, Miss Lark! You ever need a ride, you ask for Tamren! Thank you! Thanks!"

There was no sign to tell me where to go, no other kids to stand with. As I approached the gate, all my fear came slamming back, making each step forward a torment. There was a guard in the gatehouse, watching my trepidation with some bemusement. When I finally reached the gate and opened my mouth to speak, he anticipated me.

"Lark Ainsley?" he asked. When I nodded, he got down from his seat and walked over to the gate, unlocking it and pushing it open a fraction for me to enter. The lock on the gate was heavy iron—no amount of magic would free me after it shut behind me. But I had no other choice than to keep going.

I took a deep breath and stepped inside.

The building in front of me was a huge, square, white monstrosity with faux columns and a massive pair of iron doors on its front. I could just make out a copper-colored dome above the façade. Carved into the marble over the doors were the words *"Vis in magia, in vita vi."* In magic there is power, and in power, life. Latin was the language of the architects, a language forbidden to the rest of us. I only knew the phrase from one of the battered history books I'd read to pass the time in school after I'd outgrown the curriculum.

Before the wars there had been people able to regenerate their innate power—Renewables, they were called, though they'd been called many things before that: Witches, sorcerers, magicians. Demons. But there hadn't been any Renewables born in generations, not since the Wall went up, and those left outside destroyed themselves by abusing the Resource.

A young woman in a blue assistant's coat came hurrying down the steps toward me. "Sorry!" she called out to me, coming to a halt a few feet away. "Sorry I'm late."

She cradled a clipboard against her chest, face peeping at me over its top. She could have been my older sister, with hair a few shades darker than mine, looking almost black in the shade of the building. Her face was round enough to reflect the heavier rations given to the employees of the Institute. With the physical and mental labor expected of those employees, they needed the extra food.

I gave her my best cold stare. If it protected me from embarrassment in the face of schoolyard mockery, it might help with my panic, too.

She only glanced at her clipboard and then smiled, moving close enough to put a hand between my shoulder blades. "So you must be Lark." She ushered me forward. "My name's Emila. Sorry it's just you this time. I know you must be nervous, but I promise you have nothing to worry about. You won't feel a thing when you're harvested."

She led me through the doors and into a vast hall topped by a breathtaking rotunda—the inside of the dome I'd seen from the steps. Intricate machinery lined the ceiling, a metallic gold replica of our sun disc in miniature, a tribute to the Wall. The clockwork mechanisms purred, a steady whirring punctuated at intervals by the clink of a shifting component of the masterpiece. It was morning inside the rotunda as well, but there were other tracks and gears in the process of dipping below the lip of the dome as the sun rose on the other side, carrying objects I didn't recognize from the sky of the Wall outside: a crescent of gleaming silver, shapes picked out in precious gems that glinted in the light.

What must this place look like at night? Emila was hurrying ahead, reading her clipboard and paying no attention to me, and I reluctantly kept moving.

Shafts of light shone through remote skylights, illuminating the exquisite tile floors in dappled gold. The tiles radiated from the rotunda's center like a compass, arrows pointing toward doors that led to various wings of the Institute. Bronze plaques declared the destinations of each branching corridor.

As Emila veered toward one of these doors, the plaque told me she was headed to the Department of Harvest and Reclamation. Below it was a second plaque with arrows pointing right and left, describing the passages further along the rim of the rotunda room. The Biothaumatic Laboratory lay to the right; the Museum and Hall of Records to the left.

I stopped walking, a shoe squeak echoing through the rotunda. I cringed, but Emila didn't lift her head.

We weren't taught much history in school. We knew that the Institute had saved us from the fallout following the wars over a century ago, and that was enough. The Institute held the details of our history in trust for us, so that nothing would be lost or changed by the retelling of it. The glimpses I had in school of the world before the wars were electrifying and frightening all at once: a world full of Renewable sorcerers and vast machines operated by magic, of mechanimals, of struggles for power unlike anything we had to endure in the peaceful city today.

"Hall of Records," I whispered, the final sibilant echoing around the rotunda and returning distorted to my ears. Inside were all the records of the past century—including, surely, those of the only experimental exploration beyond the Wall since its creation. Somewhere in there was a piece of paper with Basil's name on it. When would I ever have another chance?

I took one last glance at the now distant, retreating form of Emila as she hurried down the corridor toward the harvest department. I was far enough behind now that I'd have to run to catch up. I could just as easily say I'd gotten separated while admiring the rotunda. It wouldn't even really be a lie.

I took a deep breath and ducked down the other corridor.

Without the skylights in the dome, the hallway was lit by long glowing panels in the ceiling. It was possible to create light by raw Resource alone—it just took a lot of power. A skilled vitrarius, however, could direct the Resource through tiny glass filaments that would glow with the concentrated energy.

I had known the Institute was lit this way. From the roof of our apartment building at night, I had seen the whole compound sparkling in the distance, lighting up the dome of the Wall above and behind it. My father used to take me up there after he came home from the recycling plant. We would sit at the edge of the roof with our legs dangling over empty space and watch the lights blink on, one by one, warm and golden, as the sun disc faded into violet darkness.

After Basil and the other volunteers crossed the Wall in search of power to supplement the Institute's stores, my father and I went up on the roof every night—almost as if we were hoping for a glimpse of him, even though that was impossible.

For six long weeks, we had no news of them. Then, abruptly, the Institute issued a citywide notice declaring them permanently missing, presumed dead. An unharvested child with his or her innate Resource stores intact could survive for a time outside the Wall. But no one could survive indefinitely.

No death, no Adjustment—nothing final, nothing to hold on to. He was just gone. We were compensated for our loss with extra ration chits and a few days off from school and work to mourn, but we were never told anything more.

My oldest brother Caesar barely reacted, throwing himself into his job as a Regulator, finding comfort in ensuring the city ran as smoothly as the finest prewar clockwork. My father, though, became obsessed with trying to find out what had happened, pressing until he began speaking out against the Institute and the way it hoarded information. He was summoned before the Regulatory Board for his disruptive behavior. Even Caesar couldn't predict whether Dad would come home, or if the next time we saw him it would be for his Adjustment. The father I remembered never did return. But a quiet, tight-faced drone eventually came home in his place. He barely spoke to me or my mother, who compensated by doting on Caesar, cooking him dinner and packing him lunches even though he technically lived across town.

And my father never took me up onto the roof again.

I tried once to see it on my own—the comfort and the wonder of the magical glow of the Institute—but I saw only a faint smear of light against the domed Wall, like grease clouding dirty dishwater.

To see those same lights directly above my head now, however, washing me in their steady golden glow, was another matter entirely. They lacked the flicker of our home oil lamps and produced no warmth. And yet, my skin tingled as though some heat touched it. I could hear a faint hum, like the sound of pixie mechanisms, above the muffled sound of my footsteps. The sound wasn't as grating as the dawn, but it showed no signs of fading either. It rested at the base of my skull, a steady pounding.

The corridor had a polished, reflective stone floor, forming the illusion that I was walking down a tunnel of light. My heart pounded in time with the magical pulse of the lights, but I'd made my choice—even if I turned around now, Emila would be long gone. I was already lost, and this could be my one chance. I would be caught, and punished, but if it meant I had a chance of knowing Basil's fate, it would be worth it.

The long hallway ended in a sleek wooden door, which I edged open a crack. I could hear nothing on the other side, and so I eased it open the rest of the way.

Ahead of me lay an immense gallery, lined on either side with fantastical sculptures. I closed the door behind me and paused at the first, a huge monstrous creature I didn't recognize. It was covered in brown, shaggy fur, standing on its hind legs with its clawed forepaws upraised. Its jaws were parted in a soundless roar, teeth glistening. With a jolt I realized it was no sculpture at all, but the remains of an actual creature, skinned and stuffed. Horrified and fascinated, I bent my head to the inscription on the plaque at its feet.

"*Ursus arctos horribilis*," I read. *Horribilis*, indeed, I thought, taking a step back from the glare of its glassy, dead eyes.

My steps echoed as I made my way along. Overhead, long-extinct birds hung motionless from wires, wings outstretched in a parody of flight. There were flying creatures ranging from tiny things I could barely see to one mighty creature with a wingspan larger than I was tall. All along the sides of the gallery, examples of creatures gone extinct during the wars stared back at me, haunted and blank.

There were mechanimals in the gallery as well, clockwork simulacrums of the creatures themselves, dormant without magic to power them. *Canis lupus familiaris*, I read at one such exhibit.

A glass case toward the end of the gallery caught my eye. I headed over to peer down at its contents—and started back. Inside was a pixie, as real and clear as the one I had annihilated.

My heart pounded against my ribcage, but the pixie was dormant. It couldn't see me—or else it would be halfway to the Administrator by now, to inform her that a harvestee was not where she was supposed to be. I swallowed and forced myself to look closer. Its squat, copper body was supported on six spindly legs, delicate mesh wings outstretched and poised as if ready to fly. No eyes, only the bulging multifaceted sensors attuned to the Resource, and long delicate antennae for reception of orders.

The plaque beneath the case said it was a prototype, from back when pixies were just amusements for the rich, before the Institute altered them to suit its purposes. It looked just the same, though, as cold and calculating. I backed away from the case, skin crawling.

The next room opened up into a cavernous, dark space broken up by long tables and rows of shelves, and I squinted as my eyes adjusted. Something moved in a pool of light cast by a lamp and I realized with a jolt that there was a person at one of the tables—I darted to the side, ducking behind one of the shelves.

Willing my pounding heart to slow, I peeked around the shelf. At the other end of the room, an ancient architect with a neatly trimmed beard and wild eyebrows sat hunched over a desk piled high with books.

My heart leapt. I'd read the few books in the classroom countless times—never had I realized so many books even still existed. The entire room was full of them, thick with the smell of leather and dust. Even the shelf I was hiding behind was lined with them. An entire world of knowledge locked in here, far exceeding anything I could have imagined. Beyond the architect's desk was row upon row of shelves stacked with papers and boxes. The records.

The architect hadn't moved since I first noticed him, and for a wild moment I considered inching around him in the gloom to get at the papers. Before I could move, though, a flare of magic jolted through my brain and a dim musical chime pierced the musty silence.

"All code-red clearance personnel to Administrator's office, please," said a pleasant, tinny voice. From my vantage point behind my shelf, I saw the architect's head lift and then, with a dusty sigh, he rose and made his way toward me. I withdrew behind the bookcase and held my breath until I heard the door open and close.

Now or never. I wove through the bookshelves, aiming for the records at the far end. It would take days just to skim it all, and if "code red" had anything to do with me, I might not have more than a few minutes.

With any luck it'd be alphabetical, and my brother would be filed under our last name. I stood scanning the folders, searching for anything I could recognize. The entire top of the shelf was lined with boxes, and after a few seconds my eyes flicked up to them—and my breath stopped. *Ainsley, Basil.* My eyes darted to the side: another box, labeled the same. I moved slowly down the row of shelves, counting at least a dozen boxes all labeled with my brother's name. Only the last box bore a different label: *Ainsley, Lark.*

I stood there staring upward, the letters of my own name burning through the gloom, when the sound of the door banging open jerked my attention toward the entrance. A pair of women wearing blue coats came through the door. I fled behind the shelves again.

"Yes, but why would she come here?" The woman's voice sounded exasperated. I heard the scrape of a chair and a wooden creak, not far away.

"How would I know? Do you really want to be the one to question the Administrator?"

The first woman gave a nervous laugh, punctuated by the sound of fingernails tapping on the tabletop. "Good point.

Still, if I were a kid loose in the Institute, this would be the last place I'd aim for."

"Well, this one's not exactly a kid anymore."

There was a door not far away on the back wall. I might be able to make it undetected, but . . . From where I hid I could just see the edge of one of the boxes bearing my brother's name.

"I suppose we just wait here until they find her," sighed one of the assistants. "They're setting the pixies loose, so at least it'll go quickly."

A jolt ran through me. I took one last look at the box overhead and then tore myself away, heading toward the unmarked door on the back wall. I slipped through, shutting it silently behind me.

I stood with eyes closed in the corridor, willing my racing pulse to calm and my aching head to ease. I pressed the palm of my hand against the door I'd come through, as if somehow I could summon the answers through it. I'd been so close. I had no idea why they had an entire shelf of boxes devoted to my brother. The sum of information they'd given my family after his death would have fit on half a sheet of paper.

And why would they have any records at all about me?

It was only a matter of time before the pixies found me, and I couldn't be found here. It was clear I wasn't supposed to know about those files high on the shelf.

Ahead of me stretched a much more utilitarian corridor than the other I'd passed through, the lights overhead stark white, the floor dull gray. The hall branched into three a few paces away, but only two of the paths had plaques. The right-hand path pointed the way to the Biothaumatic Laboratory while the left read ROTUNDA. All I had to do was follow that corridor. I could say I'd just gotten distracted by how astonishing the rotunda itself was, and ended up separated from Emila.

I turned to head down the hallway when a flicker caught my eye. The third path was unlabeled, nothing to indicate where it led. I stared down the corridor, head throbbing with the magic hum of the lights, willing whatever I'd seen out of the corner of my eye to return.

It had a barely perceptible curve, making it impossible to see what lay at the end of it. As I watched, a section of the lights flickered and went dark for a brief second. Just a malfunction of some kind. I started to turn away again when the panels overhead went dead with a sudden, blessed cessation of the awful buzzing of the lights. Before my eyes could adjust, they came on again with a blaze of painful magical backlash, leaving me gasping. It was dark now a few steps down the path, and I staggered into it to escape the sound of buzzing Resource slicing into my brain. The lights went out just ahead of me again. A ripple of darkness continued on down, lights going out and coming on one by one, around the curve and out of sight.

I took another step, and the patch shifted one bar of lights. It was responding to my movements. It was *leading* me.

I hesitated. I knew I had to head back to the rotunda, pretend I'd seen nothing I wasn't supposed to see. I shouldn't draw any more attention to myself than I already had. I should forget everything I'd seen.

Slipping my hand into my pocket and curling my fingers around Basil's paper bird, I followed the lights.

The corridor stretched for what felt like miles. I couldn't be sure, but it seemed to have a slight slope as well as a curve, a gradual downward spiral. In the distance, a door came into view at the end of the corridor. I stopped dead for a second and the lights went still. As I stood there, they shifted once in the direction I'd been going, then ceased again.

"Okay, okay," I said, glancing up at the dark lightbulbs overhead.

The door swung open soundlessly at my touch.

The space behind the door lay shrouded in darkness at its edges, although the impression was of a huge spherical cavern of a room. At its center hung a blindingly bright mass, with streamers of light connecting it to the most complex machinery I'd ever seen, hanging above and around it. The noises of meshing gears were only rivaled by the sound of magic mated with machine twanging in my mind.

On the other side of the door began a metal walkway that spiraled down toward the light. My feet took me down of their own accord.

As I got closer, the light powering the machines became more distinct. It was long and slender, with the faintest suggestion at the top of something like a head. . . .

It was a person. Though it wore no clothing, the light was too bright at this distance to make out any features or its gender. Glass filaments seemed to plug directly into its skin, stretching up into the mechanisms overhead and carrying the Resource away from it. Just as iron was an insulator of magic, glass was the best conductor of all.

The room vibrated. Although I had never felt the Resource in such quantities, there was an undertone to it that I recognized from Basil, from my own ill-advised experiment. Barely detectable beneath the harshness of the harnessed energy rang the pure, sweet notes of raw magic. Light dazzled my eyes.

I stopped walking and leaned closer over the railing of the catwalk, gazing at the creature. My breath stopped, and I stood transfixed, horrified.

There was no doubt it was a living person. I could see the face more clearly now, my eyes accustomed to the light.

White skin, closed eyes, wasted, delicate features, lips set in a strange, hollow *O*.

While I stared, the eyes opened. I shrieked and fell backward, banging hard into the opposite railing.

The pain brought me to my senses. I could still feel that overpowering need to run, but there was a part of me that was detached, freed from it. With a shocking clarity I realized that the need to flee was *not* coming from me.

Sucking in a deep breath, I got to my feet and turned toward the gleaming-white creature suspended by glass. She—I wasn't sure how I knew, but I was certain now it was a woman—was looking directly at me. Her irises were as white as the rest of her, the black pinpoints of her pupils fixing on mine.She opened her mouth, lips cracking. A viscous, brownish-gray liquid spilled onto her chin.

"Run," she gasped.

CHAPTER 4

My thin shoes clanged painfully against the metal as I sprinted away, lungs heaving.

I barely made it through the door before I slammed into what seemed like a red wall. I would have ricocheted back onto the walkway, except that the wall extended hands to catch me.

Reeling backward, I saw that it was the Administrator.

I'd never seen her so close. Her, short, black hair curled inward under her double chin, with a fringe cropped straight across just above her perfectly tweezed brows. Around the high collar of her red coat coiled a thick copper wire, on which hung the insignia of the architects: an ornamental drafting compass, its sharp end gleaming in the light. For an instant she gaped at me, thin lips parted in surprise, small eyes narrowing. Like she was examining me.

Then the expression cleared. "My goodness!" she exclaimed. "You look like you've just had a fright!" Her round face gleamed with a faint sheen of perspiration, as if she'd just been hurrying somewhere.

"There's a—" I gasped, unable to articulate anything for my trembling. "And she looked at me, and— and—"

"Heavens," she said. "Come along, poor gosling. We've

had quite enough delay for one morning, don't you think? We'll get you through the Machine and on to your feast, and all the lovely things we've got planned for you. Won't that be nice? You'll love all the delicious food we've cooked up."

With a mixture of cheery cajoling and brute force, the Administrator ushered me through the corridor. She took the second door we came to, sliding a badge into a slot beside the doorknob until there was an audible click. I barely noticed where we were going until we reached a set of tall doors that slid open sideways with a faint whirring of gears.

She led me into a tiny room, and the doors hissed closed behind us.

"But what was that—" I began, before the floor rushed up to meet me with a scream of grinding machinery.

I flung my hands out to catch myself, and realized that the entire room was moving. There were no windows, but I could feel it rushing upward. The Administrator bent down to help me up. "I'm sorry, duck," she said, beaming at me. "Elevators can be quite the ride if you're not used to them. Don't worry, it's quite safe.

"This will all be over in no time at all," she added as the room stopped and the doors hissed open. "The Machine's just up ahead."

I had a fleeting image of myself in place of the light creature, with glass wires protruding from my veins. I nearly threw up all over the Administrator's vast red coat.

She propelled me into a grey room containing a single low bench against one wall. The Administrator gave me a cheerful little wave before bustling back out through the doors again. "Just relax, and we'll be done before you know it," she said, as the doors whizzed closed. The unique mechanical sound of the Institute was quickly becoming familiar.

There was no sign of any machine in the room, only a

dim gray light from a panel overhead. The room had only the one door, and after a few seconds I crossed over to it, to ask if there'd been some mistake. I nearly walked into it, when it failed to slide open the way it had for the Administrator. A bubble of panic rose in my throat. Maybe they were punishing me after all.

I was about to bang on the door when the dim lights wavered overhead. A strangely tinny voice coming from all around me said, "Please remove your clothing and leave it on the bench."

I moved toward the bench and then hesitated. Most girls who came through here were eleven or twelve at the oldest. I was sixteen. The thought of being naked was intolerable. No one had told me about this part. But then, no one had told me much of anything about what it was like to be harvested, other than that it was great.

"Um," I called, directing my voice upward in the hope that someone would hear. "Can I just—"

"Please remove your clothing and leave it on the bench."

The voice spoke in an identical tone. This time I heard it catch in places, unnatural brief clicks in the voice. A machine's voice.

I shuddered and pulled off my shirt and pants, leaving them in a crumpled heap on the bench. I kicked off my shoes and nudged them underneath. When I straightened up again, the voice came a third time, repeating its message. Someone, somehow, was watching me. Even in the dim lighting, who-ever it was would be able to see everything. Shivering, miser-able, I took off my underwear, too, tucking it under my pants. As soon as I did so machinery clanked and whirred, and a sec-ond door appeared opposite the first. It had fit so seamlessly into the wall that I'd missed it before.

Why had no one prepared me for this?

I swallowed the humiliation and confusion, watching the new door as it slid aside. Beyond I saw a lighted pathway leading into darkness. At least it was darker in there—I hurried through the doorway, eager for a little more concealment.

As soon as I was through, the door clanked shut behind me. Suddenly I remembered the paper bird folded in my pocket, and what I had done. What if they could sense the magic on it? I turned and pressed my hands against the door, trying to find some way of opening it—but found only smooth metal.

The lighted pathway brightened a little, leading to a chair ahead of me. A voice coming from all around me said, "Please be seated in the chair. Once you have been seated, please remain motionless." The same voice, the same metallic hollowness.

I headed for the chair, which was lit with its own light. My bare feet made sharp sticky noises, echoing strangely, as though the room was an odd shape. I couldn't see beyond the pool of light ahead of me.

The light pulsed, emanating from glass panels in the chair. I could feel a faint ache beginning in my temples, and knew that if the lights got any brighter my headache would return with a vengeance.

Suddenly I realized that this was the Machine the Administrator had mentioned. I saw no glass wires waiting to trap me. I listened to the tinny voice repeat its command two more times before I climbed gingerly into the chair.

It was warm. My skin crawled, trying to shrink away from it. My body blocked out most of the lights in the chair as I settled in. A band swung down from the top of the chair to encircle my forehead, touching lightly at either temple.

Don't panic, I commanded myself, closing my eyes and trying to breathe normally. I tried to imagine Basil's voice chastising me for being silly and scared, but even that failed me. Basil, I thought, would be afraid, too.

When I opened my eyes, there was still faint light coming from the chair beneath me. I tried to see the shape of the room around me, but the dimness of the light only played tricks on me. I got the impression of other machines, shrouded in shadow, my eyes picking out the faintest edges of metal just beyond the pool of muddy light. I waited, my skin prickling, for something to happen—for the chair to come alive, or the voice to give me my next order. But nothing happened.

In school, the harvest was always spoken of as a transition. It was the rite of passage into adulthood, the process by which our childish pools of Resource were drained away and we were ushered into the roles that would be ours for the rest of our adult lives. We grew up being told how wonderful a feeling it was to contribute our Resource to the city. People spoke of the feast, of the joy of becoming a functioning piece of the larger clockwork, of the satisfaction of leaving childhood behind. But no one had ever spoken about what the harvest *was*. I'd looked forward to the feast, and to moving on, getting out of limbo. Why had I never asked what they'd actually do to me here? Why hadn't I asked if having my magic stripped from me would hurt?

The waiting was agony enough by itself, every inch of me twitching against the sticky warmth of the chair, which still hadn't adjusted to my own body temperature. Every involuntary spasm of my nervous muscles made the light from beneath me jump and shiver in the dim air. I couldn't lift my head. A flash of memory—the sewer tunnel, being unable to move. I struggled for breath.

Without warning the lights in the chair went out. The blood rushed past my eardrums as vertigo swept through me, leaving me fuzzy-headed and dry-mouthed. My skin tingled as all the hairs on my arms stood to attention. I tried to lift a hand to scratch at my elbow, but found I could not move.

My lungs constricted, panic gripping me. The darkness closed in around me, and no matter how I pulled, I couldn't unstick my body from the chair. It was as if I was made of metal and some giant magnet had collected me.

My dizziness swelled as a sound, the same dissonant humming I'd heard from the lighted panels in the hallways, started from the chair itself. This time I could feel it through my bones, and after only a few seconds it began to feel as if I would shake apart. Every molecule of my body was vibrating.

I tried to cry out to whoever was operating the Machine, get them to stop, but something had paralyzed my vocal cords. No one had ever told me their harvest had hurt like this. Something had gone horribly wrong.

Unless they had found out. Perhaps *this* was my punishment.

Just when I was certain I'd disintegrate from the throbbing vibrations, searing pain lanced through my back. Something jabbed into my skin, slicing deep along my spine. In front of my eyes flashed a vision of the glass wires piercing the creature I had seen.

I opened my mouth and screamed soundlessly until the darkness smothered me.

CHAPTER 5

I became dimly aware that someone was helping me out of the chair. My back ached and my legs shook, but the person I clung to was steady.

"There now, that wasn't so bad, was it?" A round, cheerful face swam into focus.

"No," I croaked, my mind still a blank. "Not . . . bad."

The lights had come on again at some point, a soothing glow all around me. The round-faced person helped me into a tunic and ushered me along, her hands under my elbows. We went through a door that opened up in front of us and then clicked shut again.

"You must be hungry now. The harvest process always has that effect. We can go directly to your feast, get you some of that delicious food. Would you like that?"

I *was* hungry—ravenous, in fact. "Yes," I said, my voice sounding much more normal now. I was rapidly becoming steadier on my feet. What had I been so upset about? No matter, there was a feast awaiting me.

"Fabulous," exclaimed the round-faced person. I remembered her now—the Administrator.

And I remembered—something. There was a fading

image of a glowing chair, a vague notion that something had touched my back. And something else, too. A person made of light, eyes that sought and held mine. And glass. I remembered glass. . . .

"Right over here, darling!" said the Administrator, putting her hand between my shoulder blades and shoving me into a tiny, strangely familiar room.

"Hang on when the elevator starts," she said, squeezing her larger body into the box after me. "You're in for a treat!"

With a lurch, the ground rose underneath us. My legs buckled, but I kept my balance. The sensation was hauntingly familiar.

It wasn't a very long ride, barely enough time to grow accustomed to the sensation of movement inside the box. The doors hissed open.

"Wasn't that fun?" said the Administrator, laughing. "Right this way, duckling—please have a seat.

In front of us was a long hall dominated by a huge wooden table. It was more solid wood than I'd seen in one place. The table was clearly meant for dozens of people, and I chose a seat near the end of it. The chair was strangely cold against my back, as if the skin there had been recently irritated.

The Administrator moved to stand at my elbow. The entire space was done up in the style of an old-fashioned dining room, with lush carpet covering the floor and soft lights overhead. I had the strangest feeling that the lights should have made my head ache. They didn't. A fireplace complete with the mechanical illusion of flames adorned one end of the room. A mechanimal dog lay dormant on the rug in front of it. I'd never seen mechanimals outside the museum trips we took every few years in school. I stared at the dog, willing it to move, until the Administrator joggled my elbow to catch my attention.

"Let me introduce myself properly," said the Administrator, beaming at me. Something about her saccharine smile and sing-song voice made me shift uneasily in my seat. "I am the Harvest and Power Administrator here at the Institute, but you can call me Gloriette. My entire purpose is to help you make the best out of your time here, and I hope you'll think of me like a substitute mom for the next few days. I really just want to make this a wonderful time for you."

As she spoke, a young woman in the blue coat of an assistant came out from another room bearing a napkin and silverware, which she laid in front of me. My stomach began to growl noisily. I'd tolerate a room full of people talking down to me, for the chance to eat my fill for once.

"Normally we have four or five children here all together," said Administrator Gloriette, as I tried to ignore the sting of being described as a child.

"Over the next two days, you'll be interviewed and tested. The job assigned here will be yours for the next five years. At the end of this period you'll be allowed to petition for a reassignment, or in the case of poor performance," and she gave a sad little smile, "you'll be reviewed for Adjustment." I'd noticed the Administrator had a habit of sliding a fingernail along the wire that held her architect's compass on her collar. She did this now as she let the word "Adjustment" hang in the air. Fiddling with the ornamental tool wasn't just a nervous habit. It was a subtle but definite reminder of her rank. Somehow, despite her sad tone, I couldn't imagine her shedding a tear when she ordered an Adjustment.

"When you've finished eating, please come find one of the assistants up here and they'll help you to your room." She inclined her head, round face gleaming slightly with perspiration. It was warm in the dining hall, and Gloriette's body bulged with a lot more insulation than mine.

As if on that cue, the assistant returned, this time bearing a tray. She set it down in front of me, and all thoughts of the Administrator vanished as I stared.

It was a tray for one, but it was more food in one place than I'd ever seen before. All of the food that fed the city was grown beyond the Wall, planted and harvested by machines designed to survive the harsh conditions there. Most of what was grown, though, people like me never saw—at least not in recognizable forms. Except on Harvest Day.

Mountains of food crowded the tray. There was a large bowl of soup, a plate piled high with vegetables, a small dish with bread and—my stomach lurched—margarine. The vegetable oil for margarine was so energy-intensive to make that even those at the Institute didn't eat it often. The smell wafted up to me, and I dragged my gaze away to look up at Gloriette.

She laughed, the folds on her face jiggling. "It's okay, duckling, I'm done. Go ahead and tuck in."

I wasted no time. I nearly dove face-first into some smashed potatoes on the side of my plate, drizzled with a vegetable gravy that smelled better than anything I'd ever had in my life. There was a dish of mixed vegetables that I didn't have names for, green and yellow slices cooked in oil. Soy curd in a brown sauce. Shredded carrots soaked in vinegar. Tamren's potatoes, fried golden and crispy.

I tried to taste a little of everything, but each new thing I tried was so good that I found myself stuffing my mouth with as much of it as I could fit. I had never been full before. I found the heaviness in my stomach to be hugely uncomfortable but also strangely satisfying. And I kept eating.

Gloriette left the room, replaced by a number of assistants in blue coats. I lifted my head to watch them, uneasy at being the only one eating in the big banquet hall. But they came bearing new plates to replace my old ones, and I forgot my discomfort. The new dishes were full of pastry and fried sugar beet stalk, cakes with caramelized syrup drizzled over them, balls of fried dough that had been soaking in sugar water. I saw a neat stack of dark pink wedges and lunged for those. I recognized it as watermelon from pictures in history books, but I was totally unprepared for its taste. Cold, crisp, bursting into delicately sweet juice when I bit into it. From that taste on I touched nothing else. They replaced the nearly untouched plates of cakes with more watermelon. I devoured it all, right up through the bitter fruit at the edge of the rind.

By the time I forced myself to stop eating, I was feeling none too brilliant. All the rich food was catching up to me. There was also an odd uneasiness at the pit of my stomach that had nothing to do with feeling overfull. I couldn't place it, only that something in the back of my mind kept telling me something was wrong. I had some reason to be afraid, if only I could remember what it was.

I kept picking at my last watermelon slice, not wanting to leave the table full of food even though I couldn't eat another bite.

Eventually, a young man with dark, wavy hair and a slight stoop to his shoulders came to collect me. He wasn't much older than I was. He was wearing a red coat, which meant he'd been born here at the Institute. His face was like sculpted marble, all strong angles and smooth planes. I stared openly, forgetting my manners.

"I'm Kris," he said, flashing me a quick, but genuine, smile. "Ready to head to your room?"

I nodded, and before I could stand, Kris moved behind my chair in order to pull it out for me. Confused and pleased by the courtesy, my face warmed as I trailed along behind him. He was not as tall as my brothers, but still significantly taller than I. He lacked the characteristic fuller face of the other

Institute residents, nor was he built strong like the laborers in the rest of the city. He stood slim, trim, with an easiness about him that just made my blush worse.

He held the door open and stood to one side so that I had to move close to pass him. I tore my eyes away with difficulty, staring instead at the mechanimal dog—still dormant by the fire.

"He's just for show," Kris whispered as I came near and let the door close again behind me before he led me down the hall.

I was glad for his guidance. The corridor we were walking down looked identical to the others I had seen.

"So watermelon, huh?" Kris said, slowing to a halt in front of a door.

"What?" Lost in trying to keep track of where we were going, I had almost trod on his heels.

"I saw you singlehandedly devour an entire platter of it." He grinned at me, revealing even, white teeth.

"Oh!" Humiliated, I could only stare at the floor. I was absurdly conscious of how short the smock they'd given me was.

"I like the cakes myself," he said cheerfully, as if he hadn't noticed my discomfort. "To each his own, eh? Here's your room."

He touched his badge to the handle of the door and opened it for me. Lights overhead came on automatically.

I had expected a dormitory of some kind, or at least rooms that would have held four or five kids, if I weren't the only one. Instead, Kris had shown me to a small but private room with one bed and a small chest of drawers at its foot. In the corner was a door that, as he demonstrated, led to a small bathroom.

"No water rations, so you can use the shower as much as you like. Temporary clothes in the chest there," he went on. "You'll probably want to find something that, uh, fits you a bit better."

By now I was so thoroughly embarrassed that I wished I could just slip down the drain of the little shower. Was it my fault I was older—and taller—than most of the kids who came through here? "This is just what they gave me when I—" I began to protest.

"Oh, I know, don't worry. I remember it well. At least I was scrawny and little when it was my turn."

I had to stifle the urge to blurt out my doubt that he was ever little and scrawny. Luckily, he saved me from that humiliation by continuing.

"Okay, rules. When you're supposed to be in your room, stay in your room. They're very strict about that here. There are experiments and equipment that could hurt you if you go wandering around on your own. Once you've settled a little, you'll discover you're really exhausted. The harvesting process does that to you. You've got the rest of the evening to rest, and the tests start tomorrow. Any questions?"

I wished I could think of something clever to say, something that would make him want to stay and talk to me. All that came to mind, though, was the memory of how greedily I'd stuffed myself at the feast, and that he'd seen it all. I was so used to avoiding contact, fending off stares and jeers with prickly animosity, that I had no idea how to seek out attention.

"Uh, no," I mumbled. "I guess not."

"Don't worry, you'll feel better after you get some rest." He grinned. My chest tightened.

"Thanks," I said, smiling awkwardly, my face more accustomed to a scowl. His smile was so contagious that I couldn't help myself.

"The lights will turn out automatically. If you need anything, ask for Kris, okay?" He waved and backed out of the room, shutting the door behind him.

I checked the chest for something to sleep in, but found only stacks of the same tunic I was wearing, and drawstring pants to match. None of it fit me. It was like I was living in a doll's house—the bed was too short, the clothes too small, the shower head jutting out from the wall a good three inches below my forehead.

I didn't want to sleep in the tunic I was wearing—it was clingy and scratchy, and had a strange smell, like sweat and fear. There was nothing in the chest to fit me any better, though, and sleeping naked was an abominable thought. So I gave up and collapsed on the bed. Only then did I discover how exhausted I was. I couldn't believe it was already evening. It felt like only moments had gone by since I was stuck in the pipe under the school. My mind was too tired to recall the time in between my arrival at the Institute and the feast. It was much easier to lie on top of the sheets and savor the sensation of being completely, utterly full. I thought of Kris, and that infectious smile, and the delicate perfection of his hands.

The lights cut out, leaving me in soft, warm darkness.

Again I felt that strange, nagging sensation that something was missing, even as I began to drift off to sleep. There was a piece somewhere that I'd forgotten in between my nervousness about coming to the Institute and my ravenous assault on the feast. It was as if I'd been dreaming and the dream had vanished upon waking, but I knew clear as day that there was something I ought to remember.

CHAPTER 6

The lights woke me in what I could only assume was the morning, and a voice projected into the room. "Good morning, duckling!" Though the voice was distorted by whatever process made it possible for me to hear, I recognized the cadence and tone as Gloriette's. Her voice continued, asking that I dress and report to the testing station. I groaned, remembering the chest full of children's clothing, and sat up.

Sitting neatly on the chest was a set of clothing that I *knew* hadn't been there the night before. The new clothes fit—at least well enough that I wasn't embarrassed to show my face in them. There was no sign of my old clothes—or my brother's paper bird.

I didn't see Kris at breakfast. A pang of surprising disappointment shot through me when another assistant led me off to testing.

All morning I completed booklet after booklet of questions testing mathematical and linguistic abilities, spatial awareness, and memory. They brought lunch on a tray in my testing room, and in the afternoon the same assistant led me through the maze of corridors to a large gymnasium full of unidentifiable equipment. The assistant walked me through each of the machines, making notes on her clipboard as I completed the tasks.

At dinner I could barely keep my eyes open, exhaustion for once overtaking hunger. They had been paying attention to what I ate, and brought only those dishes I liked. When Kris arrived, he found me nearly facedown in my last piece of watermelon. "Come on," he said, putting a hand on my shoulder. "Let's get you to sleep."

"I'm not sleepy," I protested, aware of how idiotic I sounded with eyes half closed and voice slurring.

With a hand under my elbow, he guided me toward the door. My skin tingled and prickled under his touch. "It's a rough couple of days. You'll feel better once you're tucked up in bed."

I scarcely remembered the walk to my room. My head pounded with exhaustion.

"Here you are," he said, pushing open my door and gently propelling me inside. "Sleep tight," he added. He stepped back and bowed, folding one arm across his chest. A day ago I would have scowled, knowing him to be teasing me—but now I just smiled in spite of myself. His charm was infectious. A pang shot through me as he straightened and closed the door behind him. Only one more day left—and I certainly wouldn't be seeing Kris anymore once the Institute doors closed behind me.

I gazed up at the lights. Their brightness made my head throb. Somewhere in the back of my mind, I remembered this headache, but I couldn't place it. There was something about a corridor, and a gentle, dark patch that eased my pain. I needed a moment to think. I had to force my mind to function despite my sudden, unnatural weariness.

I closed my eyes, hoping to somehow re-create that patch of darkness in my mind to stop the throbbing. It continued regardless until, unable to fight it off anymore, I slept.

· · ·

The next day they spent interviewing me—endless questions about my family, my hobbies, my abilities, my knowledge both of the city and of prewar history, and of the current theories about the world beyond the Wall. I wondered if they asked everyone these questions, or if my testing yesterday had shown my interest in prewar history. It was impossible for me to imagine myself as a historian working inside the Institute, but maybe there was some sort of assistant's position they were considering me for.

For lunch, I was brought to a little room that held only two chairs, one already occupied. A young architect sat making notes on her clipboard as I ate. She didn't seem to be observing me, but her presence made me uneasy and I didn't eat much of my meal.

When I pushed aside the tray, she lifted her head and smiled at me. She also wore the compass symbol, but it hung innocently on its wire, the point nowhere near as sharp as the Administrator's. Unlike Gloriette, her smile didn't make my skin crawl. "Just a few more questions and one last test, Miss Ainsley," she said. Her smile widened a little, and I realized that she was only a little older than I was.

She asked if I preferred a specific job. She showed very little reaction when I blurted out "historian." My heart sank as she made notations on her clipboard. How many other kids had spouted similarly outrageous preferences? I was going back over my test answers the previous day when she asked a question that drew me up short.

"Have you ever used the Resource illegally, Lark?"

I looked up, startled. The assistant's round eyes gazed back at me.

"What? No. No, of course not." I felt as though she must be able to hear my hammering heart.

"Okay," she replied, ducking her head again to make a notation on her clipboard. She continued writing for some time, during which I was certain she knew I was lying. Why couldn't I have said a simple "no?" Habit prompted me to check my pocket for my paper bird, but the linen trousers had no pockets—and the bird was missing, perhaps forever, perhaps sealing my fate if they had found traces of the Resource.

After a few more questions, she opened a case and removed a copper sphere. When she handed it to me, every hair on my arms stood up. The headache I'd been trying to ignore burst into brilliance and then, just as suddenly, faded into almost nothing. Skin tingling and heart racing, I looked up at the architect in confusion.

"It's a logic puzzle," she explained, her eyes flicking back to her clipboard. "You twist it and try to get all the patterns to line up."

I looked back down at the sphere. It was clearly magical, though I couldn't see why—it seemed to be a mechanical puzzle. It was made up of tiny copper panels inlaid with glass, each etched with different designs meant to line up with their neighbors. Each panel was slightly concave, fitting my fingertips exactly.

I gave it an experimental twist and was rewarded with the low, quiet hum of some mechanism within the object. Strategy was not my strong point, but my future possibly hinged on completing the puzzle. I saw a few panels that would line up easily, and twisted the ball until they did. The glass lit up with a discordant hum that set my teeth on edge.

The architect didn't seem to notice. I kept at it, working the puzzle until I had a few more adjacent panels lit and humming. I found myself becoming engrossed in how each new panel required longer patterns of twists to line up without disrupting those I'd already put in place.

It wasn't until I had half the sphere glowing that I looked up again—to find the architect staring at me. Her clipboard was in her lap, and her face suddenly looked even younger than mine: round eyes, parted lips.

My windpipe closed. What if this device detected whether I'd used magic before?

She cleared her throat when she saw me looking and summoned a labored smile. "I'm just going to run to the restroom," she said, getting to her feet with a metallic scrape of the chair legs beneath her. "You just—just carry on." Her eyes flicked down to the puzzle and back to mine, and then she backed out of the room.

I sat rooted to my chair, still holding the magic sphere. My whole body tingled with that magical buzz, which grew stronger every moment. I put the puzzle on the floor, hoping that would help, but not only did the panels on it stay lit, but my skin prickled more.

My jaw clenched so tightly that I felt it pop. I tried to look unconcerned—who knew what methods they had of spying on me? I nudged the puzzle with my toe, sending it rolling across the floor. Even distance brought no relief.

After an eternity the door opened. A plump red form bustled inside, wearing a wide, toothy smile. "Hello, hello, gosling!" said Administrator Gloriette. Her tendency to refer to me as various types of birds—all extinct now—gave me visions of how people used to eat them and use their bones to make soup. Gloriette's smile made me think she might be imagining what kind of soup my bones would make.

She continued, "I'm hearing some exciting things about you!"

Exciting things? My vocal cords felt frozen, but I was saved from trying to force something out by the Administrator herself.

"Are you enjoying yourself so far, here at the Institute?"

I nodded, still not able to speak.

Gloriette beamed her wide-lipped smile at me. "How perfectly fabulous," she cooed. "We so rarely see someone of your potential come through here, you know. You could be anything you wanted to be. Maybe even an architect's assistant! Would you like that?"

My head spun. Maybe this was a mind game—to throw me off-guard and convince me to blurt out the truth. With a huge effort I found my voice again. "Thank you, ma'am, but I'm more interested in history."

Gloriette's smile faded to something a little less brilliant. Apparently, this wasn't the response she expected. "Well, aren't you sweet? I think you would make a perfect historian. Of course, we'll have to keep you here for a few days so that we can run a few more tests. A historian is such a rare thing that we need to make absolutely certain, of course."

I found myself nodding, although my mind still roiled. I was certain that being kept behind meant something terrible, and yet Gloriette was smiling and telling me I was gifted, that I could be anything.

Still chattering, Gloriette reached for my elbow and pulled me to my feet. "I'll just take you back to your room, duck."

"I could find my way," I offered, shrinking from her heavy touch. "Especially if I'm to stay here as a historian."

"No, no," replied Gloriette, ushering me down the hallway. "I won't hear of it. It's rude to make you run around unescorted." She stepped back toward the door as she said this, and in the process, she crushed the puzzle with her left foot. She didn't even look down.

I managed to plaster a smile across my face in response. My mouth said, "Well, I've loved it here so far. I'm so glad I get to stay here even longer."

My mind whispered, *Why are they so afraid to let you out of your room alone?* An image formed in my mind of the boxes I'd seen on my way in, labeled with my name and my brother's.

By the time we arrived back at my room, I was almost stumbling, kept upright only by Gloriette's fleshy grip on my arm.

"Could I see my mother and father?" I asked, as she sat me down on my bed. "Just to let them know I'll be here a little longer?"

"Oh, we'll take care of that, dear." Gloriette smiled more widely. "They're going to be enormously proud of you!"

I tried to arrange the chaotic tangle of thoughts running through my mind. I wanted to insist on seeing my family—surely they couldn't keep a daughter from her parents?—but I couldn't form the words. In the end I only stared at her. "Proud of me?" I echoed stupidly.

Gloriette's eyes narrowed, and yet she kept smiling. The effect was horrifying. "Yes," she said, looking down at me and testing the needle-like point on her compass with her thumb. "You're going to do great things for your city."

As soon as she left, I lurched to my feet and headed for the door. I knew what I would find when I tried the handle, but the wave of despair still choked me. The door wouldn't budge.

CHAPTER 7

I awoke in darkness, with no buzzing lights to tell me whether it was day or night. I must have dozed off after Gloriette left. I had been awake only seconds before the door opened, sending a shaft of light slicing into my room. I kept quiet and still, but couldn't keep up the act when a blue-coated woman came to my bedside and shook me awake.

"Up you go, Miss Ainsley," she said, giving my arm a little tug.

When I stood, I felt dizzy, groggy. It felt as though I had slept only an hour. The overwhelming weariness that followed Gloriette's visit was unabated. "What's going on?" I mumbled. "Am I going home?"

"Time for your harvest," said the woman, whose face was painfully familiar, though I couldn't place where I'd seen her before. She introduced herself as Emila. "Don't worry, you can wear what you slept in."

"But," I protested, my voice coming out slow and distorted, "I've already been harvested. It's time to get my assignment. To go home."

"Have you?" Emila sounded surprised as she led me from

the room. "No, I'm sure we wouldn't have done that. Everyone is always harvested on their way out."

"But I remember. . . ."

"What do you remember, Lark?"

I realized that I could not remember a thing about being harvested. I remembered the feast, and the hours of testing and interviews. I remembered something about a faulty door lock, and I remembered being afraid they'd find out I had done magic. I remembered Gloriette telling me I could become an assistant. I remembered Kris and his dark, handsome hair, and his privileged, smooth hands. I must have dreamed something about being harvested. Even now, as I began to wake up a little more, the dream drifted away into nothing, like a cloud of steam.

"You'll be able to see your family again when it's done," said Emila when I didn't reply. "Would you like that?"

My family. Yes, I had wanted to see my mother and father. "Yes, please," I said eagerly, and stopped resisting.

As soon as I stepped into the corridor, the lights stabbed into my eyes. When I shut them, I felt harsh magic buzzing against my temples, my head bursting into a pain that was strangely, achingly familiar. "Wait," I said, but Emila pulled me onward.

"Don't worry, that'll go away after we harvest you."

She led me through a maze of corridors, my light-dazzled eyes failing to track where we were going. I was both floating and heavier than lead at the same time.

She brought me to a room full of red coats, who crowded around me to stare at my face, to shine another light into my eyes, to prick my skin with tiny needles I barely felt. I heard them talking in low voices, though I couldn't understand what they said. The sounds melded with the rushing in my ears as though they were speaking underwater.

Then abruptly I was in a different room altogether, without any surprise that I was there. In this room a woman in a black coat—what did black mean?—took off the tunic and the drawstring trousers I wore and scrubbed me from head to toe.

Then there was another room, this one filled with a huge red coat and Gloriette's simpering face and saccharine voice. I threw up on the floor, and she barely seemed to notice. She connected strange clips to the tips of my fingers and asked me questions while staring at something I could not see. I couldn't understand what she was saying, nor could I understand the words I spoke in response.

A room full of green things. *Plants*, I thought dimly. *Am I in the museum?* A vine with pale, sickly yellow flowers all in a row that turned toward me when I entered the room.

Then a room so cold my breath steamed in the air, and I shivered. From somewhere I had acquired a simple, thin white shift that went down to my knees. I gasped and shook, the cold stabbing my body. Our world was strictly climate-controlled inside the Wall. I had never been cold before.

A room lined on either side with mirrors, so I could see myself repeated endlessly, stretching around a barely perceptible curve. Dimly I saw the farthest-away reflection shake itself and lean out so that I could see the empty holes where my eyes should have been.

I cried out and tripped as I turned to run—and then found myself on my hands and knees in a different room altogether. Warm, familiar hands helped me up. Kris. I reached for him, but my hands slid past him. He stepped aside, and the dream fell away in tatters.

They had brought me once again to the Machine. And with sudden cold clarity, I remembered everything. My illegal Resource use, my panic, the trip to the Institute. Emila, my paper bird torn from me, wandering the maze of corridors alone. The tortured creature of light in the huge spherical room. *"Run."*

The Machine.

The chair was in front of me, long and squat and black. Lined with the glass panels that would turn into the shards and pierce my back. And there, pulsing, the field of magic that would hold me to it.

I turned to run and hit Kris square in the chest. His hands came out to take hold of my arms and I found I had no strength. He led me, sobbing, to the chair. I remembered the pain so clearly now that it was as though I was feeling it again, already.

"No," I gasped. "Please, no. No. I've been harvested already. There's been a mistake."

Kris squeezed my arms and pushed me down into the chair. "Please try to relax, Miss Ainsley," he told me loudly. "It'll be over soon, and then you can see your family." He bent low over my face, lip caught between his teeth and brow furrowed. Pretending to make sure I was settled, he said in a voice barely louder than a breath, "Just hang in there for now. I'm going to get you out of here, Lark. I promise."

And then he was gone, the room went black, and I was screaming before the vibrations reached my skull.

• • •

Out of the burning darkness, a voice.

?

No, not a voice. A touch. Questing, curious, wild. My body kept screaming under the torture of the Machine, but my mind seized that touch like it was a hand outstretched.

!

The touch, recoiling at my desperation, struggled and withdrew. With nothing now to feel except the knives sliding through my skin, nothing to hear but the screams, my mind surrendered and I slipped into unconsciousness.

· · ·

I awoke once more in my room. This time I remembered everything. Apparently, they no longer bothered to toy with my memories. I rolled over on the bed, and the pain of movement was so violent that I retched, sending the last liquid remains of last night's dinner splashing onto the floor.

I fell, narrowly avoiding the vomit on the floor, and caught myself on my knees and elbows. The shock of my impact sent jolts of pain through my spine. With sparkling afterimages dancing in front of my eyes, I dragged myself to my feet.

I staggered to the shower unit and pressed the button for water. Someone had undressed me at some point; I scarcely noticed.

When the jet hit my back it exploded with pain, and I bit my tongue to avoid shrieking. Wiping water out of my eyes, I craned my neck to try to look at my back. What little bit of it I could see was red, covered with puffy, shiny lines.

I tasted blood from where I'd bitten my tongue and spat, sending watermelon-colored tendrils swirling down the shower drain.

The first time they harvested me, I had recovered in no time at all. This second time, it was clearly taking much longer. How long would it take if they did it a third time?

Despite the jet of warm water full in my face, a trickle of ice ran down my spine as the significance of that thought sank in. A third time. To have harvested me twice was unheard of. How was such a thing even possible? The machinery must have failed in some way the first time around. The only other possibility was that they had successfully stripped me of my Resource—but somehow, impossibly, I had regained some measure of magic in the days since my harvest.

The last Renewables had destroyed themselves in the wars. They were barely myth now. No more real than the wolf-men living outside the Wall.

I turned off the water and stood in the shower, shaking. The nausea had passed and the water had helped with my back, but nothing eased the knot of panic in my belly.

If they sent me home, then I would know it was only a malfunction of their machinery. With any luck they would make me forget everything again. The thought of losing the memory of the Machine again was blissful.

• • •

The days passed in silence, my world shrinking down to the inside of my cell and the trays of tasteless rations they slid under the door for me. Shortly after I woke up on the third or fourth day, the skin on the back of my neck began to prickle uncomfortably as I picked at my breakfast. When I looked up at the Resource-lit panels overhead, the sensation flared into a dull throb at the base of my skull. I pushed it away, dropping my eyes, unwilling to believe.

That night I slept with the pillow over my head, pressed against my ears, trying to drown out the impossible hum I knew I shouldn't be able to hear.

No one regenerates. No one.

By the time they brought me out and took me to the Machine again, I couldn't even summon surprise. There was only a dull ache, the numbness of trying to understand impossible things. This time when they forced me into the chair, I didn't scream. I had to bite my tongue so hard that my mouth filled with blood, but I didn't scream for them. I pulled until my bones shook and my muscles burned but I couldn't escape the chair.

Just as the edges of the world began to fade, the voice—the touch—the presence—whatever it was—came to me again. A frightened, wild blow against my mind, nonsensical with pain that felt strangely familiar, similar to mine. It spoke to me—not in words, but in something far more primitive, screaming directly to my gut and my heart and my bones— and I listened.

You, it said. *You are like me.*

And then a roaring surged in my ears and I fell away.

• • •

My mind wandered when it could. Memories long buried came bubbling up to the surface, painfully vivid. Everything then was clean, orderly, the peaceful world of my city spinning around me in its precise dance. I knew the rules. I knew my place in it all.

When I was little, no more than four or five, a friend of my father's at the recycling plant required Adjustment. He was unhappy in his job, my father explained, and unfit for any other. His work was slow and inconsistent—he wobbled from task to task without purpose and without regularity. His meeting with the Regulatory Board was quick, a formality only.

Basil held my hand while we stood among the other families who knew this man, whose name my memory failed to recall. The ceremony was outside, not far from where we all lived, where one of the broad streets vanished beyond the Wall. The energy of the Wall sang in the background as everyone crowded around the man; the adults couldn't hear it, but the un-harvested children twitched and swayed to its music, the discordant, hypnotic strains. My hand tingled in Basil's.

The man kissed his wife on the cheek, ruffled his son's hair. Said good-bye to his friends at the plant, shook my father's hand. There were no Regulators there, only his friends, his family, the people who cared for him. I remember everyone smiling.

When there was no one left to thank for coming to his Adjustment, the man turned to face the Wall.

"What's he doing?" I whispered urgently to Basil. It was the first rule we learned as children. *Never go near the Wall.* One wrong move, one slip, and you're gone forever.

"Watch," my brother replied. I'd never heard that voice from him before. He was only a few years older than me but he sounded like an adult. He sounded tired.

The man lifted his head, and without looking back at the friends and family who had gathered to see him off, he strode forward through the Wall.

The violet film of energy in front of us rippled with his passage, sending cascades of light and color racing away, out of sight. I saw the man's wife put an arm around her son's shoulders, a gentle squeeze.

Shock kept me silent, staring. There were always stories of what lay beyond the Wall. Monsters, ghosts, a barren world, all that remained from the warring Renewables. Caesar in particular liked to give me nightmares describing carnivorous stones and shadows that bled.

But never had I actually thought of a person going beyond the Wall. I couldn't stop shivering despite Basil's hand warm around mine, squeezing tight. All around me the crowd stood still and quiet. Almost as though they were waiting for something.

Then, without warning, a dull thud. The whole crowd flinched in unison as the Wall rippled with the sound. The sound came again, a muffled pounding. The energy was too opaque to see anything on the other side, but with each thud the light shimmered from the force of the blow.

Basil's hand around mine was so tight it hurt, but I didn't pull away. We stood there, silent, listening to the frantic pounding from outside the Wall. The crowd held vigil as the knocking grew louder, more insistent, hysterical. Pleading. A few people gazed up at a nearby clock tower. I looked at the face of the man's wife—it was quiet, calm. Gentle.

We listened as the pounding rose to a frantic drum roll. And then, in the space between one breath and the next—it stopped.

Nothing. Silence. Only the ever-present singing of the Wall, now still and gently shining.

That night, the neighborhood's rooftops were alive with lanterns as everyone honored the man's sacrifice and celebrated how smoothly the city would run in the morning.

The memory should have been frightening. Now, I felt only the ache of something lost, all the more wrenching because I never knew I wanted it. There would be no Adjustment for me. No family gathered around to see me go, no city lights to mark my passing. I would just vanish, gone forever. Like Basil. Like something too broken to fix.

I thought of my parents, and what the Institute had told them. Perhaps they thought I was to become an architect. Perhaps they had told them I was dead. Perhaps they had told them I had volunteered for a mission the way my brother had. At some point I realized I would never see them again.

My life retreated into a hazy darkness, the dim waking hours between sessions in the Machine haunted by the pain behind me, the pain in front of me. My world became a maze of corridors and unfamiliar faces, masses of red coats crowding around me. I ate the food they gave me because I didn't have the will to stop eating. I showered when told. I slept when the lights commanded. Kris's face swam out of the haze sometimes, drawn with concern, his warm hands holding me up, his eyes reflecting my pain.

Help me, I wanted to cry, but my voice never worked properly. Once he touched my cheek, his hand soft against my skin. His bottom lip was between his teeth, and he stared at me for a long moment before his face twisted and he turned away, retreating back into the haze.

After the third session in the Machine, the fourth, the fifth, I lost track of time utterly. The wounds on my back never healed now, and I slept naked on my stomach with the sores open to the air.

The only times I woke, the only times I came to myself, were when the voice came to me from the Machine. It began to teach me. As though taking me gently by the hand, it led me through the steps of pulling my mind away from the torture my body was undergoing, giving me moments of relief. I would have gone insane had I not learned how to slip away from myself.

Some time after I completely lost count of the days, they led me, shuffling mindlessly after them in the corridor, to the room I had been drawn to on my first day in the Institute. I recognized the clang of the metal catwalk under their shoes before anything else. Though my feet were always bare now, I had been wearing shoes the first time I came here. Memory prompted me to look up.

This time when I saw the woman of light, I recognized her instantly. It was the shape of her mouth, the same fixed *O* that had transfixed me that first day. I saw it now for what it was—a silent scream.

She is like me.

They led me past her and toward a platform, where assistants stripped off my shift and began to measure my body with cold metal tapes. Beyond them I saw some vitrarii, glassworkers even less commonly spotted outside of the Institute than architects. They were shaping glass filaments and cutting them with a concentrated fire-spitting torch. I let my head fall back, gazing up. There was a bundle of glass cables extending from the ceiling, a glass wire spinal cord with nerves branching off in every direction. The nerve endings terminated in nothing. Waiting. Grasping.

I stared again at the creature suspended in space as they hustled me back out of the room again, my measurement complete. She did not look at me—I don't think she could see anyone. The light was being pumped from her. I could see it trailing away up the wires into the very walls of the Institute itself.

I knew her now for what she was. *Renewable.* The magic they stripped from her would power the Wall, the automatic harvesting machines, the generators that allowed us to breathe. I wondered how much of the Resource that kept us alive came from the kids they so publicly harvested and how much came from this creature. I wondered if the harvest's sole purpose was to find another like her. If so, they had achieved their aim.

I wondered how long she had been there; I wondered how long she would continue to live. How long would I live?

• • •

I had no memory of the walk back to my cell. I woke only when the door opened and the lights came on. I was lying on my stomach, half on the bed, one arm trailing to the floor. Weakly I pressed my palm against it to try to lever myself back on the bed.

A hand grasped my arm, gently, and lifted me into a more comfortable position. I tried to turn my head to see, but the motion tugged on the raw skin on my back and I whimpered.

"Shh. Try to stay still."

Kris. I tried to remember that he was one of them, was as responsible as any for what was happening to me. Instead I could only start to weep with relief.

He rubbed my arm as one would comfort a child. "Shh.

It's going to be okay. I brought something for your back. May I?"

I tried to say yes, but my throat was so hoarse that all I managed was a little moan.

Without further warning he lifted the edge of my tunic and touched my back with his hand, and I stiffened. Even as smooth and uncallused as his fingertips were, they felt like sandpaper. The pillow muffled my cry. No sooner had he touched me, though, than a blissful coolness spread. He worked his way across my back, slathering it with something that smelled acrid and chilled the insides of my nostrils.

My sobs quieted as he worked, and by the time he finished I was silent. Facedown in the pillow, I didn't lift my head when I felt him stand. A few seconds later I heard him washing the pungent salve from his hands in the shower. Then footsteps, and that gentle weight making the bed creak and depress by my hip.

He plucked a few strands of hair away from my neck, freeing them from the sticky salve. I remembered my mother doing something similar so that she could tickle me there. I couldn't bear the thought of Kris doing the same, and made a sound into the pillow.

Kris stopped, but didn't rise from the bed. After a few seconds of silence, he spoke.

"You won't be going back into the Machine."

One second passed, then two. Then, spots exploding in front of my closed eyes, I was forced to breathe again. I didn't dare linger on the significance of those words.

"We want you healed up, Lark. You'll get some time, let the Resource fully recharge." His voice was very, very quiet. Subdued. There was a deadness to his tone, the charm vanished. The skin on the back of my neck prickled in warning.

I started to speak, but he put a hand on the back of my head, stopping me.

"At least you're back on normal rations now," he said, evidently spotting my barely touched tray of food. "Just as well. I never could stand those little cakes at harvest time."

I had barely enough time to register confusion—just days ago he'd been telling me how much he loved those—before his hand tightened around a lock of my hair, giving it a painful tug.

"Listen to me, Lark," he said when I tried to protest his painful grip. "*I'm to tell you* that you'll be monitored closely and any attempts to disobey will send you back to the Machine. We expect you to behave and do your duty. Think of your family, your friends, everyone who is counting on you to do this. One broken piece and the whole machine breaks down. We need you."

There was tension in his grip on my hair. I realized that we must be being monitored. He was reciting a script. The emphasis on "I'm to tell you" said everything. There was urgency in the clench of his fingers. Suddenly the pain in my back, in the roots of my hair, wasn't the sole focus of my attention anymore. What was he trying to tell me?

"We expect your recovery to take about a week," he went on. "During this time you are to rest and eat to replenish the Resource within you."

I lifted my head very slowly so that I could turn it, free my mouth enough for speaking. He didn't shift his grip on my hair. "And then?" I asked. I didn't recognize my own voice.

There was a pause. "And then you'll go home," he said, and twisted my hair so hard my eyes watered. I didn't cry out, though. I heard his message:

We're lying.

"Okay," I gasped.

He let me go and then, very gently, stroked the back of my head so that the hair lay flat. "Good girl."

And then he was gone, the door closed and the lights off, leaving me in the dark again.

The blackness was so complete that it made no difference whether my eyes were open or closed. Instead, as if burned into my retinas like some blinding afterimage, I saw that empty spinal column, the fingerlike tendrils of glass wires, waiting. Waiting for me.

Home, I thought. Where I'd be spending the rest of my existence. *Home*.

CHAPTER 8

I lay there for a time, facedown on my mattress. I know I should have been frantic, weeping, panicked. But instead the predominant sensation was one of relief. The past week—or had it been weeks?—had been full of pain, but now my skin was numb, and I knew I would not be going back into the Machine.

One week, I thought, Kris's words echoing in my mind.

They had had no problem putting me in the Machine when my back was still raw and my magic half-charged, but perhaps it was different when it came to—my skin crawled at the word—*installing* me in the web of glass wiring. It seemed that they needed me to be at full strength.

With a groan, I pushed myself up on my arms and gasped as the wounded skin stretched. The pain woke me, made me sharp.

And I'm going to need to be sharp if I'm going to get out of here.

The very thought was ridiculous. The Institute was the most heavily guarded and sophisticated place in the entire city. And even if I could break free, then what? There was nowhere to hide. There was nothing after escape except death outside the Wall or recapture within it.

But the tiny trickle of a thought ate away at my reservations bit by bit. *Escape.*

I knew that the moment they deemed me fit they would slot me into those glass wires, and I would become something barely human.

I would rather die. The thought came to me one night with all the fury of the Machine, echoing through my body and vibrating in my bones. Out of the black, I saw the Renewable creature's mouth set in that constant, soundless scream. *I would rather kill myself.*

"Yes," I whispered aloud, staring into the darkness. In my mind I saw the tangled wires of glass reaching for me. "Oh, yes."

For the first time since this place had become my prison, I slept soundly and of my own free will.

• • •

In the morning I rose and choked down the dry ration bread in the dark. They were careful to give me plenty of food, and I had realized quickly that it was linked to the regeneration of magic in my system. Energy in equaled energy out, no matter the form.

They rarely turned the overhead lights on anymore. I climbed onto the bed in darkness and stretched up toward where I knew the light to be. I imagined the paper bird, cupping my hand around it, making it wake up and fly. A faint roaring in my ears rose and then subsided again as the image vanished. I concentrated again, this time seizing the image and the feeling and thrusting out toward the dark light.

Something snapped in my mind, and one bulb of the light burst into brilliance. I fell back, stumbling against the wall. My eyes were dazzled after so long in darkness. My head ached from effort and from the hum now emanating from the light, but it was nothing compared to the surge of triumph.

The Institute was strong because it had the Resource, relied upon it, needed it. It sucked it away from us, had been doing so for centuries. I had never once questioned them; we needed it, after all, to keep the horrors beyond the Wall from reaching us. But that reliance was exactly what was going to get me out of here.

Magic, said my brother's voice in my mind.

If I could manipulate their lights, I could do anything. My gaze fell upon the door, dimly lit now by the single square of light overhead. I fell upon it, seizing every scrap of power within myself and hurling it at the lock.

I strained until my vision swam and sweat rolled down my temples, but the lock made no sound other than vibrating once, and only briefly. When I tried the handle, it remained immovable.

But that lone vibration was enough to tell me that I wasn't wrong to think that I could blast my way out of here; I just wasn't strong enough yet.

Perhaps magic was like any ability. Perhaps all I needed was a little practice.

I threw myself into my new routine. Every morning after eating I would stuff spare clothing against the crack under the door to hide the light and stand over my bed in order to focus my magic on the ceiling panels. At first I could only light one before I had to rest, and then two, and then three. After four days I could turn them all on, one by one, without having to stand on the bed to be close to them. I would turn each of them on, and then, with the same tiny surge of power, turn each of them off again.

The feel of the magic was drastically different from what I had felt when I'd made the paper bird sing. That had felt sweet and clear, ringing like a bell and leaving me lightheaded. Now it felt thick and heavy, twanging out of my body like an alien thing, painful and harsh. But it worked.

I ate ravenously. As the days passed, I found that after turning the lights on and off a couple of times, the hunger would be so great and so sudden that it would nearly make me black out. I saved a few pieces of the dry bread for these occasions, hiding them inside my mattress.

Now and then, I tried the door. Only once did I ever get it to vibrate again. Still, I was growing stronger by the hour. I knew it was only a matter of time.

. . .

On the fifth night, as near as I could estimate, the door banged open unceremoniously. Three red coats. I recognized them only vaguely through my eyelashes, and tried to feign sleep.

"Miss Ainsley," one of them said firmly. "Will you please come with us?"

They were always the soul of courtesy. Almost friendly. "Where are we going?" I asked, my heart hammering in my chest.

"Almost time to go home," said another red coat. It stretched a red sleeve out toward me, offering a hand. "We just have one last test to run."

They led me through the maze of corridors once more, down an elevator, and up another hall. With so much time between me and my last trip to the Machine, my mind was more clear and lucid than it had been in weeks. And yet, I still couldn't recognize where we were going. Every time I thought I recognized a turn, it opened up into a hallway I was certain I'd never seen before.

When we reached the Renewable's chamber, I balked. I had little strength but I began to struggle anyway, for all that my efforts did to stall the two techs gripping my arms. The empty spinal column of glass stood waiting, side by side with the one occupied by the creature. It was finished.

Administrator Gloriette stepped out from behind a curtained alcove, and beamed at me. The expression was half-lost in the rolls of her face. My gut roiled at the sight of her. How had I ever thought her harmless, even jolly?

"Poor duckling," she oozed, gliding toward me. "You must be really ready to get settled, aren't you?"

"I'm okay," I said, unable to speak except through clenched teeth. "Really."

"Such a brave chicklet," she replied, delighted. "Still, we can't have such a brave girl suffering so much. We just have one more measurement to make. Then you can go home."

No. No. It was too soon. I hadn't figured out yet how to escape. "But—"

A burning pinch on my neck interrupted me. I started to whirl around but my knees buckled. I had a brief image of one of the red coats holding something long and glinting, and then Gloriette's face. She was no longer smiling. And then her face began to melt, like a piece of glass in a furnace. Long rivulets of pasty, fat flesh, pooling and swirling and burning into blackness.

• • •

I woke nauseous, feeling as though I was barely touching the mattress. I knew this sensation. They had put me in the Machine. I felt raw and stretched and hollowed out. I leapt off of my bed, staggering. My knees didn't bend right. Nevertheless I craned my neck, trying to get a look at my back.

The scars there were clean, pink, shiny—no new gashes. And a slight thrum of power fluttered at the edge of my mind. The magic of the door lock, perhaps. Fainter than that of the lights, which were off, but I could hear it. Which meant my magic was still intact.

In a panic I reached out for the door with my mind, stomach convulsing with the effort. Nothing. I still couldn't budge the lock. I was trapped.

And tomorrow would start the rest of my life.

There was a tray of food by the door. I still felt nauseous, but something caught my eye.

In addition to the usual rations of dry bread and soy protein paste, there were two round cakes on the corner of the tray.

Kris.

A treat on my last day. I wanted to feel something: gratitude or grief, maybe. Instead I stared at the cakes numbly.

There was a tiny point of gray-white sticking out from the edge of the cake. When I lifted the cake, whatever was beneath it stuck to the bottom. I peeled it away, and then sat cupping the thing in my hands.

How long I sat there, gazing at the paper lark my brother had made for me, I couldn't say. Tears came and went, and my nausea subsided. I tucked the little bird into the palm of my hand and held it against my heart, reaching for the other cake.

As I lifted it, something else peeled away from the bottom of the cake where it too had stuck. It fell with a metallic clatter against the tray.

A key.

CHAPTER 9

I lurched to my feet. How much time had I wasted? There was no way of knowing how long I had until they were at my door, ready to take me to the Renewable's chamber. To put me into that glass cage forever.

I dug a pair of the drawstring pants from the chest at the foot of my bed. Tying the legs together, I loaded my makeshift bag with my untouched bread rations and the rolls I'd hoarded. I drained cup after cup of water. When I could hold no more, I threw the cup in the bag with the rations.

It was an awkward backpack, but it would hold for now. I tried not to think about what I would do when I got home. What would my parents do? What *could* they do? Sucking in a deep breath, I shoved the key into the keyhole and twisted.

There was a click, and the door swung outward at my touch.

The corridor stretched away on either side. I could hear movement to the left and so I went right. I passed door after door—the rooms that had been occupied by other children. They were all unlocked, giving me easy places to hide whenever architects passed.

My mind remained oddly detached. As though subconscious memory was leading me, impulse told me without hesitation which direction to go whenever I reached an inter-section of hallways.

I came to a door at the end of the hallway that was built more solidly than the others, designed to swing outward rath-er than slide open. I saw a strip of light below it. I couldn't know what was on the other side of the door. A room full of architects, a corridor lined with guards, or alarms sounding throughout the building—but I couldn't wander the halls for-ever. I placed both palms against the door, willing myself to go through with it.

A sound, behind me. A clatter of a door opening, voic-es exclaiming. Footsteps, running. Someone had realized I wasn't in my cell. It didn't matter now whether I set off an alarm or not.

I threw my body against the bar on the door and daylight exploded against my eyes as I staggered over the threshold—and onto empty space.

My momentum turned me in midair, giving me a glimpse of the open door above me. There would have once been a fire escape there, but no longer, only a long drop from several stories off the ground.

My mind worked clearly, efficiently; it seemed I fell for hours. I had time to picture the oddly comforting image of my broken body once it hit the ground. I had said I would rather die than be their magical slave. So be it.

The air rushed past me, and the wind whispered, *Just like you, Lark.* An imaginary shoulder jostled mine, a broad palm cradled a little bird made of paper. A rustle of wings, a breath, and then stillness.

NO. Something flew from me with such force that it sent me tumbling sideways in midair. I collided heavily with the wall opposite, striking my head so hard that my vision spotted with black. I hit something else, something yielding and buzzing with power, and then bounced onto the cobblestones.

. . .

I lay there stunned and gasping. My body tingled and roared. I rolled over and the motion sent a ripple of pain and dizziness that triggered a spasm of nausea. I fought the impulse to retch—I couldn't afford to waste the food.

My hands were resting on something sticky and warm. I lifted one, staring without recognition at the aggressively bright red color coating it. It wasn't until I saw something drip past my vision and into the crimson puddle that I clapped my hand to my head. A wave of dizziness swept over me, and this time I did vomit, a thin stream of acidic, vile liquid. *Head wounds bleed*, I reminded myself, trying not to panic. *It looks worse than it is.*

With a groan I hauled myself up against the wall. I aimed my steps toward the mouth of the alley. I was still within the Institute complex, but at least I was outside the building.

By the time I emerged from the alley, I felt a bit better. Now I could see that the sun disc hung low in the west, just past the four-o'clock tick mark on its track. The Institute was on the eastern edge of the city, and since I knew I couldn't leave on its east side—and go through the Wall—I went west.

The lane ended in another doorway. With no other choice, I pushed through it, slipping down the hallway beyond. My head throbbed in time with the buzzing lights overhead, and my mind slipped into a waking doze. Again I had the strange sense that I was being led.

Too late, I recognized my surroundings. My concussed mind hadn't grasped that I was walking down a spiral. I had been led down this path once before. I froze, and then spun around to retrace my steps, and found instead a door I didn't remember coming through. I shoved it open and staggered inside.

The blinding column blazed in the room's center. Filaments of glass traced outward, stretching toward the spherical walls and disappearing into them. Crystals lined the edges of the walls, storing the magic emanating from the creature.

Gripping the railings in each hand, I made my way toward the being in the center column. Her face was still split by that silent agony, and she gave no sign or expression that she was aware of me.

The vacant suffering in her gaze made me stare. She was naked, the features of her body easily visible. I had balked at the idea of undressing in a dark room, alone. Now this was my future, hanging suspended and laid bare for all to see. The violence of her existence hit me like a blow. She was tense with agony, skin twitching now and then as the glass filaments plugged into her skin pulsed.

I shivered and forced my eyes toward her face. Her hair and her vacant eyes were as white as her skin. Each eyelash glowed white-hot, searing against the darkness around her. Her pale lips were cracked and caked with a substance like blood drained of its color. Her skin was strangely mottled, tiny specks that blocked out the light shining from her every pore.

She had freckles. We didn't get freckles in the city, with no sunlight to cause them. Suddenly she stopped being "the creature" and became a person, a woman, once a girl not unlike me. And she was from beyond the Wall.

In that moment I realized that I had no more strength. Nauseous, dizzy, exhausted beyond the point where my mind could function, I collapsed, slumping against the railing.

And this was my future. Hours of trying to escape, and I walked right back to the chamber that would be my tomb.

"Lark." It was scarcely a whisper, but in the eerie cavern, silent but for the hum of magic and machinery, it was electrifying. My head jerked up.

The woman's eyes had not moved, still gazing out into the middle distance, fixed on blackness. But as I watched, her lips moved, shaped the single syllable of my name again.

Something moved near her waist. A filament withdrew, shining in the glow of raw magic, and moved toward me. I scrambled back as far as the railings on the opposite side of the walkway would let me.

"Lark," came the whisper again. The movement of her lips cracked the skin, causing a fresh flow of grayish-brown blood. The glass wire twisted once, twice. Beckoning.

"No." Speaking took more energy than I thought I had left. "I won't. I won't."

The tendril of glass curved low, moving slowly, as a person might approach a frightened child.

The woman groaned, as if making a massive effort. Then: "Trust."

I stared at her, and at once I saw that what I had taken for agony in her gaze was desperation. She could only speak to me as she had before when we were connected—she to her cage, I to the Machine. Networked through the web of glass that was the Institute's heart.

The wire beckoned again, and the woman's body shuddered, sending the glass filaments dancing and shimmering in the glow from her skin. I forced myself away from the railing. I pushed back the sleeve of my tunic, and held out my shaking arm.

The wire twitched once and then plunged into my wrist. I felt nothing at first, staring as the filament slid under my skin, forming a transparent bulge surrounded by the blue of my veins.

There was a moment of silence as the woman's eyes closed, her chest falling as she exhaled a soundless sigh.

My arm exploded into fire. I screamed and screamed and

saw the harsh metal catwalk surging up to meet me as I fell.

I thrashed and kicked, my skin burning and every hair stiff. I screamed for her to let me die.

My wild gaze fell upon my arm as I tried to tear the glass wire from it, but the slightest touch multiplied the pain. I stared at it for some time in anguish and terror before I realized what I was seeing.

Both times I had seen this creature of light, the glass wires had been carrying that energy away from her body, sucking it free, draining her. But as I watched, the light came *into* me through the filament, in fitful starts and stops. The memory of her assistance while I was in the Machine came crashing back, and I yanked my mind away from my body's pain.

I knew my body was lying crumpled on the catwalk, but that knowledge didn't lessen the wave of bliss that washed over me at the sudden cessation of pain. I had only time to gasp for air before a wall of light, sound, and feeling collided with me.

With her magic came her memory. Bright flashes of meaning, inextricable from my own thoughts, and yet incomprehensible parts of an incomplete whole. I felt the edges of her insanity crowding in upon me.

There was a city, somewhere beyond our Wall. No, not a city. I could see something like buildings, but not—massive and delicate and strange. There were people living in them, around them. People I had never seen before, each one alive and humming with power. *Adults* who had magic.

You must find them, said a voice that had become familiar to me over the past weeks.

Who? I was struggling to breathe the thick air.

The others, she said. *The others like us.*

Where can I go? There's nothing beyond the Wall.

Find the Iron Wood. You will know now where to go. Follow the birds.

The images were hazy now, nothing more than a strangely muddled memory, viewed from behind warped glass.

And you? Will you come?

They will come for me when it is time.

I could feel the agony rushing back at me, and I tried to force it away. Anything was better than returning to that tortured body lying in a heap on the corrugated metal walkway.

Please! I don't even know where to go!

Go south, she said. *Across the river. Then follow the birds.*

And then the wire was whipping out of my arm. As it retracted, it flailed up and struck my head with a flash, and she glowed so brilliantly that I felt that my eyes must be burning, blinded. Then it was all gone.

CHAPTER 10

When I came to I was outside, and the sun disc was dipping below the lip of the buildings. I had no recollection of how I'd come to be there. The last thing I remembered was the Renewable, her gift of power, her instructions.

The world was washed in the lavender glow of sunset, the Wall shimmering over and around me. For a tiny, quiet moment I forgot everything and gazed at the violet sky.

Then I heard a siren in the distance, and the moment fled.

I got to my feet, staggering at first but growing more steady. I shoved back the sleeve of my tunic and saw delicate silver lines tracing across my skin. As I watched it began to fade. The only mark that remained was a shiny pink dot of a scar below my wrist.

My head throbbed, but I could no longer feel the dreadful slow trickle of blood dripping through my hair. When I lifted my hand to the spot, the hair there crackled and fell away. I thought of the burning glass wire catching me as it whistled away into the dark. She must have cauterized the wound.

I was in a part of the city that I didn't recognize. The buildings were better preserved here. Tall brick row houses lined each side of the street. Each had a crisp white door, as impassible as stone. I wasn't going to find anyone here among the richest quarter who would help me, not looking as I did now.

Glancing up the street I saw a cluster of carriage drivers standing around, chatting. They were tossing stones at a manhole cover.

I saw my reflection in the gleaming windows of one of the houses. "They'll never take me," I croaked to myself.

Sure enough, the drivers recoiled as I approached. I knew I looked like something from beyond the Wall. I couldn't blame them for their revulsion. Suddenly a name rose unbidden in my mind. I saw a pair of improbably large ears and red hair.

"Tamren," I choked. "I need Tamren."

The smallest of the drivers took off as if all the shadow monsters on the planet were after him, vanishing into one of the buildings. The others retreated back to where their carriages were parked, talking together in urgent whispers and sending me frequent, horrified looks.

The kid was gone for maybe five minutes before he reappeared, dragging a skinny, familiar form behind him. Tamren was chattering away, and for this more than anything I recognized him.

"—and I was just all, you know, you can't tell me where to piss, mister, and *he* was like, oh yes I can, you little—oh, holy *mother*." He skidded to a halt.

"Hi," I said, leaning against a fire hydrant. I hoped it looked as though I was merely doing it to be casual, and not that it was necessary to prevent my falling over.

". . . Miss Lark?" He gaped at me.

"I need you to take me home," I managed.

The other drivers were all staring at Tamren. He continued to stare at me, but abruptly straightened, aware of their scrutiny. "Of course, miss," he said, as if I were any well-paying customer. "This way."

He took my arm. The gesture was gentlemanly, but the way I leaned against him was certainly not ladylike. He said nothing, for once remaining blessedly silent.

"I don't have anything to pay you with," I said awkwardly.

"Nah," he said, unchaining his bike from the rack. "You're paying me in street cred. The other drivers are too chicken to drive someone looks as bad as you do now. I'll be king for a month with this story."

Tamren didn't speak as we pulled away, his muscles straining as he built up some momentum. It wasn't until we were out of sight of the other drivers and had crested a slight hill that he slowed to a halt and turned to stare at me. "Miss Lark, what *happened* to you?"

For a tiny, overwhelming moment I wanted to pour out to him what had been done to me. I longed for sympathy. I wanted him to be horrified, wanted him to comfort me. And I knew he would. But what would telling him accomplish? Better leave him out of it. Better keep him safe.

"Just take me home," I whispered. I felt hollow, scooped clean.

"But I need to take you to the hospital—all that blood—"

"Tamren, if I tell you anything, you'll get in trouble for it. You might get in trouble just for giving me a ride." Why had I said that? There was no way I could walk so far as my building. I wasn't even entirely certain where I was.

Tamren's ears were turning a furious shade of dark pink. "Miss Lark, if someone's hurt you, you tell me and I'll whoop them."

I laughed. "Just take me home, Tamren. That's all I need. Please." I gave him my address.

Tamren spluttered and protested but in the end he gave

in. When we arrived it took some serious convincing to prevent him from accompanying me up all the stairs to our apartment, but eventually I was able to start the long climb to my apartment, alone.

As my feet hit the familiar solidity of the steps, I realized I had no plan. I had nowhere to go. Even if I could hide from their pixies, my tiny stash of food wouldn't last long. Still, something made me long for home.

It took all my strength to climb the steps. I collapsed against our door—which turned out to be ajar. I fell inward. Looking up, I saw Caesar's face.

"Lark?" He sounded uncertain.

"C," I gasped. "Please. Please, I need your help."

This was pure desperation. Caesar was a Regulator. His entire function within the city was to ensure that it ran smoothly. And what would make it run more smoothly than apprehending a Renewable capable of sustaining the city for a few more generations? His talkie device hung quiet at his belt; with it he could summon an army of pixies here in seconds.

But he was my brother. Suddenly I was telling him everything.

At some point in my story Caesar guided me into the living room, to the couch that served as my bed. I noticed that it was still made up for me. Whatever the Institute had told them, it wasn't that I was dead.

When I finished speaking it was more due to my voice failing than because I had reached the end of my story. "Please don't call them, C," I begged him. "Please don't report me. They won't even make an Adjustment; I'll just vanish again. You have to believe me, I haven't done anything wrong. Please—" My voice gave out.

Caesar leaned toward me and put an arm around my shoulders. "Of course I'm not going to report you," he said, hoarsely. His gesture was awkward—I'm not sure he had ever hugged me—but the touch was so welcome that it brought a fresh flood of tears as I turned into his shoulder.

He held me for a while and then very gently disentangled my arms from around his neck. "I'm going to get you a glass of water," he said. "Are you hungry?"

I nodded, wiping the tears from my face.

"Get changed into some real clothes," he said.

I shrugged out of my backpack and tore off my blood-stained tunic and pants, and slid into my only other clothes. Then I snuggled down against the arm of the couch and fell into a stupor. For a brief moment I was safe again. I was in my brother's hands now.

He was making a ton of noise in the kitchen. Dishes clattered and clanked. Now and then he'd mutter to himself, low and unintelligible. When he turned the spigot on the water tank, and I heard it tinkling into the cup, I realized that I desperately needed to use the bathroom. I forced myself up off the couch and down the hall, listening to the comforting sounds of Caesar in the kitchen as I went.

On my way back, as I passed by the doorway to the kitchen, I could hear Caesar's stream of murmuring more clearly.

"...think she'll stay put," he was saying. "No, I don't think so." A pause. "A few minutes?"

I stopped dead in the doorway. With one hand, Caesar was stacking plates, keeping up a steady clatter of activity. But in his other, he was holding his talkie. It was pulsating the red of a steady connection. I could feel the hum of the Resource from here, throbbing against my temples like a bruise.

I stood frozen, my mind unwilling to accept what my eyes were seeing. He didn't notice me at first, continuing to speak into the device.

"Yeah, she doesn't know anything. No problem, she's about half-dead—" He saw me and stopped speaking.

The moment stretched into an eternity, the pit of my stomach roiling though my mind had yet to understand.

"Lark," he said, his voice low, steady. "Just listen—"

I whirled, grabbed my pack, and sprinted for the door.

I heard him thumping after me. "Lark!" he shouted. "Get back here! It's not what you think!"

I flew down the fire escape, scarcely noticing how the metal grid cut into my battered bare feet.

His heavy footsteps started clanging down after me. "You need a doctor!" he shouted. "They know what's best for you, Lark; they were keeping you for a reason—you're sick—jeez, Lark, slow down!"

My legs were shaking with effort, but I could hear his footsteps getting closer. I couldn't afford weakness.

He was just above me now, one floor up. As I turned a corner, he swung himself over the railing out over empty space, letting his momentum carry him back in. He landed hard on his feet in front of me, between me and the next flight of stairs down. I skidded to a halt.

I darted to the side, looking down over the railing. Five stories.

Caesar saw my sideways movement. "Uh uh," he said, stretching his hands out so as to make it clear there was no way past him. "Stop it, Lark. Just come back in with me and we'll have some food, okay? I know you think all that stuff is true, but you're sick. It isn't real." He smiled at me, showing his teeth.

There was no escaping him. He was twice my size, and, like he'd said into his talkie, I was half-dead. "Do you *really* believe what they told you?"

His false smile faded. "Where are you going to go except

back?" he asked, shaking his head. "It's better if you go voluntarily. Don't make a fuss. Go quietly, smoothly. You have to understand your function in this city."

I tried to catch my breath, too angry and too frightened to find words. How could he believe my function should be a lifetime of enslavement?

He must have read something of my thoughts from my expression. "Let me take you in."

"Is this all so you can get your precious promotion?" I spat.

Caesar shrugged. "We are who we are, little sister," he said. He came toward me.

I backed up until I was pressed against the railing behind me. "I'd rather die than live there." My voice was steady as I stepped up onto the bottom edge of the railing.

"If you jump here you won't die." Caesar rolled his eyes as if I were six years old. "You'll just break a bunch of bones, and it'll hurt like hell, and then you'll end up back there anyway. Might as well make it easy for yourself."

My stomach lurched as I realized his words were true. Maybe if I'd run a little more slowly he'd have caught up when I was still high enough. Now I couldn't even kill myself.

My despair must have been clear on my face. Caesar nodded. "Good girl," he said, and without warning, lunged for me.

I thrust out my arms and felt the sickening, now-familiar lurch, the world spinning. There was an audible crack as my vision went black for an instant, and then I heard a strangled cry. Caesar's body sailed over the railing and then dropped down, down. I saw his legs kicking feebly until he struck the ground with a wet, meaty smack.

I had killed my own brother.

He betrayed you, said a whispery little voice in the back of my mind. *You asked him for help, you cried, you trusted him. And he betrayed you. Didn't he deserve it?*

The only answer I could hear was the sound of his body hitting the ground, over and over again. I somehow found myself at the bottom of the stairs and forced myself to move closer, reached out to touch him—

He groaned, his hand twitching feebly. I jumped back. Not dead. *Not dead.* Relief so palpable it was like a torrent of hot water swept over me.

Sirens. I'd only ever heard them once or twice in my life. If I'd been in my apartment still, I probably would have been high enough up to see the police walkers crawling down the streets, hissing magic and clanking. How badly they must want me, to use the Resource-powered machines to chase me down.

Of course, said that venomous part of my mind. *If they had you, you could power a thousand machines for them before you die.*

I ran. I didn't know where I was going, except away from the sirens. Down a side street. Another turn and I was on a road little more than an alleyway between two crumbling buildings. My lungs burned. The alley ended in a brick wall; no, wait. It turned to the right. My momentum ricocheted me off the bricks, and I came to a screeching halt.

The Wall gleamed not two yards away from me, stretching up, up, into its massive curved dome. The sun disc was nearly down, setting somewhere to the right of where I stood, lighting the Wall a violent shade of purple-red. It crackled, the hairs on my arms standing up in response to the surge of energy, and I stepped back.

End of the road, Lark. My feet were burning. Now that I had stopped, I realized that the soles of my bare feet must be torn to shreds.

End of the road? End of the *world.*

My head buzzed with exhaustion. I tried to think through it, but the sound only grew louder. It was familiar. I had felt something like this before. Felt? No, heard.

It wasn't in my head. Something in the distance was humming. The sound surged, drawing closer at an astonishing rate. Pixies. Terror swept over me. Of course they had sent the pixies. A wall of screaming metal, a hundred clockwork mechanisms each buzzing with magical power as they thundered toward me. They were at the end of the street but streaming toward me faster than any person could have ever moved.

I turned.

There was nothing—nothing except a mass of violet energy pulsing before my eyes. No one had left and lived in hundreds of years. We were the last city, the last of human civilization. The world beyond could be anything.

Supposedly the Institute harvested crops outside using machines, but I could no longer trust anything they told us. The world outside could be full of flesh-eating mutations, barren of life, burnt to nothing or a frozen wasteland. I thought of my father's coworker, pounding desperately from the outside until silence. It could be nothing but the vacuum of space.

It could be beautiful.

The thought came unbidden, almost as if it were not my own. An image flashed in front of my magic-dazzled eyes of the glowing Renewable in her cage of glass wires.

The pixies had slowed their pursuit. Now that they had me cornered, they advanced more slowly. I realized they were containing me until the Institute arrived.

You said you would rather die. I closed my eyes. *You said you would rather die.*

Images stirred in my imagination and memory. A paper bird, stretching its wings for the first time. A woman of light, whispering, *run.*

Would you rather live?

I leapt.

PART II

CHAPTER 11

I struck cobblestones and rolled, the rock stinging my palms, my chin, my elbows. I had jumped through the barrier with all my strength, expecting . . . what? Resistance, certainly. Bone-shaking agony, maybe. A quick crackling sound and then oblivion. But not this.

My surroundings looked so like where I had just been that I would have thought I'd misjudged my jump, had I not leapt straight at the shimmering force field.

I took inventory of my body—nothing broken, nothing burned, nothing sliced off by magic. Only the sting of skinned elbows and chin.

From the outside, the Wall was a smooth, reflective dome of tarnished silver. I saw myself reflected in a warped monochrome of grays and silvers, the curve of the wall spreading my eyes grotesquely. I crawled toward the Wall. Bracing myself, I touched it and then jerked back in anticipation of—

Nothing. Just the slick, wet feel of cool metal. On the outside, the Wall was like iron. I dragged myself to my feet, laying one palm then the other against the cold surface. It was as solid as the ground on which I now stood. No turning back.

Above me the sky was gray and thick. *Clouds.* The word was unfamiliar but the effect was not. I could've just as easily been inside the Wall. I couldn't help but feel disappointed; I had imagined the sky to be something unimaginably beautiful. Instead it was like an ugly version of what I'd seen overhead my whole life.

The sky was darker out here, but the clouds were deceptive. Inside the Wall it had been dusk. Here, though, the diffuse light was coming from the east. Dawn. That seemed somehow appropriate.

My heart hammered as I stared at the sky. Even a cloudy sky was vaster, heavier, deeper than anything I'd ever seen in my life. My knees buckled without warning, and I shut my eyes. I could still sense gray vastness overhead, but so long as I didn't look, I was all right.

There was a crackling above and to the right, and my head jerked up in time for me to see a pixie shoot out of the dome, sending ripples across its surface. I leapt back. The clockwork bug spiraled sideways and flew back against the metal surface of the Wall. It ricocheted off with a clang and then fell to the ground. The pixie buzzed around in a circle on the cobbles and then stopped, wings fanning feebly for a while before going still.

Two more shot out and suffered the same fate.

I nudged one of the dead pixies with my bare foot.

If I needed proof of how harsh the world outside the Wall was, I had it. The Institute maintained that the world outside the Wall was stripped of magic in some places and ravaged by supercharged storms in others, that the wars had irrevocably damaged the delicate balance of background energy. That balance was necessary, we were taught, to sustain life, and the magical imbalance would drain anything unshielded— like the pixies. I knew I had some resistance to the vacuum because I generated my own magic—but did I generate it quickly enough to avoid being sucked dry?

And what would happen if I didn't?

Regardless, I couldn't stay here. They wouldn't stop chasing me just because I'd left the city. I was too valuable. They had machines capable of functioning outside the Wall; otherwise they wouldn't be able to harvest the crops out here. They could probably reconfigure the pixies, too. If my time was limited, I had to spend it finding the Iron Wood. The Renewable's instructions echoed in my mind.

I took a last look at the cold metal dome that had protected me for sixteen years, and then I set off down the deserted street.

• • •

The city had contracted over the years, as our energy reserves grew smaller and our population dwindled. The Wall had to be moved, the perimeter contracting every decade or so. I was standing in what appeared to have been a part of the city that was inside the Wall only recently. The cobbled street was lined with row houses and apartment buildings that seemed only slightly shabbier than mine.

I wasn't sure what I had been expecting to find outside the Wall. I thought of the forests I'd seen in history books, deserts and lakes and fields of snow. I had expected the world to be transformed into something out of a fantasy. Instead it was exactly like the world I had known, but for its silence.

And oh, the silence. I had never in my life heard such quiet. It shook me to my bones, made my head throb with every minute touch of my foot to stone. Each tiny noise of my passing was a crashing alarm.

Go south across the river, and then follow the birds. Within the Wall, directions were based on the sun disc—its track traveled east to west. Was it the same outside? From the maps we had studied in school, I knew there was only the one river nearby, the one that divided the city from the suburbs. I also knew that the automated gardens were nearby, and I decided I would head there first for supplies and then cut due south to the river. Or what I hoped was south.

I passed a pothole in the street and stopped short. I could see my reflection in the water pooled there. Though I knew I shouldn't waste the time, I knelt down, shrugging off my makeshift backpack—I'd have to find a better way of carrying supplies—and began to scrub at my face and hair with the water. When the worst of the dirt and blood was gone, I straightened and kept walking.

A skin-crawling sensation of being watched washed over me gradually, my skin tingling at what felt like searching eyes. The gloomy daylight revealed nothing that I could see, but the feeling persisted. As I stared into the darkened alleyways, the shadows seemed to dance and slink after me.

Somewhere ahead of me I heard a sound. Very quiet, little more than a soft cough. Nevertheless, in the silence, it sounded like a crash. I darted into a doorway, trembling all over.

I heard another sound, this time the softest of scrapings. A footstep on the street.

I held absolutely still, struggling to see through the shadows of the alley half a block ahead. Imagined light and movement danced across my straining eyes like an afterimage. Each illusive twitch set my heart racing, so much so that when I actually did see movement, I almost didn't recognize it.

Something dark and low to the ground slid out of the alley. *A dog*, I told myself. Dogs had once been ubiquitous among people, but they were carnivores unable to live off of what we grew, and when people retreated behind the Wall, dogs stayed behind.

But would a dog make a sound like that? It had sounded like a step. Like a human step.

The shadow paused just inside the mouth of the alley, keeping to the gloom. I saw it lift its head, stretching up, sniffing the air. I still could not see it in the half-light well enough to tell what it was, and yet it didn't have a dog's profile—and it was the size of a man. As I watched, it made a quiet, chuffing sound and then let out a heart-wrenching cry.

I froze. The scream was abrupt, loud, desperate. *Inhuman.*

It dropped its head again and slunk back into the alley, rejoining the shadows and vanishing.

I stayed in the doorway, shaking, long after I was sure the thing was gone. It wasn't until I heard the cry again, far in the distance, that I forced my body to peel away from my hiding place and keep moving.

I wasn't alone out here. *There are stories*, I thought to myself, *of what lies beyond the Wall. . . .*

The sky was getting lighter. I could see a brighter spot in the clouds above the Wall in the distance. The sun. It felt less powerful even than our sun disc, and I reminded myself that it was behind the clouds, concealed. Still, I could not help but feel another surge of disappointment.

I kept walking, forcing myself to move my bruised and battered feet.

In the city, night would be falling. My weariness made my knees buckle. But I couldn't risk staying so close to the Wall. And it wouldn't be enough to hide out of sight. Out here, in this magical desert, my power would shine like a beacon.

I'd been walking for half an hour when something caught my eye in the street ahead of me. I drew up short, taking half a step back—but whatever it was lay still. I crept closer until I could see—and then froze.

Sitting neatly, side by side, and squarely in the middle of the street where I could not possibly miss them, was a pair of shoes.

I stared at them stupidly for several long seconds. Then my lungs constricted. They could not have been left from the time when this part of the city was abandoned. It was easily ten years ago that the Wall was rezoned, and even the mortar of the streets was crumbling. There was no way a pair of shoes could still be sitting here neatly after all that time. And that shoes were the one thing I needed most? I could not believe that coincidence.

As alarming as those two shoes were, the hope they offered was even stronger: *Is there someone out here like me?*

I nearly tore the shoes apart searching them for any clue of who had left them, what Institute trick was concealed somewhere inside them. A tracking device, maybe. A secret poisonous compartment that would incapacitate me on command. And yet, if the shoes were from the Institute, why hadn't they just grabbed me outright? I had no answers and neither did the shoes.

A careful look at the shoes presented only questions. These were not the flimsy, recycled slip-ons that we received inside the Wall. These shoes felt durable, made of a material from before the wars. And they were absolutely filthy, except that clearly some effort had been made to clean them up. There were swipes where someone had scrubbed away the dark brown grime.

Suppressing everything, I tried them on, slipping my poor, bruised feet inside. I should have been surprised that they fit me more perfectly than any shoes I'd ever owned, but I felt as though I had no more capacity for surprise or shock. If they were a trap, I couldn't figure out the catch. And I knew I wouldn't make it much further barefoot—I had little choice.

I didn't know how to tie them properly, and eventually just stuffed the trailing ends of the laces inside the shoes.

I walked southwest, where I believed the automated gardens to be, hoping to find something to sustain me until I could cross the river and "follow the birds." If there were birds, there would be food. Fruit or grain or something I could eat, I was sure of it. If I could only escape this graveyard of stone and brick, I would be okay.

I'd seen plants before. There were a few growing in the museum in our city, and optimistic weeds would sometimes pop up in the cracks in the streets. Still, nothing I had seen in my life prepared me for what I saw when I rounded the corner of the next block.

A vast garden spread out before me in what had once been a park. Benches and lamp posts were overgrown with pale green vines, while crumbling pavement walkways bordered the patches like gray rivers. All the plants were lined up in rows, with dark rich soil beneath and leaves spread to the gray sky. The garden stretched as far as I could see, following a creek that twisted out of sight in the distance. The plants themselves were heavy with produce. I couldn't identify everything that grew there, though I saw cucumbers and tomatoes nestled like gemstones in the rows nearest me. I darted forward.

I tore off a tomato and bit into it. Its juice stung the scrape on my chin, but no amount of stinging was going to slow me down. I devoured the fruit, core and all, and grabbed another. It wasn't until I was halfway through my third tomato that I slowed and shucked my backpack so that I could start stuffing it. I went for the tougher vegetables, the cucumbers and the carrots. When I knew I couldn't carry any more, I reshouldered the bag, wincing at its weight.

I headed down toward the creek that wound its way through the park and retrieved the cup from my pack, drinking until my stomach sloshed. If only I'd had more time before leaving the city, maybe I could've found a bottle or a canteen to take with me.

Munching another tomato, I wandered back through the rows of plants. The earth I crushed underfoot smelled strange and alien, a wet richness that felt soft and springy. As the leaves whispered by against my arms, I let my mind wander.

The Iron Wood, the Renewable had told me. I had never heard of such a thing, but when she spoke of it I felt as though I could almost see it. *South. The river. Follow the birds.*

Many species of animal went extinct during the wars, and some—like honeybees—disappeared even before, like warnings unheeded. Birds had not gone extinct before the wars the way the bees had, but they were certainly some of the hardest hit animals afterward. Some theorized that there were still some birds alive in the world, but there was no evidence. Birds were a legend, like the Renewables themselves.

How, then, was I meant to follow something that didn't exist, to a place I'd never heard of? If my fearless, brilliant brother hadn't survived out here, how could I? I pressed my hand against the pocket where my paper bird lay, folded tightly against my thigh.

The faintest of sounds, easily distinguishable in the silence, caught my attention. No, not just a sound—a hum of power. Magic.

I whirled, and as I moved there was a roar of machinery so loud that it sent me sprawling. A huge brass monster loomed over me. Its steps shook the plants around me, quivering as if in sympathy with my own terror.

They'd found me. Somehow the Institute had traced me, sent their brass and copper monsters, located my tiny form in the sea of cold iron, brick, and stone. I hoped it would crush me quickly, rather than drag me back.

CHAPTER 12

The thing, which was half again as tall as a man, extended tiny, spindly arms with branching fingers, each tipped with glass. The fingers scraped against each other with a delicate metallic whine as they spun and oriented themselves. I counted six arms, three on each side, and covered my face with my hands as they stretched toward me. Frozen in terror, I waited for it to tear me apart.

Time slowed, stretched, and after a while I realized that it hadn't touched me. I forced my shaking hands down and saw the machine's arms flashing out and retreating, grasping at the plants and withdrawing again, vanishing into its cavernous body. Each hand cradled a red tomato on its way in, and reemerged empty again. The thing didn't have any sensors to detect my presence. The hands navigated by feel, the glass tips of the fingers touching leaf and stem and fleshy fruit alike with incredible delicacy. There was a spot for a human driver, but it was empty—the Institute had altered these machines to operate automatically beyond the Wall.

One of the hands came scrabbling across the earth toward me, feeling out the path ahead of it. I felt frozen to the earth. As I watched, the delicate fingers caught the tip of my toe and scrabbled forward, learning the contours of my shoe with a whispering, spidery touch. When it reached my bare ankle there was a sudden jolt between a glass-tipped finger and my skin, and the machine gave a strange lurch, all hands pausing in their jobs. There was a second, stronger jolt, and then the hand tightened in recognition. Glass, a conductor of magic.

I jerked away, wrenching my ankle as I scrambled to my feet. Dropping my half-eaten tomato, I bolted.

The hum and whir of the machinery grew fainter until I had to pause for breath, and I looked over my shoulder. The machine was still where I'd left it, its hands all sagging, scrabbling in the dirt. Searching for me, and that familiar jolt of magic. I slowed to a rapid walk, trying desperately to calm the terrified gallop of my heartbeat. I limped on my twisted ankle until I could no longer hear the machine behind me, and came out of the garden onto a city block once more.

This, however, was like no part of the city I'd ever seen. It lay in ruins, no building standing higher than a few stories. Hollowed out, tarnished, most of them barely more than rubble, I felt as though I had stepped forward a thousand years into the future. Humans were little more than memory.

This must be the part we abandoned during the wars, I realized. It had been only a hundred years. How had it gone so quickly?

Large portions of the street were caved in, and whole buildings had fallen into the sinkholes. The soil here was a thick, red, soggy clay that looked like it couldn't possibly support life—and yet, plants had clearly taken hold of the city.

Thick undergrowth had pushed through the cracked streets. There was no way around it, so I tried to find a path over the portions of the street that were most intact and still preventing the brush from growing. I passed what had once been a storefront of some kind, some of its glass window still improbably intact. Through it I could see part of a tree trunk, far larger than the spindly things we got inside the Wall. I tilted my head back and saw a canopy of leafy green spreading beyond where the roof of the building had once been. Suddenly it wasn't a shop with a tree growing inside—it was a tree with the remains of a building still clinging to it.

Here and there ancient walkers still stood, frozen, overgrown with vines and moss. I began to notice other abandoned machines, carriages and street cleaners, even the occasional mechanimal. I scraped away the overgrown vines on one lump to see the copper-sculpted, expressive face of a cat peering out of the undergrowth. I'd only seen pictures in books before. It was still crouched, tail erect, as though about to pounce on an invisible toy.

The sky overhead was growing mottled, gray-on-gray patterns becoming visible. I thought perhaps that meant the clouds were clearing. I could more easily see the bright spot of the sun, bright enough that I couldn't look at it for more than a minute. It was well past the zenith now, and I tried to imagine the sun disc's perfectly measured gradations to tell the time. Perhaps one, two o' clock? But past midnight, in the city. Exhaustion dragged at my feet.

The river was not far away, and between the buildings I caught glimpses of an old bridge and knew it was my way across. When I reached it, though, I found that it was a lot less intact than it had looked from a distance. It had once conveyed the Resource-powered carriages and cycles across the river but now I wasn't sure it would hold me. The metal skeleton of it was still standing, and chunks of its rotting stone body still clung to it, but there were large, gaping holes. Marking the beginning of it were two massive bronze statues, so corroded and overgrown I could not identify them. One outstretched limb resembled a hoof—perhaps they had been horses, once.

Trying not to think about how firmly the remaining pieces were attached, I set out across the bridge. I had never learned to swim. No one in the city could; why bother? I tried not to look down, when my path took me close enough to the gaps that the water was visible below. It was a wide, sluggish river, but no less deadly. If I fell, I would drown. That is, if the fall itself didn't kill me.

Stone and concrete crumbled into the water as I stepped. The river was too far away for me to hear the splash. I had still not grown accustomed to the quiet. My ears yearned for any familiar sound. The clamor of the hateful artificial sunrise would have been welcome.

The far side of the river was lined with trees, and I could see them stretching away to the south before the horizon was lost in the mist. This must be the forest the Renewable had mentioned. I was to continue south through it until I found birds. I tried to imagine the sight of a bird, something I'd only ever seen in pictures, but couldn't give the image life. My birds stayed flat, two-dimensional in my mind. Like paper.

I reached the other side of the crumbling bridge, distracted by my imagination enough that it took me a few moments to register the faint hum of magic.

I could hear no clockwork, and usually the gears and mechanisms were louder than the magic that powered them. I shifted my pack and moved as quietly as I could toward the sound.

As I rounded a massive pile of plant-covered debris that had once been a building, I found the source of the sound. It was like a miniature version of the Wall, only instead of tarnished pewter, it had the same violet sheen of energy that characterized the Wall from the inside. I drew back and stared.

Though I stayed for what felt like the better part of an hour, nothing came in or out of the bubble. The Institute had theorized that when the remnants of magic settled after the wars, they did so unevenly. They told us that while the vast majority of the landscape was barren of magic, there were little clumps of highly concentrated power, far more concentrated than the uniform fabric of magic had been before the wars.

This was what they'd sent my brother to find. I couldn't help but wonder if Basil had made it this far.

I crept closer, my skin prickling, alert. All was still, but for the hum of the magic and the flicker of energy across the intangible surface of the dome. I estimated it to be no more than two hundred yards in diameter.

I reached for it, stopping with my palm about half an inch from its surface. The hairs stood up along my arms as if a static charge was about to go off. I stooped and plucked a blade of grass, and then dipped the tip of it into the gently twisting pool of energy. Back home, the Wall was one-way. You could poke things out of it, but when you tried to pull them back in, it would shave off whatever was left outside.

I withdrew the blade of grass. Completely intact. The piece of grass wasn't even warm to the touch.

A faint sound interrupted my inspection. It was either very far away or very quiet, a thin, buzzing whine that rose above the magical thrum that was all around me now.

Pixies. How had these survived outside the Wall when the others had died instantly? And if I was hearing them so clearly, they could not be far—

A cluster of them rounded the debris pile and screamed straight at me in precise formation. I dropped to the ground, curling into a ball.

I expected to feel them ricocheting off my head and arms, whining mad triumph at having located me. Instead, their buzzing took on a strange, meandering note. Cautiously, I lifted my head.

They were flying in disarray, meandering around the bubble, jerking and spinning. Pixies were designed to track magic. I could only guess that this pocket, this superconcentrated magical field, was camouflaging me.

I had never had an opportunity to observe pixies flying for any length of time. They flew gracefully even when confused, their hum quiet and jangling when not aggravated into a fullthrottled screaming whine. The knot of magic at their core, powering them, gave off a faint, golden glow that set the edges of their copper bodies afire.

As I stared, I realized that one of them was different: easily twice the size of the others, for one thing, and giving off a much brighter glow.

A queen pixie? No, more like . . . a general, marshaling its forces. Maybe it had something to do with why these pixies hadn't died like the others outside the Wall.

It had stopped its meandering and was hovering in place, darting side to side—as though it were thinking. And then, with great deliberation, it opened its eyes.

Unlike its sightless troops—and all the other pixies I'd seen—this one had tiny, jewel-like, multifaceted spheres affixed to its head. They shone with shocking azure-blue clarity.

The copper lids blinked once with mechanical precision, and then the bug turned in a slow semicircle—until it was facing me.

The lids blinked shut. When they opened, the faceted eyes had changed to angry red-violet. The general gave a shrill, whistlelike buzz, and at once the other pixies stopped their confused stumbling and formed up behind it.

I barely had time to register that they'd seen me. Another thrum, this one low and constant, and the whole formation darted directly at my face.

I had no choice. I threw myself backward into the magical barrier.

Again, there was no pain or resistance. Less concerned this time with impending death, I noticed that the sensation of static charge grew unbearably intense as I passed through, but as soon as I was on the other side, the sensation vanished.

Ahead of me I saw the barrier from the inside, exactly as it had been on the outside, a violet, flickering dome of energy. I could not see through it but for the occasional hint of a tiny shadow, swooping close and darting away into invisibility. I could hear, very faintly, the sound of their clockwork fury as they tried, and failed, to understand where I had gone. I flinched every time I saw a shadow or heard that whine, but soon they slowed, and then ceased.

I was safe.

A prickling sensation on the back of my neck prompted me to turn around. *Where was I safe?*

I had expected it to look like the ruins of the city outside. Instead, a deep, thick, twisted forest lay before me. All was silent, but for the distant sound of water trickling somewhere.

Huge, ancient trees clogged the area, twisted in their age. Yellow-green tendrils of moss draped from huge, low-hanging branches that seemed to reach for me. Gnarly roots made the ground more treacherous than the worst of the ruins. No sign, not even a moss-covered mailbox, that there had ever been a city here.

I pushed up onto my knees, gazing around. Though it was only a few hours past midday outside, the tiny amount of light that made it through the barrier left the forest in dim, violet twilight.

Something flickered in my vision, like bright light seen through wet eyelashes. I turned my head slowly until it flashed again, iridescence that sent an electric tingle through my body. *Magic.* The place was full of it. Pale stone caught my eye, and I got to my feet to move closer. The study of rock and earth was one of many disciplines that had been lost since the wars, but this rock I knew: limestone.

Natural crystal was by far the best substance at capturing and storing magical energy, and even manmade crystals could serve, as they did in the Institute. Certain other natural stones, particularly limestone, could work the same way, though limestone was so inefficient that it was useless for practical purposes. I reached out to the bit of exposed stone and felt a jolt of energy leap up my arm, intense enough to make it fall to my side, numb, for a few seconds.

Well, I guess that explains why the magic is concentrated here, I thought, rubbing my arm, legs wobbling a bit.

A thin, musical call pierced the silence. A brief quiet followed, and then came an answering call from another part of the jungle. The forest had quieted at my entrance, and had now decided I was no threat. The place suddenly burst into life.

An insane cacophony of sound assaulted my ears and it took me long moments to understand what I was hearing. Animals. Whoops and cries and calls for which I had no name split the air, some shrieking, some musical. I moved slowly, the moss underfoot muffling my steps. Droplets of dew glinted darkly in the violet half-light, and everywhere was the rich, dark, wild smell of dirt and wet and life.

I passed a tree full of unidentifiable fruit, and I plucked a piece from the branches. I had no idea if it was edible, but I peeled away a strip of skin with my thumbnail. It had pale, yellow-gold flesh that smelled unlike anything I'd ever encountered. I couldn't help tasting it, and once I did, I devoured it right down to its hard, woody pit. If I died, at least I'd die happy. I took a few more for my pack and kept moving.

Following the sound of trickling water, I found a fast-moving creek that carved through the overgrown forest. The water was clear and cold, better-tasting than any we had behind the Wall.

I found a place to sit, a flat, moss-covered stone in a hollow between two waist-high roots. Gazing up, I could see very little of the dome above me, only glints here and there of lilac through the ceiling of leafy green. I scratched at the moss covering my stone seat and discovered that it was not a stone at all but a section of collapsed brick wall, crumbling and overgrown. So it had, at some time, been part of the city. I wondered how long it would take for the silent, hollow graveyard outside to be so transformed.

Lulled by my full stomach, the oddly comforting animal noises, and the sense that I was finally safe for a while, I dozed. Here I was inside, shielded from the emptiness of the clouds overhead. I couldn't think how many hours had passed since I woke in darkness in my cell at the Institute. It was warm in the hollow, and the smells of earth and life overcame me.

CHAPTER 13

When I woke, night was falling outside the barrier. Inside it was dark; only a faint violet sheen from the bubble of magic gilded the trees. I thought at first that it was this shift in the light that had awakened me, but then I realized what had changed. The forest had gone silent again. *Well,* I thought, *perhaps all the animals go to sleep when it grows dark.* But that didn't ring true to me. There had been a passage in one of our textbooks in which the cacophony of noise that erupted after nightfall had kept an explorer from sleeping during the night.

Then there *was* a sound, a tentative whoop. It was cut off mid-cry, ending in a horrible gurgling wheeze. Above and some distance to my right, I saw the branches leap and wiggle with movement, the leaves hissing against each other wildly.

I pressed myself against the tree at my back. Until now, I had managed not to think too much about the stories we had been told as children, about the things that existed beyond the Wall.

I listened as hard as I could, but I heard nothing else, only the slight creaking of wooden tree trunks as if in a breeze. I closed my eyes, trying to hold absolutely still, breathing shallowly. The wooden creaking grew louder, and then the hot pit of fear in my gut turned to ice.

It isn't windy.

Above me, the branches were moving. Not rustling as if the wind or an animal were moving them, but moving from within, with deliberation, with dexterity. As I watched, a branch disentangled itself from one of its neighbors and very delicately plucked a curtain of moss from itself. On either side of me, the wall-like roots that had been such a comfort were now arching toward each other, enclosing me.

I screamed and threw myself and my bag out the rapidly shrinking opening. I lurched to my feet and looked behind me.

The tree loomed over me, huge, dark, and inescapable. Its branches enclosed me, its trunk opening in a huge, gaping maw. The faint light coming from the barrier above edged row upon row of tiny, razor-sharp teeth in violet. They pointed backward, lining what would have been its throat. I saw no end to them.

A touch just behind my ear shattered the hypnosis holding me in place. I shrieked again and flailed out with all my strength, and felt the branch that had made a grab for me snap. A wooden groan issued from that gaping hole in the trunk. I flung myself away and sprinted into the dark forest.

As far as I could tell I was near the center of the pocket. I had thought that the further I got away from the edges, the less likely the pixies would be able to sense me. I had no time to curse my own stupidity. Instead I picked a direction at random and threw myself through the wood.

Just there—ahead of me. The faintest glimmer, a lighter patch among the hungry blackness of the tree trunks. The edge of the magic.

Though my chest and my legs felt as though they would burst, I forced in a lungful of air and pressed forward. The patch grew lighter, larger. The border. I would make it.

I was only a few yards away when a tree crashed down in front of me. Its mouth was inches from my face, all its teeth bared, its razor-lined throat hungry and moaning. My momentum would carry me straight into its jaws. I threw my hands up, felt my head spin and the air go out of my lungs. A burst of blinding light, a clap of sound so loud it left my ears ringing, and the tree exploded. My momentum carried me forward, and I half fell, half threw myself through the barrier.

I struck the ground and had only time to look up and see the empty blackness of the overcast sky above before I shut my eyes. The vastness overwhelmed me. I clung to consciousness with grim determination, only the knowledge that I couldn't stay here keeping me from lapsing into oblivion.

I rolled over onto my stomach and pressed my forehead against the cool earth. A wave of exhaustion so intense that I nearly retched swept over me. This, then, was proof that I should avoid using magic if I possibly could.

Still, better weak and nauseous than eaten by a tree.

In my weariness, I could not spare a moment's reflection for the strangeness of that thought. I could only drag myself into the meager shelter provided by a nearby collapsed building. I collapsed onto my knees and then onto my face, and was asleep before my brain registered the jolt of my body hitting the ground.

. . .

I dreamed I was in the pipe under the school again, enclosed in brick and mortar and thick, warm air. The stone pressed into my arms and my knees and I couldn't move, but this time there was no terror. I was cocooned and safe. The whisper of the air cleaners echoed through the tunnels, rising and falling, and somewhere in the distance I could hear water coming closer and closer.

Somehow I knew the water would be warm, and I put my cheek down on the brick to wait for it to wash me away. The rushing sound grew louder and louder, and just as the oncoming wave was about to reach me I lifted my head, and woke.

The sound that in my dream had been the comforting whisper of machinery and water was real—something I could not identify. A voice, inhuman, whispering and howling by turns. The warm closeness of the dream fell away, leaving me shivering, blinking, trying to remember where I was. A cold fear sparked somewhere in my mind, pressing me to the earth where I had been sleeping. It was not a human sound, and not anything I could have guessed would come from an animal.

The sound swelled and fell again, sometimes a tired whistling and sometimes a full roar that sounded like a chorus of a thousand voices. As far as I could tell it was not moving, either closer or farther away. It sounded like it was coming from directly outside my building.

I forced myself to my feet. It was much lighter outside than it had been the previous night. A faint sheen of pearly white filtered through the trees. A clearing stood not far ahead, where for whatever reason the trees had failed to reclaim the concrete.

There was nothing there, but the trees thrashed and shuddered as if an army of pixies inhabited their branches. I tried not to think of the last cluster of trees I'd seen thrashing. I was outside the magical pocket now. They were only trees. *Just trees.*

The thrashing and the howling rose and fell together. As I leaned forward to get a better look, a gust tossed my hair back from my face, startling me so that I jerked back.

Wind. Relief and wonder made my knees weak. I thought I had known wind. I'd felt it on my face while riding in the carriage. But nothing, none of it, nothing in my life had prepared me for this.

I stepped out into the clearing, which was half-lit with that pale silver light. The air rushed around me and threw back my hair, plastering my clothes to my body. The air's movement was fitful and gusty, inconsistent at best and startling. There was a strange wildness to its smell. I walked through the whispering, knee-high grass in the clearing, listening to the wind sigh and scream through the trees and the rubble. It robbed me of breath, stole my soul. Wind.

The shadows writhed and swayed, and my skin prickled with the sense that my every movement was being observed. I looked around but could track nothing for more than a breath. Only the shadows cast by the strange silver light. Then I looked up.

And saw the sky.

The wind had blown the day's thick cloud cover away, and a bottomless blackness yawned above, pockmarked with stars. A sliver of moon cast the sickly, color-leaching hint of light across the ruined city. There was no end to the sky, nothing holding me down on the ground. I felt it reach down to me, threaten to swallow me. I seemed to fall upward, and threw myself down to stop it, knocking the breath out of my lungs.

Digging my stubby fingernails against the dirt, I clung to it and clenched my eyes shut so tightly I saw spots, inverted echoes of the stars above. I pressed my forehead against the ground hard enough to make it throb. At that moment, I would have welcomed the sound of the pixies.

I could still feel the sky above me, waiting. The hideous gaping sky glittered with stars like shards of glass, like rows of teeth. The trees seemed like a child's nightmare compared to this . . . emptiness. Terror more complete than any I had felt since leaving the Institute crippled me. Gravity could not possibly be enough to keep me from falling up into that pit of blackness.

Though my heart hammered, I focused on breathing, sucking in huge lungfuls of air. With oxygen came a glimmer of reason. I uncurled my fingers from the grass below me. I shifted as far as I dared and then grasped for the ground again, focused on the other hand. Moving my feet was harder, but the desire to get the roof of my rubble shelter between me and the sky was stronger than my fear of movement.

Inch by tortured inch, I dragged myself back toward the ruined building. Though I had taken only a few steps outside it, getting back took far longer, at the pace I was forced to move. My breath came in ragged pants, and cold sweat dripped down my face.

A groan escaped my lips as I pulled myself into the barely defined line of shadow marking the doorway. After another few inches, I let my body fall, my muscles trembling with fear and effort.

How could I ever have thought the sky would be beautiful?

CHAPTER 14

Sunlight woke me. I lay there in the patch of sun with my eyes closed. It was still cold from the night, and so warmth was welcome on my cheek. The temperature difference was tangible in a way the sun disc within the Wall never was.

Hunger eventually forced me to move. I sat up, and my stomach cramped so sharply that my eyes watered. This was clearly the price for that uncontrolled burst of power to destroy the tree. It had saved my life, but at what cost? So that I could die slowly of this accelerated starvation?

I opened my pack with shaking hands, my eyes blurring with my need. Two pieces of bread left, one of the fruits from the forest, a couple of cucumbers and a handful of carrots. I tore one of the pieces of bread apart and stuffed half of it in my mouth, telling myself I needed to eat it slowly. Still, the bread was gone in seconds, and I stared at the second piece, trembling. No. I had to ration.

But I lasted only seconds before I reached for the fruit, a compromise. It, too, was gone in moments. I tossed away the bag and temptation, and I leaned against the wall. My eyes shut. I waited for the intense, cavernous hunger to die away, and in time it did, a little. Not enough.

Hunger blunted, I took stock. My face was covered in tiny scratches from the branches during my flight the previous night, but nothing serious. My muscles screamed in protest when I tried to stretch them out, but I knew they would loosen when I began walking.

My feet were bruised but whole, and again I whispered a tiny word of thanks for whatever—whoever—had brought the shoes to me. They had not failed me yet, nor given any indication that they were a trick. If I had been barefoot last night, I would not have been able to escape that pocket of magic.

There was a strange smell in the air, a musky tang that I could not identify. It made my stomach twist with uneasiness. I slipped on my pack and turned to leave my rubble shelter.

Lying not two feet inside the empty doorway was the corpse of an animal. Headless, disemboweled, lying in a pool of its own blood. I lurched back against the wall, suddenly wishing I hadn't eaten. Squeezing my eyes shut, I willed the grotesque vision to vanish. But when I opened them again, the sight remained.

I could not have missed such a thing the night before. I had dragged myself over that very spot.

Something brought this thing to the door while I slept.

A message? A warning? A threat? I pressed the back of my head against the wall, eyes closed, but I couldn't get rid of the sight of its body, stiff and furry and bloody, its tail curled around itself as if it were sleeping.

The carcass lay between me and my exit. I was forced to step over it, averting my eyes. Despite my attempts not to look, I saw that it was mutilated as if by something far bigger and nastier than I cared to imagine.

Though the terror of the sky made me break out into a cold sweat, I wasted no time in leaving that place.

I stepped out into the clearing and the sunlight fell full

on my face. My eyes squinted of their own accord. This, then, was sunlight. It could not have been more different from the light of our sun disc. The sun disc was diffuse, gentle, pale. This was harsh and yellow-white, angling sharply through the branches and the ruins and casting hard-edged shadows unlike anything I'd ever seen.

I caught a brief glimpse of a soft, empty blue before I jerked my gaze away and shut my eyes. The jolt I felt wasn't as bad as the one the nighttime sky had given me, but the huge emptiness was still too monstrous to look at.

The panic that welled up in me would not be quieted by reason. Now, I would have welcomed a claustrophobic pipe. I forced my eyes open, blinking in the impossibly bright light. I felt my nose clench up. I sneezed once, twice. I kept my watering eyes on the ground as I moved out.

Adrenaline and terror swept through me as I walked. My mind was screaming at me to relax, that it was only the sky, that humans had lived under its emptiness for thousands of years. I had worse things to be frightened of. I tried to listen, but the physical terror wouldn't be stilled.

The forest here was much thinner and younger than the one inside the barrier, for which I was grateful. I made slow progress. Even with frequent breaks, ducking into the ruins to feel a roof—even a broken one—over my head, I tired quickly. I sweated and shook, and every step in the open was a terrified one.

Every now and then, something caught at my peripheral vision. Occasionally it was the copper-gold of a pixie searching for me, but often it was something I couldn't identify—a deep flicker of a shadow. Even in the high midday sun, when the shadows were at their smallest, I saw darkness darting around the edges of my sight. I recalled the sensation of being watched and followed, before the pixies had even found me.

As afternoon rolled on, the temperature began to drop significantly despite the sun. I guessed that it was approaching autumn, and I wasn't dressed for it. Inside the Wall, there were no seasons. Inside the Wall, we were never cold.

I could sense another pocket some distance along the road, and I needed to try again to cover my tracks. I'd heard the pixies twice earlier in the day. Once, I'd caught a glimpse of the large, copper-gold of the general. It looked as if it were alone, but even alone it could lead the Institute to me. It was clear they were still on my trail. I was going to have to hide out in the camouflaging magic again, hope to throw them off more completely.

The sun was setting when I reached the pocket. It neatly intersected a row of crumbling buildings—hopefully a sign there would be shelter inside it. It was far smaller than the last one had been; I didn't know if that meant it would be less dangerous, or more. It was still light out, though the sun was crossing the horizon. Taking a peek inside couldn't hurt. And if there was the slightest hint of a forest in there, even one spindly little tree, I'd take my chances with the pixies.

The hairs on my arms and legs and neck rose as I stepped through the barrier, the static charge familiar now. I was braced to run, leap back out backward again if I needed to.

I saw to my relief that the only plants were overgrown bushes dragging at the rusted iron railings of the steps leading up to a house. The trees and undergrowth choking the world outside the barrier were gone, leaving the house much more intact than the buildings in the ruined city. Where time had sped up in the last bubble, the forest taking over to the point where the city was unrecognizable, here it was all but stopped in its tracks. The house looked as if only ten years had passed since people had lived there—not one hundred.

The door was locked, but a stiff jerk of the handle freed the rusted hinges from the rotting frame. I leaned the door aside and stepped into the gloom.

The windows were all shattered, blown inward, but the sun was setting and there was little light coming through the barrier outside. The air was thick with ancient dust. Under my feet the stone of the stoop gave way to soft carpet, each footstep releasing puffs of dust and mildew. Paper peeled from the wall of the front hall. I tried to flatten a curling strip of it to see what was pictured. It crumbled at my touch.

There was a stairway to a second floor, and doors all along the hall leading to other rooms. A tarnished mirror stood at the end of the hall, reflecting parts of me back in the dim light. Pushed against the wall was a cabinet with a vase that had clearly once held flowers. Only a tiny pile of dust and un-identifiable shards of decayed matter remained.

I wondered about the people who'd lived here. All their things were still here. Had the backlash from the wars killed them instantly, with no time to move away to safety?

Would I find their bones somewhere within, still locked in the poses in which they'd died?

I shivered. If the Institute knew how the fallout from the wars had killed people, it chose not to share that informa-tion—for our own good, I'm sure. There were rumors that the fallout wasn't always lethal—that there were fates worse than death.

I was only here because I could create magic to sustain myself, so long as I could fuel my body. And I was quickly running out of food.

My vision flickered with that same fleeting sheen I'd no-ticed in the other pocket of energy, and I paused at a junction in the hall. I stepped through an open doorway that led from the entry hall to a big room, clearly a family space with the kitchen attached. A long, L-shaped couch divided the space, and a rectangular dining table sat in the center, six chairs clustered around it.

I made a slow circuit of the room, inspecting the kitchen with awe and confusion. It was big enough that our entire living room could have fit inside it. There was a broad stone countertop and a large pantry full of cans and boxes so covered with mold and grime that I couldn't identify them. A clock hung high on the wall, its hands frozen and nearly invisible through the dust coating its face.

I could imagine what it must have been like to live here, work in this kitchen, have seemingly unlimited ingredients at my fingertips. If I half-closed my eyes I could see the kitchen restored to its original splendor, stone countertops polished, the tile floor gleaming, exotic food piled high on plates.

Against one wall behind the couches was a machine I recognized, and as I turned toward it the air flashed with power. Every Yuletide, the Institute brought out a device they called a phonograph, a device that used to exist in every household. A windup handle released a diamond-tipped needle to read engraved cylinders, translating the etchings into prerecorded music amplified by magic. The only one left in the city was the one the architects kept in the museum.

I reached out to touch it and experienced a similar jolt to the one I'd felt at the limestone deposit, though not as strong. As I ran my fingertips down the arm leading to the needle, the thrumming of magical energy grew stronger and stronger, until I was forced to pull my hand away. Diamond. It was clear that the pockets weren't random after all. They formed around objects, substances that were somehow significant.

I could almost hear the chatter of the family that had lived here, reliving the events of their day around the dinner table.

I heard the clatter of silverware against china, the clink of ice cubes in a glass. Someone—a child—laughed.

And then it was no longer my imagination. While I had been exploring, the sun had finished its trek to the horizon outside the shimmering barrier. Darkness had fallen outside the windows. And yet, in here, there was light. More than light. Overhead, panels cast a gentle, magical glow. The tile floors shone and the windows were once more intact. The phonograph, suddenly shiny and new again, crackled to life. The haunting strains of a woman's voice floated on the air, singing a song I'd never heard.

And from the next room, voices. Conversation. Words. It was the first speech I'd heard since I'd thrown my brother from the balcony. The room came alive.

CHAPTER 15

I ducked behind an armchair, trying to make myself as small as possible. People. Real people. Alive beyond the Wall.

"Well, I hope you gave her hell for it," said the sarcastic voice of a girl a bit older than me.

"Kacey!" gasped another voice, high and quick, belonging to a much younger girl. "You're not supposed to say the H-word!"

"I won't tell Dad if you don't," said the older girl, laughing.

They continued chattering. I heard the scrape of stools that I hadn't seen at the counter. They didn't *sound* like monsters. All I wanted to do was leap out of hiding and rush to them, explain everything, and beg for help.

Again my mind showed me the rows of razor-sharp teeth that I'd avoided so narrowly the night before. Inside the pockets, things were never what they seemed. I shut my eyes and squeezed myself more tightly into the corner.

A woman came in, older. She asked the girls about their days. I heard pots and pans, a knife on a cutting board, a hissing kettle. Plates, silverware. Laughter. I could even hear the once-broken clock ticking in the background.

A man joined them, distinct in his weary baritone. His steps thumped on the tile while the steps of the girls were almost noiseless. I listened to them eat, talk, laugh. A family.

I knew I had to leave, make a break for it. People living outside the Wall could not be trusted. At least I knew what I faced with the pixies. But I could not quite bring myself to flee. Monsters they might be, but they sounded like home.

The need for survival had so dominated my thoughts that I had never quite realized just how lonely I was.

"You girls finished your homework?" the mother was asking. After an unintelligible chorus from the two girls, the mother added, "Where is Jed? Not like him to be late for dinner."

"Probably working on his bike," said the older sister. "He doesn't like casserole anyway."

After a time, the chairs scraped back away from the table. Footsteps. Suddenly, I realized they were aiming for the couches in the living room. They were coming my way. If anyone sat in the chair, they'd see me clear as day. Now was my only chance to escape. Perhaps if I stayed low, they wouldn't notice me.

I darted out, and as I straightened up to run out the door, someone came in from the other side.

I froze. The boy, a teenager about my age, was walking directly toward me. There was nowhere I could run.

He didn't stop, didn't even slow down. And then, without any indication that he saw me, he kept walking—straight through me. He flickered and fuzzed as he reached me and reappeared on the other side as he moved to join his family in the living room.

"Mom, could I have my allowance early? I need a new chain for my bike."

Gasping, groping at myself to verify that I was, in fact, solid, I couldn't quite hear the response. It must not have been satisfactory, though, because the boy turned and stomped out of the room and up the staircase. I leapt out of the way, but he gave absolutely no sign that he could see me.

Baffled, I shoved my fears aside and stepped back into the family room. They were all seated now in the living room, the parents reading while the girls played some sort of game with cards.

"Hello?" I croaked. My voice was hoarse, shocking, and strange. I swallowed, tried again. "Hello?"

Nothing. They all seemed riveted to what they were doing.

I walked between the girls and the cards on the floor, placing myself so that my body would be blocking their view. When that failed to garner a response, I walked up to the oldest daughter and waved my hand in front of her face, shouting in her ear. I tried to tap her on the shoulder, and my hand passed through.

There was a strange crackle, and the whole scene flickered. For the briefest instant I saw the room as I had when I entered, only pitch-dark now, only the edges of rotting furniture barely discernible. But only a flash, and then the family was back.

The phonograph buzzed and hiccupped with static, and then with a tiny snap, went quiet entirely. The father stood and crossed over to it, giving it a sharp rap on the side.

"Honey?" said the mother. "What's going on? Is the record broken?"

"I don't know; give me a sec." The clock in the kitchen had stopped ticking.

The youngest girl, who would not have been more than eight, was gazing out the window. "Do you hear that?" she asked.

"Hang on," said the father, preoccupied.

"No, that buzzing," said the girl. Her voice suddenly jumped in pitch, to a scream. "Look, the window!"

Driven by the sudden urgency in the girl's voice, the family turned to gaze out the window. I did the same, but I saw nothing, only vague, blurry shapes. Whatever they saw, though, electrified them. Everyone was shouting, and the mother threw herself on top of the children, barely a second before the windows all shattered inward and the room flashed brighter than the sun.

The scene flickered again and without warning the two girls were back in the kitchen.

"Well, I hope you gave her hell for it," the older girl was saying.

"Kacey!" gasped the child, who seconds before had been pointing, horrified, at the window in the living room. "You're not supposed to say the H-word!"

The scene flickered again.

"Kacey! You're not supposed to say the H-word!"

Another flicker, and this time the figures were only half-present, superimposed over the dark, abandoned house.

I leaned back against the wall, sliding down until I hit the ground. One of the more popular stories about the world beyond the Wall was that it was inhabited only by ghosts, roaming the wilderness, hungry and lost. As a child I had imagined pale, dead-looking things that floated and moaned. In the stories they were always wretched and angry, vengeful for having died before their time.

These people, or memories—or whatever they were— didn't even know I was there. They kept living their lives, that last day, that last night. It must have been during the wars, when some strike from a power-hungry Renewable knocked out this neighborhood.

I thought back to the first Yuletide festival I could

remember, when the Institute had brought out the phonograph to demonstrate holiday music from before the wars. The sound popped and fuzzed, full of static. At one point later in the festival, the needle of the device had stuck and the record repeated the same few bars endlessly, the melody transformed into a grating parody of music.

I was reminded of that skipping record, watching the fragmented last day of this family play itself over and over. The house remembered them, or else the magic did, writing the memory and engraving it into the very bricks of the foundation. I could have left, gone upstairs to see if there was a place to sleep, or changed houses, but I stayed. Even fragmented, tinny with age, the voices felt familiar to me. It wasn't my family but it was *a* family. I was lonely. And to them, I was no more than a ghost.

I curled up in my corner, listening to their laughter, covering my ears when the phonograph skipped and the little girl screamed. Though the vision of the family came with light, it brought no warmth, and I shivered through the night, sleeping only fitfully, torturing myself with the sound of this family living and dying again and again.

The scene became more fragmented as sunrise approached, the increasingly fitful skips and starts waking me from my doze. I had moved in the night, lying down on the mildewed carpeting, head pillowed on my hands. From this vantage point I saw that the boy had returned, something I'd never noticed from the previous versions of the memory.

He crouched underneath the counter, gazing toward his family and the chair I was curled behind. How had I not seen him before? Perhaps he sneaks in, later in the memory, to listen to the music but not make up with his mother?

I sat up. Wait. No. It wasn't the boy. It was someone new. He was older and thinner. He was absolutely filthy, his clothes tattered. His hair was so grimy that the dirt concealed its color.

And he wasn't looking at the family after all—he was looking straight at me.

The scene flickered again but the boy remained, solid and real. He looked to be in his late teens, though it was hard to tell underneath the dirt and the intensity of his face. His gaze was full upon me, fierce. The boy was slim, every limb taut and tense. Feral. Despite the dirt, the wildness, the frightening intensity, something about his face made my stomach tighten, my breath catch.

The sun was rising. As the scene flickered again I saw that it was growing lighter. And as I watched, the family gave one more flicker—*you girls finished your homework?*—and vanished entirely, leaving me and the wild boy alone in the empty house. In the light of the just-risen sun through the barrier beyond the broken windows, I could just make out the boy's eyes, glittering in the gloom. I never saw him blink.

Perhaps if I ran now, I could make it outside the barrier before he caught me. Maybe the gloom would work to my benefit, hide me somehow. And yet, as the light grew stronger I was able to make out more of his features. He was dirty, absolutely filthy, his face stained with rusty-brown—*blood*, a fearful voice in my mind supplied—and his clothes tattered. *There are cannibals beyond the Wall.*

He saw me watching him. His eyes grew round, but he never took them off of me. There was not a flicker of intelligence behind those eyes as they met mine. The hairs stood up along my arms as a near-electrical jolt passed between us. My heart threatened to break free of my ribcage, so frenetic I thought it might burst.

My resolve cracked and I lurched to my feet, prepared to run. My legs blazed with pins and needles and I staggered, dizzy after such a long night spent curled up on the cold floor. My dazed vision barely caught his movement. Silently, he unfolded from his crouch and made a breathtaking leap for the window and was gone.

. . .

Though my restless night gave me little energy to face the day, I struck out as the sun began to trickle through the tree trunks. The morning was chilly, goosebumps rising on my arms.

And despite everything, the mist-filled morning was also beautiful. I hadn't yet been outside so early, and the way the sun, mild and peach-colored on the horizon, lit the mist was beyond anything I'd seen behind the Wall.

The day passed swiftly, and I made good time. My pale face burned in the sun, but I couldn't afford to stop in the shade except where I found creeks with clear enough water to drink. The ruins seemed endless, trees and buildings together in a strange stone forest. As afternoon crept toward evening I picked up my pace, to cover more ground and to keep warm. I was still waiting to see the Renewable's birds. *Go south through the forest until you find the birds.*

How far south? Would I know if I went too far?

I remembered the frantic desperation in the touch of her mind against mine, the shreds of sanity lacing the edges of her thoughts—but only the edges. Would she have been more specific? Would she have known how?

I was so lost in thought that I didn't notice the hum until my head began to throb. I now recognized the differences between the sound of city magic and wild magic. The magic here in the wilderness hummed like a huge tuning fork, deep and resonant and powerful. The city magic, tied up in the hearts of the machines, twanged uncomfortably, jangled with a disharmonic quality that set my teeth on edge. My own magic had this sound now, too, but I refused to contemplate what that might mean.

The approaching magic was harsh and discordant. Machines. Pixies. They must have picked up my trail again.

I closed my eyes, trying to listen. Just there—to the southwest—the tiniest flicker of sweet humming. Natural magic. I veered west and broke into a run.

A machine, still and silent, came into view between the ruins, one I had no name for. I knew it was from before the wars. It looked like a giant walker with a cabin on top for sightseeing. A tourist's machine, maybe. How it was still upright I didn't know, but the pocket I had sensed clung to its legs, and I made for it.

This pocket was the smallest yet, barely larger than our apartment in the city. Still, it would conceal me for the night—and if it was small, perhaps that meant nothing dangerous could be inside. Nothing big, anyway.

But how big did something need to be to kill me?

The inside of the pocket looked the same as the forest on the outside had looked. The trees inside looked a little worse for wear, as if the barrier prevented them from getting enough sun. The ground was littered with broken, dead branches. One of the dead machine's legs was inside, the metal corroded by time. Old leaves carpeted the area. I could see nothing that explained the pocket's presence, felt no jolt or pull or energy—it must be something below the surface of the earth. Panting from the exertion of running, I pushed the leaves around until I had a little mound, something to cushion me from the cold, hard ground. I sagged to my knees in the moldering leaves, closing my eyes. Two nearly sleepless nights, too little food, and too much walking.

The light, already dimmed through the violet filter of the barrier, was fading. I ate a carrot for dinner, telling myself that I'd eat more in the morning. For now the carrot would have to do. I tried to imagine Administrator Gloriette trying to survive out here in the wilderness—the thought of her bulk subsisting on a meager carrot for dinner made me smile.

The light went from palest violet to deep, dusky gray. When I looked to the west I could see the faintest glimmers of gold shimmering against the barrier. The sun was sitting low beyond the horizon.

I explored my face with my fingertips, finding scratches and hot, scorched skin from the sun. My lips burned when I licked them.

I had worked up the barest of sweats as I ran for the barrier. As the temperature dropped, my damp skin chilled despite the unfamiliar heat of my sunburn. I emptied the supplies in my pack and pulled it over my arms, hugging myself beneath the thin material.

I hunkered down, ears and eyes attuned for the slightest shift that would warn me the pocket was about to change with sunset. I waited until my eyes had to strain to see through the darkness, but as the time ticked by nothing happened.

I was beginning to understand that every pocket of concentrated magic was different. One had twisted the landscape, animating the trees. Another had imprinted the moment of cataclysmic backlash from the wars, to repeat endlessly. This one, apparently, was simply still and quiet. Empty. Perhaps it had something to do with the fact that whatever had attracted the magic of this pocket was beneath the earth, making this edge of magic small, weak. I hoped it was enough still to shield me from the pixies.

I began to shiver. I tried to pile leaves over myself, closing my eyes and willing myself to sleep until morning warmed me again, but the shivering wouldn't let me rest.

There were dry leaves and dead wood all around. I

gathered some, clearing a space near my makeshift bed. I had a vague recollection that you could start a fire by rubbing two sticks together—*friction*, I thought.

Though I kept at it well after the moon rose, I never got anywhere with the fire. The sticks were only slightly warm where I had been drilling one into the other, and my palms were raw from the effort.

Darkness had brought an edge to the chill that set my teeth to chattering, and I clenched my jaw. My limbs quivered, and my mind grew sluggish. I had never been cold, not like this.

Part of me longed for the soft warmth of my mattress in the Institute, for their hot soup, for a simple cup of tea to soothe my aching muscles and pounding head. I wanted a blanket. I wanted socks. I wanted to sleep without shivering and without fear of what might find me as I slept.

I tossed the sticks aside and tried to gather in some of my precious power to start a fire by magic. But I was cold enough and weary enough that every time I began to gather momentum, the energy slipped from my concentration.

I finally gave up and curled against the leg of the ancient machine as tightly as I could. The metal was cold and hard at my back, and never warmed to my touch. I wrapped both arms around myself, the makeshift backpack covering my front as much as I could. I ducked my head and tried to let the hot dampness of my own breath warm my chilly skin.

I dozed like I had the previous night, my exhaustion too great for consciousness but my discomfort too much for true slumber.

It was not quite a sound that woke me from my daze. I opened my eyes to the sensation that I was no longer alone. I thought I saw a shadow move amongst the other shadows, a furtive, sideways scuttle.

A dry, brittle leaf somewhere scraped against another. I held my breath, listening, shivering. I strained to see, but the filtered moonlight was too weak.

Without warning, he was there. The wild boy from the dawn, crouched low, slipped from a shadow and gazed at me, the faint light defining his cheekbones and brows. He looked less filthy, the darkness concealing the caked-on grime. There was still a wildness about him, though, something that made my heart ache and hammer at the same time.

There are cannibals beyond the Wall, said a child's voice in my mind. My shivering was no longer from the cold.

The boy darted forward, and with a metallic *shhnk* drew something from his boot. All I could see was the light glinting off the edge of a short blade.

I gave a tiny, half-strangled shriek and tried to scramble aside. The boy leapt back, the knife held low. His other hand he extended, palm out, his breath catching audibly. I couldn't see his expression, but the gesture was unmistakable. *Wait. Be still.*

I stopped, mostly because my stiff muscles refused to co-operate. He saw that I was half-crouched, frozen, unmoving.

He eased forward, the knife held between us. I tried not to stare at it. I knew my best chance to tell if he were about to lunge would come from his face, and my gaze locked with his. He never took his eyes from my face. With a quick, smooth movement he reached for one of the dead sticks I'd gathered. He could not have been more than two yards away.

He put the edge of the knife to the wood and began shaving off tiny curls, his hands speeding up until the shavings were flying from the branch. Soon he had a small pile of them, and he carefully eased the knife back into his boot. The thumping of my heart, however, didn't ease at all.

Eyes still fixed on me, he gradually lowered his hand and

dipped it into a pouch hanging at his waist. It emerged hold-ing an object I could not quite recognize, only half-visible in the near-total darkness.

Finally he broke his gaze from my face in order to look down at his hands. I should have bolted, but instead I stared at what he was doing, magical in its own right. He was glancing his thumb along the object, eliciting a scraping sound. Sparks darted up and away from his hands like pixies in the sun.

One settled in the pile of wood shavings, fizzled, spread. He ducked his head and exhaled slowly, gently, with all the care of a mother brushing an eyelash from a child's cheek. The growing spark lit up and with a tiny sound, burst into a single lick of flame.

The boy took a step back, grabbed up a handful of tiny sticks, and slowly began laying them over the flickering fire, building it carefully. He glanced up at me and then laid the sticks next to the fire. He stepped back and then crouched again, setting the thing that had created the sparks on the ground in front of me.

I could barely see him, my eyes robbed of their night vi-sion by the orange glow of the fire. He inclined his head, a gesture that was both alien and gentlemanly at once. Then he was gone.

I crept close to the little fire and fed it a few more sticks from the pile the boy had left. It was clear that, had I managed to coax any sparks from my attempts with the sticks, I would have smothered the flame with the big pieces of deadwood that I'd lugged back from the surrounding trees.

I examined the fire-starter in the glow of the blaze. It was a solid, heavy silver lighter, rectangular and rounded at the edges. Tobacco was not something we had inside the Wall, but a few people still had these, relics from times past. I turned its wheel with my thumb, scraped against something below it.

After several tries, a single spark emerged. No flame, but then, the fuel inside the lighter was long gone.

As the fire popped and whistled, every sound made me jump and stare intently into the darkness. My vision sparkled with afterimages and phantom movement. But the wild boy was gone, and with him my will to stay awake, and so as soon as the fire was crackling on its own with one of the larger logs slung over it, I fell into a deep, thorough sleep.

• • •

Sunrise failed to wake me, the morning light too weak through the barrier to warm me more than the fire smoldering at my side. Instead, I woke to the sound of magic. And not natural magic—the discordant, angry sound of magic powering a machine.

Unmistakable. I was so used to it behind the Wall that it still felt comfortable, familiar. I didn't notice it starting; it must have been humming away since before I woke. I opened my eyes.

There, sitting quietly on the moss-covered foot of the dead walker machine, was the pixie general. It sat so still that I thought maybe it was dead as well, that perhaps it wasn't constructed for cooler temperatures. Then it opened its crystal-blue eyes and blinked slowly, lazily. The clockwork inside it began to turn with individual clinks and clatters, a metallic, musical heartbeat. So much for the theory that they couldn't follow me inside the barriers.

I held my breath, gathering my meager power to strike, as I had done with the pixie in the tunnels below the school in the city. It blinked again, its eyes shifting from blue to an intense red. Then, head tilting gently to one side, it spoke.

"Hello, gosling."

CHAPTER 16

The voice that emerged from the squat copper bug was tinny and strange, one I would not have recognized had it not been for the words it spoke. Its eyes glared red, pulsing like Caesar's talkie.

"We've been so worried about you, duckling. What happened? Did someone frighten you, poor thing?"

I was so baffled I couldn't speak. I stared at the pixie, which sat with its wings fanning the morning air lazily, its tiny mouth hanging open.

"Oh, duck," said the voice of Administrator Gloriette. *"Speechless, you poor dear. It's over now, we'll have you home before you know it. Your brother's been worried sick about you."*

I found my voice again. "My brother is the one who turned me in," I croaked. "He betrayed me."

The pixie—or, rather, Gloriette's voice from within the pixie—gasped. *"Good heavens, no! Who told you that? Never mind,"* it continued, before I could answer. *"No, your brother only wanted to help you, poor chick. We've all been searching high and low for you. We need our most promising new citizen back."*

I pressed back against the leg of the machine as far as I

could go, my shoulder blades digging into the rusting metal. "I don't believe you."

"*Oh, gosling.*" The tinny, distorted voice managed to convey sadness well enough. "*Who has been filling your head with nonsense? We've always done what we could to keep you happy while still helping your city.*"

That was so ludicrous that it snapped me out of my horrified stupor. "You were going to make me a slave!" I cried. "Worse than a slave, you were going to make me a *thing*. You were going to chain me up like that Renewable and turn me into a nothing!"

"*We certainly were not,*" said the Gloriette-pixie, aghast. "*Poor gosling, such a silly misunderstanding! She was a creature from the outside, and she tried to infiltrate our city. We would never, ever do that to one of our own! We just want to bring you back and keep you safe.*"

I forced myself to my feet, my stiff muscles protesting the sudden movement. "You'll have to kill me first," I said through gritted teeth.

There was a pause before the Gloriette-pixie replied. When it did, the voice carried a stiffness underneath the artificial crackle of magic. Still saccharine and smooth, but hard as glass. "*I don't know that there's any call for such theatrics,*" it said. "*It's time to stop this nonsense, Miss Ainsley. You cannot survive out there on your own.*"

"I've managed so far," I said, sounding far more confident than I felt. I tried not to think about the mysterious gift of the shoes or the wild boy's lighter. "You won't bring me back in one piece, so you might as well stop wasting the energy to find me."

"*If you come back now, you will face no punishment for disobedience. And you can take up any career you want once you've recovered from your ordeal. You can continue living with your mother and*"

father if you like, or we'll set you up in your very own apartment. But only if you come back now."

Now that the shock of hearing the pixie speak had faded, I found to my surprise that laughter was fighting its way out of me. Did they think I was so stupid? They'd waited until I'd spent some time on my own, seen the horror of the sky, learned what it's like to be truly hungry. They'd given me enough time to get desperate, before offering to *let* me come back. As if all I wanted was to return to the Institute's glass cage.

I swallowed the bile rising in my throat. I ignored the pixie and pushed away from the ancient walker, striding past it.

"Wait!" snapped the Gloriette-pixie, the word accompanied by a whirring of clockwork as it turned to track me.

My back to it, I stooped to retrieve my meager supplies. I turned toward the edge of the barrier and took one step.

"We know where your brother is."

I froze.

"What did you say?" I didn't turn around, my hands clenched into fists around the makeshift straps of my pack. I knew she wasn't talking about Caesar anymore.

"He suffers greatly. You could save him, if only you knew where to look."

She was lying. Of course she was lying. Basil had vanished with his entire group of volunteers the day they had set out in search of Resource pockets. Basil had died years ago.

I closed my eyes.

"My brother is gone," I said, my voice trembling through my teeth. "We scattered his ashes."

"You burned his belongings and bid farewell without another thought," said the pixie. The metallic voice grated and cut into my mind. *"But it takes years to die from Resource withdrawal. Long, lonely, painful years. He's alive, but only barely. Even so, it*

isn't too late. Come back and you may use whatever resources you want to find him and bring him home."

Beneath the voice I heard a faint whir of clockwork, and I turned my head enough to see its source. Something was unfolding slowly from beneath the pixie's abdomen. A long, wicked-looking needle glinted in the light.

I wrenched my gaze ahead again.

"We can bring him back, bring your family together again," the pixie went on, Gloriette's voice low and hypnotic. *"We can give you everything you've ever wanted."*

I sucked in a deep breath, my voice dead calm. "Go to hell."

The Gloriette-pixie screamed, half voice and half clockwork whine, and flew at my face, stinger extended and seeking flesh. I snapped my power up, deflecting the pixie and then crushing it into the earth.

Fury made me stronger, more accurate. I inspected the ruins of the bug, its gleaming body half-destroyed, making visible the gears inside. A tiny core of magic fluttered and pulsed within its diamond shell, like a heartbeat made erratic from pain or fear. Shimmering the same faint violet as the inside of the Wall, the longer I stared at it, the more light-headed I grew. Dizzy, like I'd been just before I destroyed the pixie in the sewers. The pixie general said nothing else, and the red-violet eyes were dull and empty.

As I lifted a foot to crush it, the pixie gave a pitiful groan of gears. Then, with effortless beauty, it trilled in a pitch-perfect imitation of a bird call. I would not have recognized it but for the sound I had heard once before, from a paper bird briefly given life by magic.

I stopped so abruptly that I nearly knocked myself over, stumbling where I had meant to stamp the machine into bits. The core continued fluttering, pulsing. The eyes flickered blue, struggling, no longer red-violet. I saw no sign of the stinger—had it broken off? Again, it trilled, the exact same sound.

Follow the birds.

Where had this thing heard such a call, to be able to re-create it?

I had seen not a feather, heard not a hint, of any birds since the Renewable had spoken to me. And yet, this pixie had managed to re-create a bird call.

I couldn't afford to leave this clue behind. The countryside was vast, so much vaster than this tiny city and its suburbs that the scale of it terrified me if I thought too much about it. How could I hope to find the Iron Wood without help?

And so I sat, watching the ruined pixie, catching my breath, trying to still the hammering in my chest.

"Pixie?" My voice emerged as a thin, reedy whisper. Annoyed at my own fear, I swallowed and tried again. "Gloriette?"

Silence. Not a flicker in the dark, empty eyes. Nothing to signify that pulsing connection, like I'd seen with Caesar's talkie.

Still, I had no way of knowing the extent of the Institute's deception. I leaned closer, resisting my body's urge to scramble away and run.

"Gloriette," I tried again, in a low voice. "I changed my mind."

My whole body trembled with the lie. But if there was one thing that would get it to shed its deception if it was only faking destruction, it was this.

"I'll go back with you."

The eyes were dark, the machine silent. I stared at it, eyes watering, every sense attuned for the slightest shift, my head spinning and dizzy, ready to slam it again.

Then again, its eyes had been blue when it sang, not the red of the Institute's communicator devices. If Gloriette wasn't behind the birdsong, who—or what—was?

As I watched the thing, the pulsing knot of power at its core grew more steady. Less like a flame about to flicker out, more like the constant thrum of the overhead lights at the Institute. It had tried several times to move, gears turning and clanking, mismatched and broken. But now, it extended tiny, needlelike appendages. They moved falteringly, each attached to a set of the tiniest, most delicate gearwork I'd ever seen.

Unable to help myself, I leaned closer, staring.

The appendages—fingerlike wisps of copper—set about straightening gears, setting them back on their correct axles, fitting the teeth of one into the spaces of another. Though filament-thin, the fingers were strong enough to bend the pixie's body back into shape. It folded up the copper-plating covering its glowing heart, but not before I saw it flare with power.

The pixie was *healing* itself.

The fingers scrabbled on the ground, and for a wild moment I thought it was trying to crawl toward me. Then I saw a tiny cube of copper a few inches past the tips of its fingers, something that had clearly broken from its body when I smashed it. I stooped and picked it up.

"Oh, no you don't," I said, heart hammering away in my chest. At least I could keep it from being fully operational. Maybe.

"*Don't,*" said the pixie, a bizarre echo that caught me short.

Startled, I took a step back. Its eyes still glowed the soft, clear blue. Maybe I had been wrong in guessing that red meant connection to the Institute, to Gloriette. But then, it hadn't spoken in her voice.

It had spoken in mine.

"*Don't,*" it said again, and giving a little shake, it lifted off the ground, wings a blur. It flew at me, and before I could dodge, collided blindly with my arm. I shook it off and stepped back, cornered against the ruins.

"What the—stop that!"

"*Stop that!*" The pixie dropped and buzzed against my fist, the one holding the piece I'd taken from it. Hearing my own voice changed and mutated by the pixie's metallic body made the hair on the back of my neck stand up.

"You're repeating me," I said, darting past the creature, walking backward so I could keep it in my sights.

"*Repeating you.*" It buzzed toward me, but when I started to back away again, it stopped, hovering a few feet away.

"But that's not a repetition," I accused, as some part of my brain screamed at me that I was going mad, talking to a machine as if it could understand me.

"*Ohnoyoudon'twhatthestopthatyou'rerepeatingmebutthat'snota repetition,*" it said.

The words were all in my voice, exactly as I had said them, a perfect replica, strung together without the natural pauses and cadence of human speech.

"You need my voice to create sound," I whispered, staring. "You don't have a vocabulary of your own."

"*Create sound, your voice.*" The pixie darted to the right, and then the left. It was an oddly impatient gesture.

"But you spoke earlier in Administrator Gloriette's voice." I was still poised to flee. "You couldn't have had it all recorded; she wouldn't have known what I was going to say. When was that vocabulary created?"

"*Gloriette,*" said the pixie. "*Not created. Not recorded.*"

"Can she hear me now? Are you still connected to her?"

The pixie bobbed in place, hovering uncertainly. I could hear the turning of its gears, the hum of its wings, and under it, the now-steady thrum of magic in its heart.

I realized what was causing its hesitation. "Oh! Yes or no?"

"*No,*" said the pixie, instantly.

"How come you can't use the words you heard from Gloriette to talk to me?"

More turning gears. "*Create your voice,*" it said. "*Create create. Not Gloriette. Not recorded.*"

"Guess you don't have the words to explain it. And I certainly can't give them to you if I don't know what they are."

The pixie continued to hover, waiting, quiet.

"You only answer direct questions?"

"*Yes.*"

"Does the Institute know where I am?"

"*No. Yes. No.*"

"They think they know?"

"*No.*"

"They know the general location?"

"*Yes.*"

"Are you supposed to report the specific spot?"

"*Yes.*"

"Do you need this thing to make it back?" I opened my fingers and held up the little copper cube on the palm of my hand. It had tiny lines and patterns engraved on it, so minuscule I couldn't see the details of them. Intricate pathways that must have been etched with the thinnest possible needle.

The pixie gave a desperate whine and lurched forward. I closed the cube in my fist again and the pixie stopped. "Uh uh," I said, shaking my head. "Answer the question."

"*Yes,*" it said. Always the same syllable, the same way. No hint of emotion but that which I had given it when I spoke.

"What is it?"

"*Specific spot. Location. Where I am? Answer.*"

I had no idea what that meant. "Um. A map?"

"*Yes. No.*"

"But you can't find your way back without it?"

"*Can't,*" it agreed.

"I should just smash you," I said, my fist tightening around the cube. "To be safe."

"*No.*" The pixie did not beg; the word was as calm as when I had spoken it.

"How do I know you're telling the truth? You're just one of their machines, and all they ever did was lie to me. You're no different from them, just programmed to hunt me down."

"*Machines. Don't. Lie.*"

I bit my lip, rattling the tiny cube around in my hand, the little piece that was, apparently, all that stood in the way of this pixie telling the Institute exactly where I was.

"Just as I was about to step on you, you made a sound," I found myself saying. "How did you make that sound, if you can only repeat sounds you've heard?"

"*What sound?*"

"It sounded like a bird."

"*Bird. No bird.*"

"But I heard it!"

"*No bird,*" it repeated.

Stalemate. It was unlikely anyway that it could lead me to the Iron Wood. If the Institute knew such a place existed, they would have found it and harvested all the people long ago.

I tucked the metal cube into my pocket. Hearing the pixie speaking my own voice—however warped—made it hard to decide to destroy it, but I had little choice. I couldn't trust it. I gathered up my power, trying to ignore the ravenous, gnawing pit of hunger in my stomach caused by the first blow.

"*Stop that!*" cried the pixie, in my voice. "*Don't.*"

"Quit talking to me," I said, frowning. "You're making it harder. You're just a thing, it's not like pixies have a sense of self-preservation."

"*I have,*" said the pixie. "*Not a thing. Programmed me different.*"

The gathered power faltered and slipped, and I lost some of it around the edges of my concentration. It was true that I had never seen a pixie like this, with eyes, with speech. "There's no reason for me to keep you alive." As I said it, I cursed myself. The thing wasn't alive. Just a collection of gears and magical programming.

"*Bird,*" it said.

"You said it wasn't a bird. If it's not a bird call then you can't help me."

"*Wasn't a bird,*" it agreed. But then, infuriatingly, added, "*Bird. Location. Answer.*"

Suddenly, I understood. "You can take me to where you heard that sound?"

"*Yes.*"

"You don't know where the Institute is, but you know where you heard the bird call?"

"*Bird sound alive, different. Can't sense the Institute.*"

"You can track living things, if they're close enough." Could it sense my excitement? "Why would you help me?"

"*To keep me alive.*" Its speech was getting better, more complete, with every sentence I spoke.

"If you could, would you turn me in?"

"*Yes.*"

"But you can't as long as I have that cube?" I put a protective hand over my pocket.

"*Yes.*" The thrum of its wings sped and slowed again. Irritation? From a machine?

I could destroy the pixie, here, now, with a moment of concentration. But then I would be stuck drifting aimlessly across an unfamiliar world. As long as I kept the cube in my pocket, I was safe.

"How do I know you're not leading me off a cliff or straight into a forest of carnivorous trees or any one of a thousand dangers I haven't discovered yet?"

The color left the pixie's eyes, leaving them glowing an empty white, and its mouth opened wide. The voice that emerged was not mine—and not Gloriette's. A man's voice. *"First directive: Keep Lark alive."* Its mouth closed again, and the blue of its eyes returned.

I recognized that voice. Even tinny, warped, miles away from the source, it made my heart pound painfully. "Kris." I was seized with such a sudden, intense longing to see him that it nearly brought me to my knees.

"Kris," it repeated. *"Keep Lark alive."*

"So as long as I don't let you figure out how to get back, you're harmless. Right?"

The pixie did not respond at first, hovering calmly in front of my face.

"Are you safe?" I pressed.

The pixie blinked slowly, lazily. *"What is safe?"*

I swallowed. The thing couldn't form its own words, but it could equivocate. I tried to ignore the shiver that crept down my spine. "But you can take me to the bird sound."

"Take you to the bird sound?" it said, and paused. All I could hear was the mad turning of its gears. *"Yes."*

"Then let's go."

• • •

I had expected the pixie to lead me back the way I had come. Either it would betray me and lead me toward the Institute, or it would be retracing its steps to where it had heard the bird. Instead, the pixie headed away, toward the wilderness.

It said little when I spoke to it, unless I pressed for answers. At some point in the one-sided conversation, I had uttered the phrase, "I'm not certain," and it had become the pixie's favorite way of dodging my questions. The pixie couldn't lie—or, at least, it certainly seemed that way—but it could avoid answering truthfully.

"Was it a recording of a bird?" I trudged along, trying to keep up despite the way my feet ached. The pixie kept to a faster pace than I would have done on my own, forcing me to move quickly or lose sight of it.

"*I'm not certain.*"

"A phonograph, inside one of the pockets?"

"*I'm not certain.*"

"A bird that's not a bird," I muttered. I had run out of ideas, and fell silent.

By the time the sun dipped down toward the hills to the west, we had covered more ground than I ever would have done on my own. The ruins gave way to a broad sea of waist-high grass, spotted with trees and skirted on either side by dense woods. The pixie turned abruptly west, leading the way into a much thicker forest, something that had clearly been forest long before the wars. An old forest—a hungry forest. I hung back.

"No forests." I searched each tree for the telltale lines of mouths, the unnatural shiver of leaves. "Let's stop here for the night."

The pixie paused, hovering. "*No,*" said the pixie. My own voice, echoed back to me, sounded far more firm and confident than it ever did coming out of my own mouth. "*To keep Lark alive. Let's stop for the night. Forests.*"

I groaned. "Of course you would say that. Are you trying to imply that it's more dangerous out here than in there?"

"*Yes.*"

"I don't suppose you're going to tell me why?"

"*I'm not certain.*"

"How much further until the bird?"

"*I'm not certain.*"

"Well, are there more machines from the Institute coming after me?"

"*I'm not—*"

"Never mind." Empty as my pack was, my weary shoulders felt its slight weight as if it were full of rocks. "Look, I don't like forests, okay?"

"*Okay.*" The pixie darted around and sped off, vanishing into the gloom.

"Hey!" I shoved aside my exhaustion to jump after it. It occurred to me again that this could be an elaborate trap, but I chased it anyway.

I couldn't help but remember the last time I had run through the forest. Although these trees gave no sign of being animate, there were still plenty of roots to trip me and branches to claw at my face. I ducked underneath them and kept on, listening for the thrum of magic that told me where the pixie had gone.

And then, abruptly, it was there, hovering a few feet away. Still. Calm.

"You're *not* allowed to do that anymore," I gasped, slipping in the leaf mould as I skidded to a stop. "You hear me?"

"*Okay,*" said the pixie. Then: "*Look.*"

The pixie drifted past me, crystalline eyes directed back the way we had come.

I turned, wondering again if I'd made a horrible miscalculation in allowing the pixie to live. No, not live. Exist. It wasn't alive.

I could still see a good portion of the field across which we'd been walking. At first I saw nothing, and started to say as much, when the pixie buzzed impatiently, interrupting me.

Then, all at once, I saw them.

A chain of six figures, low to the ground, moving fast.

Heading north. There were no details in the gathering dusk. They were darker than the oncoming night, no more than shadows slipping between the tall grasses, silhouetted by the setting sun. Another day I might have marveled at the sunset, the first I'd seen out in the open, but I was too fixated upon the shadows in the grass.

While I watched, the one in front straightened, becoming a silhouette so familiar I nearly darted out of hiding. A human.

The pixie hummed low, gears growling and grinding. A warning. I kept back, wondering how it had sensed my eagerness. Not counting the wild boy, and the ghosts in the townhouse, when was the last time I'd seen another human face?

The silhouette dropped back down, and some of my exultation dimmed. I'd never seen anyone move with quite that strange, low gait. No *human* moved like that—did they? They kept to a loose formation, fanning out behind the leader, and moving fast.

I took a step back, wishing the tree I hid behind had a broader trunk. I let my eyes drift ahead of the shadows, trying to figure out where they were headed. And then I saw it: a seventh figure, similar in shape. Not moving so quickly, but with the same low, sinuous motion. Smooth, but for a slight hitch. It was limping.

I had barely time to realize this before the pack of six had caught up to the lone figure, speeding up as they caught sight of him. A guttural cry went up, echoing eerily across the plain, reverberating within the forest. Something—the seventh figure—screamed.

And then they were upon it, and I could hear the sounds of their slaughter as far away as I was. I stared, unable to look away, as all six people—but they could not be people, they could *not* be people—fell upon the wounded one. The clearing echoed with the sounds of tearing flesh and cracking bones interspersed with whoops and gurgles of delight.

The sunset blazed behind them on the plain. I saw one of the six rip an arm off of the corpse, the motion silhouetted against the bloody setting sun. I retched and covered my mouth with both hands.

Two of the figures lifted their heads. I couldn't tell, in the deceptive light, whether they were looking in my direction. The pixie hummed another warning, but I didn't need it this time. I held my breath until the two heads dropped back down, the monsters returning to their feast.

I tore my gaze from the sight and turned away, spine pressing against the tree at my back. The pixie drifted on into the gloom of the forest, and when it spoke, the sound was so slight as to be barely distinguishable over the continued sounds of carnage behind us.

"Let's go. Keep Lark alive."

CHAPTER 17

The next hour was a miserable haze of fear and exhaustion. My spine tingled constantly, expecting the monstrous creatures to leap at me at any moment. The pixie kept me marching through the darkening wood, staying just far enough ahead that I could still see and follow it.

The forest could not have been more different than the one in the pocket. There were old trees, yes, but in the deep of this forest, the trees stood tall and lean, with nary a branch between the canopy and the floor. Here, where the trees were thickest, the undergrowth was stunted and low, made up of tangled briar patches and broad-leafed ivy.

"Will we be safe in here?" I asked, catching myself before I stumbled to my knees again into a thorn bush. I shivered in the now-freezing dark.

"*Maybe,*" said the pixie.

"Will those shadow men come into the woods?"

"*Shadow men,*" repeated the pixie. For the briefest second, I imagined I had detected amusement in its voice. Which was impossible, of course. It was only repeating my own tones. "*Not the shadow men,*" it answered, finally.

"But something else might?" I pressed.

"I'm not certain."

I was too weary to protest, and from then on walked in silence that was broken only by the crashing of leaves and twigs as I blundered my way through the forest. It had grown so dark that I began to spend more time on my hands and knees than on my feet, and when I had crashed into a bush for what felt like the fiftieth time, the pixie came to a halt.

"Let's stop for the night."

I dropped to my knees where I was standing, one tiny part of my brain grateful for the moss underfoot that could have easily been rocks or more thorns. It didn't even matter, for the moment, that I was being ruled so completely by a machine. All that mattered was rest.

The pixie made a wide circle and buzzed back toward me. It didn't speak, but instead bumped insistently against the pack slung across my shoulders.

"What, you want food? You don't eat." Uncertainty tickled at my mind. "Do you?"

"You eat," said the pixie. *"I don't."*

"Such concern," I said, making no effort to keep the chill out of my voice. I leaned forward, shrugging out of the bag and loosening the drawstring. Despite having stopped midday to eat my last piece of bread, I was still ravenously hungry from having used magic to smash the pixie.

All that came from the pack into my groping hands were two carrots and half of a cucumber. I swallowed the saliva that came rushing to my mouth, and took up the cucumber. The broken end of it was dry and wrinkly from exposure to the air, but I ate it anyway, too hungry to care about its rubbery, chalky texture. It was gone all too soon, leaving me holding the two carrots. I willed my stomach to settle.

"Eat," repeated the pixie, invisible in the gloom.

"If I eat them now I won't have anything to eat in the morning." My voice sounded hollow even to my own ears.

"You will look in the morning."

"For more food?" My hands tightened around the carrots. "Out here?"

"Yes. I will help you."

"And lead me straight to something poisonous." I gritted my teeth. I knew I shouldn't eat the carrots. But the stabbing in my gut was too strong to ignore.

The carrots, sweet and only a little soft, were gone as quickly as the cucumber.

Now that I was still, the cold had begun to creep in around me. I had been so preoccupied with my hunger that I hadn't noticed it. The aching emptiness was only slightly lessened by the vegetables, but it was enough that I could focus on the lighter the wild boy had given me.

The pixie sat some distance away as I gathered a little pile of leaf litter. Striking the wheel with my thumb without being able to see it was harder than I had expected. By the time I was able to coax a spark out of it, I was shivering so violently my vision blurred.

By sheer good fortune, the spark fell full upon the little pile of leaf litter—and smoldered there, uselessly, until it winked out. Echoes of its brightness danced in my fuzzy vision as I stared into the darkness where it had been.

Only the pixie kept me from throwing the lighter across the clearing. I would not admit defeat in front of a machine.

Wait—the pixie *had* been there, humming faintly some yards away. It was no longer. There was only the quiet and the cold and the utter darkness closing in around me.

All the day's suspicions crashed in on me. To have trusted one of the Institute's machines, believed that I had rendered it harmless, with one lucky blow? I deserved to be caught. I cradled the lighter, warm from my futile attempts to make it work, against my chest.

I heard the pixie's return long before it spoke, and so when it buzzed into the clearing and said, *"Here,"* I managed not to jump.

Something soft and light dropped down onto my lap as the pixie buzzed past my face. I groped, and my fingertips discovered a loose ball of dead moss. Dry, thin, airy—the perfect kindling. I looked up, but the pixie was invisible in the dark. I swallowed a "thank you" and bent my head once more to the fire.

I coaxed sparks out of the lighter much more easily this time, but they seemed only to fly up, out—everywhere but onto the little ball of moss. My fingers were stiff with cold now, throbbing with every movement.

When a spark finally caught in the moss, I held my breath as it smoldered, one tiny filament glowing in the darkness. The glow spread to another. And then another. And then, as I exhaled over the smoldering moss so gently that it barely stirred at my breath, the flame caught.

I groped around, cursing that I had not gathered twigs and sticks beforehand. Luckily the spot the pixie had chosen to stop for the night was full of them, and I found enough fuel to turn the wisp of flame into a tiny little fire that shed enough light for me to see my surroundings.

I was in a clearing. The trees around me stood tall and straight, but for one that had fallen, uprooted at its base. It had to have been recent; the dirt still clung to the roots.

The pixie settled onto a dead branch of the fallen tree, rustling and settling its wings in an odd parody of grooming. The hum of its magic was discordant, but rapidly becoming as familiar to me as the sun disc inside the Wall had been. Now that I was growing warmer, my body began reporting various aches and pains I hadn't noticed before. Somewhere, between the sound of the pixie and the faint aching of my body, I let exhaustion take over and fell asleep.

Once I thought I woke in the night to see a face at the edge of the firelight. It was a face I was coming to know. It was softer by firelight, the orange glow smoothing his dirty cheeks and highlighting the hair. His features were younger than I had first guessed. I should have been frightened, but the lethargy of sleep kept me quiet, calm.

"Who are you?" I whispered.

The wild boy looked at me, crouched in the moss and leaves, one hand on the ground to steady himself. "Nobody," he whispered back, his voice raw and young and startling. I had not believed he would answer me. "Go back to sleep."

I fell helplessly into oblivion, the face swimming back into darkness. I tried to call out, "Wait!" But he was gone, and I knew nothing else until dawn.

• • •

I woke to the dappled sunrise, narrow shafts of light making their way through the treetops. I had almost forgotten the sound of the sun disc, the sound that had woken me every morning for sixteen years. Instead, I heard the pixie's faint whirring and the tiny hiss of the embers of my fire.

I had slept more deeply and more soundly that night than I had since that first night in the Institute. I remembered a face and an electrifying *human* voice whispering, "Sleep. . . ."

The pixie had not yet woken, or started up, or whatever it needed to do to snap out of its hibernation. I chose to stay where I was, curled up by the fire, savoring the extra rest.

As I dozed, my mind turned over something that had been bothering me since the pixie first spoke. It was such a tiny creature, its diamond heart so small that it couldn't possibly carry much power. In the city, all machines—pixies included—returned often to the Institute to be recharged. How, then, was this one still going, days away from the city? How had it regained power after I had damaged it to the point where its heart had been barely flickering?

My stomach began to roar for food. I remembered, with a sinking heart, that I had eaten the last of my rations the night before. This was no natural hunger, either; this was the price of having used magic. I could feel it gnawing away at me, exploding in my brain with the power of a migraine.

As if awakened by my digestive system, the pixie gave a sharp click and then whirred into life.

"Sleep well?" I had no way of knowing if it could detect sarcasm; it was probably just as well if it couldn't.

"*Yes*," it said, giving its wings a flutter and a shake, sending a spray of tiny droplets of dew shimmering into the air. "*Thank you.*"

My stomach roiled and lurched. Had I taught it that phrase?

"*You should eat*," it went on, continuing to rustle and shiver its wings as if grooming them.

"Eat what?" I shut my eyes against the painful emptiness in my body. "You convinced me to eat all I had last night, remember?"

"*Look*," said the pixie.

When I sat up I saw it across the blackened remains of my fire. Nestled on a leaf, in a neat conical stack, was a pile of little purple berries.

My throat seized with confusion, as my stomach gave a painful lurch. "Where did those come from? Did you—"

"*No*," said the pixie, before I'd managed to finish the question.

"Then who?"

"*You don't know?*"

The image of a face, dimly seen through the flames, swam into my mind's eye. But that had been a dream.

Hadn't it?

"I have no way of knowing if they're safe to eat." I was unable to tear my eyes away from the berries. For a blind, aching moment I didn't care if eating them would kill me—I wanted to fill my empty stomach. My head swam from hunger.

"*They're safe*," echoed the pixie.

I stared at it. "How would you know? You've spent your life—existence—whatever, behind the Wall."

The pixie fluttered its wings again, lifting a delicate copper leg to scratch at its abdomen. "*As did you.*"

"I know!" Hunger twisted my mind. I wanted to smash the bug. "And that's why I don't know if they're safe!"

"*I know.*" Its voice was firm.

I had little choice.

My fingers trembled as I reached for one of the berries. "Just one," I whispered. "Even if they're poisonous, surely one won't kill me." The berry was slightly warm from the fire, and gave under my fingers like flesh. I shuddered and popped it into my mouth.

It was so tart that my mouth felt as though it was shriveling up. I gasped as the acidic juices touched cracked lips, and swallowed. Now to wait, to try to ignore the overwhelming urge to stuff my face.

And yet, why would the wild boy have left them, if I wasn't meant to eat them? If he wanted me dead, he could have killed me in my sleep a dozen times over by now.

Even before I had followed the thought to its conclusion, my fingers were reaching for more berries. They stained my fingers purple-red as I ate, but I didn't care. Their tartness was unbelievably satisfying. Before I could stop myself, I'd eaten every last one.

I threw myself onto my back, staring up at the treetops above me, waiting for my stomach to process the news that I had fed it. I was by no means sated, but I would at least live a little longer. I wondered how long it took to starve to death.

How long does it take to die from poisonous berries?

My stomach was roiling a bit, having trouble with the acid of the berries, but nothing more dramatic than that.

Berries. Berries meant a flowering bush. And a flowering bush meant pollinators. At the Institute, they had developed strains of berry fruiting shrubs that could self-pollinate. But in the wild? Was there a place, then, that bees or butterflies still existed? My heart skipped a beat. Or birds?

I sat up again, running a hand through my hair. "Do you know who that was?"

"Who?"

"The boy—man—whoever it was, who brought me these."

"No."

"I can't keep relying on him to bring me things when I need them."

"No." The pixie's sedate agreement infuriated me.

"We need to find some food I can take with me."

"We are close to where you want to go."

"Close?" My hands tightened around the moss underneath me. "How close? A couple days? One day? Less?"

"Less than one day." Finally its wings settled into stillness as it finished grooming the dew from its mechanisms.

I hesitated. A search for food might take us farther from the source of the sound the pixie had replicated. And if there were birds where we were going, they had to be eating something—hopefully something I could eat, too.

The pixie's path would take us deeper into the forest, further from the plain that I thought would be my best hope for finding food growing wild. Further from the city, further

CHAPTER 18

The pixie's pace was much less harsh than the headlong flight the night before, but I still felt like a blind follower. With the thick ceiling of leaves overhead, it was impossible to tell time or to guess what direction we were heading. More than once, the uneasy pit in my stomach lurched, reminding me that I couldn't know if I could trust the thing.

Only the memory of Kris's voice—*keep Lark alive*— kept me from smashing the machine and searching for food on my own. Kris was the only reason I hadn't become the city's human power source. I wouldn't have taken a step outside my cell if he hadn't brought me the key. If Kris had programmed this pixie, then I had to believe it would help me.

The pixie and I talked now and then as we moved. I was always the first to break the silence, but the pixie answered readily enough. Its vocabulary was growing.

The conversation was scattered, inconsequential. Nonsensical things, mostly. I spoke to hear the sound of my voice. I had never been a friendly person—and yet, out here, stretched thin to breaking, I discovered that I was lonely.

"Pixie." The pounding of my feet and the ache of my

stomach had grown too strong. "Break?" I was too winded to form complete sentences.

The bug slowed and then turned in a wide circle back toward me. I braced myself for its reproach, but the command to keep moving never came. The pixie settled onto a fallen log and folded its wings demurely.

"I don't like that," it said eventually, gears whirring. I had come to recognize the rapid buzzing of its mechanisms as a warning signal, heralding conversations in which the pixie had to be particularly clever about piecing together its stolen vocabulary to say what it wished to say.

"Don't like what?" I dropped onto the log as well. The rotting wood gave a little under my weight. It smelled of earth and green, and I closed my eyes.

"'Pixie'."

My eyes flew open again. "What? You don't like me calling you pixie?"

"I am different."

"Clearly. The other pixies never would have given me this kind of trouble. It's what you are, why shouldn't I call you that?"

"Should I call you Human?" It had pulled that word out of my terrified questions the previous night, when I'd seen the shadow people and asked what they were. My own voice as it named my species sounded disgusted.

"My name is Lark," I said.

"Then I, too, need a name."

"You're a machine." I ignored the way the bug buzzed and hummed in response. "Machines don't get names, just labels and model numbers."

"I have a sense of self-preservation. I can make decisions. I have speech. I have will." The pixie's blank sapphire eyes gazed up at me. *"Do I not deserve a name?"*

My head spun, and not only from the exhaustion and hunger tugging at me after our few hours' travel. "Fine, then. What do you want me to call you?"

"No creature can choose its own name."

"So I have to name you?" I would have stalked off had I the energy, but I wasn't sure the muscles of my legs would support me if I tried to stand. "Don't be ridiculous."

The pixie said nothing in reply. After a few seconds, it shook its wings and launched itself off the log again. It waited a few feet away, expectant. Break time was over.

We walked in silence after that, which proved to be far more exhausting than scattered conversation. I had no distraction from my fatigue. I was cold; I was hungry; I was exhausted and weak. I was sunburned and blistered, dizzy from exposure. More than anything I was thirsty, something I only realized now that I wasn't speaking. The only water here, though, was lying in stagnant pools that even I knew I shouldn't drink.

We were, with every step, moving further from the last place I'd seen something to eat or drink. I was, perhaps, walking placidly to my death. *At least*, I thought to myself with grim satisfaction, *my use to the Institute will die with me.*

The forest had descended into a low-lying marsh, with swollen ridges crisscrossing its surface and offering safe places to step. The pixie slowed its pace so I could watch where I was placing my feet. The water all around was still and dark, spotted with vegetation and rotting tree stumps.

Lost in thought, I stepped too close to the edge of a ridge. My foot rolled painfully on the curve, and I staggered sideways. I tried to grab something to keep myself from falling, but my fingers closed on leaves that tore as I fell. Terror flooded my mind as I crashed into the swamp, flinging both hands in front of me as if to catch myself.

I hit the water—which was only a few feet deep—face-first, both arms sinking up to the elbows into the mud at its bottom. Relief at how shallow the water was turned to panic as I tried to pull my arms free of the muck. It felt light, smooth to the touch, but it sucked at my limbs with a cruel tenacity. I struggled, heaving my arms free in one panicked jolt, giving me enough room to throw my head out of the water and gulp a breath of air. The movement forced my legs deeper into the mud.

I shrieked for help, though I didn't know who I expected to help me. The pixie, so tiny, could do nothing. It was a glimmer in the darkness, hovering, watching as the swamp sucked my legs deeper and deeper.

As I watched, the pixie *changed*. Its body shifted, elongating. It sprouted a second set of wings from nowhere. Its torso unrolled, the squat body lengthening into something slim and elegant. I blinked my eyes, which were streaming tears and swamp water, certain I was hallucinating. And then, without a word, the pixie vanished into the wood.

I choked, coughing up the water I'd swallowed. I grasped for the ridge, but I was facing away from it and the mud had such a hold on me that I could not turn. I twisted my body, trying to reach for anything I could use to pull myself out, but my struggles only drove me deeper.

The water was above my shoulders now. I could feel the weight of it pressing on my lungs, making it harder to breathe. Air came in and out in frenzied gasps. I had no magic in my core to save myself with; I was too hungry, too weak.

I gasped for breath again, the sound of it echoing in a terrified sob. The water closed over my lips and I tipped my head back, trying to keep my nose above the surface of the water.

Not like this. Somewhere from deep in my gut rose an unfamiliar longing to see the sky again. What had once been such a terror for me was now all I wanted to see. Overhead there were only leaves. In the distance I heard the crashing of footsteps through undergrowth, inhuman noises. Shadows.

I gave a last desperate jerk, kicking with all my strength so that pain lanced through the muscles of my legs. My body lurched upward. But it was not enough. I rose a few inches, enough to open my mouth and gasp one complete breath— and then the weight of my body dragged me back down, and the water closed over my head.

The light danced and rippled above my eyes, the surface of the water shining like the Wall. I clamped my lips, holding my breath. The exertion made spots dance in front of my gaze, that last lungful lasting all too briefly. I could still see the leaves, a wavering green mass that sparkled and shone, broken and torn by the bubbles that escaped me despite my attempts to hold onto that last breath of air. My body burned as the swamp swallowed me down into its cold belly.

Shadows flew across the surface of the water above me, unfamiliar sounds coming distorted to my ears. *Too late*, I thought, watching the shadows dance and rage above. *I'm already dead, and you can't eat me.* At any moment I expected the howls I had heard the previous night, when the shadow people had attacked. My lungs gave way, and the last of my air left in a rush of bubbles. I gasped for more, chasing the bubbles, but they were dancing up, away. The swamp rushed in, cold and burning and final.

Something warm wrapped around my shoulder. Finger-like claws dug into my armpit. I struggled as the trees overhead began to fade, the light to go dark. I would not become some monster's meal. My head snapped back as I was jerked upward, and as soon as I got one foot on solid ground I twisted, throwing my elbow back hard against the thing that held me.

I heard a grunt of pain, but the hand at my shoulder only tightened in response. I twisted again, jerking my shoulder away so hard it wrenched painfully.

The hand let go, but not without shoving me hard enough to send me sprawling onto the ground. I started to scramble up again but my feet slipped on the muddy ground and I fell onto my hip. I looked up, gasping for breath, expecting to see teeth aiming for my throat.

The wild boy stared back at me, half-crouched, feral. Time stopped for a moment as I tried to blink swamp water from my streaming eyes enough to focus on his face. Then he lifted a hand and rubbed gingerly at his ribcage, where I'd elbowed him.

For a fleeting moment, his eyes were so cold I thought he was about to throw me back into the deadly muck. Then he gave a quick jerk of his head, an unmistakable command to follow him, and turned to lead the way through the swamp.

• • •

The wild boy led me through the darkening wood. If I'd thought the pixie had set a grueling pace, it was nothing like what this boy expected. He didn't turn around once to check I was following, moving so fluidly he was more like a shadow zipping through the trees than a human being.

My progress was a constant struggle to stay upright despite my shaking legs and burning lungs. Eventually exhaustion won, and I went sprawling face-first into the undergrowth. The air jolted out of me and for a moment I was too focused on trying to breathe again to care whether my rescuer stopped or not.

By the time I picked myself up, he was standing only a few feet away, motionless and silent, and staring at me. I could feel bits of leaf and dirt sticking to the mud caking my face. The wild boy saw that I was trying to sit up and came to crouch right in front of me, eyes flicking back and forth between each of mine. Too close.

I scrambled back.

His eyes, a shocking ice-blue amidst the general grime coating his face, narrowed.

"Who are you?" I tried to ask. It emerged only as a croak, my throat so hoarse that it burned as badly as my lungs.

He retrieved a canteen from where it hung across his chest and rolled it toward me. The movement was so precise that the canteen stopped inches from the tips of my fingers. He said nothing, only watched as I picked up the canteen, heavy with water, and took a drink. The water scorched my throat, but I began to feel better. As I drank he straightened up again and stepped past me, looking back the way we'd come.

"Are there shadow men coming?" I asked, screwing the cap back onto the canteen.

The boy held up a hand sharply without looking at me. The line of his shoulders was tense, the corded muscle visible beneath his T-shirt, which was worn so thin it was nearly transparent. They were a man's shoulders, and yet, when he turned to face me again, a boy's wary curiosity stared back at me. He held a finger to his lips, flashing me a look so intense that all my questions died instantly. Then he returned to scrutinizing the rapidly darkening wood.

I tried again, in a whisper this time. "My name's Lark. Thank you for—" There was too much to name. "Everything," I finished lamely.

He ignored me, turning back and reaching instead for the canteen, to replace it over his shoulder. His clothes had been city-made, but they were so old I didn't recognize the fashion. His shirt had once been white, and the pants had been patched so much that I could not tell what color they'd been. A number of small fur pelts hung from his belt, and I shuddered.

Without another glance at me, he started off again, through the trees. This time there was even more urgency to his step, his gait low to the ground, quick.

"Wait—" I called breathlessly. "I need food; I haven't eaten in . . ." I couldn't remember the last time I'd had food.

He dug a hand into his pocket and pulled out a strip of something, tossing it back to me without looking to see if I caught it. It fell in the dirt, but I was too hungry to care. I gave it a sniff as I staggered along in the wild boy's wake. It was stringy, a dark brown that smelled like charcoal. Something smoked over a fire. My stomach lurched uncontrollably, and I bit into whatever it was.

Chewy, extremely tough—my jaw popped as I tore off a bite-sized piece. It certainly resembled nothing we ate in the city, oddly rich and flavorful. I was about to ask what it was when my eyes fell on the pelts dangling from his belt.

Meat.

I gagged and threw the rest away, spitting out my mouthful and trying not to retch. Leaning against a tree for support, I spat again, trying to rid my mouth of the rich, meaty texture. Animal flesh, stripped and cooked—I shuddered and summoned every inch of willpower to prevent myself from throwing up.

Out of the corner of my eye I saw the wild boy crouch to retrieve the strip of meat and sniff at it himself.

"I can't," I managed, shaking my head violently. "It's—it's awful."

He was eyeing me flatly when the sound of magic, dizzying and light, pulled my attention away. The Institute.

Before I could panic, the pixie general came whirring out of the forest, making straight for me. It was aiming for my shoulder—I swatted it away, and it instead alighted on a fallen log, wings buzzing madly.

"Where have *you* been?" My throat was working better after having had some water.

The pixie shuffled its wings, turning its head on one side. "*I got help,*" it said after a long silence, as if it had been hunting for the proper vocabulary.

I knew my own voice had never possessed such a quiet dignity as that. "You can't mean you brought him here," I said, glancing at the wild boy, who had dropped into a half-crouch, ready to flee—or strike. "You and I are going to have to have a serious talk about what you did back there," I added. "I didn't know you could change shapes."

"*Neither did I,*" it said, and began its habitual meticulous grooming routine.

The wild boy made a disgusted sound and turned away to leave.

"I don't think I can do this," I murmured, trying to summon the strength to leave the solid support of the tree I was leaning against and follow him. All the rescuing in the world did no good if I collapsed from exhaustion while hiking through the forest.

The pixie flew from the log to hover not far from my face. There was urgency in the buzz of its wings, the same urgency shown by the wild boy as he started making his way back through the woods. Uneasily, I remembered the shadows flickering across the surface of the water as I sank in the bog. Were they coming after us?

"*Follow him,*" the pixie said. "*This is what you were looking for.*"

"What?" I felt the anger rise in me; anger that I was the last to understand everything, anger that I had required rescuing *again*, anger at my own inability to put all the pieces together. "Have you been leading me nowhere this whole time?"

The pixie flew after the boy as he left, then returned to

me, every movement betraying impatience. *"This is your bird sound."*

I stared at it stupidly.

With an exasperated grinding of mechanisms, the pixie let out a piercing version of the bird call it sang to stop me from destroying it.

The wild boy stopped, going still. Then, slowly, he turned and moved back toward me, his eyes on the pixie, glinting gold in the last of the sun as it set.

All this time, the pixie had been lying to me. Leading me to this boy, instead of to the birds I was supposed to find. How could I have trusted it? For all I knew, this boy was working for the Institute as well, ready to lead me right back to the cold glass arms of my cage.

Just as I felt tears sting at my eyes, the wild boy cupped his hands around his mouth. I thought for a moment he was about to shout, but then, instead, the most unimaginable trill emerged. Birdsong.

Silence stretched for long moments as I tried to understand. "What *are* you?" I gasped.

"You ask too many questions," he hissed. "You should be quiet. It isn't safe." The boy licked his lips, gazing at me with his animal eyes. "My name is Oren."

CHAPTER 19

His voice was quiet and a little rough, but very human. How long since I'd heard another person speak, who wasn't a machine or a ghost or a dream?

Oren—it could have been the name of any of my classmates back in the city. And yet it took only one look at him, the finely muscled shoulders, the wild eyes, the ill-kempt hair and dirty skin, to know he could never be mistaken for one of them.

"You said it isn't safe," I managed. "Is it the shadow people?"

"If you must talk," he said in a low voice, "talk while you're moving."

The pace he set was even more grueling than it had been before. Perhaps he knew that I couldn't really talk if I was moving so fast I could barely breathe. Every now and then he'd dig in his pocket for that strip of smoked meat and tear a mouthful off with his teeth, causing me to shudder and look away.

He didn't stop often, and when he did stop he never spoke, just tossed me the canteen of water and moved away to scan the woods around us. During one of these breaks, the pixie hovered closer. *"You should've eaten the meat he offered."*

"A machine is giving me advice on how to make friends?" I gritted my teeth, closing my eyes. "Just don't talk to me. Why are you even still following me?"

The pixie said nothing, but I heard the sound of its wings darting away from me again. After a few moments I cracked an eyelid briefly to see it sitting on a nearby shrub, its back to me, unconcerned.

The machine had said it brought the boy to me. How else would he have found me, just in time to prevent me from drowning? Or worse—being attacked by the shadow people? The shape it had changed into, just before the water closed over my head, was long and slim, built for speed.

Could it have really been trying to help me?

I watched it, where it sat looking for all the world as if it was sulking. I felt something in me relent a little.

"Nix," I muttered, closing my eyes again and leaning back against a tree.

The pixie buzzed, sounding almost quizzical.

"Nixies. They were these creatures from mythology. I remember reading about them. Shapeshifters."

"Yes?"

"Well, you said you couldn't name yourself. Will that do?"

Silence but for the breeze stirring the leaves overhead, and the tiny noise of the pixie's mechanisms.

"That will do."

I took a long, slow breath, trying to marshal my strength. I knew Oren would be back soon, ready to move again.

"You know, in stories, shapeshifters are never to be trusted."

"No," agreed the pixie calmly, and returned to its meticulous grooming.

. . .

We walked into the night. I fell asleep during one of Oren's pauses for water, but I don't think I slept long before he nudged me awake with the toe of his shoe.

"Time to go." His voice was hoarse, as though the habit of silence was easier than speech.

I picked myself up and we set off. The pixie—Nix—acted as sleepy as I felt, and settled on my shoulder. I thought about swatting it away, but I was too tired to summon the energy.

In the dark I couldn't see Oren, and he moved so silently that I often lost track of where he was. What little noise he made was drowned out by my own crashing and rustling as I stumbled through the undergrowth.

He moved like an animal, with an unconscious, unstudied grace, as if he'd been living out here his whole life.

But that was impossible. Unless—my heart seized—he was like me. The Renewable had said there were others like us, after all. She had said to follow the birds to find the Iron Wood, whatever that was. I hadn't seen the slightest glimpse of a feather, but this boy had spouted a torrent of birdsong like I'd never imagined.

"Oren," I said, trying out his name for the first time. "You can do magic, right? Like me?"

"Magic?" His voice emerged from the darkness ahead, ghostly and disembodied.

"Yes, like . . . doing things by thinking it. Magical power. It's what they use to power machines, you know? In cities?"

He didn't answer immediately. I strained through the darkness, but heard only the humming of the pixie. Finally he said, "No. Never heard of it."

"But how are you out here?" I blurted. "And not dead? Or twisted like the shadow people?"

"Who are these shadow people you keep talking about?" he asked abruptly.

"Those—things. I heard them coming for me when I was sinking in the bog. I saw them eating each other the other day. They're—twisted. From the absence of magic."

"I don't know any magical anything," he said, the words clearly unfamiliar in his mouth, "but the others have always been like that. The dark ones."

"But how are you—" I struggled to articulate the question, but my exhaustion was like a dark fog in my mind, preventing me from thinking. "Are there others like you?"

"Depends what you mean," came the reply.

"I mean like—living out here, like this. Do you have a family? People you live with?" My hand crept into my pocket for the paper bird, but I'd put it into my pack to dry after my dip in the marsh, and my fingers closed around nothing.

There was no reply.

"Look, you're the first person I've seen since I've been out here that hasn't tried to eat someone," I said. Why was he so determined to move in absolute silence?

"Do you never stop talking?" he asked tightly, as a twig cracked just in front of me. He'd stopped. It was just enough warning to keep me from walking straight into him in the dark. "What do you want? I'm keeping you alive, aren't I?"

"But why?" I felt that familiar sinking in my stomach. The Institute wanted me alive, after all.

His voice was clipped but quiet. "There aren't so many of us left. You were different. So I followed you."

"You were the one who left me the shoes!" I gasped, realization spreading like ice water.

"Shoes?" In the dark, he wouldn't be able to see the now-filthy shoes in question.

"I needed them and suddenly they were just sitting there,"

I said. "You were the one who left them for me, weren't you?"

Oren hesitated, and the uncharacteristic moment of uncertainty gave me the strangest impulse to reach out to him in the darkness, decipher his expression through touch. Eventually he grunted, the only reply I was going to get.

"And the bloody corpse?" I asked, as my toes tingled inside their stolen shoes. "Why leave me that if not to scare me?"

"You were supposed to eat it," he said, a hint of impatience coloring his voice.

"Oh." I felt my cheeks warming with embarrassment, grateful for the cover of night. "I thought it was a threat."

"What would I have to threaten you about?" Oren said. "If I wanted you dead I'd just kill you. It wouldn't be hard."

Oh. "Yes, but—" I struggled to explain the terror of those first few days. I wished I could explain the terror that *still* ruled me. "Never mind."

"You didn't answer my question," he said. "What do you want? You're fed now. Probably strong enough to move on by tomorrow."

"Those bird sounds you made." I took a deep breath. "I'm looking for a place called the Iron Wood. And I think you might know something about how to find it."

I hadn't realized how close he was standing until he leaped back, barely more than a shadow darting away. I felt the wind of his movement as he staggered, snapping leaves and twigs in an uncharacteristic display of clumsiness.

"No," he said, his voice low. "I don't."

"You do," I argued. For once, my voice didn't shake. "Why else would you react like that? I need you to take me there."

He was silent for a moment. "I'll take you to a place where you can find food, water, rest. No further."

"But—"

"It's a bad place." His voice emerged through gritted teeth.

"I don't care," I said. "That's where I'm going." I tried to ignore the way my heart surged. He *did* know where it was. I'd be able to find others like me. I'd be able to stop running. Sleep in the same place for more than one night, eat a meal that didn't leave me aching for more. Talk to people who actually wanted to talk back.

"You don't understand," said Oren. Something in the coldness of his voice made my excitement falter. "I won't take you there. I can't. It's a terrible place. If you go there, you die."

Before I could even absorb what he'd just said, an unnatural howl rose some distance behind us, no less terrifying for its remoteness.

I staggered—the darkness was suddenly more terrifying than the sky had been. Anything could be concealed in it, just a few feet away.

A hand emerged from the darkness and closed around my wrist. As I opened my mouth to scream, another hand clapped over my lips.

"We have time," Oren breathed, his lips not far from my ear. "But we have to move quickly. Nod if you understand."

My skin tingled unnaturally where he touched me, despite the frantic pounding of my heart. I nodded. The grip of his fingers over my mouth relaxed.

"This way."

CHAPTER 20

Though we heard the howls of the shadow men twice more, each time they were more distant. In the pitch-black of the night forest it was impossible to tell the passage of time, but it wasn't long before I realized I could make out Oren in front of me. The trees thinned, and soon we broke out of the forest at the edge of a broad plain.

Despite the lightening indigo sky to the southeast—Oren must have let me sleep for longer than I'd thought—a few stars were still visible overhead. I leaned against a tree, trying not to show my exhaustion, and looked up. There had been a moment, in the bog, where I thought I'd never see the sky again. Troubled, I looked away, toward the wild boy at my side.

Oren's gaze swept the hills rolling away ahead of us. Clumps of forest and the occasional patch of magic scattered the plains, which stretched up toward a ridge of wooded mountains that loomed blue and misty in the distance.

"How much further?" I asked, breaking the silence that had stretched since we began our headlong dash through the night.

He didn't answer my question, only grunted, "Wait here."

In a manner that was rapidly becoming familiar, Oren disappeared into the forest the way we'd come.

"And you claim I am difficult to talk to," said the pixie from my shoulder, in the unnaturally tiny voice that passed for a whisper. It was gaining more personality all the time. I wasn't sure that was a good thing.

"Is Oren from the Institute?" I asked, not sure what I expected the pixie to say.

"No."

I scrubbed at my face with my hand, as if I could wipe away the exhaustion that made it hard to think. I didn't want the wild boy to be a spy. Incomprehensible as he was, I felt better with him nearby.

"But you could be lying."

"Yes, but I'm not."

I groaned and rolled over onto my stomach, resting my forehead on my hands.

"If he were from the Institute," said Nix, *"then surely they would have given him a bath."*

He didn't act like he was from the Institute. Dirty, wild, stronger than any of the architects, skilled in ways no city-dwelling citizen would have reason to be. I pushed away thoughts of Institute spies and turned to the other mystery. "Nix, how is it that he's not twisted like the others?"

"I do not understand the question."

"Why isn't he a monster? Like the ones we saw a couple of days ago?"

The pixie ruffled its wings. *"I don't see any difference between them."*

I grimaced. The idea that it couldn't tell the difference between slavering, cannibalistic monsters and people like Oren and me was ludicrous. Before I could retort, I began hearing the subtle signs that Oren was returning. Already I was adjusting to the sound of another person existing around me.

"All right, let's go," he said, moving past me and on out of the forest.

"What were you doing back there?"

"Laying a false trail."

"What?" I scrambled to catch up with him, summoning the energy from somewhere to get to my feet. "A false trail for what?"

"For whatever might want to follow us. It's a hungry world. And you don't walk very quietly."

I glanced over my shoulder before I could stop myself, half-expecting to see shadowy faces and teeth between the thinning trees.

"It looks like a storm is coming," he said, tilting his chin briefly toward the sky. "We don't want to be stuck out in these hills when it hits.

"A what?" The architects had spoken of this—theorized that while the majority of the postwar landscape was barren and empty of magic, storms of energy sometimes swept across the wilderness, obliterating everything in their path.

"A storm. We'll be fine if we get to the edge of the forest." He stopped and looked back at me. Without input from my brain, my feet had stopped moving. His face changed, only a flicker, as he looked at me. "You've never been in a thunderstorm before?"

I shook my head. It seemed I would spend my life trying, and failing, not to show how afraid I was. He'd mentioned thunder, not magic—but still, that sounded no safer.

He watched me for several long moments and then jerked his head in the direction of the foothills. "Let's keep going. Best thing to do is get to cover before it hits. We should get to a place where you can rest before nightfall."

Out on the plains, the clouds were unimaginably immense. As we walked, the old terrors began to catch up with me, the feeling that at any moment the vastness of the sky would suck me up into its depths and tear me apart. Each time I glanced up, I instantly wished I hadn't. I tried to keep my eyes fixed on the ground until the vertigo passed.

We were maybe half an hour from the edge of the forest that dotted the base of the mountains like stitches along the hem of a skirt when the rain began. The moment I dared a peek at the sky, something splattered against my forehead. I stopped dead, reaching up with astonished fingers to feel the water dripping down my face.

Oren stopped a couple steps ahead. "Best keep moving," he said, without looking around.

"Rain," I said. Something in my voice must have struck him, for he turned around. I held out my wet fingers as proof.

"Usually comes with thunderstorms," agreed Oren. "You'd think you'd never been rained on before."

I tipped my face back again, a second drop and a third splattering against my muddy cheeks. "I haven't." Each drop brought a rush of adrenaline and fear, all coalescing into this moment.

"Come on, let's go."

But my feet wouldn't move; I stood there shivering, staring at him. What had once been unfounded fears of undefined space and horrible emptiness were now turned real. The sky became a vast sea overhead, and I struggled not to drown.

He looked at me again and hesitated. "Just take one step," he said quietly. "We're almost there."

It was easier to do as he said than refuse. I was so unsteady when I lifted my foot that I slammed it back down, closing my eyes as the world spun. The rain was falling faster now, a chilly roaring in my ears as the pixie huddled against my neck, humming madly. For once, the sound was a comfort.

Oren took a step toward me and then reached for my hand. My skin jolted the moment he touched it, every hair on my body standing on end. It was like the moment of static electricity when stepping through the barriers, only visceral and immediate as though I could feel energy flowing through each pore of our skin. I shuddered, but his expression gave no sign that he had noticed anything. He gave my hand a gentle tug, and I took another step, and another.

Oren coaxed me to the edge of the wood. Once the branches overhead were thick enough to block out most of the rain, I found it easier to breathe, easier to move. I let go of his hand and held on to a tree for support, resting my forehead against its bark. My skin was damp from sweat and rain, my shirt sticking to my back.

"Are you okay?" Oren was standing not far away, hands tucked into his pockets.

"Fine," I said. "Just—the sky scares me." There was no point, now, in trying to pretend I was anything less than a coward.

Oren frowned. "How can the sky possibly scare you? It's just the sky. There's nothing up there. Except water right now, I guess."

"That's just it." I shut my eyes and swallowed hard. "Nothing. I only saw the sky for the first time when I left the city." I shook my head. "It's huge, and empty, and awful."

"The sky is just a thing in the world. Like any other. Of all the things you have to be scared of, Lark, the sky's the least of your worries."

Perhaps he meant it to be comforting, but his quiet voice triggered something in me that had been building since the first time we spoke. "Look, maybe you know everything there is to know about this place but I'm new to this! I'd never even seen the sun until I escaped. So stop treating me like a child!" My voice cracked on the last word.

Oren waited until my breathing had calmed. His head was tipped lightly to one side, expression set in familiar neutral disinterest. "We've got another couple of hours to walk, and then we'll be there. Let's go."

He said nothing after that, although it wasn't much of a change from the morning. Water dripped through the canopy, seeking out the collar of my shirt and the nape of my neck. I regretted my outburst—I'd told him to stop treating me like a child, in the midst of a tantrum so childish it was a wonder he stayed with me at all. I tried whispering once to the pixie, but it didn't answer. I found myself missing my former solitude. At least then silence felt like a choice rather than a judgment.

The sky grew darker as we walked, so much so that I felt we had to be inside another pocket. The only glimpses of the sky through the treetops were of a blue-gray so dark I felt it must be illusion.

In the distance I heard the rumble of a machine. I stopped dead, my heart pounding. Oren kept walking, and my eyes fixed on his back as I stood waiting.

There, again—the sound of something enormous stirring. The harvester I encountered on my way out of the city was huge but it didn't sound nearly so loud. How much larger must something be to make a sound like that?

Oren realized I was no longer behind him. He stopped and turned. "Still an hour yet," he said, in that maddeningly even voice.

I swallowed, throat so dry it felt like sandpaper. "You don't hear that?"

"You mean the thunder?" Oren glanced up. "Storm's still a ways off. We've got time."

Thunder. I heard it again as I started walking, a deceptively low rumble, quiet, swelling beneath the sound of rain on leaves. The rain surged overhead, falling more heavily as we headed deeper into the forest. The canopy was no longer enough to protect us, and we got drenched. Oren seemed not to notice, running a hand through his hair to slick it back out of his eyes every few steps.

"At least the rain might wash his face a little," the pixie whispered, its voice barely audible above the sound of the storm.

The rain was washing away the mud caked onto my skin, as well. I smiled, grateful for the sound of another voice—even if it was the voice of my enemy. Technically.

"Will there be shelter where we're going?" I shouted ahead, struggling to make myself heard.

"It won't be raining there," was Oren's cryptic reply.

"How far now?"

His only answer was to walk faster. The pace forced me to adopt a strange, half-skipping gait—I walked a few steps and then ran one or two, struggling to keep up.

The sound of thunder and rain drowned out the hum of magic, so I had no warning of the pocket's presence until it loomed up in front of us, shimmering and dark in the gloom. Oren continued walking with not a moment's pause, and without so much as a backward glance at me, vanished inside.

Oren clearly expected me to follow. So far, he'd done nothing but help me. I had to trust that he knew what he was doing.

I took a long, slow breath and stepped inside.

He was right. Inside the pocket, it wasn't raining.

I stood, dripping and staring, in a meadow. Oren was halfway across it, heading for a forest that, while sparser than the one outside the barrier, looked very similar.

The meadow itself stretched away in front of me, the

grasses still but for where Oren had pushed his way through them. The color of the meadow was strangely pale, reflecting the violet light and looking like a sea of purple—

Flowers. Every inch of the meadow was blooming.

I dropped to my knees, spread my arms, and gathered an armful of the blossoms, burying my face in them. They were barely scented, carrying the merest hint of something crisp and wild and heady. The blooms were white, reflecting the purple dome overhead and glowing in the twilight. Their petals brushed my cheeks and lips and eyes, growing damp from the rain dripping off my nose and the tears clinging to my eyelashes.

"How many times am I going to have to stop and wait for you?" Oren's voice came from just behind me, but I didn't even lift my head. "I suppose you've never seen flowers before either," he said, more quietly.

I shook my head, and with a great effort, straightened a little. I released my armful so that they sprang back into place, bobbing their pale faces at me as if in enthusiastic welcome.

"Come on," said Oren, stooping to offer me his hand. The tears still stubbornly clinging to my eyelashes gave everything a fuzzy halo of sparkles, but through it, I thought I saw him smile. "There's a lot more to see."

I let him lead me through the meadow. He didn't speak again, but this time his silence felt reverent rather than rude. His hand still conveyed that strange buzzing sensation where our skin touched. His was rough, callused, strong—so very different from Kris's hand.

The pixie launched itself from its perch and went flitting crazily around the meadow as we walked, brushing the flowers and looking for all the world like a—

My dreamy, drifting thoughts came to a screeching, electrifying halt. There couldn't be flowers out here—not without something to pollinate them. Bees, butterflies—or birds.

Oren had reached the edge of the forest, and dropped my hand in order to pull a bit of undergrowth away so I could step inside. And I all but forgot the meadow and its flowers.

The forest was alive with movement and color and smell, animals bounding away from our intrusion. I smelled more flowers and the sharp tang of fruit, mixed with the nutty smell of the damp earth. The branches of the trees were laden with fruits, hanging like teardrops. And covering the bushes were berries of every color. Patches of green covered the floor, tiny red gems of berries nestled in the vegetation.

I heard a buzz swoop past my ear and looked for the pixie, but then caught sight of its telltale copper gleam back out in the meadow, where it was still playing with the flowers. I gazed up and around, and finally saw something swooping away. I followed its movement and saw more and more of them.

Bees. *Bees*, which had been extinct since before the wars. I felt my knees waver and buckle, and kept myself upright only through sheer force of will. They bobbed and danced, sometimes chasing each other, sometimes skittering away in search of nectar. They didn't fly like Nix or the pixies in the city; there was no purpose or direction to their movements, just a lazy delight in the art of flight that I had never seen.

I trailed along behind Oren as he made his way deeper into the wood, weaving his way in between the strawberry patches toward a small bare space where he had clearly been before. A charred fire pit told of many nights spent in this place. He tossed his bag down and sat, leaning against a fallen tree and spreading his arms to either side along his backrest.

I let my own makeshift pack drop and stood, gazing all around. I wanted to find words, something to express what it meant that he had brought me to this place, but my tongue felt thick in my mouth.

Eventually exhaustion and weakness forced me to sit, and I tore my eyes away from the bees dancing amidst the trees and blossoms. Oren was watching me, and started imperceptibly when I turned to look at him, as though he'd been smiling up until the instant I looked his way.

"This is—" I had no word with which to end the sentence, and gazed at him helplessly.

He nodded. "I come here whenever I can. Plenty to eat, and it's safe."

It was more than that, and I started to argue the point until I saw how the tension had drained out of him, saw the easy languor with which he was leaning back against the fallen tree. He knew it was more than that. He didn't need me to tell him.

Oren stirred himself to build a fire and gather us some dinner, telling me to sit. Though I felt some small stirring of guilt that he was doing all the work, the weakness in my muscles still plagued me, and after a day's hike I felt as though I could do no more than collapse. I fell into a doze, watching the bees and occasionally the pixie, wheeling overhead in the strange violet light.

I had little sense for the passage of time, but when the tingle of his hand touching my shoulder woke me, the light was nearly gone. Only the faintest violet shadows edged the world beyond the circle of our firelight, making my eyes throb as I peered into it.

"Dinner," he said, and placed a plate into my hand.

I had only a moment to wonder where on earth he'd managed to find a plate—did he have a stockpile of utensils here, inside this pocket?—before what was on the plate stole my breath away.

Toasted nuts, topped with crushed purple berries, strawberries, blackberries tossed in a salad of brilliant green leaves, whose crisp smell identified them as mint, a pile of something that looked like potato, cubed and cooked golden. I gasped.

Oren was already tucking into the food on his own plate. I half-expected him to have a dismembered rabbit on his plate, and was all set to have my appetite squashed by nausea, but he was eating the exact same thing as I was.

We ate in silence, but only because it was necessary for us to shovel the food into our mouths more quickly.

One of the bees buzzed low and landed on a bobbing blossom not far from where I sat in rapt attention. I set my plate aside and leaned close. I could see its long tongue dipping delicately into the recesses of the flower, its furry body coated in a light dust of pollen. After a few seconds, it stopped its feast and with equal delicacy wiped its legs over its face, looking for all the world like a well-mannered diner wiping her mouth.

Without thinking, I stretched out a hand toward the creature.

"Careful," said Oren, voice sharp with warning.

As the bee moved I saw the tiny point of its stinger at the end of its abdomen, and drew my hand back.

Oren set his own plate aside and glanced up. "Sunset," he said. "Watch."

A realization cut through the haze of happy satisfaction dulling my senses. In the other pockets, sunset had always marked a change. The forest had come alive and monstrous, the ghosts had emerged.

But surely Oren would not be so relaxed if the meadow was about to turn into a nightmare. Still, I leaned forward and peered through the gathering darkness, eyes straining to see what change the sunset would bring.

CHAPTER 21

All over the meadow, the bees were abandoning their work and vanishing into the shadowy woods, all zooming in the same direction. Nix shifted forms to imitate their bodies, zipping along their path and then flipping back toward us, never quite going out of eyesight. It began to imitate their style of bobbing, dancing flight, though it could not quite capture the same languid playfulness.

Oren got to his feet and reached for one of the branches in the fire. As he straightened, the burning end of the branch left an orange trail against the darkness. Its glow illuminated his face as he watched the bees. His expression was soft in a way I'd never seen before.

In that moment I knew Oren had not been sent by the Institute. If the architects knew of such a place, it would be swarming with machines. They could feed the city for months on the fruit growing here, and the magic thrumming through the air could power the machines needed to harvest it. The idea of the many-fingered harvester rolling across the meadow made my skin crawl.

I watched Oren as he turned away from the bees to look at me, the light playing on his cheeks. The rain had washed some of the dirt away.

"Come on, follow me," he said, meeting my gaze briefly. He gestured with a torch toward the darkened wood.

"Where?"

"You'll see."

He led me into the forest. Though I stumbled at first, my eyes began to adjust to the light, which flickered and bobbed with every step Oren took.

"How many other people know about this place?"

"Just me," said Oren, stepping over a fallen log. "And now you."

"You haven't shown it to anyone else?" My throat tightened.

"There isn't anyone else." His voice was quiet, firm, dispassionate.

I followed the rest of the way in silence, until we arrived at a clearing that was positively swarming with the bees. They clustered around an old, half-dead tree pocked with hollows, darting in and out of it.

"Stay there, and hold this close," Oren ordered as he handed me the torch, but for once his tone didn't make me want to snap at him. I did as he said, angling the torch closer, the sputtering smoke mingling with the frenetic bees.

He approached the tree, causing a positive flurry of activity among the bees. They swarmed over the tree, forming a moving, shimmering curtain of light between it and Oren. Slowly, very solemnly, Oren bowed. The grace of the movement caught my breath—so at odds with the animal wildness in his expression, and yet, fitting it as well.

He waited until the curtain of bees dispersed, scattering to the sides with a swell of the almost musical drone of a million tiny wing beats. Moving slowly, Oren stepped forward and dipped his hand into the hollow of the tree. I held my breath, imagining the damage those stingers could do to his unprotected skin.

When he withdrew his arm, it was covered in a swarm of bees, but they soon dispersed. He was holding something in his hand, something that glinted and glowed gold in the torchlight. He took a few steps backward, away from the tree, and then glanced over to where I stood staring in tense fascination.

He beckoned to me with a jerk of his chin, and I went to his side. "Try this," he said, swiping a finger along the thing he was cradling in the palm of his hand, and then sticking the finger in his mouth.

I recognized it now as part of the beehive, something I'd seen in books. It was dripping with viscous honey. I dipped a finger and tentatively brought it to my mouth.

Unimaginable sweetness. Far more tantalizing than the sugar beets in the city. I closed my eyes, barely aware that I was humming with pleasure at the unexpected delight.

"Go ahead, eat all you like," said Oren. And though I could not be sure in the fading light, I thought I heard a smile in his voice.

We sat there in the clearing with the torch wedged between two rocks, devouring the honeycomb whole while the bees danced and swarmed all around us. The sugar and the light and the delicious fullness of my stomach was all the more satisfying for how hungry, and how tired, and how frightened I'd been. I couldn't help but think of the last time I was so full, that first night in the Institute, before I'd known to be scared. Before I'd ever had to run.

I closed my eyes, letting myself, for once, just rest.

"Don't fall asleep," Oren warned. "I draw the line at carrying you."

"Hmm," was my only reply, lips and fingers and face sticky with honey. A day ago the thought of the wild boy carrying me off through the forest would have frightened me beyond imagining. Now, part of me wanted to see what would happen if I tested that threat.

Nevertheless, the torch threatening to burn out and the chill of night settling in the forest drove us to return to the fire. Though I stumbled and tripped along the way, Oren never put a foot wrong. After we found our way back, we lay drowsing and licking the honey from our fingers.

"Tell me about your family," I found myself saying. "Where did you come from?"

"They're dead. Killed." His words hit like a blow to my stomach.

I knew I should stay quiet, respect the flatness of his voice as a request to leave it alone, but I couldn't. "How old were you?"

"I don't know exactly. I think about ten."

"That's impossible," I breathed. "You survived out here when you were ten years old?"

"I said I didn't know exactly," he said shortly.

"But—"

"I don't *know*."

The raw edge in his voice reminded me of that ragged wildness in his gaze when I first saw him, the shock and hunger when he looked at me. And I had thought I was desperate to see another human face after a week on my own.

After a time, Oren put his hands to his mouth and whistled, a warbling call that burbled and danced.

"What is that?" I asked when he'd finished, my eyes closed. I could still see the firelight dancing behind my closed lids, warm streaks that dazzled me as I dipped in and out of sleep.

"A lark," he replied.

I opened my eyes. "Where did you learn all these birdcalls?"

He said nothing for a long time, prompting me to lift my head and look at him. I could see only his profile from where I lay. The angle of his nose cast a sharp shadow from the firelight and his lips were pressed together tightly. He blinked, and then again, and I realized he was struggling to answer.

"I'm not sure." The words were so quiet I had to strain to hear them.

"You don't remember?"

He hesitated again. I only barely restrained the urge to reach out to him. "I don't know. I—get confused sometimes."

"Confused?" I repeated.

"It's nothing. When you spend all your time out here, alone, sometimes—sometimes you get muddled. You remember things wrong."

That, at least, I could believe. Just the time I'd been alone in the wilderness, my mind spun on and on whenever I let it.

"I remember it better when you're around," he added, very quietly. The rawness in his voice, the longing, made my stomach clench. I tried to imagine living out here, on my own, trying desperately to hold onto myself, and couldn't.

He started to speak again and then cut himself off. When I looked at him again, a ripple of something electric crossed his features, amplified by the sharp firelight. His eyes flicked toward mine and he froze. His expression was all uncertainty and wanting. Then he shut his eyes, and the moment was gone.

It took me a long moment to find my voice again. "Is that why you left me the shoes, and the food, and everything?"

He shrugged, the movement throwing shadows around the clearing. When he spoke the rawness had vanished, his voice suddenly indifferent. "You were something new, something I'd never seen before. The shoes—it's all shadow, in my mind. I don't remember."

"But—"

"I said I don't remember." The coldness in his voice stopped my breath a moment. "Go to sleep."

I turned onto my side, knowing that if I stayed on my back I'd spend the night watching him, trying to decipher what I'd seen in his face for those few brief seconds. He had not meant for me to see, that much was clear. For the first time in what felt like days I thought of Kris. I tried to imagine a look of such intensity and passion transposed on his smooth, straight, handsome face, but no matter how I pushed, I couldn't make the expression fit.

· · ·

I woke in the morning to the drowsy buzzing of the bees. They had reverted to their daytime activities, a lazy bobbing throughout the meadow as they gathered nectar.

The fire had died down in the night, and I shivered as I sat up. There was only a bit of flattened earth where Oren had been sleeping the night before—and my pack, such as it was, was gone.

Before I had time to so much as wonder, much less panic, Nix swooped down from overhead to land on the hilt of Oren's knife, blade sticking down in the earth. He wouldn't have gone far without his only weapon.

The pixie still wore its bee form, fat-bodied and sleepy. *"He's fetching you supplies."*

"I don't think he's from the city," I said, stretching and curling closer to the embers of the fire.

"I did tell you."

"You also told me not to trust you."

"I agreed I was not to be trusted." Nix fluttered its wings to settle them. *"There's a difference."*

I had no time to argue. With his customary silence and ease of movement, Oren appeared again on the far side of the clearing. He had found water somewhere and washed himself. Even with his face clean, he was no less inscrutable. Though his hair was still damp, it proved to be a sandy brown when clean. He glanced from me to the pixie, which had fallen silent again, and then crossed toward us to dump the now heavy pack at my side.

"I'll get you as far as the edge of the meadow," he said, turning his back on me to kick dirt over the last glowing coals of the night's fire. "Then you're on your own."

I listened for any hint of the emotion in his voice I had heard last night. There was none. He tossed me the canteen, which he had refilled, and told me to put it in my pack. He could get another.

"You sleep too late," he told me shortly. "The sun's well up, you should get moving. It'll take about three days—no, for you it'll be four or five—to reach the Iron Wood."

A flicker of yesterday's anger stirred. How could he expect me to move as quickly as he did, with less than a week's experience living under the sky? I felt how heavy my pack was with food, though, and bit my tongue.

He led the way back through the wood. I longed to stop and bid farewell to the meadow, the sea of flowers shining violet-white in the filtered light, but Oren was pushing harder than he had the day before and I had no strength to catch up again if I stopped.

When we stepped back outside the barrier, it was raining again. The sky was monochrome above the slow, steady deluge. The last of the fire's warmth left my bones, and I shivered miserably as I trudged in Oren's wake. Where was the boy I'd seen last night, all longing and intensity? All I saw now was a dim shape through the downpour, staying far enough ahead of me that I could read nothing from his body language.

Oren led me along a creek through to the edge of the

wood, until I could see the hills stretching away toward the blue mountains. A broken, gray-green line cut through them, unnaturally straight. "Follow the train tracks southwest through the hills until they cross the river," he said, lifting an arm in that direction. His hand was steady, his voice flat. "It cuts a pass through the mountains; it'll be chilly but doable if you follow the riverbank. When you reach the falls, cut due west.

"Dig your fire pits low, and try to keep them in the woods where they won't be seen at a distance. Keep small, keep quiet. You're in their territory now. If you see them in the distance, don't stop, just run as quietly and as quickly as you can. Try to cross some water to break up your trail. If you see them up close—" He gave a strange shrug, and let his arm fall again. "Don't get up close."

I shivered. "Okay," I whispered. I wanted to shout, *Don't leave me alone.*

"You've got enough food for maybe five days if you're careful. And you should be careful. Will you be okay in the rain?"

The sky was an even gray, a two-dimensional expanse not unlike the Wall at home. The rain dripped steadily, a reminder of the empty sea above. I took a deep breath and nodded. His face was so blank that I wanted to scream at him to look at me, to see how unprepared for this I was, and to stay at my side. If I knew how to summon that ferocity of mixed desires he'd displayed the night before, I would have in a heartbeat.

"All right." Oren glanced at me once and brushed past me, heading back toward the forest. This time he moved so silently that I realized the minute noises of movement he made in the camp were for my benefit alone. I watched him go, not realizing until the shadows of the forest began to swallow him that he was leaving for good.

"Wait!" He stopped. He didn't speak, just stood there tense and waiting for me to go on.

"You're really just going to leave me?"

"Yes." His voice was as dispassionate as his face usually was.

But I need you. I only got as far as the first word before it stuck in my throat, strangled. "But—"

He made an abrupt slashing motion with his hand, cutting me off without a word. "I can't afford to need you," he said harshly. "I can't afford to need anyone." He started moving again through the shadows.

For a moment I was too shocked to do anything but watch him go. Need *me*? *I remember better when you're around,* came his voice, last night's memory searing hot through the cold. He wasn't leaving because I needed him. It was the opposite.

"Aren't you going to tell me not to go?" I whispered.

He stopped, shoulders slightly stooped as his head bowed. "Would you listen?"

I stood, shivering lightly in the morning rain. I wanted to say yes—I could learn to live out here like him. I could forget about my magic, learn to avoid the monsters, learn which pockets were full of food and which were deadly. Surely one friendly—or at least not dangerous—face now was better than a place so frightening even Oren was afraid.

The pixie's mechanism surged briefly as it stirred its wings from its perch on my shoulder.

The Institute would still be coming for me. For all the resources it took to find me, the promise of a Renewable chained to them for life was worth it. They would never stop hunting me until I was safe with my own kind.

Perhaps Oren, so skilled at tracking and hunting, read my answer in my face when he turned around to look at me. Or perhaps my silence was eloquent enough for him. He watched me for a long moment, the unlikely pale blue of his eyes stark in the shadows. Around me the rain roared, sweeping me up into its current, drowning me. I closed my eyes, gasping for breath and inhaling air and water both, and when I looked again Oren was gone.

. . .

Though the morning was cold and damp, I set a brisk enough pace that I soon warmed a little. It was faster than I would have moved before, but Oren's warnings kept me going. The sunburn on my face was healing, and the mist of rain soothed the itching skin.

I reached the train tracks he'd mentioned not long after I left the forest. Overgrown and broken, I wouldn't have recognized them for what they were: highways for the huge magic engines that at one point had carried people and goods from one side of the continent to the other. Grass and trees, and time, had ripped the tracks apart, but left enough of a recognizable trail for me to follow.

Nix and I talked, growing its vocabulary. Its voice wasn't Oren's and wasn't mine—wasn't Gloriette's voice and wasn't Kris's. It had acquired a voice that was all of them, and none of them, and something all its own.

Oren rarely spoke when we were walking, and in the silence now I imagined him just ahead, his shape visible now and then through the rain. I could almost see him, impatient, pushing faster. I quickened my pace, and tried to drive him from my mind.

The tracks cut a neat path through the hills, saving me some climbing. Though they had appeared to be little more than gentle swells at a distance, up close my legs ached at the mere thought of having to climb them.

My stomach informed me it was lunchtime when I reached the river, and I stopped at the broken and crumbling bridge that had once carried the trains over the water. I sat on an outcropping of rotting stone and mortar, letting my aching feet dangle weightlessly over space.

I opened the pack, hoping to find the nuts he'd toasted last night, though my memory told me I had eaten them all. There was a little empty space at the top of the pack, where the supplies had settled—tucked into it was a cone of grubby paper.

I pulled it out, the paper crinkling under my fingers. The rain spattered it, first one drop and then two and then a dozen, loud and shocking in the quiet. It was real paper, unrecycled paper. Old paper. Where had Oren found it? Had he any idea the rations you could get for such a treasure, back in the city?

I turned it over in my hands and caught a flash of white. Nestled inside the cone, protected by it, was a handful of the tiny white flowers from the meadow.

There was such beauty here, in the world beyond the Wall.

A wave of loneliness swept over me. Three hours, and I wanted him back. The sound of another human voice, the sight of another human face. No, not just another human face. Oren's face. I put the flowers back in my pack, tucking them carefully where they wouldn't be crushed against my body when I moved out again.

I made a meager lunch of roasted tubers and strawberries. As I ate, I felt a familiar trickle down the back of my spine that I couldn't blame on the rain.

Someone was watching me.

I immediately thought of Oren—perhaps he was still following, making sure I didn't lose it the moment he left me alone? And yet as soon as the thought came to me, I abandoned it. Why would Oren cause such a cold shudder to run down my spine?

"Nix," I said softly. "Can you see anything? Hear anything?"

The pixie buzzed off of my shoulder, and flitted up some yards above my head, darting here and there as it surveyed the landscape.

"Nothing," it reported as it swooped back down. *"Why?"*

I shook my head. "I'm imagining things now that I'm alone, that's all."

"Not alone," Nix argued, landing back on my shoulder. *"And you've been out here for some time now. Perhaps you should trust your instincts."*

I shivered again, repacking my bag, careful now that I knew the flowers were there. The stone was cold beneath me—I wasted no time moving on.

The feeling of being watched persisted. I waded through every stream that met the larger river, though the water soaked through my shoes and drove cold needles into my feet. If it would confuse my scent, it was worth numb toes.

I couldn't convince myself that the feeling of being watched was my imagination. After all, I'd felt something similar—if less frightening—when Oren was following me.

"Have you ever heard of magic giving people other powers?" I asked the pixie, which was flitting on ahead and back, scouting the trail up ahead.

"Other powers?"

"Other than what we know about, being able to move objects and things."

"I suppose anything is possible," it replied. *"Why do you ask?"*

"No reason," I said, glancing over my shoulder, half-expecting to see shadows out of the corner of my eye. "Just making conversation."

Perhaps it was possible that some extrasensory perception came hand in hand with the magic. Though no one in the city had ever mentioned such a thing, would they know? Everyone in the city had their magic taken away from them as children.

Maybe I really was sensing something. It felt like a darkness, a strange, hungry pit somewhere at the edge of my senses. It was like the flashes of iridescence I sometimes saw out of the corner of my eye inside the barriers—but instead of light, this was dark. Empty. Void.

Or maybe my fears and imagination were conspiring against me. I picked up my pace.

By mid-afternoon the rain stopped, and by sunset the clouds were thinning. The sun glowed fiery against the overcast clouds as it sank, a sliver of it showing above the horizon to the southwest. I had begun to climb from the foot of the mountains. With visions of falling off a cliff in the dark, I found a copse of trees by the riverbank and made camp.

Weariness soon took over, and I barely had energy to clear away the leaf litter, much less dig a pit. Still, fear outweighed exhaustion and I found a stone to use as a shovel. The pixie joined in, shifting forms and tunneling like some ground-dwelling insect, stirring up the dirt.

I scooped away the loose earth and lay down some kindling, starting the fire more easily than ever. *Thank you, Oren*, I thought, shoving the lighter back into my pocket. I was still shivering by the time I could sit back and let the fire grow on its own. My clothes were damp from the day's rain, and a cold wind swept down from the mountains at my back.

Though I felt too tired to eat, I forced down a handful of nuts and immediately fell into a doze, lulled by the crackle of the fire and the distant howling of the wind in the mountains.

When I awoke, the fire was nearly dead. The sky was pitch-black, and through the treetops I caught glimpses of stars, the cloud cover having completely vanished. I sat bolt upright, breathing hard, straining to hear again the sound that had woken me.

I could hear only the low hiss of the dying fire, the river, the howling wind.

I stared at the fire, listening hard, trying to figure out what was bothering me so—then, with a jolt, I realized. The flames on the fire weren't flickering. There was no wind.

I froze, listening to the howls. They weren't so distant now as the wind had been earlier. They carried no triumph, as they had when they'd devoured one of their own, only hunger and desolation and, increasingly, excitement. They were hunting.

Dimly I saw the cobalt blue of Nix's eyes appear in the firelight. *"Lark,"* it said, the word barely more than a hum.

"I hear them," I replied. My breath sounded louder than any shout. I rolled over and kicked dirt onto the fire as I'd seen Oren do. The flames went out with a sluggish hiss of protest.

As my eyes blossomed with blue-white afterimages, the howls changed. Whoops and shouts, and with it—in the distance—the rattling of pebbles high above. They'd been watching my fire. They knew I was awake.

I scrambled to my feet. *Run quickly, run quietly. Cross water. Don't let them get close.* I left the pack of supplies. It would only slow me down. Later—if there was a later—I could come back for it.

I heard Nix following me, a dim buzz in the background of the roaring in my ears. Something laughed in the distance, high and hysterical. I tripped and fell, and my hands splashed down into frigid water when I hit. I scrambled across the stream, every splash and gasp and step ringing like an alarm. So much for running quietly. I sucked in a breath of air and hurried low through the strip of woods, praying it was large enough to keep me hidden. I tried to remember what it had looked like in the daylight, and the only image that came to mind was agonizingly small.

I burst out of the copse and into a world transformed by moonlight. Every blade of grass was edged in silver, and my shadow stood ahead of me so solidly that I nearly shrieked at the sight of it. I stopped for a heartbeat, trying to figure out which direction to go. Ahead rose the mountains—but I had heard the sound of feet on rocky slopes, hadn't I? That must be where they were coming from.

I turned to head out over the grassy hills. I had taken no more than a step before I saw them. Moving quickly, impossibly quickly, three shadows raced low to the ground, the grasses whipping around them. They were still some distance away, but closing fast. I turned so quickly my feet slipped in the still-muddy earth. I caught myself on my hands and then scrambled into a run.

My eyes sought a hiding place. A cave, a ledge, some corridor in the hills in which I could lose myself. My muscles screamed in protest, but I ignored them, sprinting as hard as I could.

Something black loomed up in front of me, and my head whipped up. Not a shadow—a shack, falling to pieces. Not great, but better than being run down on an open hillside.

I could no longer hear Nix. I had no time to look around for it, no energy to turn my head to see how close the shadow people were. I aimed for the black doorway of the shack, closing in on it.

I was only a few strides away when shadows melted out of the landscape, emerging from behind rocks, trees, out of the darkness itself. They were so close I could see their faces lit by the moonlight, their white eyes staring, mouths open and pointed teeth bared in hideous, ravenous grins.

CHAPTER 22

They had once been human. What other creature, after all, could have set such a trap? Herding me like a frightened rabbit into such a dead end? They had arms and legs and feet like any person, and most wore clothes, torn and unidentifiably filthy. Their hair hung in clumps turned black with dirt.

I screamed and hurled myself at the shack. A hand closed over my ankle and yanked, throwing me down. My chin hit packed earth, and I tasted blood as I bit my tongue. As if they could sense that first blood, the air around me exploded into whoops and screams. I kicked back hard and felt my foot connect with something that crunched audibly. The hand let go, accompanied by a howl of protest and rage.

I scrambled for the doorway again only to feel multiple hands grab my legs and drag me out. Sharp nails dug into my skin, piercing through my pants, as my own fingers scrabbled at the dirt, trying to find anything to pull myself away.

They flung me over, giving me a glimpse of the faces crowding over me. Skin blanched of all color, ash-gray in the moonlight but for the darker gray veins spreading across cheeks and throats. Pointed teeth and bright, wet lips snapped at me, long-nailed fingers tore at my clothes and skin.

One of the creatures lunged for me, teeth closing over the fleshy part of my upper arm, sinking in. I waited for the agony of tearing flesh and muscle, but it never came. Instead there was a meaty, wet sound and the beast released me, flung away into the chaos.

The howling sounds took on another tone, and they abandoned me for something else. I tried to drag myself toward the ruined shack, but the bitten arm throbbed, and I couldn't gather the strength to move myself.

The beasts were now a roiling cluster of shadows and torn clothing, their attention turned inward on something I couldn't see for the mass of bodies. One flew at me and I rolled out of the way. It missed me by inches, spraying a fountain of something wet and hot over my face before hitting the ground and lying still.

The struggling form in the center of the cluster swept two of the monsters away with a low kick, and then dove for me. I saw only a pair of white eyes in the darkness, staring into me. I shrieked and tried to kick it away. My foot connected with a solid thud, and my assailant grunted with pain but didn't let go.

"Lark!" it shouted, brushing my flailing foot aside. "Lark, it's me!"

The eyes weren't white—they were palest blue. His hand wrapped around mine and he jerked me to my feet, shoving me back into the shack. It was barely more than a tool shed, and so full of rubble that there wasn't enough room for the two of us. Oren whirled, putting his back to me, to face the pack regrouping around us.

The moonlight glinted off a knife in his hand, its edge dripping blood. I tore my eyes away. There were three, maybe four of the monsters arrayed in a semicircle around us. I had no way of knowing how many others there might be still concealed by the darkness, or how many Oren had already killed.

One of the shadow people dove for him with a scream of rage, knocking him back against me. I could smell the sweat and the blood, hear the creature's snarls as it snapped at his throat. Oren's knife flashed, and the creature shrieked again, falling away.

Oren and the monsters were blurs of shadow and light, ducking and weaving. I could see the knife most clearly, its edge scattering the moonlight and blinding my straining eyes.

I saw more bodies hit the ground, but I could not see whose they were. Two left. Still fighting.

The last monster leapt at Oren, dodging the low sweep of his knife and wrapping its arms around his throat.

I started to struggle out of the shack to help him.

Oren needed no assistance. With a grunt he threw the monster down. As it struggled to its knees, Oren darted behind it and yanked its chin up with his free hand. He shifted his grip on the knife, flipping the blade the other way around.

For an instant everything was outlined by the moonlight, the entire scene edged in silver. The pulsing throat of the monster, lined with dark gray veins. Its hands desperately trying to claw free of Oren's grasp. Its feral eyes knowing what was coming. Oren's face, transformed by ferocity, the blue eyes wild and animal.

With a smooth, graceful sweep, Oren drew the blade across the creature's throat, sending a cascade of dark blood down its filthy chest. He let the body fall, where it lay gurgling for a few seconds before going still.

Oren came at me, holding out one bloody hand palm up in reassurance, saying something gently in a low voice. I threw myself back against the rubble filling the shack.

"Don't touch me!" I cried, the words tearing from my throat.

He stood there, his bloodstained body tense and edged in silver light, panting and gazing at me. Then he turned away, crouching by each of the fallen bodies. I could hear the sounds the knife made as he dispatched the ones who still lived.

He cleaned his hands in the dirt, bathing them in dust and then wiping them on his pants, doing the same with the blade of the knife before tucking it carefully into his boot. He made a point of checking each of the bodies, but whether he found anything in their tattered pockets, I couldn't say. I kept my eyes turned resolutely upward at the square of night I could see through the door of the shack.

For once, the starry sky held no horror for me.

Oren moved past me, limping. The air was ripe with the tang of sweat and blood and fierceness. "We can't stay here," he said hoarsely. "Let's go."

• • •

He led me on up the mountain, moving slowly. He didn't try to touch me again, though I struggled on the slope, my shaking legs failing to hold me upright and the bitten arm throbbing with every step.

Though the walk felt interminable, I don't think we traveled more than an hour before Oren called a halt. He made no fire, but merely sat me down in the hollow of a rock that offered some shelter from the wind. "Get some sleep," he advised. "I'll keep watch."

I hadn't spoken since my outburst, and my throat—hoarse from fear and running—closed more tightly with every passing moment. I huddled up, drawing in all my limbs tightly to my body. I knew I wouldn't sleep. I felt as though I would never sleep again.

We were out of the direct moonlight now, but I could still see his shape from where I lay. He faced away from me, keeping an eye on the slope that led up to my hiding place. I imagined his impassive face, the piercing eyes.

Hadn't I wanted the ferocity?

In that moment of victory, transformed by violence, the color leeched from him by the dark and the moon, he could have been a brother to the monsters that attacked me. That image hung before my eyes as I watched him, sitting still and silent now.

A monster who brought me flowers.

I didn't remember closing my eyes, only watching him endlessly through the night. Nevertheless, I woke in the morning to find I'd rolled over in the night, hiding my eyes in the crook of my elbow.

Oren was nowhere to be seen. I knew now that that never meant he was gone. Nevertheless, I eased my shirt down over one shoulder so that I could inspect the place where I'd been bitten.

There was very little blood. A perfect half-moon of teeth was imprinted into the skin. Each individual tooth mark was visible, a purple-red indentation against the backdrop of bruises.

If Oren hadn't come—I remembered waiting for the teeth to tear my flesh away, tear me apart as I'd seen them do before. I began to shake, struggling to push the memory away as I pulled my shirt back into place. If Oren hadn't come.

A familiar hum cut into the panic threatening to overwhelm me. Familiar, but faltering and inconstant. I looked around for a flash of copper, some movement, any sign of the pixie to confirm what I was hearing.

Something glinted halfway down the slope. I squinted in the morning sun, shading my eyes. A tiny copper form picked its way up the hill, flitting from stone to stone, never spending much time in the air.

It got to within a few yards of me and then dropped, wings fanning sporadically and mechanisms clicking with effort.

"Nix?" I whispered, pushing up to my knees and crawling toward it.

"*I tried to find assistance,*" it whispered with what seemed to be a phenomenal effort, clockwork grinding. "*I was unable—to—*"

"I'm okay," I replied, interrupting. "Assistance found me." I reached up to touch the little copper bug with my fingertips, but my arm throbbed so suddenly and violently that I let my hand fall.

"What's wrong with you?" The pixie was in clear distress, half-flopped over in the dust.

"*Power,*" it sputtered. "*Recharging.*"

"How are you recharging?" I tried to calm my fluttering heart—was I afraid the machine would die? I swallowed the feeling. "We're nowhere near an energy pocket."

"*Renewable—source.*"

It was as though a bucket of water had been tossed over me. How could I have been so stupid? I had even wondered how the pixie was staying charged despite days spent outside magical barriers. How much worse had this thing made my weakness, my starvation, by siphoning away my power? No wonder it had ridden on my shoulder, tucked itself so close to me.

"*Sorry.*"

I could leave. Walk away this moment, and without my energy the pixie would die. It clearly didn't have the strength to follow me.

And yet—it had led me to Oren, as I had asked, even though I hadn't known what I was asking. It had located kindling, sought out the easiest paths for someone on foot, given me as much information as it could. It had saved my life by fetching Oren before I drowned in the swamp.

I settled onto my knees and stretched out a hand, brushing its body with my fingertips. A tiny, jolting tingle ran down the surface of my skin, not unlike the strange current I felt whenever Oren touched me. The pixie shuddered, wings fluttering and clockwork ceasing to emit that horrible grinding sound.

"Lark?"

"If you ever lie to me again I will crush you," I scooped the pixie into my cupped hands. "Do you understand?"

"I didn't lie, I only—"

"Nix!"

"I understand."

After only a few minutes in my presence, the pixie righted itself and fluttered up to my shoulder, where it sat cheerfully whirring and clicking away, beginning to groom itself as assiduously as ever.

I was about to ask it where it had been looking for help, when Oren reappeared.

He didn't bother making any of the tiny sounds he'd used to announce his presence in the clearing, merely melted silently out of the shadows behind the curve of the rock. He dropped the thing he was carrying a few feet away from me, and then knelt to start going through it, his profile to me.

My pack.

He loosened the drawstrings and then paused for the briefest of moments before rummaging through the supplies inside.

"What are you doing?" I asked, my voice still rough with sleep, and tried to clear my throat.

"Taking inventory. Looks like it's all here." He tossed out

a couple leaf-wrapped packets, oozing red and purple, the telltale signs that the berries had been crushed. "What's this?" He held up Basil's bird.

I lurched forward to snatch it from his grasp, heart thudding. "Don't touch that." He let it go without protest, eyes narrowed and fixed on my face.

"What is it?" He watched as I cradled it against my chest, over my heart.

"A gift," I murmured. If only Basil were here now. Maybe this world would make sense if he were here to explain it. "From home."

Silence stretched for a few long moments. I looked up to see Oren gazing at me. His eyes flashed with fleeting pain or anger. When I blinked, his stare was once again flat and cold. "I see," he said shortly. He rummaged in the pack until he found the flowers he'd given me. He tossed them on the ground with the ruined berries and then closed the pack, cinching it shut with a jerk.

Before I could protest he got to his feet, boots crushing berries and flowers alike, and dropped the pack at my feet. "Let's go." He turned to move out.

I got to my feet, my eyes on the crushed flowers. *My brother*, I thought to myself. *It was a gift from my brother.* Surely Oren couldn't be upset because he thought I'd rather be home in the city? I fell into step behind him, watching him.

It was barely noticeable, but I saw that he was moving more slowly this morning. I remembered his limp from the night before.

"Are you hurt?" I asked. My voice was still hoarse, despite attempts to clear my throat. I had screamed at him so loudly not to touch me that I'd hurt something in my voice.

He moved toward the edge of the bluff to look down the slope, monitoring it. "No."

"But—"

"We need to move quickly," he said shortly.

"We?" I felt a surge of something, relief or hope or dread.

"I can't leave you alone for one day," he replied. I wanted to smile, but there was no humor in his voice. "I thought I could—" But he cut himself off with a shake of his head. "We're wasting time," he continued. "The bodies will slow them down a little if more come after us, but not for long."

"Slow them down?" I stared at him, uncomprehending, incredulous. "Surely they don't bury their dead?"

Oren turned, glancing at me before beginning to pick his way on up the slope. "They're scavengers as much as hunters," he said shortly. "And after last night they're going to be very, very hungry."

We made good time up the mountain, as far as I could tell, despite the injuries he was too proud to mention and the throbbing of my arm. I stared at his back as we moved, barely paying attention to where I put my feet. I wanted to tell him that I was grateful he'd come back to save my life, that I'd only been exhausted and half-mad with fear the night before and that nothing had changed between us.

But every time I felt my mouth begin to shape the words, I saw a flash of his face, so transformed in the moonlight, the wildness there as he fought the beasts, the unflinching grace as he drew the blade across its throat. And I kept silent, knowing that if I spoke I'd be lying.

Though the mountains looked steep and unyielding from a distance, up close they were merely long, hard slopes. Even though the river we were following cut a swift and narrow path through them, there was a fair amount of hard climbing. I stumbled and fell regularly as my exhaustion caught up to me. I couldn't be sure how much of the night I had slept, but it felt as though it couldn't have been more than a couple of hours.

As we climbed, a sound began to build at the edge of my hearing. I could sense a pocket nearby, a light tingle at the back of my mind, but the sound was separate from it—something deep and distant and rushing. We were moving toward the sound as we followed the river up the mountain. Now and then, up ahead, I caught a glimpse of the barrier, a violet shimmer in the sunlight.

The climb seemed endless, and I timed my steps to the throbbing of my arm. After a while Oren stopped, and I nearly stepped on his heels before I noticed. He nodded his head, pointing with his chin back the way we'd come.

I squinted in the midday sun, not immediately seeing what he was indicating. As if reading my mind, he stepped closer and pointed over my shoulder, his arm only a few inches from my face. The hair on my neck prickled—I could not tell if it was from fear or something else entirely. He smelled of grass and fresh water and sweat, a surprisingly pleasant combination. I tried to remember what Kris smelled like and could only think of the Institute, clean and sterile, without scent.

Then I saw it—and his closeness was suddenly the last thing on my mind. About halfway down the slope, no more than a quarter of an hour behind us, a pair of shadows darted from rock to rock. They walked one behind the other, not unlike the way Oren and I traveled.

I reached out, unthinking, grasping at a fold of Oren's shirt. "How much time do we have?"

"Maybe half an hour before they catch up," he replied. "They've been behind us a while now."

"You knew? Why didn't you say anything?"

To answer, he grasped my hand, stretching it out, palm up. It was shaking, and I stared at it, clenching my jaw.

"Wouldn't have made you go any faster. Slowed you down, if anything. We're almost there; we'll be fine."

I glanced behind me, and this time the two shadow people had vanished behind some outcropping. I could feel them back there, though, a tiny prickle of fear running up and down my spine. "How can you be so calm?"

"We'll be fine once we reach the falls, and we're only a few minutes away." He started picking a path through the rocks again.

The falls?

The jolt of adrenaline from seeing the shadow people behind us made my footing unsteady, and though I would not have said it out loud, I knew Oren had been right to keep it from me that we were being followed.

Steps had been carved into the mountainside, weathered and, in places, worn smooth enough to make climbing difficult. Holes had been drilled at regular intervals up the path. This had once been a place people visited for fun, or for sport, or some reason I couldn't fathom, and I longed for the handrails that had clearly once lined the way up. My legs shook with strain and fear, although I never caught so much as a glimpse of a shadow again.

Oren, by now, was some distance ahead. He made no attempt to help me up, keeping his gaze ahead, his energy reserved for climbing. Though he moved much more easily than I could, I thought I sensed a hesitance, a deliberation that caught at my attention. He no longer moved with the thoughtless ease he had in the forest.

I crested a ridge, the steps ending at a plateau, and saw the barrier spreading out before me. The dome of it was bisected by the rock so that only the rim was visible. Spreading out across the plateau toward the dome was a lake, so clear that I could see the clouds overhead reflected in its surface. Above the barrier, an incredible cascade of water fell from a peak high above, lost in the mist. Where it met the top of the dome, the water scattered, most falling straight through but a fine mist spraying off in every direction, shimmering over the surface of the barrier. The light danced through it in flashes of color and fleeting rainbows.

The falls. For a moment, I forgot our pursuers.

Oren kept walking around the shore of the lake. I hesitated, and only when he reached the edge of the barrier did he pause and look back at me.

"What's to stop them from following us in there?" I asked.

"Oh, they'll follow us," Oren said.

"What? You said we'd be safe!"

"We will be," he said. "I can't quite explain it. It's—I just know."

"This is not the time for one of your confused—"

"Lark. Do you trust me?"

My breath quickened as I looked at him, the dried blood on his face and hands, the dirty hair, the piercing empty eyes. I saw in my mind's eye the flash of moonlight off the edge of his wet blade.

"No," I whispered.

His lips curved, and my heart slammed against my ribcage. "Good." He slipped through the barrier and its shimmering curtain of water.

CHAPTER 23

I stayed only moments. Nix thrummed by my ear, insistent as an alarm, reminding me of the shadow creatures not far behind us. Reaching up to shield the machine from the water, I ducked through it.

Warmth enveloped me. Inside, the surface of the water was an unimaginable shade of violet-blue, reflecting the inside of the dome. Surrounding the lake, the plants were in full summer foliage, leafy green ferns and patches of moss spreading everywhere. Where outside the leaves were fading to dull gold and brown, here everything was vibrant and lush.

By the lakeshore, Oren was stripping off his clothes. He pulled his shirt off, moving gingerly. I had a glimpse of bruises blossoming across his shoulders before I looked away.

"What're you doing?" I asked, staring resolutely in the other direction. "Won't they be here in a few minutes?"

"It'll take them a while to get up the nerve to come inside," Oren said confidently. "They're afraid of the barriers. It won't stop them if they know there's food inside, but it'll slow them down."

I heard a splashing behind me, and without thinking I turned to look. I saw only a rapidly expanding circle of ripples where Oren had dived into the water. After a few moments, his head bobbed back up. Treading water, he reached up to scrub at his face, washing the dried blood from it.

"Well?" he said, slicking his hair back away from his face. "It's the summer lake. Always warm here. Coming?"

The absurdity of it, a boy asking me to swim in a lake with a pair of monsters only minutes away, made me stare at him. Eventually, I managed, "I—don't know how to swim."

Oren only shrugged, the movement causing more ripples, and then ducked his head under again.

I walked to the water's edge while he swam and bathed. Leaning over its surface, at first I didn't recognize my own reflection. Tangled hair so dirty it looked black rather than brown; thin, hollow cheeks; skin stained with blood. I remembered the hot spray over my face when Oren had been fighting, and scrambled to splash water onto my skin to wash it away. I looked as animal and as warlike as Oren.

Pulling off my shoes, I rolled up the legs of my pants and stepped into the lake's edge. The throbbing of my feet, still unused to so much walking after two weeks of it, eased in the cool water.

For a moment, I forgot where we were. That is, until I heard a voice behind me.

"Mummy," it said, piping and tiny.

I splashed noisily in my haste to turn around.

A woman stood there with a child, who could be no more than five or six. I couldn't tell how old the woman was, her face was so lined with dirt and weather. Their clothes were more tattered than Oren's, their hair and fingernails broken and caked with dirt. They were, however, quite human.

"Mummy," the child said again, half-hidden behind its mother's leg. "Lookit the mmbows." The child was speaking half-nonsense, muffled by the woman's body.

The woman didn't reply, gazing around with clear confusion, eyes wide and staring. The child—it looked like a girl, but I could not be certain—tugged at her leg.

I stared at them, unable to speak for shock. Behind me, Oren resurfaced with a splash. I glanced over in time to see a glimpse of bare, muscled skin, and a ragged red wound on his thigh before I wrenched my gaze back to the newcomers. The roar of the falls, muted though it was falling through the barrier, covered the sounds of his getting dressed again.

The woman hardly spared us a glance. She stared at the water, gripping the child by the shoulders, knuckles white. The child squirmed in her grip, making noises of protest.

"Are you okay?" My voice was hoarse with shock.

The woman's gaze snapped to me, so intense and desperate that I took a step back. There was a wildness there that reminded me of Oren. Perhaps all people living out here developed that same bestial desperation. Perhaps I would, too.

"Need—" she said, licking cracked lips. "Hungry," she said. "Food for the child."

I took another step backward, and found that Oren had crept up behind me without a word. I glanced at him, and saw his knife clenched in his hand. "What're you doing?" I hissed, taking hold of his arm. Even through the worn cloth of his shirt I felt a dull echo of the same electric tingle that always leapt between us when we touched. Muffled by fabric, it was not quite as intensely unpleasant as it had been.

"Don't talk to them," he said, without taking his eyes off the pair.

"They're hungry," I protested. "And confused. We can surely spare—"

"Nothing." Moving slowly, he stepped around me, pulling his arm from my grasp easily. When he had placed himself between me and the pair of newcomers, he stopped.

"Remain still," he said in a low voice, enunciating every word as though he were speaking to a child. "We have nothing for you."

The mother rolled her eyes at him, confusion and fear plain in them. Oren waited a moment and then moved toward them cautiously. It wasn't until he shifted his grip on his knife, flipping it blade-down—I'd seen him hold it that way before, after all—that realization dawned on me.

"Oren!" I cried. "No!"

He stopped, every line of muscle telling of his irritation. He didn't take his eyes away from them to look at me. "They're monsters, Lark."

The child's face peeped from behind its mother to stare first at Oren and then at me. The mother stood wringing her hands and mumbling, too low for me to hear. But their skin, if dirty, was pink and fair, and their eyes a deep brown. They stood upright, walked without crouching. Their teeth, what I could see of them, were as flat and unthreatening as my own.

"They're *people!*" I hissed. "How can you—"

"In here they are," Oren said quietly. The pair gave no sign that they heard us, much less understood us. "You call these places magical—well, inside, they change. Turn back into shadows of what they used to be. Confused, senseless shadows. But make no mistake, the second they set foot back outside, they'll hunt you until you're dead."

His grip on his knife was white-knuckled, his jaw clenched around each word he spoke.

I shifted my gaze back to the child. I saw the filth around its mouth. I had taken it for dirt, but the more I looked, the more I realized it was a familiar, brownish-red color, caked on with little dribbles down the chin—

I shut my eyes, stomach rebelling. "Why?"

"The magical void did this to them," said Nix, stirring on my

shoulder. It was the first time I'd heard it speak in Oren's presence. *"It makes sense that a magical surplus would turn them back, however temporarily."*

"So—so those creatures you killed last night," I managed, gazing at Oren's back, "were people? All it would have taken was a bit of magic to cure them?"

Oren shook his head. "They're not cured. They're still monsters. That one," and he gestured with the point of his knife at the child, "would kill you in a heartbeat outside. And then come back without the slightest hint of a memory of what it had done. All the magic does is disarm them for a time."

"You can't kill them," I said, gritting my teeth.

"But—"

"No!"

Oren was silent for a moment, and then turned to face me, finally taking his eyes off the bedraggled pair. "If we leave them, they'll just pick up our trail again." He looked so suddenly weary that I had to restrain the impulse to go to him, knife and all. "With any luck they'll stay here for as long as a day, but they *will* leave, and when they do, they *will* come after us. And they can move twice as quickly as we can, and they don't have to stop to rest."

"It's a child and a mother, Oren," I said, unmoving.

He watched me, the pale, fierce eyes so blank I had no hope of reading what took place behind them. Instead of answering me, he turned around and spoke to the woman. "You," he said, gesturing with the point of his knife, "go over there. If you come near us, I'll kill you. And if you leave, I'll kill you. Understand?"

The woman rolled her eyes at him, the whites showing in the violet half-light of the dome. She nodded, cradling the child in against her legs as she shuffled over to the spot he'd indicated.

Oren headed back over toward his pack of supplies. I watched the mother and child go, my heart thrumming, and then turned to follow Oren. He set about unpacking food for dinner, although it was still only mid-afternoon. His movements were jerky and quick.

I wanted to speak but could think of nothing I hadn't already said.

"I've lived out here for years on my own," he said finally, his voice low and urgent. "This is how you do it. This is how you survive."

There was a rawness to his voice that cut me more than any anger would have. "I know," I said, keeping my gaze ahead of me, on the fractured surface of the water. "I'm sorry."

There was a gritty, metallic sound; in my mind's eye I saw him stab his knife into the earth, as he'd done countless times in the past. This time there was an undeniable frustration in the sound. "You can't come crashing into the wilderness, half-starved and wholly incompetent, and imply I'm some kind of monster for keeping your skin intact."

"I wasn't," I insisted. My voice shook, despite my conviction. "I wasn't," I repeated, more steadily.

"You were." The crunch of sand and dirt and pebbles told me he had gotten to his feet again. "There's food here. Stay put and try not to drown while I'm gone."

By the time I turned around, he was halfway to the edge of the barrier, and left without another word. He'd left his knife, standing blade-down in the sand not three feet from me. I wanted to run after him and give him the knife—he needed it out there, surely.

But then, the monsters weren't out there, were they? They were inside. Here. With me.

The mother and child sat a fair distance around the edge of the lake. The child sat between its mother's knees, and she had both arms wrapped loosely around it. I heard snatches of melody over the roar of the falls, carried over the water to me. She was singing to it.

"He's certainly a joy," said Nix, the words fairly dripping sarcasm. The dry tone interrupted my contemplation.

"I hurt him," I said, rubbing a hand across my eyes. "And I have no idea why. He's only ever helped me."

"By being a murderer," reminded the pixie, flitting from my shoulder to the lake, dipping low and flirting with the water's surface.

The very word was enough to make me dizzy, want to curl up away from it all. He wasn't a murderer, he was trying to survive. Trying to keep me safe. There hadn't been a murder in the city since the Wall went up over a hundred years before—to murder a fellow citizen was to break part of the machine. It only hurt ourselves.

But for Oren, out here—did he even have a choice?

"I should go after him." I didn't sound convinced even to my own ears. I wasn't sure I wanted to venture out into the world where the shadow people existed again.

"Better let him alone for a while. Rest up, have some food." Nix landed on a boulder, tipping its head up at me. *"Such an emotional boy."*

At that, I laughed. "He's the least emotional person I've ever met. *You* have more emotions than he does."

Nix rubbed a leg over one eye, its azure surface blinking briefly. It was so like a wink that I found myself staring at the creature in confusion. *"If you say so."*

I decided to take the pixie's advice and nibbled at the food Oren had left. Though I was hungry, I had managed to grow so tired of nuts and roots that it was increasingly difficult to eat them. I reminded myself that days ago I'd been on the verge of starvation and forced myself to eat.

The rocks by the falls were warm, as if heated by the sun, and I curled up there, trailing my fingers through the water, making patterns with the ripples. Lulled by the white noise of the water, my interrupted, sleepless night caught up to me. I drifted off.

When I woke it was still daylight, although far darker than it had been. Either the sun was on its way down behind the mountains, or the sky had grown overcast. I glanced toward the camp, hoping to see Oren had returned—instead, there was a figure standing there, watching me.

I jolted upright, throwing myself back against the rocks. The woman stared at me, arms hanging loosely at her sides, eyes empty. She stood between me and the knife.

"Have you seen my baby?" she whispered, her voice sighing from between her lips.

"What?"

"She was just here. My baby. She was so hungry. Have you seen my baby?"

The child was gone. My gaze fell to the knife, which Oren had left behind. Had he another hidden somewhere?

Doubt seared my mind, followed by the briefest flash of an image of something tiny and black creeping up behind Oren, who stalked angrily along the slope, unnoticing, mind preoccupied with the stubborn burden that was me.

I pushed past the woman and snatched the knife, whirling to point it at her. "You, go back to where you were sitting. *Now.*" She stared at me, as if failing to comprehend. I remembered Oren's tone and tried as much as I could to emulate it. "You stay there, and don't move, or I'll—I'll *kill* you."

The woman drifted away, still whispering to herself about her baby, heading toward the spot where she'd been sitting with her child. I sprinted for the place where Oren had left the pocket.

The sun had just dipped below the mountain ridge at my back when I burst into the world outside. I ignored the cold as I stared around, trying to find any sign of Oren's path. There weren't many options that didn't involve a sheer, steep cliff— back down the way we'd come, or up around along the mountain's side, away from the barrier. I scanned for footprints, but the only prints I could find had clearly been left by us as we entered the pocket earlier.

I closed my eyes. *Anything is possible*, Nix's voice came to mind. I'd been able to sense the shadow people the night they attacked me. I tried to calm the racing of my heart, sense any tingle that might tell me where to go.

Please, I thought, desperately.

I heard something in the distance. It wasn't much, only the slightest rattle of pebbles—but in a world with so few creatures in it, I couldn't ignore the sound. Whether it was a sound my ears detected, or something I sensed through my magic, I could not tell.

It had come from around the curve of the mountain. I set out, trying not to think of what I was going to do if I found the child before I found Oren.

The path, such as it was, was narrow and the deepening twilight was treacherous. To the left the drop was long, the mountain falling sheer away for at least a hundred feet before curving into the distance. I kept my hand against the rock wall to my right and my eyes on my feet, picking my way slowly.

I occasionally thought that I heard something, but I could never be quite sure that my ears weren't playing tricks on me.

I had been walking for perhaps a quarter of an hour when I heard something that I knew *wasn't* a product of my frightened imagination. A low cry, the sound of something soft striking stone, and then—so close my blood froze in my veins—a tiny, piercing howl of triumph.

I abandoned caution and flung myself ahead on the ledge, sending stone fragments careening off the edge. I rounded the corner ahead of me and nearly slid off the ledge when the scene unfolding in front of me registered.

Oren was facedown on the ground; a shadow crouched on his back, tearing at his clothes. He was alive—stirring feebly.

I screamed and ran. I flew at the thing, brandishing the knife. I caught it with the edge of the blade, causing a spatter of blood on the stone and a scream of rage from the child-thing. It lurched sideways, out over the edge of the cliff. Sinking its ragged fingernails into Oren's arm, it dangled, dragging his body toward the edge. I threw the knife away and lunged for him as he began to sag over the drop. Throwing myself on top of him, I summoned every ounce of energy I had before flinging it up around us. I heard the magic connect with a crunch, the force of it launching us up and back. Oren landed on top of me, knocking the breath from my lungs, and the monster fell away. I saw its face for a frozen instant, shifting from shadow to light, my magic illuminating its humanity like a light.

Magic cures them. However temporarily.

The child's scream echoed up at me as it fell, down, down—into silence.

I lay gasping for breath under Oren's weight. I wanted to feel for his pulse, but my arms wouldn't move, frozen with dread. I heard my magic humming around us, could see it overhead glimmering faintly, a barrier of protection.

When he finally groaned, I muttered a muffled something, and he rolled off me and onto his back. We lay on the ledge, panting.

"I thought I told you to stay put," he mumbled, lifting himself on one elbow so he could look down at me.

A semi-hysterical laugh forced its way out of me. He raised a hand, fingertips just brushing my cheek, and then without warning, the backlash from the power I'd used hit me, and everything went black.

. . .

When I came to, I was by the waterfall again. There was still some light, telling me that I could not have been out for very long.

Supplies were strewn about the clearing, some of the packets torn to shreds, and there was no sign of the mother—or of Nix. Oren was crouched with his back to me, one hand steadying himself on the ground while the other sorted through my pack.

"What did she leave us?" My voice emerged as a dry croak.

Oren glanced over his shoulder at me. "Most of it is still here," he said. "I don't think she recognizes the nuts and berries as food."

"Is your head okay?" I asked. The blow to Oren's head didn't look too serious.

"I'm fine," he countered, moving closer to me and dropping into a crouch. There was a small gash at his hairline, but it had already stopped bleeding. He gazed at me, his eyes as clear and as unreadable as ever in the twilight.

"You don't look like you have a concussion," I said, clearing my throat and looking away as I struggled to sit up.

"My parents could do that." Oren was still watching me, making no effort to help me up.

"What?"

"What you did back there. Knocking the dark one away without touching it. My parents could do it."

"Your parents were Renewables." I stared at him, trying to ignore the thumping of my heart. There *were* others like me. "Did they—were they from the Iron Wood?"

Oren's face tightened, and he shook his head. "No. That's a bad place. They were—" He paused, the tight expression softening into one of uncertainty, gaze clouded with confusion. "I don't know. I was very young. But they could do that."

"But you can't?"

He shook his head. "I remember they kept trying to teach me. I can't do it."

"But maybe if you just tried again—"

He cut me off with another shake of his head, quiet. "I'm not like you, Lark."

Before the resulting silence could grow too thick, Nix whirred in from beyond the barrier. *"I chased her off the food,"* it announced. *"I tried to keep her from leaving the barrier."* There was a note of apology in its voice.

"You did right," Oren said, without bothering to lift his head. As far as I was aware, it was the first thing he'd ever said to the pixie.

Somewhere in the roar of the falls, I could hear the echoes of the child-thing's cry as it fell. Despite the summer warmth, my body felt colder than it had before Oren taught me to make a fire. I put my forehead down on my knees, cradling my limbs in close with a shiver.

"So did you," Oren added, quietly. I turned my head enough to be able to see him out of one eye. He was still watching me.

"She was just a kid," I whispered, my eyes prickling and my throat dry. "And I killed her."

"You didn't have much choice," Oren said. "It's survival."

"Maybe survival isn't worth it, at such cost." I shut my eyes, turning my face into my knees again. The world spun, dancing to my exhaustion, and no matter how hard I willed it to be still, my dizziness got worse and worse.

A hand touched my hair. For once, the jolt of energy at Oren's touch didn't jar my senses; it ran down my spine until it sat in my belly, tingling and leaping.

"Is it always like this?" he asked. He was close enough that his voice made the very air vibrate. "Using magic?"

I would have shaken my head, but I was afraid moving would cause him to stop touching me. "It's getting worse," I said. And though I hadn't dared to think it myself, I knew it to be true as soon as I said it. "Harder to recover from every time."

The hand moved, a gentle stroking motion. "You had no choice," he said again. "And I'm grateful for what you did."

"You wouldn't have been out there if I hadn't provoked you," I pointed out. His hand dropped away, making me bite my lip. Why had I said that? The pang I felt in the absence of his touch nearly robbed me of breath.

"It doesn't change the fact that you came after me."

Something had changed in his voice, prompting me to lift my head. He was still looking at me; how had I ever found those eyes to be so frightening? There was a youth to his gaze, something that reminded me he could be no more than a couple of years older than I was. Just now, there was something in them that I could not identify—something like fear.

"I'll take you to the Iron Wood," he said.

CHAPTER 24

From the summer lake, we only had to climb a short distance before our path took us downward again, on the other side of the ridge of mountains. Even so, Oren's head injury and my weakness slowed our progress. He called frequent halts, all but force-feeding me from what rations the woman had left behind. I had made the mistake of telling him that my magical recovery was linked to food. I knew we were low on supplies and should be conserving them, but whenever I pointed this out, Oren's face became unreadable, and I gave in.

We sat on an overhang to eat our mid-afternoon meal, legs dangling over empty space. In front of us spread a vast plain, crisscrossed by rivers, dotted with forests with leaves tinged in orange, red, and gold. Every so often a mound of rubble stood as a monument to the farmhouses and barns and silos that had once governed the fields, which were by now lost to wild grasses and trees.

"There it is," said Oren, after we'd finished.

I was licking the juices of the berries from my fingers, and paused when he spoke. "Where what is?"

"The Iron Wood."

I stared, but saw nothing that stood out as anything

strange. As if sensing my confusion, Oren tilted his chin in the direction of the valley. "See there, on the horizon?"

He leaned toward me, supporting his weight on one arm behind me and stretching the other over my shoulder, pointing. The warmth of him, shielding the chilly breeze, made my skin tingle. As always when he was near I could not be sure if it was fear that caused my breath to catch, or something else.

I forced myself to concentrate on what he was saying.

"See the river there that curves in on itself? Follow that bend up toward the horizon."

"I see a forest," I said, hyperaware of how close his face was to mine.

"See the gray, just at its center? At the very edge of the horizon."

It looked as though some blight had descended upon the wood, turning the trees ash-gray and dead. "That's it?" I whispered.

Oren let his hand fall. "That's it," he confirmed, still leaning on the arm behind me.

"Why are you so frightened of it?" I asked, scarcely daring to breathe for fear he'd leave, that he'd avoid the question once again.

He stayed close, eyes on the distant landmark. "All my life that place has meant death. You don't overcome that easily. Why are you so set on going there?"

"A woman once told me there were others like me there. Like your parents. All I wanted was to fit in—and in my city, that ended up meaning a lifetime of slavery and suffering. So I left. The Iron Wood—it's my chance at a normal life."

Oren was silent. He turned his head a little, watching me out of the corner of his eye. "I'm not so sure there is such a thing as normal. At least not as you'd like it to be," he said. "To me, this is normal. Until you came along, at any rate."

"Sorry about that."

"I didn't say it was a bad thing."

I glanced at him, found him watching me, and hurried to drop my gaze. More and more, I found I couldn't look at him for very long, the fierceness of his eyes overlaid with a new softness I couldn't quite withstand.

He straightened, leaning away from me again; the cold air rushed in in his absence, and I shivered. "Let's go," he said. "We should reach it in a few days if we keep moving." He got to his feet, dusting off his pants.

We reached the bottom of the mountain and set off across the plain, following the river he'd pointed out to me. Unlike the quick-rushing torrent on the other side of the mountain, this river was slow and lazy, a wide brown swath across the fields. As we drew closer to the Iron Wood, it vanished from sight. Without the advantage of height, the dense gray patch of dead trees was hidden by the healthy forest spreading between us. Though it was hidden, its presence was never very far from our thoughts.

Oren grew increasingly agitated, checking and double-checking our trail, covering our tracks with a single-mindedness that verged on obsessive. At night he built fires so tiny they scarcely warmed, and as far as I could tell, he slept only in snatches when his head drooped while standing guard. Often I would wake in the night, visions of gray faces and white eyes hovering in my mind, and look for him, only to see him standing some feet away, watching me. He never said anything, just looked at me long enough to see that I'd woken from my nightmare, and returned to scanning the surroundings.

I thought he would relax a little when we reached the edge of the forest, and we finally had cover after the long exposure of the plains. Instead he grew worse, rarely sleeping and investigating every tiny sound.

I found myself more on edge as well, but for different reasons. I had expected to start hearing the buzz of magic ahead. Surely a city, or whatever it was, full of Renewables would be clearly audible, even from a distance. Instead a strange, muffled quiet descended over me, as if some background white noise I'd never noticed before had vanished without warning. My mind rang with the silence. Nix huddled closer and closer to my neck. Now I knew what to look for, I could feel it leeching the energy away from me, slowly and steadily. Despite the silence, the heavy pit that had been growing in my stomach grew lighter with every step. Finally, I would find others like me. Finally, I could go home. With a pang, I realized I missed more the feeling of belonging than I missed my actual family—I had never realized that even as the odd one out, I was still a part of a greater whole.

On the evening of the third day since leaving the mountains, we reached the edge of the Wood.

Oren, traveling some distance ahead of me, stopped—my first warning that something had changed. He never stopped but for meals, and those came regularly as clockwork. It was some hours past mid-afternoon rations, but not time yet to make camp. He stood at the edge of it, toes not six inches from the start of the dead trees. They stood like ashen copies of life, every detail of bark and leaf etched in gray. High above, gray blossoms still clung to the branches. Nix perched on a high branch, every bit as fascinated as I was.

I stepped up beside Oren, my fears dropping away for the briefest of moments as I stared, transfixed. "It's actually *iron*," I whispered, the meager light from the forest canopy gleaming off the dull metal.

Oren didn't answer. I looked over at him, to see his jaw clenched so tightly that the muscles stood out like cables. His whole body was tense, the blue eyes no longer fierce but fearful.

"Come on," I said, softly. "You've gotten this far."

"I can't," he said, not moving so much as a hair's breadth from where he stood except to close his eyes against the metal forest in front of him. "Lark, I can't."

I took his hand, for once scarcely noticing the current that ran between us. "Just one step," I said, my voice low. I remembered his voice, the comfort of it, as he coaxed me out of the rain, and tightened my hand around his. "I'm right here."

He shook his head, resisting the pull on his hand. "I can't. I can feel it; you don't understand. It's death for me."

"Please, Oren. Don't leave me alone." It was a lower blow than I thought I was capable of delivering. I bit at my lip, cursing myself. But I couldn't bear the thought of him turning and walking away.

His eyes opened again. His hand turned, seeking mine and enveloping it. It felt as though sparks were leaping up my arm from where our skin touched. "Then don't go in. Stay out here with me."

Just days ago I wanted nothing more than him to ask me to stay. But that was before the attack, before I'd killed a child, before I knew the line between right and wrong out here was as thin as a magic shell.

"I can't live out here," I said, hollow all the way through. "You know that as well as I do. I'm not designed for it. I can't bring myself to eat meat or kill or scavenge, and I'm frightened every moment, and—"

"I'd keep you safe," he said tightly, his voice fierce. "I've kept you safe since you spent that first night in the city ruins. I brought you food; I pulled you out of the swamp. I kept you safe then; I've kept you safe since, I can keep doing it."

"That's not the point, Oren!" I said, frustration bubbling up and bursting forth. "I don't want to be kept *safe*! I don't want to have someone constantly trying to keep me from tripping on my own incompetence. I want to live in a world where I know the rules, where people are just people. Not one where they keep trying to eat me. That's the reason I left the city in the first place. I don't want to be *kept*, not by anyone."

His jaw clenched again. His grip on my hand was so tight I feared I'd hear the cracking of bones at any moment. "I could teach you." He was quiet now. For the first time I saw how young he was, my own confusion and uncertainty reflected in his face.

Speech was growing harder, trying to form words around the lump in my throat. "Just come with me."

"I don't belong in there. I can't live among people."

My eyes burned, but I refused to blink it away. "I could teach you," I whispered.

He lifted the hand that wasn't currently tangled through mine. Very softly, he touched my cheek, brushing my skin with the backs of his fingers. His skin was rough and callused, but achingly gentle.

"I would have kept you safe," he said.

I closed my eyes, forcing the tears down my cheek to break against the dam of his fingers. "I know."

His hand released mine, and his fingers fell away. I couldn't bring myself to open my eyes, knowing that the sight of his face would undo my resolve. When I finally did, he was gone—vanished, without a sound, without a footstep, without so much as a whisper of wind to tell he'd ever been there.

Part of me longed to run blindly back through the forest, shouting for him. I knew he would not have gone far—he never went far from me—and if I called for him, he would come. I stayed where I was with a monumental effort.

I stood at the edge of the Iron Wood for a time, staring into its frozen gray depths, straining for some movement, some sign of life. There was only crystalline stillness, not a leaf stirring in the breeze. Only the normal rustling of the leaves at my back and the faint noise of Nix's mechanisms pierced the silence as it darted back and forth.

Just go. I stretched out a hand across the visible threshold between nature and iron. I wasn't sure what I expected, but I felt nothing but the cool air on my skin, the tingle of imagined effect.

It's just a thing in the world. Like any other.

I closed my eyes and stepped into the Iron Wood.

The sensation of muffling fell so heavily that I almost turned around and marched back out. Nix's ever-present magical hum was reduced to the tiniest flicker, despite being inches from my ear. Though my footsteps rang as loudly as ever—perhaps more so now that the background sound had vanished—I felt as though I were tiptoeing through a graveyard.

"What is this place? It's so—quiet."

"*Iron*," Nix mimicked my soft voice. "*It's an insulator. It's cutting out the background magic.*"

I had known that, of course. In the city, iron was rare. It was difficult to use because it was impossible to magic. Iron was the only substance completely impervious to it. The most skilled metalworkers were employed by the Institute to coat glass wires in the stuff, as insulation to prevent magic from leaking.

"I never knew how much of what I was hearing before was magic," I said, touching the cold, hard trunk of a tree as I passed. "I'm not sure I could ever get used to this."

Nix gave a spirited little whir of its mechanisms. "*But it would be the perfect place for magic-users to hide.*"

"But you can't magic iron," I whispered back. "If anything happened to them in here, they wouldn't be able to do anything with magic to stop it."

We continued through the Wood, moving quietly through the silence. Despite the frightening stillness, there was a strange beauty about the frozen forest. It was as though the iron had caught every season at once. One tree was covered in frozen blossoms while the next was forever trapped with its buds beginning to open. Still others had round iron fruits clinging to their branches.

As we walked, I noticed that the trees stood in rows. They were lined up so uniformly that I knew their placement could not be natural. My skin prickled, on edge.

Up ahead I caught a flash of something. It had been so brief that I hadn't been able to detect anything other than color and movement, but I froze and stared.

From somewhere above and behind me, an unimaginable sound rang through the iron trees. For a wild, joy-filled moment I thought, *Oren!* But it was not the lark's birdcall. I whirled around, straining to catch sight of the source. A second call, this time from somewhere to the east, sounded—as if in answer. And then, the entire forest was alive with birdsong.

Disoriented and breathless, I spun, trying to understand what was happening. Then, just as quickly, the songs all cut out. A figure dropped down out of the branches, landing in a soundless crouch. My first thought was of the shadow people.

As the figure stood, I saw that it was a girl not much older than I. She wore ash-gray clothing that hung in tatters all over, and her face and hair were similarly stained with ash, but underneath she was human. She melted into the forest, even standing directly in front of me.

"Are you alone?" she asked.

"What?" All around me, other figures were dropping out of the trees, surrounding me. After such silence and solitude I struggled to keep up. "Yes!"

"How did you find us?" she snapped, her eyes fierce.

"What—I—" I spluttered. Surrounded by people after so long in the quiet, I was at a loss for words. "A Renewable. In my city. She told me—told me where."

The fierce girl was half-crouched, clearly expecting me to run or attack. "I don't believe you," she said. "If that were true, she would've given you the words."

"The—words?" I stared at her, the bottom falling out of my stomach. "Like a password?"

"I don't care who you are," spat the girl, "if you're a spy or not. You don't belong here. Either leave, or die."

"She didn't *give* me a password!" I cried. "I can't leave; I have nowhere to go. She didn't have time to say much; she barely gave me directions. She just told me to find the others in the Iron Wood, and to follow the birds."

Around me, the circle shifted, postures relaxing, only noticeable because everyone relaxed simultaneously.

"Why didn't you say that at the beginning?" said the fierce girl, straightening up out of her crouch. "What, you thought you were *actually* supposed to follow birds?" I must have looked dumbfounded. "Tell me, how far did *that* instruction get you out there?"

I stood still, not quite understanding yet. The girl withdrew a slender rod from her boot. It was a glass rod—not unlike the glass wires I had run from in the city. "Stay still," she said, coming toward me.

As far as I could tell it wasn't sharp, but I tensed nonetheless, my legs bent and ready to flee.

"Shh," said the girl. "I'm not going to hurt you; I just have to check something." She stretched out the rod and touched the skin of my wrist with it. A familiar jolt coursed through it. The rod glowed with a barely perceptible violet light and then subsided again.

The girl frowned at it for a few moments and then looked

PART III

CHAPTER 25

"Sorry for all the precautions," Tansy said as she led me through the wood. A number of the other figures that had surrounded me went with us, but most had melted back into the forest without a sound. "But we can't just take your word that you're not one of Them. They don't know they're monsters, most of the time."

The iron trees were so dense I could barely catch more than a glimpse of the sky. For the first time, I felt uneasy under cover, too confined. I shook my head, still dazed. "I know," I said. "I've seen them."

Tansy turned around to look at me, walking backward, both eyebrows lifted. She was a tall, round-faced girl with a bright smile despite the ash coloring her face. "Really? And you're not dead? Still, explains why you look—well, like that."

I had not exactly seen a reflection of myself in quite some time, except for a muddled and imperfect glimpse in the lake's surface. I started to object, and Tansy interrupted with a wave of her hand.

"I don't mean to sound critical. It's pretty impressive. I mean, it's not like I've ever had to survive out there on my own. I'm a lifer, always been here." Her tendency to chatter suited me fine, as I was having trouble stringing together more than three words at a time. I found myself thinking she and Tamren would get along well.

"What's that?" she asked, peering at my shoulder. Nix had been silent and still since the people from the Iron Wood had appeared.

"This is my—" I hesitated, uncertain what to call it. Surely they wouldn't appreciate a machine from an energy-starved city being in their hidden village. "Friend," I said, uncertainly. Nix thrummed its approval.

"Well, don't think you can use it to send a message," she went on. "Transmitters don't work here. So if you *are* a spy from one of the cities, good luck trying to tell the others where you are."

"*One* of the cities?" My knees felt weak and wobbly.

Tansy glanced at me, brows lifted in that characteristic look of surprise. "Yeah. Why, where are you from?"

"W—we just call it the city. East of here and north. I didn't know there were others."

Tansy nodded, slowly. "Yeah, I think I know which one you've come from. It's one of the ones that never made contact after the wars. Kind of sad, really, all those people thinking they're all alone. You're better off here. And speaking of here—"

We'd reached a strange curtain, a drape of fabric and leaves and paint that hung from the branches high above and stretched away on either side. She pulled it aside at a seam and pushed me through.

It was as electrifying as walking through a magical barrier. On the other side of the curtain, the world was alive with color and light and movement. There were houses, down on the ground and up in the trees, scattered seemingly at random. People bustled to and fro, wearing clothes brighter than any you'd find in the city. As we stood there, Tansy stripped off an outer coat of the ash-gray clothes, revealing much more normal-looking blue fabric underneath.

She led me down into the town. People stopped to watch me. Far from looking suspicious or afraid, they looked intrigued more than anything else.

"We don't get outsiders very often," explained Tansy, shooing away some children who came to stare at me, open-mouthed. "Usually the only creatures that stumble their way into this place are monsters. And we don't let them get this far."

There was a cold finality in her voice that made me shiver in spite of myself. Even here, in something like civilization, the only solution to the shadow people was unquestioning execution.

Tansy misread the expression on my face, and touched my elbow. "Oh, don't worry," she said quickly. "They don't come here that often. They seem to know that this is the last place they should come, and they stay away."

I shook my head. "I'm not afraid of them," I said, and as I spoke the words I realized them to be true. I pitied them.

The town was three dozen buildings that I could see and maybe more hidden from sight. Many of them doubled as both homes and shops, with wide windows overlooking the pathways through the iron trees. Half of them were in the branches themselves, connected by precarious-looking walkways of rope and wood. Children and adults alike crossed without so much as a second's hesitation, though, so I had to assume they were safe.

The shops, if that's what they were, offered pots of clay and of iron, bread, wooden furniture, a whole rack of iron tools, strings of fish and—I averted my eyes quickly when I saw them—slabs of meat hung high on iron hooks. There were bushels of produce so bright and alluring I had to force myself to keep following Tansy. Some of the baskets held things I'd never seen before—after my steady diet of nuts and sour berries, I ached to stuff my pockets with what lay before me.

"Where are you taking me?" I asked finally, with one last look over my shoulder at the vegetable stall.

Tansy snapped her fingers, bringing my attention back to her with a jerk. She grinned at me. "Don't worry, we'll come back later. Market lasts all day today; it's the rest day. I'm just taking you to Dorian."

Though she had spoken what sounded like a first name, there was a reverence in her voice nonetheless that had my skin prickling with sudden alarm. I'd heard that brand of reverence before. That was how we referred to our architects.

Tansy took me to a rope ladder that led up to one of the houses in the trees. It was no bigger than any of the others, nothing to show that it was anything special. The ladder itself twisted and shook as we climbed, and I tried not to look down as we got higher and higher. Nix whirred and clicked reassuringly in my ear, darting up to the next rung of the ladder and back to my shoulder again.

By the time we reached the top, my arms and legs were shaking, and my hands burned from the tightness of my grip. Tansy smiled and nudged my shoulder with hers as I stood up. "Don't worry," she said. "You'll get used to it in a couple of days, I promise. Wait here."

She ducked inside the door of the house. I heard voices, pitched too low to hear, and I resisted the urge to press my ear against the wood of the door. Nix zipped around to one of the windows, where it crouched, antennae waving furiously.

After a few moments, the door opened again and Tansy beckoned me inside. It took my eyes some time to adjust, but there were lamps glowing with a strange golden light scattered around the house and after a time, I made out the form of a man standing not far from the window outside which Nix was stationed.

"Tansy tells me your name is Lark," he said, walking toward me and extending a hand. "Welcome. My name is Dorian."

Behind me, the door opened and closed again as Tansy slipped out, leaving me alone with Dorian. I was surprised to see that he was younger than I'd expected, his youthful round face marred only by the faintest hints of lines around the eyes and mouth. His hair was a dark brown, and as far as I could tell, untouched by gray. As I took his hand, a strange current passed between our joined palms.

"Thank you," I said, voice wobbling.

"Please have a seat," he said, releasing my hand to gesture to an exquisitely carved chair near a small stove that radiated a gentle heat.

I sat. His voice had a quiet command that I found hard to resist.

He sat down opposite me and leaned forward, resting his elbows on his knees. "Tansy seems to think you're a Renewable like us," he said, fixing brown eyes on mine. His gaze was every bit as unreadable as Oren's, and he had none of the tiny signs and tics that told me what Oren was thinking.

I nodded, my mouth too dry to form words. I swallowed. "My city was going to keep me captive and use me for energy," I said, voice cracking.

"I see," said Dorian. "I'm not so sure."

"What?" I felt my hands tighten around the arms of the chair. "What do you mean?"

"Don't be afraid," said Dorian, with a smile that did wonders to calm my racing heartbeat. "I only mean that I'm not so sure you're like us. There's something different I can't quite put my finger on." He flexed the hand that had shaken mine, and I realized that he had somehow read me, and my abilities, when he'd touched me.

"Are you going to turn me out?" I blurted, my grip on the chair white-knuckled. The idea of going once more into the wild was almost too much to bear. I thought I'd found at last a place where I could click.

Dorian blinked at me, the first sign of genuine surprise I'd seen. "What—? No, of course not!" He laughed, leaning back in the chair and resting his palms on his thighs. "Many people here have abilities that express themselves in unusual ways. Tansy, for instance, can only access her power when it rains, or sometimes if the humidity in the air is high enough."

Relief washed over me, tinged with confusion. Magic is uniform, simply a power source—or so the Institute teaches. I should've realized that couldn't be true, after seeing the magic do so many different things to the landscape. If magic was different in everyone—then maybe I could fit in here after all.

"No," continued Dorian, "you can definitely stay. I regret to say that we'll have to keep you under a close watch for a while, because we can't be too careful. But of course you can stay. What skills do you have?"

The question, and the quick shift in conversation, threw me again. "What ski—uh, I don't know," I stammered. "I can build a fire?" As soon as the words left my mouth, I cursed myself for saying them. What use was that, after all? Just because it was a skill that had taken me so long to master didn't mean it meant anything to anyone else.

But Dorian only nodded gravely. "Anything else? What did you do back in your city?"

"Well, I hadn't been harvested yet, so I hadn't been given my assignment—"

"Harvested?" Dorian's brows lifted.

"Oh. In my city, in order to power the barrier that keeps the magic in and the monsters out, the Institute takes kids once they're grown-up enough and harvests their power. We're not Renewables there—except for me."

Dorian stood, crossing to the stove to throw in another chunk of wood. "I see," he said, not showing as much surprise—or horror—as I would have expected.

"I wanted to be a historian," I said. "I like learning about the world before the wars."

Dorian nodded, shutting the door to the oven again. "Well," he said. "We can set you up with something easy, something unskilled, until you figure out what you'd like to do."

The words were a dismissal, and I got to my feet. "Thank you for letting me stay."

"Of course. Except for the ones who were born here, like Tansy, most of us have escaped from someplace or other who wanted to use us."

I hesitated, searching for something recognizable in the set of his expression. "What am I then, if not like you?"

He shrugged, moving away from the stove and toward the window. "Some unique product of your city, I expect," he said. "Evolution works differently after the wars. There are so few of us left, compared to what there used to be. Humans have never been forced to adapt quite so quickly before. Perhaps your little spy-fly knows." He tapped on the window with his fingernail, and Nix zoomed off, startled.

I scrambled to explain, not wanting Dorian to think I was spying on him—what if they believed me to be an agent of my city come to scout them?—but he waved my spluttering away. "Hush, you aren't the only one to have brought something from your city with you. We've got a couple of machines here, even."

I shifted my gaze away from the window. His bed stood in the corner, neatly made up, its single pillow dented in the middle from long use. An exquisitely carved chest of drawers stood low against the wall, below a broad, hand-painted canvas. I recognized it from my lessons at school as a map, full of pins and covered with hand-written notes. I longed to study it, for I was still thinking of Tansy's off-hand comment that other cities besides mine still existed. But it was the chest of drawers, and the knick-knacks and trinkets that covered its surface, that drew my gaze.

Dorian saw me looking at the chest. "Gifts," he said, of the trinkets. "Advice is as valuable currency here as any."

There were carved figures, boxes beaten from the iron leaves overhead, rings and tiny puzzles. There was even a folded paper cat that could have been the twin of something Basil would have made. I felt tears sting my eyes and passed a hand across my face.

"Go on," said Dorian, his voice soft. "You're exhausted. Tansy will find you a bed for the night."

• • •

Tansy brought me home to her family, which surprised me more than it probably should have. It seemed that family units were much more of a focus here than in my city. There, once you were harvested and got your working assignment, you rarely rejoined your family except on subsequent Harvest Days if you wanted to.

Tansy's family barely skipped a beat, her parents setting up a pallet by the stove. They apologized for not having a spare mattress for me, but when I reminded them that I'd been sleeping on the ground for weeks, they subsided a little. I slept more soundly than I had done for a long time, next to the warmth of the stove, with the chatter of Tansy and her parents lulling me to sleep.

The dawn woke me, as people emerged from their houses as if on a schedule, beginning the day the moment the light penetrated the trees. I rose confused, listening to the sudden noises of life and movement, imagining myself for brief moments to be back in the city, listening to the clockwork dawn. As if nothing had changed.

When I had dressed myself and eaten a light breakfast, Tansy took me to work with her father. She explained that while she was technically a scout, she often came to help out her father when it was too dry for her magic to be sharp enough to serve her on watch. She called him a worker bee, but wandered off to chatter about something else before I could find out what that meant.

And so I tagged along with the pair of them with barely restrained eagerness, buzzing with purpose and excitement I hadn't felt in a long time. I was a part of the world again, in a way I'd never been in the city. Here I could have a reason for being, slip into the role I was best suited for and live my life.

We walked past the outer ring of houses and down a path densely overgrown with iron trees. The narrow path had been cut through the thicket, and the sharp iron edges filed down, and yet the brambles still caught at my clothing. Tansy moved through it with ease, but I struggled through the grasping fingers of iron, the gloom under the trees pressing in at me.

We emerged from the tunnel of iron thicket into a valley so beautiful that I stopped breathing. At the heart of the Iron Wood, the trees were alive and thriving. Tall, thick, with the most heady of scents drifting on the air. The only sign that these trees had ever been like the iron ones surrounding them was that they, too, were caught in every season. Flowers and buds and bright, round fruits adorned the branches. Suddenly, I realized why the trees of the Iron Wood seemed to have been planted in rows.

"It's an *orchard*," I gasped, coming to a halt.

Tansy stopped, her father going on ahead. "As far as we know, it's the last apple orchard in the world. We think it happened during the wars. When it petrified—or metallified, is that a word?—it preserved everything perfectly. And now, here, a few trees have begun to change back."

"How? Magic can't affect iron, can it?"

Tansy shrugged. "We don't really know. My dad thinks that the wars were intense enough that even iron was affected. Maybe somewhere on the other side of the planet there's an iron city that turned into a forest."

There were people scattered about the orchard, some of them walking here or there on the ground, but most of them halfway up ladders, heads lost in the clouds of blossoms.

"What are they doing?" I asked, my voice still breathless with surprise and joy. Not even the revelation that even iron could be turned by magic if it was strong enough could distract me from the beauty of the orchard.

"Taking care of the trees. Come see," was Tansy's reply. She took my hand and led me around the edge of the orchard to find her father, who had taken up work halfway up a ladder.

"Dad," she called up. "Can you show Lark what you're doing?"

Her father glanced down at us and nodded, before climbing a few rungs down the ladder. A small pouch dangled from his wrist. He dipped a brush into it.

"No bees, of course," called Tansy's father. "So we've got to do the hard work ourselves." He dabbed the brush against one of the bobbing sprays of blossoms, and moved along the row so quickly I struggled to follow the movement.

"Couldn't you just . . ." I made a gesture with my fingers.

"Use magic?" Tansy grinned at me. "It's so much harder

to do things with magic than it is to do them by hand. So if we can do something naturally, we do."

I gazed around at all the workers. "Did you turn them into real trees again? From the iron ones?"

Tansy shook her head, furrowing her brow at me. "*We* can't magic iron," she said. "No, they were like this when we found it, just smaller. Every now and then a new tree wakes up from the iron. Dorian believes that the magic is settling from the wars, and that things are beginning to return to normal."

I thought of the pockets, the trees with teeth and the ghosts. And yet—perhaps there was truth to the idea. Some of the pockets were barely distinguishable from the outside world.

"But it must take days just to do a single tree," I protested. "Why?"

Tansy gazed up at her father, the little brush flashing in and over the flowers. "Because someone has to. Because the birds do their best but they're not designed for this. Besides, it's worth it."

She went to the next tree over—this one full of fruit being harvested—and stretched up onto her toes in order to pluck one down and toss it to me.

I glanced at the apple uncertainly, half-afraid I'd break a tooth on it if it still bore some resemblance to its iron neighbors. It smelled unimaginably delicious, though, and curiosity—and greed—got the better of my caution. I took a single, cautious bite.

The flavor was delicate and tangy, flooding my mouth as I crunched into it. It was perfectly ripe, and juice dribbled down my chin. There was no electric tang of magic, no metallic bitterness—there was only apple, more delicious than I had ever imagined. The architects had never come up with a way to synthesize apples, not without pollinators.

Suddenly, the rest of what Tansy had said sunk in. *The birds do their best.* What birds? I lifted my head, about to call out to Tansy and ask, when a flicker of motion caught my eye.

A shape darted down and across my vision. At first I thought it must be Nix, who had left that morning to explore the village, but the blur had been brown, not copper-gold, and there was no whir of clockwork whizzing by.

The shape settled onto a branch not two trees away from me. I stared at it, so familiar and strange all at once—it puffed up its little breast and gave a series of chirps that escalated to a piercing trill.

"Tansy," I whispered fiercely, willing her to hear me, though I dared not raise my voice for fear of scaring the creature off. "Tansy!"

She came up beside me, following my line of sight to the branch, where the little bird was still singing its heart out. "Oh! Yeah. It's a sparrow."

"But—" I spluttered, still staring at the bird. "Birds are extinct!"

Tansy shook her head; I could see her smile out of the corner of my eye. "There aren't many of them, but every now and then, a few more show up. We don't know where they come from. But they find us somehow and come to live here in the apple grove. They help us pollinate the blossoms."

The bird, mottled brown and white, crouched low as if bowing, eyes darting all around. And then it was gone again in a flash of wings, leaving only the branch bobbing up and down behind it. As I scanned the trees, knowing now what I was looking for, I saw other birds here and there, of varying types, flitting from branch to branch.

"Kind of like you," Tansy was saying.

"What?" I blinked, turning to look at my new companion.

"They find their way here, we don't know how. Kind of

the same way you did." She handed me a shovel. "Come on, let's get some work done."

· · ·

The days passed in a rush of activity. I had thought my cross-country trek of the past few weeks had been rough on my body, but it didn't compare to the labor I put out in the Iron Wood. As far as I could tell there was no physical currency, despite the market I had seen. Work was their means of exchange. They bartered, and when someone had no goods, they'd offer hours of labor. Being a new arrival with little more than the clothes on my back, I spent much of my time performing menial tasks for various craftsmen in the village.

The market ran from dawn until midmorning, except for the rest day, when it lasted all day long. In exchange for continuing to live with Tansy's parents, I did their shopping for them, sparing them the trip out at dawn. Tansy's mother, an herbalist, also made a tangy cider from the apples in the orchard that was in high demand at the market.

The vendors would often include a little something extra—a handful of sweet carrots here, a potato pie there—for me, despite my protests that I had nothing to pay them. I was reminded of what Dorian had told me, that the majority of people in the Iron Wood still remembered what it had been like to be on the run and had found their ways here like me, bringing only what they could carry. They knew what it was like to have nothing.

There was no rite of passage, no trial to pass to be an adult here. There was nothing to set me apart from the others but that I was new. There were no formal schools, no graduations, no harvests. And despite being the first new person to turn up in over a year—a detail Tansy revealed days after my arrival—I still felt more at home than I had in the past several years in my own city. Maybe this was why I slept more soundly than

I ever had, despite waking with a jolt each morning to the sound of the village stirring at dawn.

I was never happier than when working in the orchard, where the breeze tossed the living branches and dappled sunlight snuck through the leaves and blossoms. In the Iron Wood the muffling trees were rigid and dense, a tight-knit shield all around the village. Here, at least, I could breathe.

Nix settled into the daily life in the Wood as well. It vanished for hours, no doubt cavorting with the birds in the orchard. I often found Nix, transformed into the shape of some unidentifiable bird, flitting from apple blossom to apple blossom. It always drew a crowd. Dorian tried to press it into service as a messenger, and sometimes Nix would oblige, but it made its own decisions about when it felt like helping.

It was only in the evenings, before exhaustion caught up with me, that I let myself feel a tiny pang of discontent. Unlike the abrupt dawn, dusk was slow, a lazy winding down of the machinery that was the village, like clockwork running out. It made me long for action. My feet were restless, despite my weariness, and part of me longed for something new again. I couldn't see the sky here except in the orchard, and the still closeness of the air made me itch to be on the move. For all the terror of the past few weeks, I found—to my utter confusion—that I missed the journey.

I longed to leave, to find Oren and tell him there was nothing to fear about the Iron Wood, that they'd welcome him if he chose to come. Maybe if he were here, I wouldn't feel so restless. But even if I had any hope of finding him, I still wasn't allowed outside the perimeter for fear I could signal another city. And so I tried to push Oren from my thoughts and let weariness carry me to sleep.

One morning, a hand shook me awake when it was still dark outside the window.

"Lark," said Tansy's father. "Wake up."

I struggled out of sleep, muttering blearily about the sun and the dawn and the market. I apologized for sleeping in, too muddled to understand what was happening. The smell of Tansy's mother's herbs hanging to dry from the ceiling nearly overpowered me.

"It's fine, the market hasn't started yet, that's not why I'm waking you up."

I sat up, running a hand through my hair and squinting at him in the gloom. He carried a single candle, which he handed to me. There was someone standing beyond him at the door, a dark shape silhouetted against the slightly lighter purple darkness beyond.

"What's going on?" Tansy's voice came from behind me. She looked fully alert. *Scout training*, I guessed. I envied her competence. If she'd been the one lost in the wilderness, she never would've needed Oren's help the way I did.

"There's someone here for Lark," said the person at the door. I recognized the voice as belonging to one of Tansy's fellow scouts, one of the ones who'd caught me that first day, though I could not remember his name. "He's at Dorian's."

"What?" I stared at him, sleep falling away.

"A guy a little older than you," said the scout. "He said he followed you. We brought him to Dorian. Will you come see if—"

He didn't have a chance to finish his question. I scrambled out of my blankets, not even bothering to change out of my night clothes, throwing on a coat and shoving my feet into my shoes.

I ignored Tansy's confused questions, her voice falling away as I broke into a run. I sprinted out past the scout, my heart surging. *He came after me.*

Dawn was breaking, the faintest light surging in the east. Here and there a light shone from a window, marking the house of an early riser.

A cluster of people stood near the ladder to Dorian's house. I sprinted for them, Tansy's fellow scout not far behind me.

I plowed into the knot of people, most of whom were dressed in the ash-gray tatters of the scouts. Shoving them out of the way, I climbed the ladder to Dorian's platform two rungs at a time. When I reached the top the door opened to reveal Dorian standing there, his expression quiet and grave as ever. He stepped aside, and I rushed past him, crying in spite of myself, "Oren! I knew you'd—"

I skidded to a stop, staring. The visitor turned, his face splitting into a familiar, heart-stopping smile as he saw me.

Kris.

CHAPTER 26

Kris took a step toward me, and I backed up a pace. He lifted his hands, smooth palms out. "It's me, Lark," he said. "Don't you remember?"

"Of course," I said, struggling for breath. I could not have been more floored if Gloriette herself had come strolling across the village toward me. Kris was wearing a red architect's coat. Though it was dirty and tattered, speaking of days spent in the wilderness, I couldn't help but cringe at the thought of trying to stay hidden and safe wearing a color that bright. "What are you doing here?"

"I followed you," he said, voice electrifying in how familiar it was. "They figured out I helped you; I had to escape. Lark, I—" His expression softened and he took a step toward me. There he stopped, his eyes flicking toward Dorian.

The village leader seemed to take this as his cue, and straightened from where he was leaning against the door frame. "This young man claims he followed you here," he said quietly. "And that he is on the run like you."

Dorian's voice betrayed doubt, and I nodded vigorously. "He's telling the truth," I said, words tumbling over each other in my haste to defend Kris. "He helped me escape the

people who wanted to enslave me. He's the whole rea
here."

A pair of pale eyes, grass-scented hands, a fierce sr.
the images flickered in my mind and I pushed them asid

I turned back to him, aware of the way my breath qu
ened. He was every inch as handsome as I remembered,
brown hair still tumbling just so over his eyes as he duck
his head, smiling at my scrutiny. "How did you survive ou
there? You should have been—even without the shadows, the
pockets, the void should've twisted you by now."

Kris smiled, though there was an odd sadness in it. "I'm
like you, Lark," he said softly.

I'd all but forgotten the stab of disappointment in my
breast when I'd seen he wasn't Oren. My heart leapt as he
spoke. "How is that possible? Wouldn't they have locked you
up, too?"

Kris shrugged, the bitter smile fading again. "The difference is that my parents were architects. They knew what I was
long before my harvest. I have no idea how but they managed
to hide it from the others. Every day we run tests and experiments, trying to figure out how to create more Renewables,
save the city, and I was sitting right under their noses." He
shook his head, lowering it, clearly ashamed.

I closed the gap and reached out and touched his arm; no
jolt flowed between us. His arm was warm and solid underneath his sleeve. "You didn't have a choice," I told him. "They
would've made you into a thing, wired you in like they were
going to do to me."

Kris turned his head, looking at my hand on my arm.
When he lifted his gaze there was such a shift in his expression that my stomach lurched. I was close enough to smell
him, but I could only detect the faintest scent of chemicals.
He still smelled like a laboratory. *How long will it take for that*

to fade? I wondered. The corner of Kris's mouth lifted, as he moved his face closer to mine.

Dorian moved slightly, and I jerked my hand back, cheeks burning. "I'd like to speak with Lark alone for a few moments, if you don't mind," he said, inclining his head toward Kris.

Kris backed up a few paces and nodded. He circled around us, giving Dorian a wide berth, and shutting the door behind him.

I took a long, slow breath before I looked at Dorian again. I expected—amusement, maybe, or embarrassment. Instead he was solemn, even grim. "Would you like to sit down?" he asked.

"Thanks." I sank into one of his chairs, grateful for the moment to gather my thoughts.

"This boy," he said eventually, still standing. "You trust him?"

I nodded. "He slipped me a key to help me escape. He's not like the others."

Dorian moved away from the doorway and paced across the room to the window. I assumed he could see Kris down below from that vantage point. "He had no password. No one sent him here."

"He programmed Nix—the machine I had with me," I explained. "I assume he had some way of following that."

"A way the others didn't have?"

I spread my hands helplessly. "I'm not an architect," I said. "Do you want me to go ask him?"

Dorian shook his head. He was quiet a while, watching through the window, so that his voice, when it finally came, startled me. "I'm not sure he is what he says he is."

I stared. "An architect?"

"A Renewable." He flexed his right hand, as I remembered him doing when he read my abilities the day I arrived.

"You said the same thing about me," I insisted. "You said you didn't know what I was. Maybe we just feel different, the people where I come from."

Dorian hesitated, turning away from the window to face me. "It's not the same. I can't put my finger on it."

"You weren't sure about me," I said softly, "and you let me stay. Please. He saved my life, Dorian."

More silence. I held my breath and his gaze.

"Fine," he said. He held up a hand, forestalling any celebration. "But you will be responsible for him, and you will keep track of him at all times. You will be the one to orient him here. Understand?"

I tried unsuccessfully to hide my grin. "Yes. I understand."

• • •

Kris fit in much more easily than I did. But then, he had fit so neatly into the city. By his second day in the Iron Wood, he knew more of the other villagers than I'd met in a week, and though he was new to every task he was given, his hands were quick to learn. His mind was so much quicker than mine, absorbing details and memorizing faces. I often came upon him in deep conversation with a stall owner or a metalworker or a group of scouts, asking questions I never would've thought to ask. He asked where the food came from, how it was grown, why the weather didn't affect the orchard, what the villagers used to fashion the iron trees into houses. Details I'd always thought were too boring to ask about, until he brought up the subject. The villagers were only all too pleased to share, thrilled that their lives were of such interest. Kris meshed with the machinery of the Iron Wood like he was designed for it.

The more he charmed them, though, the more I wished he wouldn't. At the Institute we saw each other only rarely, and always under supervision. True, even then the sight of his face quickened my pulse, but there was never anything more.

Here, though—there were no experiments, no machines, no bounds of propriety—nothing to keep him from me. And yet he spent more time with them and less with me. Even the family he was staying with lived on the other side of the Wood, as far from me as possible.

Nix, in its quiet and dignified way, was overjoyed to see Kris again. The pixie spent the first day following its programmer everywhere, watching everything he did and echoing his sentences. Much to my relief, however, the machine returned in the evening, and it was still my pillow on which it clicked and whirred to itself all through the night.

That second day, I brought Tansy to meet Kris. She'd offered to help him sort out his roster of duties, similar to the variety of tasks I did each day. Like me, he'd try his hand at different activities until he decided where he wanted to work for good.

"Wow," Tansy said as she and I headed across the orchard to meet Kris. "And you swear you two aren't—" Her gaze lingered on Kris as he lifted his hand in a wave and broke into a jog toward us.

I felt my cheeks growing warm, and I shook my head. "It's not like that," I said firmly. "He just helped me."

"Yeah, out of the goodness of his—hi!" Kris was near enough to hear us, and Tansy moved forward to greet him. Despite her cheer and friendliness, every movement she made oozed confidence and ability. If I'd been training since childhood, surely I'd be that strong, too.

"Tansy," said Kris, smiling and holding out his hand. "It's a pleasure."

Tansy seemed briefly thrown by his manners. I'd explained that in our city the architects were our upper class, but she couldn't quite understand. She'd lived her entire life here, in a world without classes. "Yeah," she replied, smiling in spite of herself as she let him take her hand. "Okay, so what're you good at?"

The two sat down under one of the trees to discuss his abilities, leaving me uncertain whether I should join them or leave them to it. Awkwardly, I sat down on the ground next to them, cross-legged. As they settled on chores and temporary apprenticeships, I found myself thinking back to that first moment I'd seen him standing there in Dorian's house.

How had I ever felt *disappointed* to see Kris? Yes, I thought it would be Oren who would follow me, but if anything I should have been relieved. Life with Oren was intense and confusing and sometimes filled with such horror I could barely stand it. He was all passion one moment and ice the next. Kris was everything I had longed for in the city, regular and useful, fitting in seamlessly where he was meant to be. Even here, where everything was different, he was a part of it in a heartbeat.

Tansy laughed at something Kris said, and I pulled my attention back to them. "We'll just have to make sure you spend plenty of time with the scouts," she was saying. "I'll take you under my wing."

Kris smiled at her, and I fought the urge to leave. "The scouts," he echoed. "Sounds interesting. What'll I be doing?"

Tansy shrugged. "Pretty simple stuff. Don't worry, no fighting Them off for you. We'll just do some exercises to hone your senses. Use the power to sense the shadows, that sort of thing."

I hadn't been very good at it. Tansy had done her best, but I could barely point in the right direction when asked to sense the nearest shadow person beyond the borders of the Wood, much less give distance and number and speed, the way other scouts could.

Kris lifted his head, though all I could see from where I sat was his hair. "Hone," he echoed.

"Yeah. Why?"

"I'd rather not," he said. It was the first time I'd seen him uneasy since he'd arrived.

"It's not that hard. I'll teach you myself. We have a few pieces of equipment we use, too, to scan the perimeter, but it's mostly the magic."

"It still scares me. I kept it hidden for so long that it feels weird now to talk about it. Just give me some time to adjust." Kris turned away and leaned back against the tree, his profile visible now. He grinned. "We'll just have to find some other way for us to spend time together, okay?" He turned his head toward Tansy again, and even though I couldn't see it, I could hear his smile in his voice.

· · ·

I avoided Kris the next day, which was easy enough. I was scheduled to work all day helping one of the metalworkers. Though I hated the heat and the noise of the forge, the work was a welcome distraction. Every time my thoughts started to wander, the threat of a nasty burn snapped me back. It wasn't until I was heading back toward Tansy's family's house that I had time to think.

Of course Kris was drawn to Tansy. Who wouldn't be? She was strong, independent, capable. Her every step and gesture spoke of years of training to fight and move in the wild. The only training I'd had was reading in the back of my school classroom.

I reached the house at dusk to find it dark and empty. Tansy had patrol duty tonight, and her parents were likely dining with friends in the square. If I'd been in my city, I would have come home to my parents and my brother, to dinner on the table, a nightly ritual like clockwork. Here, I had no place I was meant to be.

I reached for the latch and was about to enter when a noise inside made me freeze.

It was no more than a thud, but something about it tripped instincts I didn't know I had. If someone with a right to be inside was there, why not light a lamp? I eased forward and pressed my ear against the door, listening. There came a second sound, fainter, little more than a scrape of fabric.

I sucked in a deep breath and grabbed at the latch, shoving the door open.

It was dark inside, but there was enough light from outside that a faint shaft of it fell on a figure kneeling at the foot of Tansy's bed. The figure half-spun toward the door, falling back and staring at me.

"Kris!" I gasped.

It took him a second to start breathing again, pressing one hand to his chest and sucking in oxygen. "Lark! What were you doing bursting in like that?"

"*Me?* What are *you* doing sneaking around in the dark?"

When he failed to answer, I stalked across the room to light one of the lamps. When I turned back, Kris was still sitting where he had been kneeling—at the foot of Tansy's bed, the chest there open, its contents strewn about the floor.

Tansy's belongings. Tansy's bed. I shut my eyes. "Never mind, I don't want to know. Does she know you're here?"

Kris blinked in the light, eyes clearly adjusted for darkness. "What? Who?"

I waved a hand at the clothes and belongings scattering the floor. "That's Tansy's stuff."

Kris looked down at the clothes on the floor as if seeing them for the first time. He was struggling for a reply, mouth opening and then closing again. I'd never seen him so rattled.

"You live here, too," he said eventually, looking up at me.

"For now," I answered, nodding. "Tansy's out on patrol."

"No, I mean—" Kris got to his feet, stepping over the scattered belongings toward me. "I know that. I didn't come here because Tansy lived here. I came here because you live here. I thought these were your things."

I stared at him. "Why did you want to go through my things?"

Kris shifted his weight from one foot to the other, looking down at the floor for a few seconds. When he looked back up, his hair fell into his eyes, making my fingers itch to fix it. "The bird. The paper one that you had with you when you entered the Institute. I gave it back to you with the key?"

He was looking at me as though I might not remember. I managed a nod.

"I thought if I could find it, I could—" He shrugged, bowing his head, shoulders stooped. "It sounds ridiculous now. But I thought I could make some sort of gesture. Show things haven't changed."

"What are you talking about?"

In the lamplight, I could see a flush beginning to creep over Kris's features. "Back there you were something else. Frightened and weak and needing every inch of help you could get. Needy. But now...you're so different. You seem taller. You're strong and you know what you're doing. You don't need anyone now."

He smiled, though there was a sadness in it that robbed me of breath. Too sad, I thought, for what he was saying. "You don't need me."

"But—Tansy?" I'd seen him unleash that same deadly smile upon her, exert every bit of charm he'd ever shown me.

"She's your friend. I tried to get to know her." Kris took a step toward me, reaching for my hand. I let him take it, too shocked and confused to object even if I'd wanted to. "Why do you think I helped you escape?"

I opened my mouth, but it took a few seconds for me to find words. "Human decency?" But as soon as I spoke, we both knew how ridiculous the words sounded. There was no decency in that place.

Kris laughed, no more than a quick exhalation. His breath puffed against my forehead, stirring my hair. He reached for my face, fingers sliding across my cheek. They were soft, smooth. Architect's hands.

"Your—" I began, before he abruptly ducked his head, lips brushing across mine.

I jerked my head back, leaving him staring at me with his mouth still half-parted.

"Your hands," I said, though my eyes were on his face. "They're soft. Your fingernails are so clean."

"I work with my head, not my hands," he said. "They'll toughen up."

"But they haven't yet," I whispered. His face was so beautiful it made it hard to think. "And you don't have a scratch on you."

"You're...angry I'm not hurt?" Kris's brow furrowed in confusion.

"Your hair," I said, scarcely listening to him. "When you got here your hair was clean. I remember it looked exactly as it had the day I..."

"I was lucky, I didn't have a tough trip." He reached for me again, smoothing my hair with the palm of his hand. "I, at least, stopped for shoes before I left." That, with a bit of a smile before he leaned in to kiss me again.

This time I froze, and he stopped.

"How did you know I didn't have any shoes?"

He didn't answer, and I pulled out of his grasp. When he looked up I could see it written across his handsome features, the eyes that wouldn't meet mine, the sadness in his drooping mouth, his slumped shoulders.

Guilt.

My face burned where he'd touched me. "You didn't escape," I whispered, my eyes beginning to burn as well. "You were *sent*. You aren't like me."

He must have read my unasked question in my face. "Machines," he replied, his voice hoarse. "And stocked crystal storage. Lets anyone survive out there a little while. And it doesn't take long to get here by walker."

"But you helped me."

Kris's laugh was short and mirthless. "Lark, you don't escape from the Institute. With or without help. Do you understand? No one escapes from there. No one. Ever."

I shook my head dumbly. I didn't understand anything.

Kris clenched his jaw, dropping his eyes and looking away, toward the window. Beyond the glass people strolled through the square, laughing and enjoying their evening meals. "We needed this place. The Renewable we have isn't going to keep us wound much longer. You know that, right? Every day the city slows, the Wall falters a little more. And when it breaks, everyone will break with it. Your parents, your classmates, their families. Workers, administrators, and architects, too. Everyone."

"The whole thing," I mumbled. "All of it. You left me the shoes. You wanted me to—to lead you here."

"The Renewable talks. In her madness and her pain, she babbles. Nonsense mostly, but over the years, the Institute learned about this place. She was captured, you know. Renewables aren't born in our city anymore—if we were going to survive we had to find the others."

"But—me. I was born. . . ."

Kris took a slow breath, like a man preparing to put his hand through a flame. "You aren't a Renewable, Lark."

The words roared in my ears, surging like torrential rain,

drowning out the chatter in the square, the sound of my breath, the sound of his voice. My throat closed and I stood stunned. Kris went on.

"You're an experiment." His face twisted. I wanted to claw his handsome features, to stop his tongue. Instead, I felt my fingernails digging into my palms. "By repeated doses it's possible to infuse a person with enough power that it seems, for a time, as though she's generating it herself. But it's dangerous. You're only the second one to survive, and you—" He swallowed. "You're burning out."

How many times had they put me in the Machine? I had believed they were harvesting me, watching the energy grow back, harvesting me again. Dorian had said I was like nothing he'd encountered before.

"Why me?" My voice shook. I thought of the boxes on the shelves in the Institute.

Kris closed his eyes for a half-second longer than a blink. "The ability to survive the process seems to be genetic."

I shook my head. "I don't—" But then I did understand. *"Basil."*

"He really was a volunteer." Kris's gaze was earnest, begging me to understand. "But we lost track of him somewhere between here and there. We think he changed his mind, destroyed his own pixie tracker."

"But there were others," I protested, the words tumbling out of my mouth now. "Basil went with other volunteers; there was a whole group of them."

Kris shook his head. "Only he left the city. The others died during the infusion."

I stared at him, my stomach roiling so much I began to think I might be sick. "You sent him out here *alone*?"

"As we did you," Kris said softly.

"And why you?" I would not give him the satisfaction of seeing me cry, though my voice shook with effort.

"It was my idea," Kris whispered. "The misdirection." He looked at me for a few moments and then swallowed. "The lie."

"Why not just *ask* me? Maybe I would've done it."

"Because your brother said he would, and he failed. We had to make you think coming here was your only choice. We had to make sure you were running so fast from us that you didn't think twice about where you were running to. And you fit into the role perfectly, Lark. Like clockwork."

I caught a glimpse of copper-gold by the window, flashing in the lamplight. I gasped, and Kris flinched, thinking my exclamation was one of pain. He reached toward me but I jerked away, forcing my eyes to stay on his face. "Why were you really in here?" I asked through clenched teeth.

Kris hesitated, but when I started to turn away he hurried to place himself between me and the door, his back to the window where I'd seen a flash of the pixie. "Fine. Truth. Tansy mentioned equipment used for scanning, tracking. I wanted to find it and sabotage it. Keep them from seeing."

"Seeing what?"

Kris looked at me a moment, stricken, then dropped his eyes.

"No. Kris—they're coming, aren't they? To take them."

Outside, as a clump of teenagers passed the window, conversation swelled and receded again.

"It's us or them," said Kris. "If there was any other way, the Institute would have taken it. Would you sacrifice your parents? Your friends? Your brother? For them?"

I couldn't think about that. All I knew was that the people who had taken me in were under attack. I stepped to the side to move past Kris. "I have to see Dorian."

"Lark, no!" Kris put himself between me and the door again, reaching out to grab at my shoulders. "Listen to me. The Iron Wood has fallen. It's over. Those people out there—it's all gone, they just don't know it yet. The Institute's only a few days away. You still have time, though. I came here for you."

I made a sound in my throat, like a laugh but choked and strangled.

Kris's hands tightened. "Believe what you want, but I do care about you. I came to get information, yes, but I mostly came to get you. If you stay here, throw your lot in with them, then you'll be captured like the rest and locked up. Your borrowed magic will burn you up from the inside and you'll die horribly. All the tests we've done—you don't want to die like that. Please believe me."

I stared back at him.

"Or you can come with me." He gave me a little shake and my eyes rolled to the side. Nix was there—I could just see it, half-hidden against the windowsill. "If you come back with me now, voluntarily, it'll all be different. We can undo what we did, reverse the process. And you'll be fine. You'll return a hero, the savior of your city. You can do whatever you want. We can even help you find your brother."

My stomach turned to lead. "My brother's dead," I whispered.

"We don't know that for sure. He could be alive somewhere. We could help you find out. *I* would help you find out."

"Let me go, Kris." Even though I wasn't sure how I was still standing, my voice sounded like iron.

"No." Kris's face was twisted with remorse and feeling. Could it be he meant what he said, and he actually cared for me?

"I won't let you do this."

"It's happening with or without me," he said. "They're already coming. Lark, you're coming with me now. Whether you want to or not. I'm not going to walk away and let you—"

Something in me snapped, and I shouted, "Nix! Help me!"

The pixie burst in, and I jerked my face away, anticipating some sort of blow or outraged scream from Kris. Eventually the grip on my arms loosened and Kris gave me another, much more gentle, shake. My eyes opened.

The pixie was sitting calmly on Kris's shoulder, as it had spent so many days occupying mine. Its faceted eyes were as still and glittering as copper-set jewels.

"I programmed it," Kris said gently, watching my face as though he knew what he said would pain me. "You had to think it was real. It's hard-wired into our natures as humans— we can't resist things that speak to us, that learn from us. We had to make you believe it was sentient. So you wouldn't destroy it as your brother destroyed his."

"Even Nix," I whispered. My gaze went from Kris's face to the pixie. It looked back at me, as emotionless as ever. How had I ever believed it was anything other than a machine?

Then, very slowly, without so much as an extra whir of its mechanisms, one eye winked for the briefest second. I shot my eyes back to Kris, forcing myself to keep looking at him.

"So everything was a lie," I said, uttering the first words to come to my mind. Keep him talking. "Down to your charm and your interest in the people here. You weren't interested in them; you were interested in our defenses."

"Our?" echoed Kris. Something was happening to the pixie, a movement I didn't dare look at for fear of drawing attention to it. "You're not an 'us,' Lark. You don't fit here. They aren't your people. *We* are. And we need you to come home." He lowered his voice. "I need you to come home."

I shifted my weight from one foot to the other, feigning indecision. "But all the people here . . ."

"They'll be fine, I promise."

"Well," I said, smiling. "So long as you promise."

Nix struck with the stinger it had unfolded from somewhere underneath its body. I had assumed it had broken when I first attacked it—I'd certainly never seen it since. Until now.

The copper barb sank deep into Kris's neck—he gave a shout and swatted the pixie away with his hand. Nix struck the opposite wall and clattered to the floor.

"Son of a bitch!" snarled Kris, rubbing at his neck and inspecting his hand, checking for blood. Nix's stinger had left behind an angry red welt on his skin. "Stupid bug—I'll have you decommish—decomm . . ." He swayed, blinking hard and staring at me. "You did this, you . . ." He shook his head and reached out for something I couldn't see. "All I wanted was to help you, keep you safe. They'll kill you—they'll tear you apart. . . ."

His grasping hands found no support, and he slumped to the ground with a thud. I stood breathing hard for a few long seconds, every muscle trembling. Then I darted for the spot where Nix had slammed into the wall.

The wings were bent and twisted, but already the little spindly repair arms were at work. "*Go get Dorian,*" said Nix, its voice shattered and distorted.

I stroked the little bug's head with a fingertip. "Thanks," I whispered.

I lurched to my feet and burst into the night. I shouted Dorian awake and had him dropping down the rope ladder in moments. He listened to my frenzied explanation and then—along with a handful of scouts attracted by my racket—made his way to Tansy's house.

Kris was gone—and so was Nix.

. . .

The town was in a frenzy, work abandoned in favor of packing and fortifying. Half of the Wood's occupants wanted to stay and fight—the others, those who had come from cities and seen what they could do, wanted to scatter across the wilderness and hope to find somewhere new to hide.

I stayed as hidden as I could. No one blamed me for what had happened—at least not to my face—but I felt each glance and whisper as a knife in my ribs. I tried to leave Tansy's house, saying I would camp outside the village amongst the iron trees, but her parents confiscated my shoes until I promised I'd "stop this nonsense," as Tansy's mother called it.

Over the next day, Tansy stayed by me when she wasn't off with the scouts, although keeping watch took up most of her time.

Though I loved Tansy for her unquestioning friendship, part of me wanted nothing more than to be alone. With a few well-chosen words, Kris had taken everything from me. He'd taken my identity, my sense of power and understanding of my life, even the accomplishment of having made it from the city to the Wood. For what teenager could break out of a heavily guarded cell and escape capture for weeks? How could a girl believe she was surviving in the wilderness when she had never seen the sky?

I was an experiment, a tool. I was what I'd once longed to be: a cog in their mechanism, nothing more. And I had fulfilled my role as efficiently as anyone could have hoped. I was a valuable part of the machine. I wanted to return to the bog and let it swallow me down.

Dorian was the only person in the village who declined to choose a side, whether to stay or go. Some accused him of indecision, while others argued that there had to be some reason that only Dorian understood.

He summoned me to his house some time after sundown, two days after Kris fled. I had known it was coming, had been braced to face him ever since I'd explained that Kris was an architect come from a city bent on taking the Iron Wood's residents for its own uses.

He opened the door for me as I lifted a hand to knock, and ushered me inside. I sat in the same chair I'd sat in that first day, feeling more nauseous and uncertain than ever.

"I've been thinking," said Dorian, taking a pot of steaming water from the top of his stove and pouring it into two cups, "about your pixie, as you call it."

I blinked, caught off-guard by the topic. I had expected a discussion about Kris, or the city, or Gloriette, or my part in it all. "What about it?"

"Well, typically those clockwork type creations need to have magic added to their stores constantly, or they run down. I've seen them before. Got to have something to keep the clockwork running."

"It used me to recharge."

"That's just it," said Dorian, handing me one of the two cups and then sinking down into the chair opposite me. "We can't do that, you know. Exude magic that way. We have to concentrate to let it out. It doesn't sit about us like—like a cloud, for anything to be touched by it."

"So clearly the city's methods are imperfect," I said, weary of having my own imperfections, my differences, pointed out to me. I bowed my head, inhaling the fragrant steam. "I was leaking. It's not a surprise."

"I'm not so sure," said Dorian, curling his hands around his mug. "You're not a Renewable, no, but you're not 'normal' either."

"I won't be anything once the power runs out." I could

hear the bitterness in my voice. I regretted it, but could not quite control it.

"Are you so sure it will?"

I blinked again. "Well—no. But what reason would they have to lie?"

"At what point have they ever told you the truth? The thing is, I can't figure out why they would have sent that young man here to collect you."

"I guess because they wanted to tie up loose ends?"

"That's possible. But he risked a lot, coming in here to get you—"

"Don't try to convince me that he *cares* about me," I protested.

"No, I wouldn't dream of it." There was a faint smile on Dorian's face. For the briefest of mad moments I wanted to shout at him for it. I restrained myself. "I was going to say that to take such a big risk, there must have been promise of a big payoff. I'm not so sure you're as useless as you think you are."

"What do you mean?"

"I'm not sure. But whether it's the quality that allowed you to survive their process in the first place, or whether the process changed something within you, you're different now, Lark. You're not one of us, but you're not one of them either. I'm not certain *what* you are, or what you can do—except that to come so far, on such tiny reserves of power, you must have an ability to manipulate power that any one of us would envy."

"That's ridiculous," I burst out. "The only thing I've managed to do is flail out with it, and sometimes it hasn't even worked."

"You told me you threw a creature off a cliff, and lifted yourself and another person up in the air," replied Dorian, both brows lifting. "And after your resources were nearly depleted. Did you think magic was easy? There's a reason we don't have everything floating around by magic here, Lark. To lift even the smallest of things takes incredible concentration and effort and strength. It's much easier to just use our hands. I'm not saying you're skilled. You have about as much finesse as a toddler throwing a tantrum. But you have an ability to take the tiniest grain of power and magnify it tenfold. I've never seen anything quite like it, and I've seen as much as anyone in the world, I'd wager."

"But what does that mean? Am I not going to die?"

Dorian lifted his cup and took a slow, careful sip of the hot tea. "I can't say for sure," he said. "I won't lie to you. If it was one of us, the act of having our magic torn away from us for good probably would kill us. It's probably why your city does it when its citizens are children, and flexible. But you? After what they did to you? I don't know. For now, just try not to use your power. It does seem like they were telling the truth about the power in you ebbing, at least. You did say it had been getting harder."

I nodded, trying to swallow the lump in my throat. "What are you going to do? About the Institute? They'll be here any day."

The smile on his face faded, and he shook his head. "That I can't say," he said, his expression troubled. "It's an impossible situation. Part of me would like nothing better than to erect a wall not unlike the one you passed through to come here, in order to keep them out. But we don't have that kind of power and finesse. And we might as well scatter to the corners of the continent; because no one in the future will be able to come here seeking asylum the way you did."

I was silent for a while, staring into the depths of my tea at the dark leaves lurking at its bottom. "How do you know I didn't lead them here?" I whispered.

"Oh, Lark. You did lead them here."

My gaze snapped up—but he was smiling again.

"But you didn't do it on purpose. If you had, then you would have left with Kris. We have scouts after him. We will find him. But you can hardly be held responsible for the fact that the leadership of your city is slightly ahead of the curve of the other cities'. If it hadn't been you, it would have been someone else."

"But it *was* me," I blurted angrily. "There were signs everywhere, I was just too stupid to see them. How could I have ever thought I was capable of doing all of that, over the past few weeks?"

Dorian listened, not a hair out of place, not a sign that he had any reaction to my angry outburst. "And yet," he said, after a few moments, "here you are. So you clearly *are* capable."

"I was *sent*."

"*You* made a choice," he said firmly. "And you saw it through."

I got out of my chair. Clutching my mug, still almost too hot for my fingers, I paced around the perimeter of the one-room house. I stopped at the bureau full of trinkets, eyes raking across each one of them.

"You could have left with him and been safe, but you chose to remain with us." Dorian's calm unsettled me, so different from Oren's blank expressions—Oren's were hiding something fierce and raging underneath the surface, but Dorian gave the impression of calm all the way through. With the Institute a matter of days, if not hours, away, I could not comprehend his serenity. Nonetheless, that calm reached me, soothing me despite my agitation.

I stood looking at the rows of curios for some time before I realized what I was seeing. When I did, I snatched up the paper cat I'd seen my first day, and whirled around.

"Where did you get this?" I asked, extending my hand.

Dorian's eyebrows lifted again. "A boy made it for me. He came through some years ago, from a city as well."

I nearly dropped my mug. "Kris said that my brother might still be alive. He made figures like this. The boy—what was his name?"

"He was here only for a day or two before setting off again. I can't quite remember. Something strange, like—Rue? Sage?"

"Basil," I whispered.

CHAPTER 27

Dorian said nothing in reply, but I could see the memory in his gaze. I could hear raised voices in the distance outside but I ignored them, my eyes locked on Dorian's face.

"Where did he go?" I croaked, my voice cracking horribly. "Did he say?"

"He said he was looking for answers. I gave him the location of a city far to the north—here." Dorian rose from his chair and crossed to the map, jabbing his finger at it. "This is us, here. This is your city, to the east—see it? And this is where I sent your brother." His finger moved up the map, tracing a thick black line marked The Great Northern Road up to a blue pin to the north.

"Why send him there?" I asked, staring at the pin until my eyes began to water, as if it might give me answers.

"Last I heard, though it's information from several generations ago, the people there had been experimenting with restoration."

"Restoration?"

"Trying to turn the world back to what it was. Before the wars. Setting free the magic trapped in the pockets."

I struggled to speak past the lump in my throat, loud

enough to be heard over the rising altercation outside. "Or taking it out of people."

Dorian gazed back at me until a piercing scream had us both snapping our heads toward the window. I ran for the door, bursting through it and coming up against the railing and staring down through the gathering twilight.

A cluster of scouts was entering the village, manhandling—something. It was concealed by the press of their bodies, but I realized quickly who it must be.

Kris. They'd caught him, or else he'd come back.

I threw myself down the ladder so quickly I barely touched it. Once my feet hit the ground I sprinted for the cluster. As I drew closer, one of the scouts was flung back and I saw a flash of wild, pale eyes that brought me to a crashing halt.

"Stop!" I cried, shaking myself from my stupor and reaching for the nearest scout. "Stop it—I know this boy!"

The scout shook me off. I recognized him as Tansy's friend Tomas. "Stay back, Lark, he's dangerous!"

"He's *not!*" I shouted, charging my way into the group.

I couldn't blame them for thinking he was dangerous. As I broke into the ring of scouts he snarled, throwing one of them off with such force that the scout hit the ground and lay there, stunned. In a fluid motion, Oren snatched his knife out of his boot. The scouts lurched back as he carved a half-circle of deadly, glinting steel in the air.

I stood alone, forcing myself to remain still. "Oren! It's me. Stop!"

The way he stared at me, blank and feral, reminded me of the way he'd looked that first day when I saw him in the house of the ghosts. Devoid of humanity. Wild. Hungry. His fingers twitched around the knife, a nervous shift of his grip. "Lark," he said finally. He blinked away the wildness.

I could see Tomas standing beyond Oren's shoulder. His

expression was grave, his voice tightly controlled. "Lark, he's dangerous. He sliced up one of my guys. You should—"

"He's just not used to this many people," I cut in angrily. "If you just let him calm down he'll be fine." He'd come here looking for me—why else would he have braved this place? And the scouts had treated him no better than the shadow monsters they so ruthlessly killed. "Oren, can you put the knife away?"

Oren's eyes flickered from my face to the scouts in the circle beyond me, then back again. "I came here to get you," he said. "Never should have let you—come on, let's go." He brandished the knife, the scouts scattering in a wave before him. The moonlight scattering from the blade cut a path through the crowd.

"But I'm fine," I whispered. There was still a hint of that ferocity in his gaze. There was always a part of me that panicked when Oren was close, like a mouse that senses a cat. He was a part of that cutthroat world, and I wasn't. "Look at me. I'm happy here. Just put the knife away and you'll see."

Another quick glance away from my face. He gave no sign of hesitation or indecision, not even a shift of his weight back and forth or an uneasy look.

Tomas caught my eye over Oren's shoulder and nodded, making a rolling gesture with his hands. *Keep going.*

"I promise," I said, moving toward him. "They've been really great. Lots to eat and a place to sleep that's not the ground. And protection, they keep the shadow people out. Just give me the knife." I held out my hand, concentrating all my willpower on keeping it from shaking.

I saw Tomas frown, glance at one of the scouts next to him. I ignored him, focusing on Oren.

"This is a bad place—" he started.

"It isn't." I swallowed, continuing to move toward him. "Why would I tell you to put the knife away if it was dangerous here? Really, Oren. I promise it'll be fine. Don't you trust me?"

His eyes stopped flicking around and came to rest on mine. He had asked me that same question not long ago, and I had said no. I held my breath, the rushing of my heartbeat in my ears like the sound of the waterfall at the summer lake.

Oren's grip on the knife shifted once more, another flash of silver in the moonlight. Blade down. Killing stance. But before I could step back, his lashes lowered for half a second and he flipped the knife down so that he held it by the blade, arm outstretched. Offering it to me.

I let out the breath I was holding, taking the knife with a shaking hand. "Thanks. I'm glad you came. I wanted to find a way to—"

Before I could finish, Tomas leapt, his body crashing into Oren's and tackling it to the ground. Oren landed with a grunt of pain, chin hitting the ground with a dull crack.

"What are you doing?" I shrieked. I threw myself forward, reaching for Tomas to try and pull him off of Oren's struggling form. He lifted an arm to shove me back, and the blade of the knife caught him low across his shoulder. He hissed with pain, but didn't let go of Oren.

I stared at the line of red bisecting Tomas' arm. "I'm sorry—I—"

"Grab her, will you?" shouted Tomas, now helped by two other scouts to try and pin Oren to the ground.

I felt arms catch hold of me, my feet leaving the ground as I instinctively tried to get back to Oren's side. The knife fell from nerveless hands to the ground.

I could only watch as they wrestled him to a cage in the center of the square, one I'd always assumed was for livestock. Its iron bars were clearly crafted from frozen wood, immutable and solid. *You can't magic iron.*

Once the door of the cage slid shut, they released me. I slumped to the ground, spent. Oren threw himself at the bars of the cage and the whole thing trembled. I broke free from my captors for half a second, bolting toward Oren until Tomas stepped in between us. The scouts caught up with me, strong hands wrapping around my arms again.

"Don't," he warned, clasping his arm with his hand as his sleeve dripped red. "He's dangerous."

"Only because you attacked him and *threw him in a cage!*" I snarled.

"We attacked him because he's a monster!" Tomas shouted back, his breathing audible through his nose as he battled pain and anger. "He's one of *Them*."

"What?" My voice didn't even sound like mine. It sounded like a recording of my voice, twisted and played back on itself. "No, I traveled with him for a week. He saved my life. He *fought* them."

As I spoke, Tomas let go of the wound on his arm to hand the cage's key to one of the other scouts. From his boot he withdrew one of the long, slender glass rods that each of the scouts carried—the rod which Tansy used when she found me in the perimeter of the Wood. He approached the cage warily, as if expecting Oren to lash out at him. Instead Oren pressed himself against the back of the cage, eyes darting from the tip of the rod, to Tomas, to my face.

There his gaze held, and while he was distracted, Tomas darted forward and touched the tip of the rod to Oren's arm. My ears rang with silence, a thunderclap in reverse. I shook my head to clear it, and when I looked at the cage again, Oren was gone. In his place—

It snarled, hurling itself at the bars standing between it and Tomas. Tomas looked at me, mouth open to drive home his point, but when he saw my face, he fell silent.

The thing was as hideous as any of the beasts, its skin a sickly gray, traced all over with veins running black. Its bright, wet lips drew back to reveal a row of pointed teeth, mouth flecked with foam as it raged against its confinement. The colorless eyes stared all around, darting this way and that, seeking some structural weakness in the cage. The clothes were the same, only now I could see the tracery of veins in the skin through the thinly worn fabric of his shirt. The multicolored, patched pants were hideously out of place on its body.

"I'm sorry, Lark," said Tomas, reaching for my hand. I didn't resist, my bones all but turned to water. "Come on, I'll take you home."

. . .

Tomas turned me over to Tansy's parents. Their attempts to comfort me were fuzzy at best in my mind, the night passing in a haze of refused comfort, biscuits, fruit. Tansy's mother pressed a mug of tea into my hand after adding something from a blue bottle among her wares. *It'll help you sleep*, she said. I pretended to drink it, setting it aside.

When Tansy came home, full of news and rumor about what had happened, I tried to feign sleep to avoid her. She was all too gleeful to know about my experiences with "one of Them," asking things like, "Wow, and you never knew he was a monster?" and "To think you slept right next to him and he could have woken up and *eaten* you!" She told me I was terribly brave to have lived alongside *Them* for so long. Her amazement was typically childlike. Another day, I would have loved to hear her speak of me as brave—but now I could only see that animal snarl, superimposed over the fierceness of Oren's features.

Only once did I attempt to lift myself from my haze of misery long enough to ask, "What will they do to him?"

"Oh, don't worry," said Tansy. "They'll take care of it. We scouts are trained to do it."

There was a deadly finality to those last two words. I swallowed, my mouth dry and my voice cracking. "Do what?"

"Execute Them." Her childish directness turned my blood cold.

Eventually I feigned weariness, Tansy and her family all too willing to believe that whatever had been in that blue bottle had put me to sleep. It was only once the three of them were asleep that my mind began to work again, shuddering to life like an ancient, overgrown machine.

I slipped out of my blankets. I pulled on Tansy's heavy coat by the door and lifted the latch to let myself out.

There were scouts posted around the square. If I had thought at all, I would have expected them, but my mind still wasn't functioning very well. So I went up to the nearest, a silent gray form leaning against the corner of a house, and touched his elbow. He started and blinked at me. It was the same scout Tomas had handed the key to Oren's cage.

"What?" His voice was rough and hoarse. He swallowed and tried again. "What?"

"I'd—like to see him," I whispered.

"Sorry," he said, rubbing at his eyes. "Orders."

"He was my friend," I said. Though my voice wobbled as if with unshed tears, my eyes were dry and cold. "Please, I just want to say good-bye."

He glanced across the square at the other guards, indecision written clearly across his face even in the gloom. "I don't know," he said, glancing at the cage, which was dark and silent now.

"I won't tell anyone you were sleeping," I said, raising an eyebrow.

He swallowed again. "Just don't get too close, okay?" He gave a light, piercing whistle, two short sounds and a long one. Across the square I saw other scouts' heads lift, and then relax again as I stepped out of the shadows of the houses and into the square, lit meagerly by what moonlight filtered through the iron leaves overhead.

I walked slowly, and although I probably should have been afraid, my heart was slow and still in my breast. I came to a halt a few paces from the cage. I had thought the thing might be sleeping, for how still it was, but I saw the glitter of white eyes and knew it was awake and watching me.

There was almost nothing in that face of the boy I'd known, the malicious gleam of teeth and the powerful jaws. And yet, somewhere in the white eyes was a wild fierceness that had once so captivated me.

What was it Dorian had said? That I leaked magic, constantly, in an aura around me that any magic-starved creature could tap? Magic cured them, after all. No, not cured. Oren's voice came flooding into my mind. *All the magic does is disarm them for a time.*

I took a step forward, searching those flat, white eyes for that hint of compassion I'd learned to see in Oren's. With no warning, the Oren-creature leapt at the bars, jaws snapping inches from my face. I fell back, barely stopping myself from letting out a cry. Behind me I heard the scout start to scramble forward, and I lifted a hand. I was all right. Just caught off-guard.

I waited. Dorian had said what Kris told me was true: the magic was leaving me in drips and dribbles, stolen in tiny pieces by Nix and Oren, forced out in great torrents when I drew on it to save myself. There was still something in me, though. I could feel it lurking at the pit of my stomach, and I willed it to stir.

Nix had been pilfering it this whole time. And, apparently, so had Oren, in order to keep himself human—but he hadn't realized it. I thought of every time we touched, the jolt that passed between us, how his confusion cleared when I touched him. *Most of them don't even know they're monsters,* Tansy's voice came unbidden. I thought of the shadow woman's confused despair, by the summer lake, the pain at having lost her child even if she couldn't quite remember how it had happened. How the shadow child's scream had sounded so human, so very human, as it fell. . . .

I get confused sometimes, he had told me. I shut my eyes. How could I have been so completely, monumentally blind? He had all but shouted the truth at me, had I been listening enough to hear it.

What terror had he overcome to follow me, believing I might need his help? I opened my eyes again, to find that the creature behind the bars was still watching me, the white eyes steady and hungry. The bars, uneven and woven like the iron tree branches they were fashioned from, cut the thing's face into tiny fragments of shadow.

He had been so like an animal that first time I'd seen him. Then, I would have believed him to be a monster. The way he'd gazed at me, as the ghosts faded into mist around us, with such shock and such hunger, had shaken me to my core. The blood-stained face, the bestial grace. Why hadn't I remembered it later? *Because he saved my life. Again and again.* And because I learned, or thought I had learned, to see through the dispassionate exterior. Had I truly learned, or had he been growing more and more human, the longer he stayed in the aura of my magic?

There was little fanfare to mark the change. The creature blinked once, the white eyes vanishing for the briefest of seconds, and when they opened again they were blue. He was Oren again.

"Lark," he whispered, blinking at me from where he squatted on the floor of the cage.

I moved forward, kneeling and wrapping my fingers around the bars. "Yes, I'm here."

"What's going on?" He didn't remember what had happened. He didn't *know*. His eyes darted around the confines of his cage, the expressionless exterior rippling under the strain of captivity.

"It's a precaution." I wanted to kill myself for lying to him. "Everything's going to be okay, I promise. You're in the Iron Wood. With me."

He swallowed, but it didn't help the rasp in his throat. "They did this to you, too?"

My own throat was dry, my eyes burning. "Yes," I lied. "It's to wait and make sure we're not one of Them."

He bowed his head, coming toward me and pressing his forehead against the bars, between my hands. I could smell the wild tang of him. "I'll kill them for locking you up like an animal," he said, through gritted teeth.

"No," I said quickly. "It's not—it's okay. They're wonderful here. They've taken me in like I'm family." *Wonderful*, echoed a bitter voice in my mind. *And they want to execute you.*

"I can't be in here," he said, his voice barely more than a groan. "You don't understand, the bars—they're too close."

I shifted a hand so I could touch his hair through the bars. "Just take a deep breath," I whispered, the scene blurring with unshed tears. "Remember what you told me when I said I was afraid of the sky? There's nothing to be afraid of. This cage is just a thing in the world. Like any other. In the morning they'll let you out and—" *Kill you*, whispered a voice in my head. I choked, and couldn't finish the sentence.

Oren was trying to do what I said, breathing in and out in great, ragged gasps. He grasped the bars where I had held them, the iron still warm from my hands.

I took a deep breath of my own. "You're going to love it here," I whispered. "It's an orchard—did you know that? An apple orchard. At the center of this place the trees are alive again, covered in leaves and blossoms and fruit all at once. Just wait until you get to taste one of the apples."

I reached out and covered his hands with mine, and the whiteness of his knuckles eased. He lifted his head to look at me, the fierceness there tempered with something new that I couldn't identify. "Why would they let me stay?" he snapped. "I'm not like you."

Not like me. It took me long moments to gather myself to answer without my voice cracking. "I'll make sure they let you stay," I said. "You'll be fine."

Oren shifted until he was leaning against the bars, one hand still pressed against mine. "Tell me more about this place," he said.

And so I told him about the work the orchard tenders were doing, the slow pollination of each individual blossom. I told him about the market, how they traded work for goods, and the produce and fish and meat it offered. I told him about the paper animal I'd found, and that it meant my brother might still be alive. I told him about Tansy, and Tomas, and the scouts, and Dorian. I described the birds in the grove, and how they sounded like him when he made his birdcalls.

By the time the sky began to lighten in the east, my voice had grown so hoarse that even I couldn't understand half of what I said. Oren's eyes had long since closed, and his breath had calmed from the panicked, claustrophobic gasps of before. Carefully I slipped my hand from his and climbed to my feet, stiff muscles protesting and screaming at me. My foot kicked something half-buried in the dirt, and I stooped to examine the object.

Oren's knife, the blade dirty and dull.

I picked it up, cleaning the dust off on my pants, and then carefully tucked it into my waistband. He was going to want it back, once I got him out.

CHAPTER 28

"If I didn't know better," Dorian said, rubbing at the bridge of his nose with thumb and forefinger, "I'd say you were causing all of this trouble on purpose."

A week ago—no, even a day ago—that sentence would have had me cowering. Now, I merely stood, jaw clenched, hands balled at my sides. "He's a human being," I repeated. "And a good person."

"He's a *monster*," Dorian said gently, taking my hand and leading me to a chair where he all but forced me down into it.

"He's sick," I corrected him. "Nothing more. Look at him now! He's just a boy, and you have him locked in a cage—"

"Because otherwise he might try to eat one of my people!" he protested. "Lark, the last time I took your word that I could trust a stranger—"

He stopped, his expression briefly stricken. He must have seen the anguish in my face, for he rubbed a hand over his eyes and shook his head. "I'm sorry," he said softly. "I trusted him, too. Look, I know what you must be feeling, but I can't—"

"You don't know!" I spat. I would have surprised myself with my own ferocity—when did I grow such a spine?— if I didn't feel every word so strongly. "He saved my life.

Repeatedly. At great risk to himself. I wouldn't be here if it weren't for him, and I'm not going to let you kill him."

"As much as he *seems* human to you, I promise you he isn't." Dorian squatted in front of me. "He's a monster and a cannibal. He has killed people—and *eaten* them, Lark. And without remorse. There is no forgiveness for that. Just because he does not remember doing it doesn't change the fact of what he is. And if we let him live, he will kill more people, countless people, through the many long years until he dies himself, probably turned on by his own kind when he's too old and weak to fight back. The atrocities will never end. Unless we help end them ourselves, right now."

Was this why Basil had left? My brother would never have stood for the mass murder of people who were only sick. *People*, not monsters.

I shook my head. "I'll keep him safe," I said around the lump in my throat. "I won't use my power for anything but for him. I'll stay with him at every moment. *I'll keep him.*"

Dorian closed his eyes, bowing his head. "And you think he'd be willing to be kept? Maybe another day we could have tried—something, I don't know. But we're under attack. Just this evening the scouts reported machines approaching. They are clearing the mountain pass. Two days at the most." He lifted his head again, the hazel eyes sober and still. "Your city is coming for us."

My city.

"Have you decided what to do?" I asked.

Dorian rose with effort. He crossed the room to the low chest of drawers, covered with the curios and knickknacks collected over his years as the de facto ruler of these people. "I don't have a choice," he said. "Most of these people have either never been in the wilderness, or haven't set foot outside the Wood in decades. We have children, infants, elderly. You've been out there. If we scattered, and fled across the landscape, what odds do you give most of us to survive on our own? Do you think even a quarter of our people would make it?"

I thought of my mad scramble across the wilderness, how very close I came to death, again and again. Only a monster's intervention, and the invisible, guiding hand of the Institute, had kept me alive. "No," I whispered.

Dorian nodded, as though I had only confirmed something he had already decided. "And so we must fight." I started to protest, and he held up a hand. "I will, of course, try to talk to them first. But you know, I suspect, better than anyone, what results that will yield."

I fell silent, biting at my lip. This was a search decades in the making. The sheer investment of energy to power the machines to travel this far meant that it would be a one-way trip for the architects—unless they had an energy source at the other end to recharge. There was nothing that could convince them to leave the Iron Wood untouched.

I tried to imagine Tansy's mother wielding her kitchen knife against anything tougher than a melon. "Could you not—hide?"

Dorian shook his head. "The very iron that has concealed us all these years will be a beacon for them. No magic can hide that much metal. Not the way the metal can hide the magic. They already know where we are."

"Then build your wall," I said desperately. "It will mean no one else can find help here, but surely that's better than a hopeless fight. Because it *will* be hopeless."

"There isn't enough magic here," he said. "From what I understand, the Wall in your city is held up through machines powered by magic. Machines that can amplify it, use it as efficiently as possible. We don't have this technology here. Alone we can't hope to amplify it enough to hold them off."

Amplify it. Something stirred in my mind, and I stayed silent, my thoughts whirling.

"And anyway," said Dorian, straightening. "I'm not so sure it will be hopeless. They have their machines, but we have power, and strength. We have the home advantage. They will be on our terms, here."

I glanced across at him. Though his shoulders were set, determined, there were lines on his face that hadn't been there a week ago. His eyes were grim, resigned. He knew they stood no chance. But how could he ask his people to fight if they knew that?

I stood, my chair scraping against the wooden floor. "Give me a little more time with Oren," I said. My voice shook—I didn't have to fake the sound of emotion in it. "One more night."

Dorian nodded, keeping his eyes on his collection of trinkets. "Done," he said. I turned to go. "Lark," he said. I halted and looked back. He still didn't look at me, fingering a tiny carved stone creature—an elephant, I recognized from the history texts. "You could destroy them, you know. With what magic you have left. I've sensed it in you—you're not like us. You could destroy them all and save us."

I stared at his back, my heart thrashing against my ribs. What was he asking me to do?

I saw the desperation in the tension of his shoulders, the way he cradled the carved elephant in his palm. He knew what he was asking of me, and he couldn't meet my gaze.

I left without another word, too shaken to reply. The sun was rising as I climbed down the ladder. Oren was still asleep—and still human—curled on the floor of his cage. He looked smaller, confined. I forced myself to keep on walking, past the cage and out of the square.

The day passed in a flurry of preparations to fortify the village. The town was in chaos, with the scouts doing their best to rally the people into some semblance of a fighting force. Kids stared wide-eyed out of the windows of their houses, while their parents and siblings converted the market stalls and carts into barricades and shelters.

Dorian, who I had never seen outside of his house before, came down to direct the madness as much as he could. Wherever he went the chaos calmed a little, as though his confidence was infectious—though I had seen his uncertainty in the droop of his shoulders that morning.

I pleaded illness and barred myself in Tansy's house while she and her parents were outside. While the others thought I was sleeping, I searched for the blue bottle from the night before. I passed the next hour opening bottles of cider and adding the thick syrup in the vial. I stopped them back up and stuffed them under the stove, near my pallet.

Dorian summoned me into his house at sunset, and for a few panicked moments I thought he might have guessed what I planned. Perhaps I ought to have protested more, kept fighting for Oren—perhaps my acquiescence gave me away? But he only asked me questions about every machine I could remember from my city, their uses and their weaknesses, whether magic could disable them. I had little to offer—most of the machines operated inside the Institute or outside the Wall, not among the citizens. I told him how I had disabled Nix with magic, but even that now was suspect, given Kris's subterfuge and the fact that Nix was meant to travel with me and keep track of me.

Unable to bear too long in his company since he'd asked me to murder the incoming army of architects, I was inching for the door when he took a deep breath and let it out in a noisy sigh.

"Lark, I want to see something."

I froze by the door, waiting, knowing it would be something I didn't want. I heard him moving around the house, opening boxes until he found the one he wanted. Then he took my hand, and I looked down as he dropped something small and cool into my palm.

It was a tiny crystal, an oblong diamond shape only a fraction of an inch long. I stared at it, familiarity nagging at the back of my mind.

"It belonged to your brother," Dorian explained. "He always had it with him, fiddling with it. He called it a reminder. He left it behind when he moved on from this place."

I turned it over between my fingertips and a spark shot down my arm, buzzing as it passed from my skin to the crystal. I nearly dropped it in surprise. Watching the magic flutter and pulse within the crystal, I suddenly remembered.

Nix's heart. When I'd all but destroyed Nix and it lay in pieces in front of me, only its heart kept beating—the little core of magic that kept its clockwork running.

Kris's voice came back to me, as clear as if he were standing next to me speaking.

Your brother destroyed his pixie. . . .

Dorian watched me and the sparks of magic that kept leaping down my arm and through my fingers to the little crystal. "It's never once lit up for me," he said quietly. "You're different. I don't know what you are."

I could feel the thing draining away the tiny reserves of power that I had left, the way Nix absorbed my magic to keep running. With an effort, I pulled back at it, watching the flow of power down my arm slow, and then finally, stop. Beads of sweat trickled down my temples as I stared at the fluttering, leaping spark in the heart of the crystal. I tugged harder, and a tiny glimmer of power came inching reluctantly back into my fingers.

My whole hand throbbed as I drained the crystal of its stolen energy, a painstaking, aching process. When I was finished, the crystal was lifeless again, a dead translucent object sitting in the palm of my hand.

When I looked up, Dorian was staring at me, his face unreadable. I started to offer him the crystal back, and he flinched, taking a step back. Just for an instant, I saw something like fear flash across his features.

"Keep it," he whispered, swallowing. "Keep it."

He didn't want me to touch him. With a jolt, I realized he half-expected me to do to him what I'd just done with the crystal. I slid the pixie's heart into my pocket, where it would nestle against the paper bird.

Dorian had recovered some of his composure and stood watching me, lips tight. I understood now what he'd sensed in me when he shook my hand. If that core of magic had been inside a living, moving pixie, it would've died the second I took its magic away. I tried to imagine the harvester I'd encountered my first day outside the Wall—it would have had a similar core inside it, somewhere.

I had the power to stop a machine's heart. To stop any heart?

I thought Dorian might repeat what he'd asked of me that morning. I braced for it, and he watched me for a few moments, his gaze grim and fixed on mine. He didn't need to ask me again—the words were already out there. I could see the desperation in his eyes. But in the end he only thanked me for my help and sent me back out to rejoin the others.

As the people of the village were finishing their evening meals in the barricaded square, Dorian came out to speak to them. I tried to close my ears to his speech, for I couldn't quite bear it knowing what I was about to do, but he was the group's leader for a reason. He was passionate and confident, so much so that by the time he finished speaking I almost believed that the folk in the Iron Wood could hold out the coming day.

"The scouts tell me they'll be here in a day's time," said Dorian, palms flat against an iron railing. "So get some sleep. The scouts will be taking turns to keep watch—we're safe for now, and soon we're going to need all our strength." His eyes found mine, where I watched him from the window of Tansy's house. This time I met his gaze, and after a few moments he turned away.

I watched as the folk drifted back to their houses, most solemn but some confident enough to smile and joke. I thought of the harvester machine, its many hands and what damage they could do if reprogrammed to seek human prey. The memory of the delicate, needlelike fingers scrabbling over my ankle still made me shudder.

I had brought this upon them. It was my fault the machines were coming to capture each Renewable in the village, just as it was my fault Oren faced execution. I'd spent my life until now as a cog in one people's machine—could I turn around and become the instrument of another?

If I couldn't save the Iron Wood, at least I could save someone. Oren overcame more than I could know to come find me, and I had repaid that by allowing him to be captured by people who meant to kill him. They had done a lot for me here—but Oren had done more.

• • •

Tansy sat up with me that night, talking about the trivial little nothings of her life. She was as anxious as I, though for different reasons. She wasn't much older than I, but had been trained as a fighter since she was a child—and still she was frightened. Her parents slept deeply out of necessity, but she sat with me in the corner by the stove talking in a low voice.

As much as I needed her to sleep and be silent, I could not

quite bring myself to push her away. It had been a long time since I had had anything approaching a friend, particularly one who did not betray me or turn into a monster or run on magical clockwork. Despite my determination to remain as impassive and steadfast as Oren would, I let her continue far longer than I should have.

Past midnight, a barely audible tap at the door announced Tansy's turn at the watch. She got to her feet, stooping long enough to seek my hand and give it a squeeze.

"We'll be all right," she whispered. "You'll see."

She and the scout at the door vanished. I listened for a time to the sounds of her parents sleeping, gathering my courage. Outside the window, Oren's cage lay in shadow. Though he had reverted to his monstrous self by midmorning, he had been quiet all day, giving little reason to counteract Dorian's order that he not be killed yet.

With no sun to mark the passage of time, I had no way of knowing what hour it was. I found myself missing the city's sun disc.

I forced myself to turn away from the window, and retrieved the bottles of cider I'd prepared that day. They were hot from proximity to the stove. By the dim light of the coals in the stove, I wrapped the bottles in a towel to pour the cider into mugs, and placed each on a tray. Each clink of glass and ceramic made me flinch and glance over my shoulder at the dark shapes that were Tansy's sleeping parents, but they never moved. I was shocked by how they took the looming attack in stride. Perhaps it was not the first time a newcomer had brought trouble to their doorstep.

I took a tiny sip from one of the mugs, enough to hold the liquid on my tongue. I spat the mouthful out and prayed the blue liquid was sufficiently concealed—and that it was enough.

I stood before the door, tray of mugs in hand, the cold

metal of Oren's blade warming to my skin where I'd tucked it in my pants. I took deep breaths, willing the pounding of my heart to slow. No one would accept a mug of cider from someone whose hands were shaking badly enough to rattle the ceramic against the tray.

When I could lift my head without my vision swimming, I lifted the latch of the door and slipped out. As he had been the previous night, the nearest scout was leaning up against the corner of a nearby house, overlooking the square. From what I could see there were fewer of them on guard tonight—Oren's stillness throughout the day had lulled them, perhaps. Or, more likely, they simply needed more eyes on watch between here and the coming forces from the city.

"Good evening," I whispered, a few paces back from his elbow. It was the same one as the night before—the one to whom Tomas had handed the key.

He looked around until he saw me. "Don't worry," he said, no doubt mistaking the wideness of my eyes and the quickness of my breath. "We'll have plenty of warning before anything gets this far."

What harm was it to let him believe it was the coming attack I feared? I swallowed audibly and nodded, trying to summon something of relief. "I couldn't sleep," I said, launching myself into the few words I'd rehearsed for this moment. "I feel so awful about everything."

The scout smiled, teeth flashing briefly. "Don't worry," he said again. "No one faults you. Dorian's made it clear you're not to blame."

Nothing could be farther from the truth, but I smiled in return, and if the smile was a little strained and nervous, well, so was his. "Still, I wanted to do *something*. I know it isn't much," I quavered, "but I heated up some cider. It'll at least keep you warm while you're on watch."

Was that suspicion in his eyes? The eagerness with which he reached for a mug, though, proved it to be hopeful anticipation. He gave it a sniff and sighed. "Thanks, Lark." In the city, everyone had known my name, too, even those whose faces I barely recognized. I didn't fit here either. "You going to take this round to the other guys?"

I nodded. "If you think they'd want some," I said. "Is it warm enough?" No point in spreading it around if they'd detect the bitterness and spit out the first mouthfuls they took.

He took a cautious sip, and then a second, longer one. "Yep. Thanks."

I left him cradling the mug in both hands below his face, the steam curling up around his chin. By the time I'd visited each scout around the square I had lost any fear that they would detect the drug I'd added to it. I felt eyes on me as I made my way around the square, and knew without looking that the creature in the cage was tracking each movement I made with the patient, hungry diligence of a hunter.

As I brought the tray and leftover mugs back into the house, the guard I'd spoken to first was already nodding. His head drooped low on his chest, and he was sagging where he was propped up against the corner. I carefully took the mug dangling from his fingertips, retrieving it before he could drop it.

"Thanks, Lark," he mumbled, and then he slid down the side of the house. A sudden stab of fear coursed through me— had I put in too much? How dangerous was this drug?

I leaned the tray up against Tansy's house and hurried back to the scout. As I started to feel for his wrist he began to snore. I startled back, relief as palpable as the cold pervading the square.

All around the square I could see that the other scouts were in similar states. I stooped and quickly began going through the guard's pockets, trying to keep my fingers as light as possible. His snoring continued unabated, a gentle rumble that assured me he wouldn't wake. It wasn't until I realized I was checking the same pockets all over again that a stab of fear coursed through me. The key wasn't there.

I gazed across the square, toward the iron cage. *You can't magic iron*, I thought. I had failed him. I fought to keep my eyes dry and my throat clear. At least I would not let him see me cry.

With my ears tuned for the slightest sound of someone else coming, I crept out into the dappled moonlight and toward Oren's cage.

CHAPTER 29

He was waiting for me when I arrived. At some point during my circuit around the square, the change had occurred and he was himself again. He was watching me much the way he had been before, though the manner of his stare had changed, softened. Less animal.

He sat leaning against the bars at his back, feet crossed at the ankles and his hands loosely draped over his knees. He looked for all the world as though he was sitting comfortably by a campfire, though the confines of the cage would hardly let him assume any other position.

We stared at each other through the bars of the cage. Finally, I licked my lips and managed to whisper, "Hi."

He scarcely acknowledged the greeting, blinking once, the gleam of moonlight reflected in his eyes cutting out and then returning. After a time, he lifted his head a fraction and said quietly, "I'm one of them, aren't I?"

"One of—" My voice caught in my throat.

"The dark ones." There was little to be seen in his face, as impassive as ever. If anything his voice was flatter, emptier than I'd ever heard it before.

"How did you—"

"There are moments in the dark times," he said, "when I almost know myself. And I'm still in this cage. I get confused. Not stupid."

I gazed at him and he gazed back. There wasn't an ounce of self-pity in his face. If it had been me I would have been howling my innocence, begging to be released. He sat and looked at me, hands resting loosely on his knees.

"What do they have planned?" he asked eventually, breaking the silence.

"They gave me this night," I whispered. "A little time. And then they'll—" My jaw clenched so tightly I almost couldn't bring myself to speak. "I won't let them. That's why I'm here."

"I'm not afraid," he said, pale eyes darkening, intensifying. He leaned forward, the fierce angles of his face bisected in the middle by an iron bar that cast a sharp shadow against his cheekbone. "If this is what I am, then I *should* die." I'd heard that kind of single-minded bloodlust in his voice before, at the summer lake. When he'd told me that it didn't matter that the shadow woman and her child were human inside the magic. When he'd told me they all deserved to die.

"No," I said fiercely, before I remembered to keep my voice low. "You're not a monster. They can't see you for what you are."

"I'm only different because of the time I've spent with you," said Oren. He had yet to raise his voice at all, keeping it pitched low. He didn't whisper, but spoke with a quiet grace that made me want to tear through the bars of his cage to get him out. "It's easy to see it, looking back. The longer I stayed with you the clearer the world became. I just thought it was—" He shook his head sharply. This time, though, I recognized that flash of irritation for the intimacy it was. He certainly didn't let anyone else see his emotions. "I just thought it was *you*."

I leaned forward and wrapped my hands around the bars, as though my touch might melt them away. "If I bring you to Dorian you can tell him that you're not a monster, and he'll stop them from hurting you. I know we can make him see it. I'll stay by you and keep you—keep you human. Keep you safe." I bowed my head, pressing my forehead against the iron.

Oren reached out, brushing the backs of my fingers with his. "I don't want to be *kept*," he said softly, prompting me to lift my head again.

My face must have been a wreck with withheld tears and sleep deprivation, but he didn't flinch away, the corner of his mouth lifting. I pulled my hands away from the bars and went to the door of his cage. If Dorian believed I was powerful enough to wipe out an army, then surely I was strong enough for this.

"It's locked," Oren said, turning to watch me.

"I don't need a key," I muttered.

"Lark," he said. "It's iron. Even I know by now that you can't magic iron."

"The trees were turned to iron with magic. Iron is just a thing in the world," I said, lifting the iron padlock in one hand. It sat in my palm, heavy and cold. "Like any other." I closed my eyes, searching for that tiny grain of energy I had left.

"You'll hurt yourself," warned Oren. "Remember the last magic you did? I had to carry you back to the summer lake. You were so light I thought you might break."

"I won't," I said. "I know how to do it now." It was only partly a lie. Dorian's words—about channeling, amplifying power—had struck something in me that made more sense than I would have admitted to him. He had told me, after all, that I had an ability to manipulate magic, to amplify it, that anyone would have envied.

I found that knot inside me, the tiny last vestiges of power that were left to me from the Institute. I understood now why it had always been so painful, using that power, the way it had snapped out of me like the shattering of a bone. They'd put it there, some alien force synthesized in their laboratory. No wonder it felt as though I was breaking.

The lock grew warmer as I concentrated—but warming to the heat of my hand, or to the power I was trying to access, I could not tell.

"Lark!" Oren said sharply, reaching through the bars and grabbing my wrist. "Snap out of it! I'm not leaving this cage if you open the lock. Lark, *I need to be put down.* If I'm free I *will* kill people."

"No!" My eyes snapped open, vision blurring with weary tears. "They intend to execute you in the morning and I will *not* stand by and let them kill you, not when I can do something about it. I don't care about what you've done and I don't care about what you might do; I only care about what you are to me, and if you don't sit down and let me do this I will drug you senseless and drag you into the woods and leave you there."

I blinked the moisture away from my eyes and saw that he was staring at me in silence, all expression gone again from his face. I cleared my throat and whispered, "If it were me, would you sit here and let me die?"

I longed for him to speak, but all he did was sit there and gaze at me with that infuriatingly impassive stare. Then, slowly, finger by finger, he let go of my wrist.

I turned my attention back to the lock, grateful to have something to focus on other than the boy in the cage. My stomach was surging so that I scarcely noticed the fog descending in my head, the dizziness overtaking me. As I closed my eyes again the metal grew hot in my hand.

The blood roared in my ears as I willed that power to snap out of me. There wasn't much left. It was as though being told I was losing it had created my awareness of it. Now I could sense all too clearly that the power was almost gone.

I summoned up—for the last time?—the image of my brother's paper bird, the ringing sensation of that first magic. It had been before the Institute had done anything to me. That first time, the power had been all mine. I tried to find that reserve and instead found emptiness.

When I opened my eyes again my vision clicked and changed. I could see Oren next to me, a power sink, each tendril of energy I raised sucked away into him. He was a dark pit of nothing, whereas I could see shining tangles of energy all around that were the sleeping scouts, the families in their houses beyond, and those on watch for the Institute. It was like the flashes of iridescence I'd seen in the pockets, only they were flashes no more. Gleaming, glittering, I could see it all— the power everywhere, waiting to be tapped.

Shaking with effort, I poured all of myself into the padlock. The images of the shining people all around the square wavered, lines of their power snapping to me like lightning to a tower. My stomach wrenched so hard I was sure it could no longer be connected to the rest of me. I gasped and dropped the lock. It fell open, swung once with the momentum, and rocked off the door. The metal blade tucked into my pants burned hot against my skin.

I stood staring at the lock as Oren pushed open the door. I felt empty and hollow. What had I just done?

Oren had climbed out of his cage and had taken hold of my shoulders, was saying something urgently. He gave me the tiniest of shakes. I swam back to the present and looked up, startled.

"—need to sit down?"

"I'm—fine," I gasped. I realized as soon as I spoke that the words weren't a lie. I hadn't felt so whole since Harvest Day. The magic was gone—and all that was left was me.

Oren gazed hard at me. It was as though he was searching for something in my face, and I was glad I had not had to lie. I felt certain he would have known. That gaze was so forceful—such a mix of human concern and animal ferocity—that I had to close my eyes and block him out. I expected him to insist I sit down, rest, eat something, that my closing my eyes would make him think I was on the verge of collapse.

"You said 'what you are to me,'" he said instead. There was something strange and unfamiliar in his voice that prompted me to open my eyes and look at him, startled. It was very faint, but I had come to know that face and its subtleties, and I saw it for what it was: surprise.

"Yes."

"You know that I'm a monster."

What good was arguing with him now? I swallowed and whispered, "Yes."

He closed his eyes and then dropped his head. When he looked up again, the moment of surprise was gone and he was as quiet and unreadable as ever. My legs felt weak, felt like the weight of his hands might drive me to my knees.

As if he could detect my weakness, he let his hands fall to his sides. "We should get moving," he said, his voice rough. "Dawn is coming."

"We," I repeated. I had meant it as a question but my voice emerged so softly that it was only an echo.

He took a step back, looking at me. I had not realized how close we'd been standing. "We," he said firmly. "You didn't free me and expect me to leave you here alone?"

"I can't go with you," I whispered. The hollowness in my stomach was a yawning pit, threatening to swallow me from the inside out. Was this what people felt like in the city when they had been harvested?

"You have to," said Oren. "I need you. To stay human."

I shook my head. The pace and a half between us gaped like a canyon, and I stared across the gulf at him. "I'm not a Renewable," I said. My voice didn't sound like my own—it was as if someone had taken over to explain the situation to him. I let the voice continue, too fearful to take control back and soften the blow. "I'm an experiment. The Institute created me, gave me the power, everything. I have nothing left. I used the rest of it opening that lock. If we leave here together then it will be only a matter of time before . . ."

It was as if I'd managed to steal the years from him. His shoulders sagged like an old man's, the sharply angled face suddenly hollow-cheeked and weary. "Before I turn, and I kill you," he finished for me.

I nodded.

"You should have let them kill me," he said quietly. "You let me think that if I could suffer to be kept, if you stayed by me, I'd stay whole." His face had changed, the eyes cold and glittering. "You let me think I'd stay myself."

"I couldn't let them kill you," I said. I felt like the phonograph. I repeated the words over and over and every time they seemed to hold less. "I couldn't," I said again.

"Why would you think I'd want to live if—" His lips pressed together. I wished he'd look away, be unable to look at me, turn his sudden anger onto some other target. But he only stared, and I burned and twisted but couldn't look away.

"Because even being a monster is better than being dead."

He stood staring at me, cold and tense. My eyes began to water with the effort of gazing back at him, and I blinked the tears away and dropped my eyes. "You should go," I said tightly. "If dawn is so close, you need to be moving before daylight to avoid being seen."

Oren said nothing, jaw still clenched.

"Cut north from here," I said. "That's where the grove is. There are apples there—you can bring some with you for supplies. Keep north when you leave; that's where the scouts are thinnest."

"Lark," he said, trying to interrupt me.

"If you move quickly, maybe you can make the nearest pocket of magic before you—before you change."

"Lark!"

"Be safe," I said, staring at his threadbare T-shirt, unable to lift my head and meet his eye. "Please, Oren, be saf—"

He took a step forward and covered my mouth with his hand. He smelled of blood and grass and the wild wind. "Be *still*," he said fiercely. "Do you never stop talking?"

He curled his fingers into the hair at the nape of my neck. He touched his lips to mine. The lips of a monster. I must have made some small sound, for he drew back abruptly. He scanned my face. I was too stupid with the ringing in my ears and burning of my lips to know what he saw in my expression.

Whatever he found there changed him. He stepped forward, closing the gap between us again. This time there was an urgency to his kiss that broke my heart. I could taste him— the metallic tang of his mouth. The taste of blood.

A monster. A murderer. A cannibal.

I shoved him away, gasping for air. "Don't," I panted. "Don't touch me." I shuddered, revulsion coursing through me.

I could feel him watching me, though I did not dare lift my head to look at him. I could imagine the hurt there. How many times had I told him he wasn't a monster? I longed to turn and put my arms around him and tell him I didn't mean it, but I knew that if I did I would be lying. How could I let hands that had torn people apart touch me?

No. What I wanted was to go back, unlearn what I had learned, make him again just a boy, helping a girl, lost in the wilderness.

Neither of us spoke to fill the silence. In the distance I heard an early bird give a questioning chirp. There was a horrible lightness to the east.

"Go," I croaked.

"I'll find you," he said, turning away from me as if the sight of me was enough to remind him of what he was. He rubbed a hand over his face, leaving it clamped over his mouth so that it muffled his next words. "Even in the dark—" and I knew he did not mean nighttime when he said *dark*—"I can see you. You shine."

"Please go," I said. I wanted to change what I had done, let him leave believing things could be different. But I couldn't take back what I'd said. And dawn was near.

"Monster or human I can't not follow you. I've tried."

"Oren," I begged, shaking with the effort of staying put. "Please go. *Please*."

"If I find you—and if I'm not me—promise me that you'll kill me, Lark."

"Oren—"

"Promise me!"

He had never shouted at me, not with such force and such intensity. Once the fierceness of his gaze would have terrified me. Now I only saw the fear behind his own eyes. He was trapped like an animal in a corner. And like an animal, he lashed out.

"I promise," I whispered. Behind me I heard a faint groan, a response to Oren's shout. The scouts were waking up. "Now go."

He turned back around, as I feared and hoped he would. I knew it would be the last time I saw him—certainly the last time I saw him as he was now. He was watching me in the expressionless way that had once driven me so crazy, but now only made me feel as though my bones were slowly turning to water. The hot metal of the blade tucked into my waistband was cooling again, adjusting to my body temperature. I grabbed at the handle and stretched it toward him.

He shook his head. "Keep it. I won't need it where I'm going."

Where I'm going, into the dark. I closed my fingers around the handle of the knife so tightly my hand shook.

"I would have kept you safe," I whispered.

He smiled, the expression sudden and uncertain and surprised—but he smiled nonetheless. "I know," he said. He half-turned, reaching out to swing the cage door closed again with a tiny click. And then he hesitated for a long moment, his weight resting against the top of the cage. Then he pushed back from it and walked away, the first glow of dawn only enough to see him until the edge of the houses. After that there was only shadow, and the sounds of the birds waking to the dawn.

CHAPTER 30

I went back to the house, stumbling in the dark and shaking. I had to get my supplies, gather what I needed to survive on my own. My bird. Oren's lighter. My pack. And now, of course, a knife.

My hands shook as I began shoving things into the badly frayed fabric that served as my pack. I dropped things, cursed under my breath, bit back sobs. My mind wasn't working, instead playing back the moment. Oren's lips; his fingertips curling in my hair; the smell of grass and wind. Over and over, like the record player, like the pocket with the ghosts. I was so shaken that when a hand reached out of the darkness to cover mine I barely jumped. I just stared, breathing hard.

"Take this," said Tansy, kneeling at my side and pressing something cold and leathery into my hands. I looked down, running my hands over it. A backpack. A proper one.

I looked up. Light from outside barely illuminated her cheeks. My mouth worked, but I could think of no words.

"You're running, aren't you?" Despite the words, it wasn't a question. Tansy took over, transferring food and belongings into the new backpack.

"Tansy," I croaked. My voice had frozen in the time since Oren had left my side, and I struggled to clear my throat. "I'm not a fighter. It isn't—"

"I saw what you did, helping the prisoner escape. You have to go, or you'll be the one in the cage." She added food to the belongings in the pack, taking what I would not have dared to take. Apples, skins full of water. "You cured him."

I shook my head, eyes burning. "Not cured. He'll turn back eventually. I just couldn't—not after everything. I couldn't watch him die."

Tansy was quiet a few moments, adding the last few things to the pack. "You said you're not a fighter, but you're wrong. You fight for the people you love." She cinched the pack shut with a jerk and then lifted her head. I could just make out her expression—sad and a little hurt. But determined.

I realized I was still wearing her coat. I started to pull it off, but she reached forward and put her hands on my shoulders. "Keep it," she said. "Too small for me anyway."

Our faces were only a few inches apart, our voices low in the quiet of morning. Her parents still slept.

"Why are you helping me?" I whispered. "I've destroyed everything."

Tansy gazed back at me, her expression strange, unreadable for the first time. "Because I try to fight for the people I love, too. And still, iron bars might have stopped me." I realized what was in her expression that I hadn't been able to identify: admiration.

She leaned forward, wrapping her arms around me for a moment. It was awkward, both of us kneeling, the pack between us. But after a few seconds I put my arms around her, too.

"Thank you."

And then she was gone, pulling back and rising to her feet,

immediately on alert, on the prowl. She melted away, vanishing through the door to join the scouts on duty. It was too early for her to relieve anyone, but I knew she didn't want to see me go. I wish I could have found the words to tell her that I'd fight for her, too, if I could.

But that would have been a lie. If what Dorian said was true, I could have destroyed the incoming army. I just didn't have the strength.

. . .

I headed east. Now and then I could still see the beings of light I'd seen while trying to open the lock, as though they were afterimages burned into my retinas. It was as though opening the lock had opened something else, some second sight. I could see the network of power, the energy and the iron muffling it.

All around in the iron trees were the scouts, watching for any sign of intruders. The city's forces weren't expected until night fell again, but Dorian wasn't taking any chances. They were well-trained from the years of defending the Wood from the shadow people.

From Oren.

I pushed the thought away. I couldn't afford to think of it, not now. I could see the positions of the scouts—each a tangle of white-gold threads, shining in the muffled blackness that was the forest of iron trees.

There—a gap in their network. They were far enough apart that perhaps, if I were careful and quiet, I could slip through unnoticed. Just because Dorian was letting me go didn't mean the scouts wouldn't stop me.

I made for the gap, moving silently enough that Oren would have been proud.

My thoughts lurched and I cast the name away. My lips throbbed, and I touched them with my fingertips like a child who has burned her mouth. They would be bruised. *If I live long enough for bruises to form.*

The city would be coming from the east. When I reached the edge of the iron trees I could cut south, and give the oncoming forces a wide berth. I could make for the summer lake, perhaps, or the world of the bees, if I could retrace our path. Perhaps there I could survive long enough to figure out where to go next.

Could I abandon the Wood to its fate? Did I have a choice? I could not believe Dorian really intended for me to destroy the oncoming army. Administrator Gloriette was the last person in the world I ever wanted to see again, but I couldn't imagine actually killing her. And Kris would be out there somewhere, too.

Oren's knife lay cold and snug in my pocket, against my leg. I had kept it as a tool for survival—not a weapon for killing, as Oren had used it.

Hadn't I?

The Institute, wanting me to participate in the destruction of a whole village; the Iron Wood, begging me to slaughter an entire army of my own people; even Oren, demanding that I kill him, and every other shadow person I encountered, because there was no redemption for them. I shifted the straps on my pack and hunched my shoulders against the morning chill, ducking through the forest unseen. Running away.

Like Basil did. Now I knew why he left. But did he sneak away while everyone was asleep?

Besides, the village was well-fortified. The scouts had years of training fighting the shadow people. They knew the city was coming. They were ready. Perhaps they could win.

My mind, so desperate to alleviate my guilt, seized upon the idea, echoing it until I had no choice but to believe it could be true.

I focused upon the second sight, tracking the movements of the scouts by the white-gold trails of power they emanated. I stumbled more than once, but when I tripped over something soft my body automatically shifted its weight to avoid stepping on it, and I fell heavily.

I picked myself off whatever I'd landed on, and my heart stopped as I saw what—who—it was.

Tansy.

I stared, uncomprehending. How long since she'd left the house? She wasn't even yet to her post. Her face was lax, unresponsive. I shook her, and her head lolled to one side. Why hadn't I seen her aura of power? Unless—*Oh God, no. Please. Tansy.*

I fumbled for her wrist, too panicked to detect a pulse. I leaned close, putting my cheek to her lips. It took several long moments before I realized that there was a slight warmth stirring the hair at my temple. She was breathing. I realized that I hadn't seen her power because it was a clear, dry day—not wet enough for it to manifest as clearly as it did with the other scouts. Now that I was close enough I could see tiny flickers around the edges of my vision.

I reached again for her pulse, this time at her throat. My fingers encountered the tiniest of holes, now barely more than a red welt against her skin. I'd seen a mark like that before, once. Kris. After he'd been stung by Nix.

I stared at Tansy's unconscious form, my mind refusing to process what I was seeing. Had Nix returned? But if so, why would it attack my friends?

As I stared, I became aware of the tiniest hints of a sound at the edge of my hearing. The muffling effects of the iron kept the magical hum to a minimum, but I could hear the sound of clockwork, hissing silently through the wood.

Pixies.

One darted into the area, the dim light of dawn glinting off its wings. It looked the same as the ones in the city—lacked Nix's larger size and eyes—except that, like Nix, it bore a long needle at the end of its abdomen.

I held my breath, cursing that I had no power with which to smash it, but it didn't notice my presence. It zipped by as I ducked down, covering Tansy's body with my own.

Of course. They had no eyes—only sensors for magic. Tansy barely had any power and they still detected her. I no longer had any at all.

All across the Wood, my second sight picked out forms that were falling from trees and slumping over where they stood. The silent advance of the pixies was taking out the scouts, one by one.

But it was too soon. The city wasn't expected until tonight at the earliest. In my mind's eye I saw the harvester machines plowing through the Wood, destroying the houses, tearing apart the home that had adopted me. Walkers crushing the orchard, brushing aside the wooden bridges and rope ladders like spiderwebs. I carefully dragged Tansy toward the sheltering crook of a tree, praying no one would find her.

They didn't know pixies here. Nix was the only one they'd seen, and what reason did they have to fear it? They couldn't know—couldn't hope to defend themselves. *Unless someone warns them.*

The sun was rising to the east. Through the gaps in the iron foliage I could guess that it was cresting the mountains. Somewhere nestled in a pass was the summer lake. I took a long breath, and then turned my back to the sun, and ran back toward the village.

Pixies swarmed past me, never once registering my presence. The cold autumn air tore at my lungs until spots swam in front of my eyes. One of the pixies buzzed so closely by my face that its copper wing drew a tiny line of fire across my cheek.

When I burst back into the square, expecting to see scenes of battle and carnage and pixies screaming madly through the air, I skidded to a halt. All was silent. For one bright moment I thought I might have beaten them to the village, until I caught a glimpse of copper flitting from one of the windows.

The pixies were slipping in and out of each house, delivering whatever soporific venom they carried. The scouts posted around the square, who had been stirring and coming awake as I left, were now still and silent.

The fight for the Iron Wood was over before it had even begun.

As I stood, I saw the lines of power all around me waver and flicker again the way they had when I was trying to open the lock.

I'm not certain what you are, Dorian had told me. *But you have an ability to manipulate power that any one of us would envy.*

Without thinking, I searched for that emptiness inside me and opened it to the flickering power all around. As I reached out for them, the lines snapped to me like arcs of lightning, filling me with energy. I gasped and opened my eyes. Something in my gut tingled. Maybe it didn't matter what I was.

Maybe it only mattered what I was going to do.

From somewhere in the Wood came a crashing and groaning that made the uncertain hope in my heart plummet again. Something was tearing through the trees. I turned my back on the village, facing the sounds of destruction and planting my feet as though my body might convince my mind not to run.

I had never heard so many machines at once before. Together they made the ground shake with vibrations from countless clockwork whispers. Overhead, the iron leaves trembled.

As the sound grew deafening, I began to see glimpses of daylight through the trees. When the machines burst out of the thickest part of the Wood, I only barely managed to hold my ground.

They had cut a swath through the Wood, iron and all, with machines that bore blades and white-blue fire. Spreading across the valley of destruction before me was an army like none I could have imagined. Machines I couldn't name, had never seen before, could not have dreamed of, all rolling and floating and crawling toward the forest and the iron world it hid. There were harvesters and planters and police walkers, and mechanimal dogs baying and screeching as they leapt forward, and everywhere the seething, darting flocks of pixies. The sound of the clockwork was one whispering roar, like thunder past the horizon, only it never subsided—only swelled and swelled.

Here and there a splash of red told of the architects marching with them, some on foot, others in the police walkers. Kris must have come in such a vehicle. I wondered if he was there somewhere, lost in the sea of seething red and copper. When I gazed across the new valley cut through the Wood with the strange second sight I'd discovered while trying to open the lock, the machines glowed with the power sustaining their mechanisms.

Still uncertain what I meant to do, I walked out of the shadow of the forest and toward the approaching army. Overhead the sky was streaked with spun-sugar clouds, set aglow by the sunrise. As those at the front of the horde saw me, a ripple spread outward and, with an unimaginable racket of clockwork, the machines came to a halt.

From the middle of the army a harvester detached itself from a fleet of other machines and came hurtling toward the front on its six jointed legs. Unlike the empty, automated one

I had encountered in the city gardens, this one had a driver. I knew who was inside before it had stopped and its occupant stepped out.

"Hello, gosling," said Administrator Gloriette, clasping her hands in front of her stomach—undiminished by her apparently easy journey from the city. "We've been *so* worried about you, poor thing. How are you?" Her voice dripped with sickening deceit. Beside her, the needle-tipped fingers of the harvester stirred idly, waiting for orders.

"I've been better," I said, watching her closely. She seemed different somehow. Flatter, as though she was a character in a storybook, painted onto the glorious morning spreading across the valley. Behind her another figure came into view, sitting in the carriage of the machine and watching.

Kris.

His face was locked down, so blank I almost didn't recognize him. His teeth were clenched so tightly that the muscles stood out along his jaw.

"You've done so marvelously well," Gloriette went on. Her eyes were hard and edged like razors, despite the saccharine voice that oozed from her mouth. She was watching me as carefully as I was her. "But I always knew you'd manage it."

Something moved just at the edge of my vision—a shadow darted from one heap of mangled iron tree to another. The breath went out of me for a moment, until I realized that it wasn't Oren.

One of the scouts had escaped the pixies' advance, slipped through somehow. With a monumental effort, I kept my eyes on Gloriette. *Keep her talking.*

I lifted my chin. "When you spoke to me through the pixie, you said that you knew where Basil was," I said. "And that you would tell me how to find him if I came back with you without a fight. Kris said that if I went back with you now, you could undo what you did to me. And help me find my brother."

A flicker ran through Kris's expression as he shifted his gaze from me to Gloriette, and back to me again. The tiniest flash—of hope. Maybe he thought I was considering returning with them after all.

"Yes," said Gloriette, one perfectly shaped eyebrow lifting in query.

The scout crept closer, keeping piles of debris between him and the machines. With a jolt, I recognized Tomas. I wanted to scream at him to get back—what could he possibly do against an army of machines?

But if I warned him away, I'd betray his position. The architects would spot him.

I swallowed, meeting Gloriette's gaze. "If I come back with you now, and you leave this place alone, does that offer still stand?"

Her lips pursed in a simper. "I hardly think you're in any position to be negotiating, duck. If Kris is correct, then you have barely any power left with which to fight. And certainly not enough to be of use to us. Besides," she added as she surveyed the village, "we're about to take possession of enough Renewables to preserve the Wall for generations."

"Does the offer still stand?" I repeated, my jaw clenching.

Gloriette watched me for a few long seconds and then shrugged, turning her back. "No," she said. "There is no cure for you. But we had to tell our boy something to get him on board, didn't we?"

She turned, her bulk briefly concealing Kris. I saw a flash of his face as Gloriette climbed back into the carriage. His eyes were stricken, raw—he scrambled forward, trying to shove past Gloriette to get to me.

"Lark—!"

The door slammed. Tomas chose that moment to strike, launching himself out of hiding and at the harvester. Without even blinking Gloriette passed her hand over one of the controls, and one of the heavy metal legs shot out and slammed into Tomas's body, smashing him to the ground.

He started to crawl away but the harvester shifted its weight, one leg coming down and pinning Tomas's knee beneath it. His scream rang through the metal forest.

I stood frozen, horror turning my limbs to ice. Tomas's hands clawed at the earth, trying to pull himself away. Through the machine's carriage window, Gloriette just looked down at him, studying him like an insect, one hand toying with the architect's compass around her neck. At another twitch from her other hand, the machine shifted again. The cracking of bone was audible even over the sound of a thousand clockwork mechanisms thrumming, and Tomas's agonized scream.

I saw Tomas's power fluctuating wildly, and finally found my voice. "Stop it!" I screamed, throwing myself forward. "I said I'd go back with you! That's what you want, isn't it? Just take me and leave these people alone."

Gloriette leaned back, looking down at me with a smile. "My dear," she said lightly, "What would give you the idea that we would even want you? Your part in all of this is finished."

She inclined her head, signaling to the machines around her to carry on. All across the valley the army roared to life and began to pick up speed again.

Gloriette's harvester moved forward. The leg crushing Tomas's knee lifted, only to come down again on his shoulder. I ran to him as the machines swarmed around us, parting like the sea around a stone on the shore.

He was still alive. I couldn't tell if he saw me at all through his pain—his eyes were fixed somewhere past my face, his mouth moving as though he wanted to speak. The second blow had crushed part of his ribcage—the flattened grass around him was rapidly becoming soaked with his blood. Too much blood—too much damage. My mind was blank, panicked—there was nothing I could do except watch him suffer.

Helplessly I reached out and touched his face with my fingertips, and saw the halo of energy around him snap to my hand, electric and raw. Tomas's breath rattled painfully in the one side of his chest still trying to rise.

I bent my head and placed both my hands against him, palms flat, and felt the power surge into me. The lines of pain etched into Tomas's face eased a little, his eyes widening. The suffering seemed to ease. I closed my eyes and kept pulling, letting the energy trickle into the empty void that had once held my own magic.

It wasn't until I felt the last trickle of power leave him that I opened my eyes. His face was calm, relaxed, eyes still fixed on the sky beyond my face. His chest was still, his labored breathing ceased. I swallowed and closed his eyes, my hand shaking.

I stood slowly and watched the machines as they passed me. My new second sight showed them as different than the people in the Wood—mutated and dark. Synthesized and false, torn from the Renewable's body and injected into clockwork hearts. It twisted and flapped as if loose in a breeze. It snapped as the mechanisms turned over—snapped like the breaking of bones.

You fight for the people you love, came Tansy's voice. I saw her form lying unconscious on the ground, and something within me snapped.

I touched the hollowness in my stomach, the hole where their synthetic power had once nestled. Tomas's energy nestled there, a tiny spark in the emptiness. Suddenly I realized what Dorian had sensed in me. I let the tension drain from my body and *opened*, pulling with every ounce of strength I had.

Behind me, I heard the sound of a thousand needle-fingered hands clicking and extending, and then the screaming of iron and earth. The machines were tearing the rest of the path for the army through the forest.

Though the touch of it sickened me I cast my net wide and caught at the threads of power flapping free from the hearts of the machines. The threads snagged and caught the pull of the void, and with snaps and jagged floods came shooting to me.

The subtle roar of a thousand clockwork hearts faltered. As the noise dimmed it broke from a single thrum into a thousand different beats, and as one by one they began to fail, the cries of the red coats became audible over the din. Curses at first, a hundred people blaming a hundred different people. Then confusion and disbelief, as walkers toppled to the ground and harvesters halted mid-destruction. Then terror, slow and subtle at first and building to a wave that swept over the army like a fire.

The power was not enough. Soon they would be upon the village, and the helpless unconscious people within it. I needed more.

I opened the pit inside me as wide as I could manage, and with a silent flash, bolts of the villagers' energy arced toward me. The void began to fill. The power rushed to me like lightning, with all the magic around me flying to me in a fraction of a second.

Then came a distant sound—cries and groans of pain from the Wood. The pain of being harvested—a pain I knew all too well, strong enough to rouse them from their artificial sleep. Somewhere I heard a child scream, and in my mind's eye I saw a tiny, dirty face falling into the shadows after I threw it from a cliff.

I tried to stop, cut off the flow of energy, but it was like trying to stop a river with my fingers. It came rushing in from everything around me—the people, the machines, the ground beneath my feet. The more I took the more I hungered—the pull grew stronger and stronger until even the trees around me, iron, unmovable, gave up their magic with a dull screech of metal.

A flash of a memory came to me—a woman wreathed in white, power flowing from her veins, carried away by glass wires. If I let the memory blur, I couldn't tell whether the power was flowing away or flooding into her. I opened my eyes and saw white, the power around me shining so hotly that the air was burning.

Dimly I heard Gloriette's shrill voice commanding that someone stop me, crush me, kill me. The few machines still standing came at me, only to crumple to the ground as they, too, surrendered their magic to me. Pixies flew at me, stingers extending, screaming—only to drop to the ground, still and dead. The sick and twisted stolen energy of the machines flowed into the white flood from the people of Iron Wood and was changed, stripped of its impurities, intensified into something greater.

All around me I could hear bodies dropping. The shock of having the power stolen away in a vacuum that sucked at your soul must have been overwhelming. I was doing to them what had been done to me—and yet, once begun, I couldn't stop.

The light in the world around me flickered, draining. People fell to the ground, twitching, then going still. I tried to stop, my whole body screaming in pain, but the rush of power was so intense that I couldn't turn away.

The world outside me was silent. All the clockwork was still now and the people just as quiet. The power screamed in my ears; now that I had taken it into myself the world hummed with energy, so blinding and deafening that I was certain I would be left in silent darkness forever when it was done. Overhead clouds of roiling green and violet rushed in, singing with power and lapping at the Wood with tongues of brilliant energy. A magical storm.

All was heat, and noise, and pain. My body was nothing but a vessel, bursting with magic. At any moment my skin would crack and spill energy instead of blood, leaving me to burn in a vortex of smoke and steam.

Something collided with me, knocking me to the ground and snapping my head on the earth.

The power exploded. The vessel was left empty—and for a blessed instant, everything went black.

CHAPTER 31

I opened my eyes to see a face leaning over me, a muffled voice calling my name. I blinked, trying to clear the fuzziness from my vision.

"Tansy?" My voice was unrecognizable even to me, but it drew such a smile from the girl leaning over me that she must have understood.

"Lark," she replied, panting. Her face was as flushed as if she'd been running. As she lifted her hand to run the back of it across her brow, I saw that the palms of her hands were scorched.

"What? How?" All around us, the field of machines and people, equally still and silent, bore the evidence of what had transpired. Tansy alone was alive. I stared at the aftermath of what I'd done, unable to understand.

"I don't know," she gasped. "Maybe because it's not raining, it didn't hurt me."

I rolled onto my back. Above me the sky was wheeling, blurry and shimmering in eyes that had not quite remembered yet how to work properly. The dark green sky of the magical storm I'd summoned had vanished. Beyond, the spun-sugar clouds marking the dawn had lightened, pale pink and yellow against the deepening blue sky. Through the path torn away by the machines I could see that the sun had barely cleared the mountains to the east.

Struggling onto my elbows, I looked toward the village. Something shimmered through my vision that I dismissed as an artifact of my stunned sight. It drew my eye, however, to the trees—trees that would have been familiar had they been gray and cold. . . .

The whole of the Wood had changed. I could see pale blossoms and red apples spotting the branches, bobbing in the breeze that had picked up across the plain. And just there, at its edge, what I had dismissed as my eyes playing tricks on me: something shimmering and wavering.

It was not like the tarnished pewter of the outside of the city's Wall—it was not even like the violet shimmer of the magical pockets. It glinted in the sun, mostly invisible, only a waver in the air to tell it was there. I could see the other scouts and villagers behind it, the shimmering curtain standing between them and the city's machines.

"I think it's a barrier," said Tansy, seeing me staring. "You made it."

"I've done it once before." The force that had knocked the shadow child away from Oren, enclosing us both in that shimmering barrier of protection—but it had felt nothing like this. And had not cost nearly so much. I felt hollow, empty, all the power I'd absorbed gone in that blinding instant when Tansy had knocked me to the ground.

Nearby a red-coated architect stirred, first twitching a hand and then groaning. My heart leapt. All around us people began to stir, and a band of panic eased around my chest. On the other side of the barrier, the villagers of the Iron Wood were moving as well. I took a shaky breath. "I didn't kill them," I whispered. Dizzying relief washed over me.

"They're fine," Tansy said firmly, almost as if trying to convince herself as well. She looked nearly as shaken as I was.

"They wouldn't be if you hadn't stopped me," I said as I sat up with difficulty, lifting myself on shaking arms. "Are you okay?"

"I'll be fine," she replied. "A bit—wobbly. I've never had my power taken like that. Are *you* okay?"

"I think I am." As the shock ebbed, I shut my eyes. I was no better than the city that drove me away. Despite the sick dread in the pit of my stomach, I felt a strange thrill. It had been so easy to reach out and let all the power flow into me. It'd be easy to do it again.

"Thank you," Tansy said softly.

"I had no choice," I said, shaking my head. "I brought them here."

"You could've run," she argued. "You had a choice. That you thought you didn't, though, is oddly comforting. Thank you, anyway."

I got to my feet, finding my legs steadier than I expected. Tansy rose too, but slowly, like a woman many times her age. She moved painfully.

I turned to look across the field of dead machines and feebly stirring architects. While I watched, one tried to crawl forward through the barrier, only to be repelled by its energy. A few scouts ventured beyond the barrier's protection and back again, testing its limits. For now, the Iron Wood was safe.

As though she could read my thoughts, Tansy said tentatively, "You—could stay. Dorian would help you learn to control . . . whatever this is."

I looked back at her. She hid it well, but I could see the faintest flicker of fear in her gaze as she met mine. I swallowed and shook my head. "I have to find answers," I said. "What I am. What I can do. It's not safe."

The words were like knives—this was the only place I'd felt at home in years. But I'd nearly killed everyone in the village.

Tansy didn't argue. She only hid her burned hands in her sleeves and looked away. "Where will you go?"

"North, I think," I whispered. "Can you ask—will Dorian give them enough energy to get home?" I gestured to the architects. "They're not bad, not all of them. Most of them are just trying to do what they can to save their people."

I thought of Kris. I thought I could see, some distance away, a familiar head of wavy brown hair.

"I don't think Dorian would condemn them to die," said Tansy. "Even them. If nothing else we can't afford this many new shadow people to contend with."

I fell silent, closing my eyes. The smell of apple blossoms had made its way over to us, newly living trees quivering in the morning breeze. I remembered Dorian's plea—*you could destroy them all*—and the desperation behind it.

"I could come with you."

I opened my eyes again. Tansy wasn't looking at me but rather back at her home, at the newly created barrier surrounding it. The villagers were beginning to pick themselves up, get shakily to their feet, explore the new wall protecting them from the outside.

More than anything I wanted to say yes. She knew the wilderness, how to stay alive, how to find food and fight off the shadows. More than that, she was my friend. I'd done this for her as much as anything. But she had magic. Even now I could feel it stirring in her, and as if what I'd done had awakened something within me, I hungered for it. The desire to touch her as I had Tomas flickered inside me, and I turned away.

"I'll miss you, Tansy."

I half-expected her to hug me again, or take my hand. But

in the end she just moved silently away. After a few moments I turned to watch her step through the new barrier, which let her pass without resistance to help her fellow scouts get to their feet.

I slipped my hand into my pocket, where my brother's paper bird and core of magic nestled next to Oren's lighter. I shaded my eyes against the sun and looked to the east, my eyes automatically finding the pass through which Oren and I had come. Somewhere up there was the summer lake, and beyond it, a world of ancient bees and flowers and hungry trees and ghosts. There was no telling what the lands to the north held, except for a boy who would follow me until he died—or until he turned and killed me. And perhaps, a man I used to call brother.

A sudden loneliness swept over me as I picked my way through the rubble of the machines, weaving through the bodies beginning to stir. I had faced the wild beyond the edge of the world I had known but I hadn't done it alone. Now, it seemed I had never heard such quiet.

A tiny clank caught my ear and my heart gave a sick lurch. There was a machine still functioning—and somewhere nearby. I sought for some scrap of power with which to destroy it, but there was nothing—I was so spent I couldn't find the other sight that had shown me what to do.

There was another clank, a rattle, and then a sudden hum as whatever it was whirred to life. Something bright dashed in front of my eyes, reflecting the sun and blinding me momentarily.

"*Took you long enough,*" said a familiar voice. A weight settled onto my shoulder. "*Planning to leave me decommissioned forever, I guess?*"

"Nix!" I felt like the tiny weight might be enough to knock me over. "How—how? How are you here? How are you *alive?*"

"Kris had me in his carriage. As for the second question: They designed me to exist out here," said the pixie, rustling its wings in my ear. "It appears I'm unusually well shielded against having my power drained away. Besides, you power me."

"But I have nothing left! My power is all gone, I have nothing for you to steal."

"That is interesting," it said, sounding significantly unalarmed. "Perhaps you have something left after all. Perhaps it's not the energy about you, but something else entirely."

"That's impossible," I breathed, though something in my chest had clenched and thrummed to the idea. If it was me, and not what the Institute had given me, that was powering Nix . . . I thought of Oren, and that last fierce moment in which he looked at me before he disappeared into the shadows.

"Lark," said the pixie, in its flat and tinny voice, "who are you even talking to? I'm a machine with a sense of self-preservation who's decided to ignore programming and wander off on a—on a lark. Don't talk to me about impossible."

I laughed, and Nix responded by launching itself from my shoulder and turning midair into a copper bird, singing songs it had learned from the birds in the apple orchard, and swooping in aerial displays.

North, I thought, inhaling. There was a tang in the air, a sharpness that stung my nose. Winter was coming. I was heading for a world of ice and snow and bitter cold, but at least I wasn't alone.

We left the field of metallic corpses behind and walked on across the valley, beneath the vast and terrible beauty of the dawn.

ACKNOWLEDGMENTS

I once heard a writer say that acknowledgments were annoying and pointless because at the end of the day, a book is made only by the writer, sitting alone in a room, typing at the keyboard. My heart goes out to that person, because I never could have made this book alone—and I never would have wanted to. The journey's involved more people than I can count, and I am grateful for every single one of them.

There's no one deserving of more thanks than my amazing agent, Josh Adams. I have no words, except these: there is no one on the planet I'd rather have fighting for me and my books. So to Josh, Tracey, and Quinlan: my gratitude is endless. Thank you as well to all the international agents, scouts, and publishers that have helped bring this story to so many countries.

Andrew Karre, my editor, is insanely clever and insightful, and showed me things about my book that I didn't even know were there. It would not be what it is without him. And so many thanks go to Sammy Yuen for designing this beautiful cover. I can't thank everyone at Carolrhoda and Lerner enough for their faith in this book.

I could not have done any of this without my family. My parents, Clint and Sandra Spooner, started buying me books before I was born and have never showed the slightest doubt that I could do anything I wanted. Thank you as well to my other family, the Miskes, who have been cheering for me my whole life. And to my big sister, Josie: thank you so much for introducing me to fantasy when I was too young to resist. It was the best kind of brainwashing.

Jeanne Cavelos, director of the Odyssey Writing Workshop: You told me I could do this, and I listened. I learned so much at Odyssey, and so much of it from my fellow class-mates, a brilliant, creative, beautiful group of people. Corry, I miss you especially—and the dentist/ice skating rink too.

To my family down under, I will be forever grateful. Marilyn and Philip Kaufman adopted me while I was in Australia, writing this book. My friends there have cheered me every step of the way—Michelle, Ailie, Flic, Ian—I miss them all every day. And most of all, Brendan: thank you for letting me live in your house before you'd ever met me, for doing ridiculous things to make me laugh, and for reading on the train.

I've had so many friends chip in with support, advice, enthusiasm, and faith: Sarah, Ellen, Caitlin, Kim, Frazier, Sophie, Thara, Josh B., Kacey, Kat, Wynn, Lindsay, and everyone who has ever said, "I can't wait to read your book."

Finally, I want to thank all the teachers who, over the years, have shaped me into who I am today. In particular, Ellen Andrus, who didn't care that her class of sixth graders was too old for story time and whose reading of *The Golden Compass* changed my life; Betty Stegall, who read my first (and utterly atrocious) attempt at a novel and somehow saw within it something to nurture; and Barbara Nelson, whose lessons about *The Odyssey* cemented my love of myths and fairy tales forever, and whose friendship now I treasure.

And to the creative writing professor who gave me a B minus because I wouldn't "leave out the magic and the ridiculous creatures," I say this: thank you.

Never underestimate my desire to prove silly people wrong.

MEAGAN SPOONER

Meagan Spooner grew up reading and writing every spare moment of the day. She graduated from Hamilton College in New York with a degree in playwriting and spent several years living in Australia. She's traveled with her family all over the world to places like Egypt, South Africa, the Arctic, Greece, Antarctica, and the Galápagos, and there's a bit of every journey in the stories she writes.

She currently lives and writes in Northern Virginia, but the siren call of travel is hard to resist, and there's no telling how long she'll stay there. You can visit her online at http://www.meaganspooner.com.